# THE PILO
# FAMILY
# CIRCUS

# THE PILO FAMILY CIRCUS

# WILL ELLIOTT

Underland Press

Book design by Heidi Whitcomb
Cover design by Heidi Whitcomb
Cover art by PTK Fotosearch

Printed in the United States of America
Distributed by PGW

ISBN 978-0-9802260-2-7

**Underland Press**
www.underlandpress.com
Puyallup, WA

Second Underland Press Edition: November 2014

3 5 7 9 10 8 6 4 2

*For my parents*

# INTRODUCTION

BY KATHERINE DUNN

*"Horror, I've come to realize, is a subset of comedy. Both genres address the absurdity of life. Both genres put protagonists in complex and hazardous situations. Both mix a bit of each other into their palate."* —D. K. Holm

Australian writer Will Elliott knows exactly what the American film reviewer, Holm, is talking about. That feral team of genres is Elliott's vehicle of choice and he drives with a sure eye for moral quandary and a precise ear for colloquial power. If Sam Spade or Phillip Marlowe were sapped in an alley and woke up in a Franz Kafka story, you'd expect something akin to the wry, hard-nosed tang of Will Elliott's ferocious, prize-winning novel, *The Pilo Family Circus*.

Elliott carves out a portrait of human evil in the medium of black comedy. His form is slapstick violence viewed with a chilled eye—the Three Stooges dissected from the inside out. And for Elliott's dark purpose, circus is the perfect setting. We've all dreamed of running away with the circus, but Will Elliott sees the circus running away with us.

This is not the equivalent of being chosen from the audience to assist the magician. Elliott's visionary abduction is as brutal and perilous as being shanghaied, or snatched out of life and slammed into jail. The alternative, as usual in these cases, is painful and maybe fatal. The Pilo Family Circus is no chipper pup-and-pony show. Elliott is not interested in the great tradition of the real circus arts, which involve talent and grace, wit and courage. His terrain is the stranger circus of our imaginings.

In modern times actual circus as exotic art and transporting, transforming entertainment has receded from our lives. It has become more concept than fact, more metaphor than reality. And that concept has mutated and spread, seeping out from the confinement of tents or arenas and dream life to tint or—depending on your point of view—taint every aspect of life from shopping malls and movie theaters to our TV sets and video games, clothes closets, kitchen cupboards and medicine cabinets. Even the garage is far from safe. Circus is hard-sell marketing. For the high-minded, "circus" has become an epithet describing the showy corruption of sports, holidays, religion, and domestic rituals from weddings to funerals.

The circus as insult is probably a malignant reaction to our twisted yearnings for a sinful circus. This circus we desire, or at least suspect, is, by many lights, everything wrong. It is a neon gem crystallizing all that is anti-Puritan, and maybe anti-social. Circus is gravity defied, truth belied, nature upended, willful idiot danger embraced and coated with spangles. Circus sleeps late, flaunts its flesh, and never pays attention in class. Circus is loud and brassy, arrogant and naughty. Circus doesn't pay for its tricks and pranks, even when they are fatal. Circus is rootless, unfettered, and never cleans house. Circus just folds its tents and creeps away in the night, leaving a large yellow stain on the grass. Irresistible. And this is the circus that Will Elliott pushes to the far, bright edge of sanity.

The lure of the circus is precisely equivalent to the prim, or maybe grim, dullness of normality. Elliott's victim, villain, and hero is Jamie, the well-meaning, under-employed, frustrated-but-aware young denizen of a dumpy shared house in the bland suburbs of Brisbane. Jamie is a decent striver, burdened by empathy and a deep fear of doing the wrong thing. He is a natural target for the malevolent power of the Pilo Family Circus. He is hijacked by the most flagrantly violent element of the circus—the clown crew.

Our fear of the clown is our fear of the disguised, the camouflaged unknown. Every Halloween trickster knows the hidden monster freed by donning the mask. Elliott adds a stroke of chemical wizardry. Once the white face paint goes on Jamie becomes JJ, the rookie clown. JJ is an entirely different creature. His fellow clown, Winston, remarks, "The nicer the man, the meaner the clown," as though strenuous niceness is always a cover for exuberant evil. This Jekyll and Hyde arrangement is precarious to begin with and catastrophic once JJ decides to murder Jamie.

The Pilo Family Circus is the disputed domain of rival brothers, the giant Kurt, and the dwarf George. Kurt is a dedicated scholar of the moral design of Christianity. He studies numerous translations of the Bible, and forces his vitriolic sermons on the circus crew. He is particularly fascinated by the role of Satan as "God's policeman," who only preys on those who deserve it. The Mephistophlean Kurt seems convinced that everybody deserves it. His circus exists in a dimension abutting and infringing on this one, and all of its performers and customers are abducted—some temporarily and others permanently.

The permanent residents are frozen in time, and barring the will of the higher demons, immortal. The circus fortune teller, Shalice, says, "When age and death are not likely to trouble people, they have no need to acquire wisdom. They are unafraid to play with fire." And Elliott's circus folk are as petty, vicious, thoughtless, and selfish as the mythic gods of Olympus or Valhalla. This is significant because the circus is the source and cause of every catastrophic evil committed by and against life on earth.

Will Elliott is swimming a thematic river that reaches back to the earliest forms of literature. Homer's Odysseus endured occult captive interludes, both grisly and glamorous. Jonathan Swift's Gulliver found decency and kindness the rarest commodities in the extremes of creation. George Orwell's *Animal Farm* tap-danced on the internal sources of corruption and cruelty. Hesse's Steppenwolf is engulfed by a spiritual circus, and Stephen King planted the fear of clowns in whole generations. Elliott's world teeters on the lip of hell and is monstrously concrete, deeply disturbing, and horribly funny.

This is a profane fable about the lizard mind of humankind, but its complexity surpasses simplistic moral forms. The magic is plentiful, crudely powerful, and gritty. The central conflict is the ancient and endless Zoroastrian dichotomy of dark and light, good and evil, with good taking it in the teeth every time. Malice, greed, arrogance, cowardice, vengeance, and sheer sadistic delight are the ruling geniuses. It's an angry view in black and white.

The cool clarity of Elliott's prose keeps this strange tale grounded. The intrigue accelerates as cartoon characters reveal multiple facets of the bizarre, and we are mesmerized by the relentless torque of the action.

The classic definition of slapstick runs along the line of, "Funny is someone else ramming his face repeatedly into a brick wall." Elliott's logic is inescapable. When we all charge that wall, it's the ultimate horror.

—Katherine Dunn

August, 2008

# THE PILO
# FAMILY
# CIRCUS

*A carnival for the human race*
*Cotton candy, happy face*
*A child talking with his mouth full*
*Girlfriend gets stuffed animal*

*A festive mood is all around*
*Another world is what we've found*

CAROUSEL

•

# PART 1

## SEND IN THE CLOWNS

# CHAPTER 1

# THE VELVET BAG

*There was not one among them that did not cast an eye behind*
*In the hope that the carny would return to his own kind.*

'THE CARNY,' NICK CAVE

JAMIE'S tyres squealed to a halt, and the first thought to pass through his head was *I almost killed it*, rather than, *I almost killed him*. Standing in the glare of his headlights was an apparition dressed in a puffy shirt with a garish flower pattern splashed violently across it. It wore oversized red shoes, striped pants and white face paint.

What immediately disturbed Jamie was the look in the clown's eyes, a bewildered glaze which suggested the clown was completely new to the world, that Jamie's car was the very first it had ever seen. It was as though it had just hatched out of a giant egg and wandered straight onto the road to stand as still as a store mannequin, its flower shirt tucked in at the waist, barely holding in a sagging belly, arms locked stiff at its sides, hands bunched into fat round fists stuffed into white gloves. Sweat patches spread out under both armpits. It stared at him through the windshield with ungodly boggling eyes, then it lost interest and turned away from the vehicle that had nearly killed it.

The dashboard clock ticked over the tenth second since Jamie's car had stopped. He could smell burnt rubber. His time as a motorist had cost the world two cats, one pheasant, and now very nearly one absolute fool of a human being. Flashing through his mind was all that could have gone wrong had his foot hesitated *at all* on the brake: lawsuits, charges, sleepless nights and guilt attacks for the rest of his life. Road rage came on fast and murderous. He rolled down the window and screamed, 'Hey! Get off the fucking *rooooad!*'

The clown stayed put——only its mouth moved, opening and shutting twice, though no words came out. Jamie's fury brought him to the verge of a seizure; did this guy think he was being *funny?* He gritted his teeth and slammed on the horn. His little old Nissan wheezed with all her might, a piercing sound in the 2AM quiet.

At last he appeared to have made an impression. The clown's mouth flapped open and shut again, and it held its white-gloved hands to its ears as it turned to face Jamie again. Its gaze hit him like a cold touch and sent a shiver up his spine. *Don't beep that horn again, sport,* said its ungodly eyes. *A guy like me's got problems, wouldn't you say? You'd like me to keep my problems to myself, wouldn't you?*

Jamie's hand hesitated above the horn.

The clown turned back towards the footpath and took a few drunken steps before coming to a halt once more. If a car came the other way at speed, it would do what Jamie had almost done. Oh well, Mother Nature knew best——it was just the natural course of the stupid gene, streaming its way out of the species like the letting of poisoned blood. Jamie drove off, shaking his head and laughing nervously. 'What the hell was that about?' he whispered to his reflection in the rear-view mirror.

He would know all too soon——the next night, in fact.

.................................

'Where's me fuckin' UMBRELLA?'

Jamie groaned to himself. It was the fourth time the question had been roared at him, with each word now having had its turn at the emphasis. Standing before him was none other than Richard Peterson, sob sister from one of the national rags, *Voice of the Taxpayer*. He'd bustled through the doors of the Wentworth Gentlemen's Club in a storm of Armani and shoe polish. As concierge, Jamie was getting eighteen bucks an hour to politely endure the tirade.

There was a pause in shouting. Peterson stared at him in baleful silence, moustache twitching.

'I'm sorry, sir, I haven't seen it. Could I offer you a complimentary——'

'That umbrella was a fuckin' HEIRLOOM!'

'I understand, sir. Perhaps——'

'WHERE'S me fuckin' umbrella?'

Jamie grimaced as two attractive women walked past the doors, smiling in at the commotion. For the next two minutes he repeated 'I understand sir, perhaps——' as Peterson threatened to resign his membership, to sue, to get Jamie fired . . . *Didn't he know who he was dealing with?* Finally, one of Peterson's associates wandered through the lobby and lured him up to the bar in the manner of someone luring a Doberman with a bloody steak. Peterson backed away growling. Jamie sighed, feeling not for the first time like he was the guest star on some British sitcom.

The 6PM rush came and went. Through the doors came a stampede of beer-gutted Brisbane Personalities, from law firm partners to television news readers, AFL head honchos, retired test cricketers, members of State Parliament, and suits of all descriptions, bar young and female. Quiet descended on the lobby; the only sounds to permeate the granite walls were the muffled honking of traffic, the quieting bustle of the city's working day filing out, and its night life waking. The lobby was deserted, the peace sporadically interrupted by club members leaving drunker and happier than when they'd arrived. Once the last of them had staggered off,

Jamie descended into his science fiction novel, stealing furtive glances over his shoulder occasionally in case his boss or a stray Brisbane Personality caught him at it. This, by contrast, wasn't such a bad way to earn eighteen bucks an hour.

The clock struck two. Jamie started from a kind of trance and wondered where the last six hours had gone. The club was silent; the rest of the staff had gone home, all members were tucked into bed, comfortably full of beer, with their hired escorts asleep beside them.

Jamie walked through the city to the Myer Centre, a tall redheaded young man taking long jerking strides with thin legs, polished shoes tapping crisply on the pavement, hands shoved into the pockets of his slacks, where his thumb and forefinger played with a dollar coin. A beggar had learned his shift times and for weeks had been making an effort to intercept him on his way to the car park. On cue, the old man met him outside the Myer Centre, smelling of cask wine and looking like Santa Claus gone to seed. He muttered something about the weather then acted surprised and delighted when Jamie handed him the dollar, as though it were the last thing in the world he'd expected, and so Jamie's shift ended in profuse thanks, which was gratifying in a small way.

Wondering not for the first time why the hell he'd done an arts degree, he started his little Nissan. Its engine rasped like an ailing lung. On the drive home he saw another clown.

His headlights swept past the closed shops in New Farm and there it was, standing out front of a grocery store. This clown was not the same as last night's; it had dark clumps of black hair sticking like bristles out of a head as round as a basketball. Its clothes were different too—it wore a plain red shirt that looked like old-fashioned cotton underwear, clinging tightly to its chest and belly, and pants of the same fashion, with a button-up seat. Its face paint, plastic nose and big red shoes were the only things 'clown' about it; otherwise it might have been any fifty-something booze hound lost on his way home, or in search of back-alley romance.

As Jamie's car passed, the clown looked to be in the throes of despair, throwing its arms up in exasperation and mouthing some complaint to the heavens. In his rear-view mirror he saw it ducking between the grocer and a garden supply store, disappearing from view.

Jamie would have happily left it at that—there were psychos loose in the neighbourhood, no surprise in New Farm. He'd have driven home, crept up the back steps to shower, put out some cat food for the legion of local strays, slunk back to his room, masturbated to some internet porn then collapsed into bed, set to repeat it all tomorrow. But his car had other ideas. There was the grinding noise of a big metal belly with indigestion, then the smell of oil and smoke. Halfway down the street his little Nissan died.

He thumped his hand on the passenger seat, sending cassette tapes scuttling in all directions like plastic cockroaches. Home was four streets away and up a hill. He was stretching his calf muscles to begin pushing the mutinous wreck home when he heard a strange voice say, 'Goshy!'

Jamie's heart skipped a beat. The voice came from behind him again. 'Goshy?'

He'd forgotten about the clown. It was a clown's voice all right, a silly voice with exaggerated worry and a childish whine, from the throat of a middle-aged man. In Jamie's mind the tone conjured an image of the village idiot pounding his own foot with a hammer and asking why his foot hurt. The clown called out again, louder: 'Gosh-*eeeeeeee?*'

Goshy? Was that some kind of swearword? Jamie about-faced and headed back towards the grocery store car park. The streets were silent and his footsteps seemed very loud. Obeying some instinct that told him to stay hidden, he crept behind a hedge next to the car park and, through the leaves, he saw the clown standing outside the gardening shop, staring at the roof and going through the motions of a distressed parent, running a hand over its scalp, tossing its arms to the sky, now making an extravagant swooning gesture like a stage actress: hand to the forehead, a backward step, a moan. Jamie waited until its back was turned before darting from the hedge and crouching behind an industrial garbage bin for a closer look. The clown called out that word again: 'Gosh-*eeeeeeeeeee!*'

A thought occurred: '*Goshy' is a name. Maybe the name of the clown I nearly ran over. Maybe this one is out looking for it, because Goshy is lost.* It seemed to fit. And, as he watched, the clown found its friend. The clown from last night was standing on the roof of the plant shop, still as a chimney. The suddenness with which it caught Jamie's eye almost made him cry out in alarm. On its face was the same look of naked bewilderment.

'Goshy, it's not *funny!*' said the clown in the car park. 'Come down from there. Come on, Goshy, you come down, you *just* gotta! Goshy, it's not *funny!*'

Goshy stood motionless, up on the roof, his fists bunched at his sides like a petulant child, eyes wide, lips pursed, gut sagging like a bag of wet cement under his shirt. Goshy stared unblinking down at the other clown; he wasn't coming down, that was for sure. He seemed to be throwing some kind of passive tantrum. He gave one mute flap of the lips then turned away.

'Goshy, come down, *pleeeeease!* Gonko's comin', he's gonna be *soooo maaaad . . .*'

No reaction from the rooftop.

'Goshy, come *onnnnn . . .*'

Goshy turned back to the other clown, gave another mute flap of the lips, and without warning took three stiff-legged paces towards the roof's edge, then over it. The drop was about twelve feet. He plummeted to the concrete headfirst, with all the grace of a sack of dead kittens. There was a loud sickening *crack-thud* as he landed.

Jamie sucked in a sharp breath.

'Goshy!' The other clown rushed over. Goshy lay face down with his arms locked stiff at his sides. The clown patted Goshy on the back, as though Goshy were having a mere coughing spell. No good—Goshy would probably need an ambulance. Jamie looked uneasily at the payphone across the street.

The other clown patted Goshy's back a little harder. Still lying face down, Goshy rolled from side to side like a felled ninepin; he looked to be having some kind of fit. The other clown grabbed his shoulders. Goshy began making a noise like a steel kettle boiling, a high-pitched squealing: 'Mmmmmmmmmm! Mmmmmmmmmmm!'

The other clown pulled Goshy upright. Once on his feet, still making that awful noise, he stared at the other clown with wide startled eyes. The clown held his shoulders, whispered 'Goshy!' and embraced him. The kettle kept squealing, over and over, but with each burst the volume lowered until the noise ceased altogether. When the other clown released him, Goshy turned to the plant shop, pointed a stiff arm at it and silently flapped his mouth. The other clown said, 'I know, but we gotta hafta go! Gonko's comin', and——'The clown patted Goshy's pants, then dug into his pockets and pulled something out. Jamie couldn't see what it was, but it sent the other clown into throes of distress again. 'Oh! Oh oh! Jeez, Goshy, what're you *thinking*? You're not meant to, not s'posed to have this here. Oh, oh oh, Gonko's gonna . . . the boss'll be *sooo* . . .'

The clown paused and looked around the empty car park before tossing the small bundle away. It landed with a sound like a wind chime striking a single note, and slid into the hedges by the footpath before Jamie could get a good look at it. 'Come *on* now, Goshy,' the clown said. 'We gotta hafta *go*.'

He grabbed Goshy by the collar and started to lead him away. Jamie stood up, unsure if he should follow the pair or run for the public phone——one of these idiots was going to get himself killed if they were left to their own devices. Then something caught his eye: a *third* clown. This one stood by the door of a copy centre two doors down from the plant shop, arms folded across its chest. Jamie shook his head in disbelief and crouched back down out of sight. He knew immediately that whatever maladies affected the brains of the first two clowns did not affect this one; there was a sharp awareness in its face, staring with narrowed eyes at the other two as they shuffled across the car park. Goshy and his companion halted. Goshy's face didn't change, but the other looked at the new clown with something near terror. He stammered, 'Hi . . . Gonko.'

The new clown didn't move or react. It was thin, dressed in a full uniform of oversized striped pants held by suspenders, a bow-tie, white face paint, a shirt decorated with pictures of kittens, and a huge puffy hat. It squinted at the other clowns like a gangster from a Mafia movie; if it had ever intended to make people laugh, it may well have done so at gunpoint. It glanced around the car park, as though for witnesses, and Jamie found himself crouching further behind the industrial bin, suddenly convinced it was a very good idea not to be seen. The sound of Goshy smacking into the concrete echoed in his ears, *crack-thud*, and he shuddered.

The new clown beckoned the others with a single finger. They stumbled over. 'I just gotta, had to find him, Gonko,' said the clown who wasn't Goshy. 'I just *had* to, he can't look after himself out here, he just can't . . .'

The new clown answered in a harsh voice, 'Shut your fucking trap. Let's go.' Its gaze swept over the car park again, from the footpath right over to the industrial bin. Jamie ducked out of sight, holding his breath. He stayed down for a minute, worried his heart was beating loud enough for the clowns to hear——yet he couldn't pinpoint what it was exactly that he feared. Finally he risked a glance over the top of the bin. They were gone. He stepped gladly away from the stale reek of garbage. Over by the gardening shop there was a small white smear where Goshy the clown had fallen. Face paint. He touched it, rubbed it between his fingers to confirm the last ten minutes had actually happened.

The night-time city sounds hummed in the near distance, as though being switched on again after a short break. A dog barked, a car alarm beeped somewhere far away. Jamie shivered with sudden cold and looked at his watch: 2.59AM. It was going to be a long walk home.

As he passed the footpath something in the hedge caught his eye. He remembered the clown reaching into the other's pocket, pulling something out and throwing it away. He picked it up, a small velvet bag about half the size of his fist, tied at the top with white string. It felt like it was full of sand. Or, maybe, a different kind of powder. And judging by the way the clowns had acted, just maybe it was the kind of powder Wentworth Club members occasionally left little traces of on hand-held mirrors, in their rooms along with bloody tissues and straws. Interesting. He stuffed the velvet bag in his pocket, where it bumped against his thigh with each step.

Now for the fun part. He put his Nissan in neutral and started pushing it to the service station two streets away. A passing motorist informed him with a scream: 'That's what you get for driving Jap shit, mate.'

'*Arigato, gozaimasu*,' Jamie muttered.

Later, looking back on this night, Jamie would marvel that he'd believed his worst trouble was the car and the ache in his back from pushing it, that never for a moment did his mind turn in alarm to the little velvet bag in his pocket, which felt like it was full of sand.

# CHAPTER 2

# DREAM STALKING

THE share-house was a big old Queenslander on top of a hill, stubbornly refusing to crumble to the ground despite the neglect of its inhabitants. The paint was chipped, the back steps wobbled dangerously, rats as big as possums inhabited the space between the downstairs ceiling and upstairs floor, and it was possible the landlord had forgotten the place existed, for a property inspection would condemn them all to hang. Jamie's room, the only downstairs bedroom, was the cleanest outpost of this bachelor's wilderness, and when he walked in he'd sigh like someone returning to the safety of his own private bomb shelter.

Not in keeping with the bachelor spirit of his roommates, who seemed not to care for such things, Jamie's bedroom was decorated with one goal in mind: what Svetlana, the Russian girl who served drinks at Wentworths, would think if she walked in on some imagined evening after Jamie had summoned the nerve to ask her out. The plan: the computer was to give him an air of one who moves with the times. The posters of David Bowie and Trent Reznor in fishnets spoke of his open-mindedness. The CD rack loaded with hundreds of discs, the cardboard box packed to the rim with old vinyls, expressed his broad tastes and cultural depth. The pot plants, his oneness with nature. The mountain-bike in the corner, his athletic prowess. The fake Persian rug, man of the world. The fish tank, his capacity for calm reflection, his kindness to animals. The dream-catcher hanging from the ceiling, his spiritual side. The small keyboard, a suggestion of creativity. Each object was like a feather in a peacock's tail, to woo and bedazzle.

When he returned that night, as with every night, he anxiously examined each part of the display, making sure all was in order, that no roommates or roaming junkies had stolen any key articles. He peered at the keyboard uneasily, wondered whether to put it in a more visible place, and decided for the hundredth time to leave it where it was. He adjusted the rug so it ran parallel to the floorboards, turned a slow circle critically assessing his nest, then sighed, content all was in order.

He kicked off his pants, the velvet bag still in the pocket, and wondered how much he could sell it for, if indeed it was cocaine—there would be no shortage of buyers hanging around the house. For now he left the bag where it was and went upstairs for a shower. The house was a disgrace—the toilet looked like someone had thrown in a grenade and flushed. Someone had devoured twenty dollars' worth of Jamie's groceries since he'd left for work, and not had the grace to throw away the empty wrappers. In the living room, a pale junkie lay comatose on the couch, presumably a friend of one of Jamie's roommates—probably Marshall. Jamie retreated down the back steps, feeling suddenly depressed. This was not the life American television had prepared him for. There were no romantic comedy weddings, no sorority houses filled with crazy pranks and girls in wet T-shirts. Just bills to be paid and dishes in the sink.

Back in his room, David Bowie gazed down from his poster like an androgynous father figure, bell-bottoms puffing around his ankles. Jamie threw himself onto the bed, set his alarm, then paused; he had to have a look at that velvet bag first, didn't he? He dug it out of his slacks. It felt a little too heavy for its size. He juggled it between his hands and could hear a very faint noise, like marbles clinking together. He undid the white string and held the bag beneath his lamp. Inside were lots of little beads glinting in the lamplight like powdered glass. He gave the bag a squeeze. Now that it was open the sound was loud, like a small wind chime. He touched the powder tentatively with his finger; it felt soft as ash.

He put the bag on his bedside table, turned off the lamp and lay back. The floorboards above him creaked as someone upstairs made their way to the kitchen to polish off what remained of his groceries. Jamie idly wondered what would happen on the day he snapped for good, and on that not atypical note, he slept.

*The dream comes with such clarity that Jamie feels fully awake, still crouched behind the industrial bin in its cloud of stink. It seems to him that pushing his car to the service station was the dream out of which he has just snapped.*

*A voice is yelling: 'Where are you, fucker? Goddamn, this dream stalking is a con job. How many bags did that scag charge us for this? DOOPS! Step lively, you shit. We ain't on safari.'*

*'Sorry Gonko, I just, I . . .' answers a whiny voice Jamie recognises. The first voice is Gonko's, the thin clown, and Jamie sees him as he pokes his head over the top of the industrial bin. Gonko prowls around the car park, somehow able to walk with an assassin's stealth despite his ridiculous large red shoes. His face seems split into vicious creases and hard as stone; it is a face that looks to have been used as sandpaper and soaked in whisky. His eyes disappear into thin slits, gleaming coldly and touching all they fall on like the point of an icy finger.*

*Behind the bin, Jamie understands Gonko is seeking two things: the little velvet bag of powder, and the person who stole it. And his belly sinks, for the bag is not safe at home, but here in his pocket. He considers tossing it across the car park and running, but one quick glance at Gonko kills that idea. Moving like a brightly dressed scarecrow, the stalking clown seems to say with his stride alone: Oh no. I'll catch you, feller. Stay hidden. Doctor's orders. There is no doubt that Gonko will kill him if he finds him.*

Crawling on his hands and knees to the other side of the bin, Jamie spots the other two clowns. He knows their names, too. The first, of course, is Goshy, and the one with black bristles for hair is Doopy. Jamie somehow knows the two are brothers. Gonko pauses in his stalking, turns to them and says: 'Don't just stand there, you ugly pair of tits. Find him. He's here.'

His head poking around the side of the bin, Jamie sees Goshy about-face and stare straight at him. The alien eyes lock onto his and the grip of that gaze holds him still. Goshy's mouth flaps twice without sound. The other clowns are facing away from Goshy at the moment, and it's a good thing, for Goshy raises a stiff arm and points right at the bin, right at Jamie. Goshy's mute mouth flaps again and a thrill of terror flashes up Jamie's spine.

'Come out, come out, wherever you are,' Gonko shouts in a singsong voice. 'Tag, you're it. Marco Polo, sweet cheeks. Red rover, I call over . . .'

In frustration Gonko flays his boot at a parked BMW so hard the panel gives in and the driver side door falls off its hinges with a metal squeal. Goshy is still staring at Jamie, predatory coldness in one eye, bewilderment in the other. There is something obscene in the face's ability to pair these two attitudes, as though the clown's mind is shared equally between a moron and a reptile. Goshy takes some stiff-legged steps towards the industrial bin, and Jamie cowers behind it. Right above him Goshy's eyes light up, his hand stretches into the bin, and Jamie almost screams . . . But all Goshy does is pull out an empty beer can and peer at it, as though it is a puzzle he means to solve. His mouth flaps again and Doopy looks over. 'Goshy, put that down. Down, Goshy, it's not funny!'

Goshy contemplates the can for a moment longer, then drops it to the ground next to Jamie's foot and wanders back to the other two clowns. But he trips on something and falls hard into the concrete. 'Goshy!' Doopy cries, rushing over. Goshy rolls around on the concrete, arms locked stiff at his sides, making that noise like a squealing kettle: 'Hmmmmm! Hmmmmm!'

*And Jamie wakes, just as the kettle in the kitchen above reaches boiling point, its noise piercing the floorboards and finding its way down to him, squealing like a clown.*

Jamie had the ominous feeling of being too well rested when he woke. The little alarm clock verified his fears: 3PM. Without sparing a thought for the night's dream, he sprinted around the room on a mad hunt for work clothes, towels, socks, wallet, all of which had hidden themselves during the night. Up the back steps, through the back door, and of course someone else was already in the shower. He thumped on the door.

'Fuck off,' came the barked reply. It sounded like his roommate Steve, grocery thief extraordinaire.

'C'mon, man. I'm late!' Jamie yelled, thumping on the door again. Shower still running, it opened, spilling steam out the doorway. A round boyish face appeared, soaking wet and bearing a contemplative expression, one eyebrow raised ponderously. A big wet arm shot out and shoved Jamie hard in the chest, knocking him to the floor, then the door closed gently.

'That's assault,' Jamie said to the ceiling. He got to his feet and stood staring at the door, mouth open, shaking his head. *Are you just going to take that?* part of him demanded. *Stand up for yourself! Jesus, for once in your life, stand up for yourself . . .*

Not today. Instead he went to the kitchen for coffee and a sandwich. He yanked the fridge open and hissed through clenched teeth—his bread was gone, as was most of his milk. 'God, am I asking for too much in life?' he whispered. He looked around for food, a vain hope in the cluttered bachelor's trough of a kitchen; he saw only instant noodle packets spilling their remains over the counter like frozen maggots. 'Fuck!' he yelled and kicked the fridge door as a wave of white hot anger rippled through him. He ran back downstairs for his shoes, at a loss for how to evoke some kind, *any* kind, of respect in his roommates.

His eyes fell on the velvet bag on his bedside table. Hesitating only for a second, he grabbed it, causing it to tinkle like a tiny bell. If it were a drug, perhaps now was the time to find out its effects—better yet, side effects. Back up the steps into the kitchen, where he opened his near-empty bottle of milk and carefully tipped just a pinch of the powder into it, before shaking the bottle and replacing it in the fridge. If Steve was true to form, he'd be high as a kite before long, maybe psychotic by dinner time. Jamie splashed his armpits over the kitchen sink, patted himself dry with a tea towel, dressed, and left for work.

His shift passed without incident. Unbeknown to him, these were the last eight hours of peace he would have for quite some time.

# CHAPTER 3

# AWAKE STALKING

HE sensed something amiss when he stepped out of the cab. It was twenty past midnight. The street was silent and there was no visible evidence to support his feeling, but it was there: *Something's going down here . . . Something's wrong.*

As he watched, the curtain in Steve's bedroom shifted slightly as though someone had just withdrawn from the window. The light went out.

At his own bedroom door, Jamie paused for just a moment with his finger on the light switch, listening for he knew not what. Everything suddenly seemed too quiet.

He flicked the switch, then dropped his bag to the ground and made a noise like he was being choked; it looked like a cyclone had been through his room. His television had been smashed, with a fissure in the screen roughly the shape of a boot's sole. His computer monitor was similarly wounded, and had been toppled to the floor like a severed head. The window was broken, and through the jagged hole he could see pairs of his underwear hanging on the neighbour's fence. His fish were floating dead, and the letters RIP had been drawn on the tank in crayon, along with a hieroglyph of a penis. His keyboards, $1400 worth, were scattered over the floor in small pieces. On his pillow was what looked to be a giant pile of human shit, curled up like a fat dead snake. His bedside table drawer lay on the floor, its contents spread far and wide. The little velvet bag was nowhere in sight.

But what did it all mean? This had been *done* by someone. At that dizzy moment it seemed the most absurd thing of all, as though an earthquake were a more rational explanation. *Why*, for God's sake? Who would *do* this?

Backing out of his room, he hoped he could just repeat his entrance, and the whole scene would blink away like a mirage. Shoulders slumped, head shaking, he staggered up the back steps and into the kitchen. He turned on the kettle, then the smell of puke hit him; bright red vomit clogged the sink and was sprayed over the floor. His shoes were in a drying puddle of it. He stared at the puke in a trance until the kettle squealed, waking him with a start.

*Goshy.* The thought passed across his mind like background noise. He dazedly poured the water into his cup, pulled the milk from the fridge, and noted that someone had put a dead bat on the middle shelf, next to a container of potato salad. Its white fangs were locked in a scowl. Jamie stared at it blankly, sipped his coffee, and let the door swing shut.

Out of the kitchen, into the living room. His eyes roamed across more carnage and settled on the wall, where someone had written the words POLITICAL PIGGIES in chocolate ice cream. The words rang a bell, and after a moment he recalled it was the message written by the Manson family in their victims' blood after the massacre. Dangling from the ceiling fan was a thin rope tied in a hangman's noose, from which a small teddy bear hung by the neck. There was a scrap of paper stuffed into a ripped hole in its backside. Jamie took it out and read the block crayon message: GOOB BYE CRULE WORLD. On the floor were pieces of plastic and wire arranged in the shapes of letters, and he recognised the smashed pieces as the remains of the telephone. The letters spelled the words HES NOT

HOME. Jamie somewhat abstractly noted that this piece of vandalism took a degree of patience and care, as though intended to contrast with the random violence around it; there was an almost artistic attention paid to each attack.

He sipped his coffee with a slow steady hand. Next to the smashed television a small red object caught his eye. He leaned over to pick it up, thinking at first it was a rubber ball. It was attached to a white plastic band—a fake nose. He dangled it by its string on his forefinger for a moment, then dropped it back onto the rubble.

Around then he became aware of the sound of sobbing from one of the bedrooms. Slowly he walked towards it, the scattered debris in the hallway breaking and crunching under his shoes. Past Marshall's door, he who befriended junkies. Past Nathaniel's door, he who embezzled bill money. Silence from both bedrooms—the crying came from Steve's. The door was open, the light switched off. Jamie stood waiting in the doorway, sipping his coffee. The sobbing stopped. He could hear Steve breathing in huffing gulps, his nose loud and runny. Finally he whispered, 'Jamie?'

'Steve,' Jamie said in a voice from far away, 'what's going on? Why is the house . . . Why is the house fucking *ruined*, Steve?'

Somewhere outside a police siren wailed then faded into the distance. Jamie could see Steve's dark silhouette shifting on the bed. 'I don't know,' Steve answered eventually. 'These guys came around . . . and I don't remember exactly . . . some of it . . . I did some of it, because if I didn't . . .'

Jamie blinked. '*Some guys* came around, huh, Steve? You're sure, now? Which *guys*, exactly?' In the back of Jamie's mind, he knew—the clown nose had not been a subtle clue. It was almost a deliberate game to clutch at a saner reason: that Steve had done it.

Steve broke down again. Jamie supposed he'd sensed some of the menace rapidly growing in his doorway . . . Political piggies all fucking right, only it wasn't meant to be written in ice cream. Jamie took a step into the dark bedroom. Steve writhed around on the mattress, the bed springs creaking. Jamie reached out to turn on the light. 'No, don't—' Steve began.

The room lit up. Steve's round face was smeared in a greasy rainbow of face paint. Around his lips a huge red smile was plastered on in lipstick. His head and hair were completely coated in oily white. Tears ran through the ghoulish mask, digging rivulets in his cheeks. Around his neck hung a red plastic clown nose, and he wore a shirt with frilly white cuffs and a loud garish flower pattern. The bedroom had copped the treatment along with the rest of the house. Steve's lava lamp was no more. His stereo was disemboweled. Half the floor had black scorch marks, like scars from a whip.

Jamie dropped his cup. It broke and splashed his shoes with hot coffee. 'Steve?' he whispered.

'Those guys,' Steve said between sobs. 'They came in and just . . . held me down here, and put this . . . stuff on me. I think they must be Marshall's friends, druggies. Maybe he owes them money or something, and they came here to get even. They were dressed like . . . clowns.'

Of course they were. Jamie crouched down on his haunches with a sudden headache. 'How many?' he said.

'Three, I think. They started downstairs. I heard all this banging, glass breaking . . . I thought it was you, so I went down there to tell you to shut up, you know? The skinny one grabbed me, and . . .' Steve made a fluttering gesture at his face. 'There were two others. One of them kept saying, *It's not funny, it's not funny.* The other one just kept making some . . . some *weird* noise . . .'

'Like a kettle boiling,' Jamie murmured.

Steve didn't seem to hear. 'The skinny one had a knife. He told me if I didn't help them trash the place, he'd slice me up. So I helped them.'

'You helped them,' Jamie echoed.

Steve gave him a look of reproach. 'What was I meant to do? It was three to one. The guy was gonna cut me, you should've seen him. He *wanted* to do it, he really did. I had to do what they said. They broke the TV. . .'

'That writing on the wall, in ice cream. Who did that?'

'The skinny clown,' Steve said. 'I don't know why. I don't even know what it means.'

'And the puke in the kitchen?'

'Mine.' Steve whispered, wiping his nose with his sleeve. 'But that was before they got here. Had a drink, came straight back up. Been happening all day.'

A drink. Jamie's eyes settled on a cold half-empty cup of coffee on Steve's bedside table. Then he looked to the broken mug at his feet, where cooling coffee was spreading out over the floor. A nasty memory surfaced: he saw himself tipping a little of that mystery powder into the milk, revenge for Steve being in the shower, revenge for the stolen food. Jamie had just enough time to smile mirthlessly before it hit. Nausea clutched his belly as though he'd been punched. It hit the back of his throat and gushed into his cheeks. He sprinted through the hallway, tripping over smashed bits and pieces, and made it to the kitchen sink with barely a second to spare.

When it was over, he scooped tap water into his mouth with two shaking palms and tried to rinse the taste out. Little white lights were dancing behind his eyes. He stared at his reflection in the kitchen window. *Now what?* he wondered.

Now the clowns were coming. It made no sense at all, but somehow he knew it: they were on their way.

Which, as it turned out, wasn't entirely true. They were already there.


Jamie was in the bathroom rinsing his mouth with toothpaste when he heard a faint noise from his bedroom below. He paused and cocked his head, hoping he'd imagined it. Half a minute of silence passed, then the clowns announced themselves. Bump, scrape, mumble, kettle sound, SMASH.

It came from his bedroom below. He groaned and sprinted from the bathroom, into the kitchen, slipped on the puke and crashed to the floor. It hurt and it was noisy. Below, the sounds of demolition ceased and a watchful silence followed, to be broken by a muffled voice crying out, 'Gonko, it's not *funny!*', then the sound of wood being ripped apart.

Jamie got to his feet and dug around in the drawer for a nice big knife, but the best he could find was a rolling pin. That in hand, he barrelled out the back door, feeling ridiculous; it was probably not a weapon Genghis Khan ever used to take care of business. Once down the steps he stopped and listened. 'Gonko, please!' said the whiny clown in an impassioned voice, right before a huge crash, then a quieter and more ominous *woof*, the noise of something bursting into flame.

Jamie gave a panicked whimper then ran for his bedroom. An orange glow flickered through his bedroom door. The three clowns had their backs to him. The whiny one with black bristling hair was carefully lifting the pillow from Jamie's bed; he seemed to be rescuing the mound of shit from the flames spreading over the blanket, as though he held a sleeping infant. Next to him was Goshy, who turned to give Jamie a view of his profile. That surprised look was still on his face, still seeing it all for the first time. He shuffled around further, spotted Jamie, and his gaze narrowed into something utterly calculating. His mouth gave a mute flap.

The thin clown turned too, squinting at him with a face of sharp creases and lines, demonically lit in the dancing shadows of the fire. 'Ah, hello sport,' he said with false cheer. 'We were just talking about you.'

All three rushed him; Goshy with his arms out like a three-year-old in need of a hug, the thin one like a British soccer thug, the whiny one stumbling and tripping as he came. Behind them the fire spread out over Jamie's bed; planks had been torn from the wall and tossed onto the mattress to feed the flames.

Jamie took a step backwards and raised his hands for combat, but he knew he was doomed. He had never been in a fight with anyone—the closest he'd ever come was an exchange of death threats in a traffic jam. His knees buckled in fright and he hurled the rolling pin as hard as he could. Surprisingly, his throw was on target; the rolling pin spun end on end, straight at Goshy. The rolling pin hit his sagging belly then, rather more surprisingly, rebounded and flew straight back at Jamie—a flash of wood rocketing at his eyes. He turned to protect his face and the rolling pin belted him on the side of his head. He fell to the floor and blacked out, completely at the mercy of the clowns.

As consciousness returned, Jamie remembered only that the waking world was an unpleasant place, and he willed himself back into the blackout. It worked for a minute or two, but it was hard to stay there when someone was pounding a tent peg into the side of his head at a steady 4/4 rhythm. He clutched at his head and moaned pitifully, then felt there was something wrong below the waist, too. Something was lodged in his rectum—God help him, there was. With a shaking hand he patted his backside and felt something stiff jutting out. He pulled it free, grunting at the nasty scraping pain. It was a rolled-up paper note.

*Bam, bam, bam.* The spike being hammered into his head beat faster as he sat up. Next to hit him was the smell, an utterly putrid reek of old beer and garbage. He peeled his eyes open and saw his room had been redecorated. The wall had gaping holes of torn wood; it looked as though the clowns had been working at ripping some kind of pattern— there was the beginning of what may have been a smiley face—but the job must have proved beyond them. The bed was now a pile of ash with a few springs and wires sticking out. Someone had dragged the recycle bin in from outside and spread its month-old contents of smashed bottles over the floor.

He stood up, swayed on his feet and sank back to his haunches. His eyes fell on the light switch; nails had been hammered into the wall around it from the other side, so their tips would jab any hands fumbling in the dark. He almost admired the effort the clowns had gone to.

Over on his desk was something that made no sense: a vase of daisies, undamaged and as pretty as a picture in the middle of the carnage. And there, on the charred mess that was once his bed, was what looked to be a greeting card. He staggered over, shoes crunching broken glass, and picked it up. It was in the shape of a red heart and said 'For a Special Guy'. A kiss had been smudged on it with lipstick.

Like a failing engine, his mind's gears ground and squealed. Why these *niceties* amidst the ruin?

He looked at his wardrobe, which was now empty. On top of it was a neatly folded pair of work clothes, ironed and pressed ready for his next shift at the club. On the rear panel of the wardrobe, someone had nailed a dead possum in a parody of crucifixion.

Something wet dripped from the ceiling and splashed on his head. He brushed at the damp spot, headache thumping in time with his pulse. On the floor his outline was engraved in the broken glass and garbage. Next to it was the paper he'd pulled from his rectum. He unfolded the note and read the neat handwriting in gold ink.

> *I dig the rolling pin gag. We could use that. We could use YOU, too. You have two days to pass your audition. You better pass it, feller. You're joining the circus. Ain't that the best news you ever got? The fuck it ain't. You're just lucky the new apprentice ain't working out. I will kill that sonofabitch, you see if I don't.*
>
> 

*Gonko, on behalf of Doopy, Goshy, Winston and Rufshod
Clown division, Pilo Family Circus*
> 
>
> *PS Steal from me again and I will cut your balls off.*

Jamie crumpled the note in his fist and dropped it to the floor, wondering what kind of sense it was supposed to make.

According to the clock—which, somehow, was still working—he had an hour to get ready for his shift. Passing the downstairs toilet he saw the rest of his clothes had been stuffed into the bowl. Another wet drop slid through the floorboards above and landed on his head. Again he wiped it away, almost without thinking, but it had brought a new smell which caught his attention. On the back of his hand was a brown streak across the knuckles. Baffled, he stared at the ceiling. Through the gaps in the floorboards above, sewage was trickling like melting snow.

Jamie managed to walk calmly outside and run his head under the laundry tap before he keeled over and was silently sick.

Upstairs, the house was the stuff of nightmares. It seemed the clowns had somehow rigged the plumbing to reverse and expunge everything that had been put down the tubes in recent memory. The mess had spread over the floor in the kitchen, bathroom and hallway, and was creeping gradually towards the bedrooms like a slowly rising tide.

With the resilience of a postman, he made it to work. When he got to the club, other staff and a couple of the members asked him if he was all right. He told them he was fine as he stared 1,000 yards into the distance. After the 6PM rush of suits, he took two phone calls. The first was from Marshall, calling from a public phone, demanding an explanation. Jamie hung up on him. The second call was also from Marshall, only his tone had changed to hysterical panic. He begged for an explanation. Jamie hung up on him again, then unplugged the phone.

He was barely able to respond to anyone he came across. Gradually the thumping pain in his head dimmed down to something tolerable. When the clock struck two, marking the end of his shift, he grabbed the master keys and made for one of the spare rooms, hung a 'do not disturb' sign on the door, and fell onto the bed.

Moonlight poured through the window. Jamie savoured the quiet as the thick granite walls kept the city noises out. Metres away the streets were teeming with the last round of nightclubbers looking for more booze and a mate, just a normal summer Saturday night in Brisbane. The women, dressed up like glazed hams and glistening in the heat, were trying to look like they belonged on the set of *Sex and the City*. Watch them closely and you could see the mannerisms of the American starlets they idolised; the gestures, the nuances of speech, grabs at being *sassy*. Meanwhile the menfolk, oblivious to it all, were squeezed tight into denim and sweat-soaked collared shirts, each one primed for a rodeo, staggering around in horny packs. The curse of the working class was in full swing. It was a comforting thought for Jamie as he lay there, just to know things were in order. There are times when even the most insipid environments can be a comfort—knowing they'd never change meant at least there was *something* you could count on.

He had not expected sleep tonight, but he found himself drifting close to it, and gladly closed his eyes to take the hour or two of respite that came his way.

Something was digging at the back of his neck. The room was still dark. He woke like someone coming up from under water, gulping for air and clawing at the blanket. His dreams had been unkind again—more clowns, this time interrogating him for his whereabouts. *See you soon*, the thin one had promised.

It was half past four. Jamie reached behind his head and grabbed at something that felt like plastic. He fumbled about for the bedside light. As he'd guessed, there was a red clown nose in his hand. He had to fight back an urge to burst into tears, because this felt like the last straw. But he knew it wasn't. They weren't done yet. *The clowns could still be here, you know*, he thought.

He jumped to his feet, suddenly wide awake as it hit him: the clown nose was not just a natural extension of his nightmare. *They had been in here.* They were almost certainly still in the building. Maybe still in this bedroom.

He stared about wildly, under the bed, in the wardrobe, in the ensuite. All clear. He straightened the covers, but as he turned to leave saw something on the inside of the door. Another dead bat, of course— what else? It had been stuck in place with a nail through its skull, its vicious little face locked in a snarl. A piece of paper was lodged in its mouth like a cigarette. Jamie winced as he took the paper out, unrolled it, and read:

*Sleep tight? Thirty hours to pass your audition. Make us laugh, feller. That's the assignment. We don't care how. We don't care who gets hurt or killed. Make with the chuckles, you pass. Ditto for your friend. He has twenty-two hours to pass his audition.*

*Gonko, on behalf of the Pilo Family Circus*

Jamie stuffed the note in his pocket and opened the door, grimacing at the dead bat which grimaced right back. Out in the hall all was quiet, with the faintest of dawn light trickling in through the high rafters. There was no trace of movement in the gloom. He could faintly hear the sound of vacuuming coming from one of the bedrooms. He ran to the elevator, pressed the button, and as the doors slid open he heard a distant voice yelling: 'It's not *funny!*'

He froze and made a choked sound, but after a second or two passed in silence, he supposed the voice had been in his mind alone; the thought was not comforting. The lift took him down to the lobby, where the front doors were shut and locked just as he'd left them. There was no sign of life in the arcade outside, its gates locked at either end. How did the clowns get in here if not through the front doors? He thought of the door by the kitchen, which opened out to a small alley used for garbage pickups. They could have scaled the fence and somehow broken through the door, but a street full of people would have seen them. The only other way he could think of was to scale the side of the building, like Spiderman, and climb through a high window.

At the front desk he sat for a moment and listened. All he could hear was the somehow peaceful sound of muffled traffic outside as a fleet of taxis carried drunk night-clubbers home. He switched on the two security monitors beside him, the little screens casting a thin greyish light in the dark lobby. The camera showed a black and white view of the kitchen, which was deserted. After a few seconds the view shifted to one of the hallways, also empty. Next, the back alley, the rows of black bins. All quiet out there. Next, the basement.

And there they were.

It took a few seconds for the scene to truly chill him. Goshy the clown was staring up into the camera, right at Jamie, and the sense of eye contact was quite real. Goshy's arm was extended and in his hand was a cigarette lighter, its little flame dancing around like an extension of his thumb, flaring in the grey screen, distorting the picture around it. Behind Goshy were . . . one, two, *three* other clowns—they'd brought a friend along. Those three were busying themselves in the background. Jamie saw the thin clown swing an axe before the monitor's image shifted to show another empty hallway, then the kitchen again.

*Why the basement?* Jamie thought. *A lighter. Fire. Why? What are they . . .?*

Then the chill set in. Built into the basement walls were three giant wooden vats, attached to pipes that led up through the club walls like veins, into the kitchen, bar and utility rooms. Sloshing around in those vats were many, many litres of cleaning products, isopropyl alcohol, turps and ethers. All of it highly flammable; all of it set to blow.

A moan escaped Jamie's lips and he clutched the front desk with both hands. The fire would spread up through the tubes, igniting the walls from within on each floor. Before any fire crew could get here, the club would become a spectacular blazing death trap. They would be too late to save the Brisbane Personalities charred in their beds.

Jamie grabbed the phone. His hand was shaking. The monitor did its rounds again, showing no sign of other people. He dialled for an outside line and called emergency services. It rang three, four times. The monitor switched views to the kitchen. Finally a female voice answered: 'Police, fire or ambulance?'

The monitor shifted to the hallway. 'Police,' Jamie whispered hoarsely.

'Police,' said another female voice.

'Hi. I got a problem with some clow— some guys. I think they're going to . . .' He trailed off as the monitor switched back to the basement. There were no clowns. In the background, the wooden vats sat embedded in the walls as normal.

'Yes?' said the voice in the earpiece.

Jamie stared at the monitor until the picture shifted back to the kitchen, where one of the chefs was ambling over to fire up the ovens, yawning.

'Yes? What is your location?'

He hung up. He sat staring at the monitors as they did their circuit twice more: no clowns in the basement. Maybe there never were.

Out the door he went, through the arcade, unlocking the gate and striding away in quick steps. Ringing in his ears was the question, *Where were you on the night of Saturday, February tenth?* He checked back over his shoulder twice to make sure the place was still standing, then jogged to a taxi rank on Edward Street, eyes peeled for puffy flower shirts, striped pants and painted faces.


He waited in line for a cab with the last wave of drunks to be rounded up and sent home to their hangovers and rude awakenings. A few could be seen staggering determinedly to the casino, the only place in Brisbane selling cocktails at breakfast time. Jamie felt as bleary-eyed as the drunkest of them.

It was a while since he'd been here in communion with the tribe, waiting for a cab as the sun came up, liver struggling with the backlog. With the sounds and smells about him now, he wondered what appeal it had ever held. It was just the done thing in this town . . . A person's twenties were the drunk years—or the drug years, if you swung that way. A year ago he'd been up to ten beers a day on weekdays, the top shelf for weekends. No one noticed a problem—people made approving noises, *praised* him for Christ's sake. Looking back, it almost defied belief. Every home he visited was adorned with collections of empty bottles, posters that read *Tequila: have you hugged your toilet today?*, pub humour, pub knick-knacks, bottle caps glued to the walls, entire shrines to binge drinking. It was everywhere you looked, so no one noticed.

In the taxi rank the drunks jostled around him, a danger to themselves and others, playing out their slurred melodramas. No flower-printed shirts, striped pants, red plastic noses. Out here, the clowns did not even seem possible.

A cab pulled up in front of him. A drunk couple jostled with him for it. Jamie shoved past them with a rare show of backbone and closed the door before the male could try to butt antlers. He told the driver New Farm, patted his pocket for money and found the note he'd pulled from the dead bat's mouth—material proof in his hands that the clowns existed.

*Thirty hours to pass your audition. Make us laugh, feller . . .*

The cab headed down Brunswick Street, through quiet traffic made entirely of other cabs. The breaking dawn pulled the night away like a blanket from an unmade bed, showing the last of the clubbers and street girls slowly wandering home.

They pulled up beside the house, a big wooden Queenslander atop a hilly street. Jamie paid the cabbie and tried to muster enough energy to be curious. Marshall was standing on the back steps with a hose in his hand. This was a first: the boys were cleaning up. Marshall's face was frozen in shell-shocked bewilderment—and who could blame him? Water ran down the back steps, leaving nasty streaks of crap down the side of the house.

Jamie shook his head in disgust and went around to the front door. Water trickled slowly past him down to the gutter. There was an awful stink in the air. At the doorway he caught sight of the neighbours staring at him through their window, heads shaking. There was not much he could say. He waved apologetically, shrugged and went inside.

Most of the debris had been cleared from the living room and hall. Someone had broken out the air freshener in a futile attempt to cover the smell. POLITICAL PIGGIES had been washed from the wall. From Steve's room came a muffled cry of alarm as Jamie passed. The door opened and out popped Steve's head, eyes wide and panicky. 'Jamie? Thank God.' For a moment he thought Steve was going to hug him; there was a strange light in his eyes. 'Jamie, they were back.'

Jamie watched him in a tired way and waited for the rest.

'The *clowns* were back,' said Steve by way of elaboration. 'You know?'

'I didn't think you meant Jehovah's Witnesses. What happened?'

Steve grabbed his arm and pulled him into the bedroom. Steve sat on the bed, Jamie on a chair, the only two objects spared from damage. Steve's round pink face looked to have been thoroughly scrubbed, but a faint tinge of colour remained from the face paint.

'They came back when I was sleeping,' Steve said, leaning forward and talking in a whisper. 'They want me—both of us, I think—to pass some kind of test. If we don't, they're going to keep coming back. I don't know what they are, but they're serious. I think maybe they're part of a—what do you call 'em? Religious . . .'

'Cult.'

'Yeah. You know, like that serial pest guy who's always on the news, interrupting grand finals? Maybe there's a *hundred* guys like that, all organised, you know?'

Jamie shrugged. 'I don't think so, but it's better than anything I can come up with. What happened?'

'I woke up and the thin one was sitting on my chest with his legs crossed. The others were standing behind him, just staring at me. It was fucking *creepy*, man. I screamed and the thin one pulls out this kind of spray can and fills my mouth with shaving cream. I almost choked. He said something like, *You have twenty-two hours to pass the test.* I asked 'em what the hell I'm supposed to do, and he said: *Make us laugh.* That was it. Then they left.'

Jamie nodded. 'They were at the club too. Threatened to blow the place up.'

Steve reached forward and pawed Jamie's leg. 'What are they? Where did they come from?'

Jamie shrugged. 'Your guess is as good as mine. What did you tell the others? About the mess, I mean.'

'Told them what I told you. Some guys came around. But I told them it was bikers, looking for one of Marshall's junkie friends who owes them money. Marshall was kind of spooked.'

'That's not a bad story. He believed it, huh?'

'Yeah. He's shitting himself. Nathaniel believed it too. He drove off somewhere. Said he won't be back until it blows over.'

Jamie stood to go. The reek of sewage was getting weaker, but it was still there like a stain in the air, and he didn't want to know how Steve had managed to sleep in it. 'The clowns didn't tell you anything else?' he said at the doorway.

'I dunno, they said all kinds of weird stuff. That thin one—he's a fucking *psycho*, man. I think his name's Gonka.'

'Gonko.'

'Yeah. Hey, Jamie . . .'

*He's going to tell me he's scared*, Jamie thought. *This is great, now we're comrades in arms. Me and him against the world. Just great.*

'I'm scared, Jamie.'

Steve made as though to hug him. Jamie walked quickly away. Down the hall, a shaken Marshall was scrubbing and hosing and sweeping with almost superhuman vigour. It looked like he'd broken out some crystal meth for the job, his preference to coffee. As Jamie passed him he blurted out some rapid-fire talk: 'Listen Jamie, I'm sorry about the mess. Look, don't worry, the bikers won't be back, I guarantee it, I made some calls, got the whole thing sorted out, just a misunderstanding I think, I'm really sor—'

Jamie slammed the back door on him in pretend anger. Down in his room the floor was still carpeted with broken glass. The only change was a light sprinkling of crap over the mess which had leaked through the floorboards above. The vase of daisies and the valentine card were where he'd left them. He made the first tentative moves towards cleaning up the nest. It took him a couple of hours to remove every last trace of the sewage and soak the place in disinfectant. He swept up the ash and wires that had been his bed and put some seat cushions in their place.

Lying back amidst the wreckage, his eyes fell on the card, and suddenly all he could do was laugh. For minutes he lay there, in the light grip of a hysteria which threatened to clutch him tighter and never let go.

# CHAPTER 4

# STEVE'S AUDITION

HE woke from fitful sleep to find the headache from the rolling pin 'gag' was finally gone. The late afternoon sun glinted on the broken glass, sharp points of light shooting off the army of jagged edges. He stood and threaded a path through the shards to the door, then paused in his tracks: a piece of paper was taped to the handle. He took a step backwards and grunted as a sliver of glass jabbed into his heel. Eyes watering, he pried it from his foot, adding a few drops of blood to the carnage. He clawed at the note with a shaking hand, and understood then that he was hanging onto his sanity by a fairly thin thread.

The note read:

*Twenty hours to go, feller. Hope you got something planned.*

*Gonko for the P.E.C.*

Jamie stood for a moment with a sinking feeling, like he'd swallowed a fist-sized lump of clay. For a moment everything inside him trembled on the brink of collapse. Then he muttered, 'Fuck it.'

And that was that: he no longer cared about the clowns. Seriously, what could they *do* to him? Kill him? No. He'd grown up in the suburbs and knew death was merely a distant bogeyman from movies and newspaper headlines. If they showed up again, he was calling the cops. If they kept at him, he was going to ask one of Marshall's criminal friends where he could buy a gun.

He managed to find a band-aid in the rubble and plastered the cut in his heel. He had nothing to wear but his work clothes, so he put them on and headed up the back steps, where the shit streaks had dried into sun-baked patterns down the side of the house. Upstairs the stink had lessened and someone had been at work with methylated spirits. A few plates and cups had survived the whole ordeal and sat in their usual spot, unwashed by the sink. Jamie made a coffee and strolled through the house in a serene state of calm. From the hallway, something in the living room caught his eye.

There, sitting on the couch and staring up at him, was a man with a billowy flower-patterned shirt, a white painted face, a big red nose and big red shoes. It was Goshy. Goshy the clown.

Jamie's heart fluttered. He blinked—no one was there. All in his head. No problem. Just some kind of psychosis, stress induced. 'I really am losing my fucking marbles,' he muttered in amazement, then had an attack of the giggles. He took some deep breaths, fought down a more serious panic attack, almost burst into tears, then heard someone sobbing. Steve. Jamie knocked on his door.

'Who is it?' Steve said. He sounded panic-stricken, poor bastard. When it came down to it, Steve was one of those guys so used to kicking the dog he couldn't handle being kicked himself. Jamie had that much going for him: he could take a psychological blow. Lots of practice; he knew when to brace himself, how to distribute the impact.

He fought an urge to make the kettle noise outside Steve's door. 'It's me,' he said instead. He opened the door and saw his roommate sitting on the bed with red eyes and wet cheeks. To think, Steve had been alpha male not forty-eight hours ago. Jamie felt a distinct sociopathic thrill; he didn't like to but couldn't help it. With agreeable detachment he watched Steve wiping his eyes and sniffling. 'Did they come back?' said Jamie.

Steve pointed at his dresser. Next to a framed photo of his mother and a porn magazine was a folded note, identical to those Jamie had found. He unfolded it and read:

*Fourteen hours, you snivelling cocksucker. Get cracking.*

*Gonko, P.F.C.*

'I don't know what they want from me,' Steve moaned. He began babbling about calling the police, about how he'd never asked for any of this, and so on, but Jamie wasn't listening; he was pondering. First, the tone of Steve's note was not friendly. On the desk were two others the clowns had left, and Jamie read them.

*Thirty hours. Clock's ticking, fuck face.*

*Gonko, P.F.C.*

*Nineteen hours. Stop blubbering. Faggot.*

*Gonko, P.F.C.*

Jamie's own notes were courteous by comparison. Second, there was a gap between Steve's remaining time and Jamie's. Ah yes. Jamie had been at work when the clowns first dropped by. That meant roughly six or eight hours difference—which meant he would get to see what happened to Steve if he failed the 'audition'.

'I'm afraid to even sleep at night,' Steve was complaining. 'I'm afraid to leave the house. I can't even wank without thinking about those bastards.'

Jamie left him to suffer alone. He stole a pair of boots from Marshall's bedroom, went downstairs and braced himself for the cleanup.

His eyes never left the clock. Two hours passed in which he cleared the bigger bits of glass. Then he fetched a shovel and scooped the remaining slivers into piles.

The clock struck ten. He'd begun to tackle the stains and smells, and to sort out the salvageable items from the write-offs. By then, Steve had about six hours to go, give or take.

Tick tock. Tick tock.


He'd settled down for a moment's rest on the seat cushions and drifted again into unexpected sleep. Someone banging on his door woke him with a start. He got up and flung it open. It was Steve.

Jamie's heart eased back to a frantic sprint. 'What do you want?'

Steve's face looked haunted. 'I got to think of something.'

Jamie shut his eyes. 'What are you talking about?'

'To pass the audition. You know?'

Ah, yes. Steve's was not exactly a mind brimming with creativity. Jamie said, 'Look, forget about it. If they come back here, call the cops. That's all.'

'Yeah, but . . . you know, what *if* . . .'

'Did you get another note?'

'No. But . . . I can't sleep. I can't stop watching the clock. I'm trying to come up with some kind of plan, just in case, but I can't think of anything.'

'No surprises there,' said Jamie, a remark he would not have dared utter aloud this time last week. 'I guess you just weren't cut out to be a clown, Steve. Go away. I'm sleeping.'

Steve gave him a beaten-puppy look over his shoulder as he left. Jamie lay back down.


It was seven in the morning when he woke, having had far too much sleep. He scrambled to his feet, unsure if he was scared or not. Steve's deadline had now passed.

He went upstairs. From the kitchen window he saw a police car parked by the side of the house. *The police!* his mind screamed like a siren. *Something happened—they blew up the club! I'm DOOMED.*

From the hallway he could hear voices. He crept into the living room and listened. The cops were talking to Marshall. 'Yeah, I dunno,' Marshall was saying. 'Last I saw he was on the roof. Dunno what he was doing there.'

'And there's nothing like this in his room?' said one of the police.

'I dunno, man!' Marshall wailed. 'I don't know who keeps fuckin' drugs in their room and who doesn't. Why don't *you* go take a look? You're the cop, aren't you?'

Jamie crept back into the kitchen and waited for the police to leave. When they were gone he heard Marshall swearing and throwing things around.

'What happened?' Jamie asked him from the doorway.

Marshall turned. He was unhealthily thin, with a pointed goatee that was meant to look druidic. His room was adorned with Celtic symbols, many bearing slash and burn marks from the clowns' visits. In his hand was an order to appear in court. He held a shaking index finger just below Jamie's nose. 'Those ... *fucking pigs* ... found a pipe and a clip bag. It had leaf in it, for Christ's sake. I got done for having *leaf*!' He spat and shook his head. 'It's not even quality pot. *Do they know how much speed has gone through this house?*' He pointed to a shoe box on the floor by the bed and whispered, 'Last month I was minding fifty grand of heroin in that. *AND I GET DONE FOR LEAF!*'

Jamie had long ago ceased to be surprised by Marshall's outlook on life. He shrugged. 'Look, have you seen Steve today?'

'I dunno, man. I can't *believe* this ...'

'Did I overhear something about him climbing onto the roof?'

'Huh? Yeah, he was on the roof.'

'Why?'

'I don't know. Dude was fucking high or something. He was shouting something about hoping it was good enough. If he's the one who called the cops on me, I swear to God ... *leaf*!'

Jamie left him to it. Climbing onto the roof ... Surely not, surely that wasn't Steve's idea for an audition? It almost worked for banality alone. Shaking his head, Jamie knocked on Steve's door. No answer. He barged in.

And stood dead still.

There was blood on the bed. Blood on the pillow. Blood on the floor. On the walls. A hand streak of red down the wall.

Jamie tottered and nearly fainted. His belly gave a heave. Blood . . . He had never seen *so much blood.*

On the pillow was a little piece of paper, folded just like the other notes. He tried to walk over, pick it up, but his legs refused to take him any closer to the red nightmare. He coaxed them to back away from the door slowly, and he shut it quietly behind him.

*Don't worry,* he told himself. *There's still time. Plenty of time. I can pass the goddamn audition.*

From up the hall he could hear Marshall wailing about the drug bust, oblivious to what lay in the room beside his. Jamie glanced at the clock, and wondered how his life had come to such ruin in so short a space of time. A week ago, hadn't things been normal? Not particularly blissful, maybe, but . . . normal?

He was supposed to be at the club in an hour. Somehow he didn't think that would happen, one way or another.

'Let's settle this,' he whispered.

CHAPTER 5

# JAMIE'S AUDITION

'WHAT'S the time, Gonko? Gonko, what's the time?'

Gonko, clown leader, waited a minute or two before answering Doopy. Doopy got worked up in those two minutes, till he was whining like a dog. These little worry-fits didn't bother Gonko. Doopy's whiny voice was like wallpaper; it felt like home.

'C'mon, tell me Gonko, it's not *funny*!'

Gonko took a watch from his pocket, letting its silver chain dangle around his wrist. The chain was fashioned like a tiny hanging noose. The watch said young Jamie had twenty minutes left to pass his audition.

'Gonko, it's not—'

'Twenty minutes, Doops,' Gonko said quietly.

The three clowns, Goshy, Doopy and Gonko, sat in their tent on the showgrounds of the Pilo Family Circus. It was the grandest show on Earth, although, apart from Jamie, not a person in the living world knew its name.

'Where's Rufshod, Gonko? Gonko, where's Rufshod?'

Doopy knew very well. He was only asking to be denied an answer, so he could fret and fuss and shit bricks. Gonko obliged by not answering him—if he did, another question would follow moments later. The answer would have been that Rufshod was in bed, for Gonko had beaten him unconscious. Rufshod had thoroughly enjoyed the beating, but that was beside the point—he had to be punished for his prank. It was Rufshod who had put the bag of powder in Goshy's pants right before Goshy wandered outside and got himself lost.

Once the powder was recovered, the plan had been to fuck with Jamie for a while, then kill him, but the rolling pin gag had had Gonko in hysterics, or as close as he was likely to come to hysterics (which amounted to a slight sideways tilting of the straight line of his hard lips). He'd taken a closer look at Jamie, with the reluctant help of the fortune-teller, watching him in her crystal ball, and he'd liked what he'd seen.

Gonko looked at his watch again and muttered, 'Where is that fucking clown?' He was referring to the apprentice.

'Uh, gosh, I'm not sure,' said Doopy, who was busily wiping Goshy's mouth with a handkerchief. Goshy was blinking contentedly while Doopy groomed him, arms locked to his sides, hands loose. 'I think I saw him, um, at Shalice's. That's what I think I saw, Gonko. And who I think. I think.' Doopy frowned. 'Remember when you asked me where he is, Gonko? Remember? You just did before. You just—'

'Shh.'

'Sorry Gonko, I just, I . . .'

Gonko looked at his watch a third time and sucked at his teeth with displeasure. It had cost him a fortune in bribes to borrow the crystal ball to watch this audition—he was not on the fortune-teller's Christmas card list.

Doopy turned to him suddenly. 'I don't *like* the 'prentice, Gonko. I don't *like* him!'

Doopy wasn't playing. The apprentice had rubbed everyone up the wrong way and reeked of sabotage waiting to happen. Not good. There were enough enemies on the showgrounds without one in your own crew.

At that moment the apprentice appeared at the tent doorway. He slunk in with his shoulders slumped, the fortune-teller's ball of glass in his hands. Gonko gazed at his sullen slinking gait with distaste. The apprentice's every movement seemed to say: *I'm waiting until your back is turned.*

Gonko looked him in the eye. A smarter performer than the apprentice would not have met that gaze; he stared back insolently. Gonko rushed to his feet in one fluid motion, to make him flinch. It worked. With extreme gentleness he lifted the crystal ball from the apprentice's arms, set it down on the table and said, 'Get out.'

The apprentice slunk back the way he'd come, slowly. He waited by the door, just inside it, deliberately disobeying to make the clown leader repeat his order. This also was unwise. Gonko stood and reached a hand into his pocket, for he'd suddenly decided to kill the sullen clown where he stood. But at that moment the apprentice crept out.

Staring after him, Gonko fingered the blade he'd pulled from his pocket for a moment, then he spat and set it down. Goshy made a beeping sound. Expressing mild disapproval, Gonko supposed, but the only one who knew for sure was Goshy.

Candlelight gleamed on the crystal ball's surface like a single yellow eye. The clown leader placed his palm on the cool glass and muttered the word, 'Jamie.' The glass fogged up like someone inside it was blowing smoke at its smooth surface. Gonko's watch said Jamie had fifteen minutes to go.

*I'll cut him a little slack, time-wise,* Gonko thought, as he considered the young man. Beneath Jamie's attempt to live a rational life where all was clearly marked and set in order, there was a wellspring of eccentric behaviour waiting to be tapped, which Jamie seemed instinctively at pains to keep from spilling over. It looked to be a daily battle. And the more fight he put up, the more impressive the results when the guy either temporarily cracked, or permanently bent. No one bends further than someone made of completely straight lines.

The glass cleared, and there was the new recruit. Gonko figured the stalking had put him within a hair's-breadth of nervous breakdown, and he was pleased with the campaign; the timing had been perfect, and now the guy would be just about ripe. The other two clowns crowded in beside their leader and bent over the glass ball. Goshy gave a small toot, best signified as 'Oo.' There was no telling what it meant—perhaps a signal of recognition as the tall redheaded young man strode over the glass ball's surface. 'Hush, Goshy,' said Doopy to his brother. 'Goshy, hush. He's starting.'

Queen Street Mall was packed with tourists enjoying the heat, and locals wishing they could escape it. The first load of Monday's evening commuters were trudging to the train station in their suits and ties. At 4.02 there was a disturbance in the crowd and a hush came over Queen Street as people turned their heads. A noise sounded from the top of the mall, so loud and piercing it was only vaguely recognisable as a human scream. Directly after it, a cluster of explosive noises like machine gun fire came from the same direction. Everyone stared; at the top of the mall a cloud of grey smoke was drifting languidly skyward.

The scream came again, shrill and drawn out, filtering through the crowd: 'There's a BOMB! *THERE'S A BOOOOOMMMMMBBBB!*'

Five years with terrorism in the headlines had taken their toll; everyone froze and panic swept through the crowd like a ripple through water. The popping bangs continued. Two police jogged cautiously towards the smoke, hands on their belts. Suddenly, bursting through the shoppers, a tall thin redheaded and, most notably, naked man was pelting down the street in a gangly sprint. A thatch of red pubic hair sat just above his frantically wobbling penis. His stride was fit for a Monty Python sketch: knees raised in a kind of goose-step, taking leaps rather than strides, elbows flailing like wings. His face was hidden beneath a pillow case. He peered through its eye slits at the crowd around him, seeing only blurred shapes and obstacles as he charged past.

There was green paint on his chest, a backwards swastika. On his back, a smiley face. Sweat was causing the paint to run, and soon the symbols were reduced to a green smear. On his trail were three baffled policemen, middle-aged men who'd expected the day's work would involve no more than a few shoplifters. They tried to keep up but, despite his bizarre stride, Jamie was fleet of foot. He swerved like a footballer between families, university students and Japanese tourists, who were aiming cameras at him. Jamie screeched again at the top of his lungs, 'THERE'S A BOMB! *THERE'S A BOMB!*'

His pillow case slipped out of place and he was momentarily blinded. Without time to regret it, he plucked it from his head and left it to float gently to the pavement for the police to collect at their leisure. Over towards the casino the smoke was spreading out into an impressive grey fog. The pops and bangs reached a crescendo, then ceased.

There was no bomb. The pops and bangs came from fireworks he'd bought from an obscure shop in Fortitude Valley. After painting himself in a public toilet and stalking up Queen Street in nothing but a raincoat, he'd wrapped a thick roll of fireworks around one of the shrubs at the top of the mall. He had no idea if all this would impress the clowns, or even if they would somehow see it, but it was all he could think of. Were it not for the jolts his mind had received from the clowns' harassment—Steve's blood the last straw—he might have just called the police and saved himself some trouble.

But as he sprinted down the mall, the troubles of the last week were as good as gone. The adrenaline was like nothing he'd ever felt. His mind ticked over like a tape on fast-forward. He couldn't feel the pavement beneath his pounding feet, the stretching muscles in his legs, or the slapping of his balls against his thighs. He felt like he could take off and fly.

Of course in the crowded mall he couldn't keep this up forever. He came to a wall of people and saw no way through. He careered into two schoolgirls in uniform, who screamed as they fell. He felt his penis brush against one of their schoolbags, and it was a miracle he avoided landing squarely on top of them. From the ground, he saw a Seven News crew stopped at the lights at the bottom of the mall. A cameraman was leaning out the window, a grin on his face, his camera pointed at Jamie.

Jamie scrambled to his feet, belatedly covering his crotch, and the schoolgirls screamed again. This would not look good on the news. Over his shoulder he saw the police closing in. Two more officers ran straight for him from directly ahead. He sucked in a deep breath and took off towards King George Square. The park was full of pigeons, tourists, commuters, students reading on the lawns. He ran through them, adrenaline still coursing through him and numbing the aches and pains. Numbing the repercussions. There would only be repercussions if he stopped running. And he wasn't going to do that . . .

It ended with a handcuffed naked walk of shame through King George Square. A policewoman tossed him a towel to cover himself, a look of complete neutrality on her face. 'You don't understand,' he'd screamed at them as they had tackled him to the ground. 'The clowns . . . I had to . . . the clowns made me . . .'

In the interview room he'd been read the charges. Indecent exposure, disorderly conduct, assault (the schoolgirls), possible indecent assault (the schoolgirls), disrupting the peace, possession of illegal fireworks, perverting the course of justice. They said they would get back to him regarding an additional charge after they consulted federal police—there were new anti-terrorism laws which made bomb hoaxes punishable as genuine threats. Which meant Jamie could be, officially, a terrorist. That was the point Jamie went from feeling like crying to actually crying.

On top of all that was the matter of Steve's possible murder, which he didn't dare mention. He should tell them, he knew, but answering their questions was enough to deal with at the moment; he'd been struck by a terrible weariness after the adrenaline high of the streak and wanted nothing more than to crawl into a warm place and close his eyes.

It was midnight when the police let him go. Around then a new and more terrifying thought occurred to him: *It might actually be, every bit of it, inside your own head. You might have imagined the entire thing, from the very first time you saw the clown on the road. If you're really that crazy, guess what?*

*You might also be responsible for those blood stains in Steve's room. Maybe you did it in your sleep. Maybe you crept up there and hacked him apart. Maybe you're the one who vandalised the house. You could be in deep, deep trouble, not just with the law. You're in trouble here, inside your own head. You may never see daylight again.*

To all this he could offer no protest as he made the slow march home. If by some miracle Steve were there, alive and well, maybe he could quietly check himself into an asylum and try to forget all this.

When he got home he saw a note lying on the seat-cushion bed. He stood in the doorway, staring at it, swaying a little on his feet. He stayed that way for nearly five minutes in which his heart seemed to stop beating. The entire city went quiet outside.

He went to his bed and picked up the note. It read:

> *Congratulations.*
>
> —*Gonko, Pilo Family Circus.*

In the clowns' tent, Goshy had been making fluttering whistles like a lorikeet chirping. The sounds meant nothing especially, just an indication that some of his circuits were still on and running, that in his own way Goshy was still ticking.

In the crystal ball the clowns had watched the spectacle from the time Jamie painted himself to now, as he was being crash-tackled out front of City Hall. Two officers were holding him down, his legs thrashing. Through it all Doopy had been offering commentary, which amounted to: 'Oh . . . gosh . . . what's he? . . . where's he? . . . gosh . . .'

Gonko's mouth had turned on its axis—a smile, to the trained eye. As Jamie was led off, hands cuffed behind his back, a look of dawning mortification on his face, Doopy turned to Gonko and said: 'Did he done do it okay, Gonko? Gonko, did he? Gonko, remember when I asked you if he done did it okay?'

Gonko's eyes moved sideways in their sockets. 'I think he did just fine.'

'Yeah, that's what Goshy thinks too, don'tcha, Goshy? Don'tcha?'

'Oo.'

Gonko placed his palm back over the glass, like someone smothering a candle. 'Beats climbing on the goddamn roof,' he muttered. 'I'll give him that much.'

Goshy gave a toneless whistle. The clowns stood. For a couch, they'd been using a bound and gagged man. The man's name was Steve, and he was out cold. 'Give young JJ a couple of hours to stew, then we'll go fetch him,' said Gonko. 'Ruf can send up a note when he comes to. And get this one,' he poked the unconscious lump with his boot, 'out of my sight.'


Jamie didn't wake that night as hands gently lifted him from the floor; Gonko saw to that. Of all the weapons in the clown leader's arsenal, chloroform was a little orthodox, but the stuff worked, and he never went kidnapping without it. He held a white handkerchief to Jamie's sleeping face for six seconds then stuffed it back in his pocket.

Rufshod and Doopy were with him. They'd been there for the acquisition of Steve, too. The blood in Steve's room had in fact been Rufshod's, just spilled for effect. The three of them slid Jamie into the body bag they'd brought along. Gonko liked the idea of a man waking unexpectedly inside a body bag; his mouth slanted sideways as he zipped it up. The other two clowns picked up the bundle and hauled Jamie out to the road. A pickup truck was parked beside the house, its motor running, the only sound on the moonlit street. They put the bag down on the tray. Doopy and Rufshod battled fiercely for the shotgun seat, their clown shoes scuffing the roadside. Doopy won. Rufshod jumped up on the tray with Jamie. Gonko sped off, swerving on the way to annihilate two stray cats. Doopy told him it wasn't funny.

One kilometre away they pulled up next to a construction yard on which an apartment block was being built. It was from here Gonko had borrowed the ute. He jumped from the driver's seat, opened the bonnet and pulled a hatchet from his pants. He gave the engine a few cleaves, just for the fuck of it, the metallic clang of his blows shooting out into the still night like gunshots. He pulled a birthday card from his pocket and wrote on it: *Thanks for the loan, Bob.* The owner of the ute was named Bob. Bob didn't know Gonko and Gonko didn't know Bob: the purpose of this exercise was to fuck with Bob's head. Gonko placed the card on the dashboard, plucked a rose from his other pocket and set it down beside the card.

The three clowns climbed the fence, manoeuvring Jamie gently down with them. Doopy complained about his back, but Doopy was full of shit. The clowns headed for a portaloo in the corner of the yard. They entered, holding the body bag upright. It was a tight squeeze. In Gonko's hand was a plastic card, which he held over the lock. A small red light flashed and a lever dropped from the ceiling. He yanked it to one side, and with a creak the floor descended like an elevator, for that's just what it was. There were several in this city alone, thousands more across the world. Above them a platform slid across to replace the floor on which they now stood. The lift lurched violently. It was a very long descent.

Finally they stopped, not before Doopy let rip a fart plaguing the small space with a stink so foul everyone burst out coughing.

'Nice one,' said Gonko, eyes watering. Doopy apologised profusely, but Doopy was full of shit. The lift doors opened.

It was night time in the circus. Around them the silhouettes of the gypsies' hunched shanties sat like rough cardboard cut-outs on dark paper. The Ferris wheel loomed above against the starless sky, like the hunched skeleton of some huge animal. Far away, something howled. The clowns went home, dragging their newest recruit by the feet.

# CHAPTER 6

# THE SHOW

JAMIE regained consciousness very slowly. A sense of claustrophobia had haunted his last hour or two of dreamless sleep. His mind tried to start as normal, booting up like a computer, but something was blocking the progressions of thought. In his mouth was a horrible dryness and the faint aftertaste of something chemical.

Something else did not feel right: he seemed awake, but everything was black. Gingerly he felt around his eye with a finger—it was open. There was a rustling sound when he moved his hand, like canvas. For a traumatic moment he was thrown into a flashback: a camping trip by the lake with his family, when he woke from a bad dream of a snake inside his tent, only to find a green tree snake really was slithering over his feet. With just a touch of panic he thrashed his arms and groaned.

There was the sound of footsteps right beside his head. Next came a ripping noise, very loud and very close to his face. Suddenly light poured into the small dark space, flaring painfully in his eyes, and the last thing he expected to see was right above him: Steve. 'Jamie?'

'Huh?' was all Jamie could manage.

'You're here too?' said Steve. 'I thought I saw something move in there. Man, you gotta come see this. It's a carnival or something. Get up. Come on!'

Jamie sat up and stared uncomprehendingly at the body bag he'd slept in. The black canvas lay open like a split cocoon. He blinked; it simply didn't compute. He wiped sleep from the corner of his eyes and tried to remember what had happened before he slept. Lying down in a body bag was not on the list.

'What the hell were you doing in there?' Steve asked, as though he could possibly answer. 'Ah, here it is.' Steve picked up his jumper from the ground. 'You're lucky I found you, I only came back to get this. Come on. You gotta see this.'

Too much input too soon. *Last night* . . . he thought. *Went to bed on the floor. Before that . . .? Cops. Watch house. Yeah . . . Caught streaking . . .* And what next?

He peered around. They were inside what seemed to be a big lofty marquee. The floor was of trampled grass, battered with large misshapen shoe prints. There was a table in the corner with playing cards and empty bottles scattered over it. On the floor were dozens of boxes stuffed with trinkets and colourful rags. A suit of armour lay on its side, covered in obscene crayon graffiti of phalluses and misspelled swearwords. Tinted sunlight filtered through the high canvas walls, lending everything a slightly sick tinge of red.

Then it hit him: Steve was alive. He was right there, standing by the marquee entrance, sunlight pouring in around him. 'Steve . . .?' Jamie croaked.

Steve looked back at Jamie with a glint in his eye—his boyish face looked more boyish than normal, as though the pair of them were in their eighth or ninth Christmas morning.

'Weren't you . . .?' said Jamie, shaking his head. 'The clowns . . . I mean, I looked in your room and there was blood . . .'

Steve ignored him. 'Will you *hurry up*, man? Take a look out here.' He bounded through the tent flaps.

Jamie noticed for the first time the sound of a marching band playing carnival music, and the babble of voices from a crowd. He went to the tent flaps, poked his head through, and the colours outside hit him like a splash of cold water in the face. It was all so bright he had to shut his eyes. When he opened them again he saw a crowd marching past, families, old people, parents, kids dressed in bright colours, babies in prams or in their mothers' arms, balloons tied to wrists, floating in the air like leashed pets. There were tents and stalls set up like a miniature city, manned by olive-skinned gypsies hawking baubles. The crowd wandered in a procession through them, talking animatedly amongst themselves. Jamie gazed around for the source of the carnival music, but he could see no band; the sounds seemed to drift like the breeze, a natural extension of the colours and the smell of buttered popcorn in the air.

He stepped out of the marquee. From the look of things, he was the only one with no idea what the hell was going on. Steve beckoned impatiently.

Jamie rubbed his eyes. 'Steve?'

'Fuck ya, *what?*'

'Are we . . .' He'd been about to ask if they were dead. '*Where* are we?'

Steve grabbed his arm. 'Will you come *on*? I heard something about a magic show over at that tent. Let's go.'

Jamie let Steve drag him down the pathway. Over in the distance he saw a painted sign: FUNHOUSE. Beyond that, a banner he could barely make out was stretched across the top of a tall tent. It said: FREAK SHOW. They passed another giant marquee, on the side of which was painted MAIN STAGE. Back over his shoulder there was a wooden archway, and behind it many flashing lights and carnival sounds: bells ringing, mechanical rides starting up, screams and cries. He could see no sign, but guessed somewhere over there was one that said SIDESHOW ALLEY.

To answer his own question, where they were was obvious: a circus. Which circus, why and how he didn't know. But suddenly none of that seemed very important; he sniffed the buttered popcorn scent, and felt a light-headedness creep into him, as though he inhaled some kind of narcotic perfume. *No, it's not important where you are,* said a friendly voice inside. *Just relax! No questions. It's the carnival. You know, the CARNIVAL!*

Indeed it was. A sudden burst of good cheer stole through him, and now he felt like he'd used to feel on a Friday night in the city, around about the second or third bourbon of the night, when the jukebox played a song by Talking Heads and the bar was packed with women. He paused to gaze about himself in wonder, and Steve snapped: 'Jamie! Are you coming to this magic show or am I going to kick the shit out of you?'

Jamie looked at him and grinned the grin of a happy idiot. 'Sure!' he said, and followed.

A chalkboard outside a medium-sized tent read: MUGABO THE MIGHTY MYSTIC. Steve yanked Jamie inside, where they saw a small stage loaded with magician's props. There was an upside down top hat, out of which a rabbit was to be pulled, no doubt; a black wand with white tips which probably drooped when picked up; bundles of coloured ribbon; and interlocking silver rings. Steve and Jamie sat in the front row of plastic seats while the audience settled in around them, and soon the tent filled with drowsy conversation. At the back of the stage was a curtain primed to be parted for a grand entrance. The audience hushed as harsh whispering could suddenly be heard behind it. '*Bunny treek?*' a strangely accented voice yelled. 'I'll do your *bunny treek*, peeg!'

'Mugabo, we've been through this,' said another voice. 'Sticks and stones, for Christ's sake. You're not going to let Rufshod—'

'That clown peeg! You friend, huh? *Bunny treek!* I can light ze fucking sky, does he know zat? I can—*GET YOUR HAND OFF*—'

There were sounds of a scuffle: a slap, a grunt, a body falling to the ground. The audience watched with interest as the curtain tugged on its frame. The apparent brawl went on for a full minute before the curtains parted, and far from a grand entrance, the magician stumbled and sprawled onto the stage as though he'd been picked up and thrown. An uncertain round of applause greeted him.

A puff of white smoke rose belatedly from the floor. When it cleared, a surly-looking black man in a turban was trying to straighten his robe with shaking hands. Mugabo the magician cut a tall gangling figure, taller still with the white turban he wore wrapped around his head like a giant egg. A jewel sat in its middle. He peeled his lips back and snarled at the audience with teeth that seemed to glow white against the blackness of his skin. He flung his arms at the rows of seats and spat on the floor. 'Stop your clapping!' the magician screamed. The applause ceased. 'Okay, you fucks. You want ze *bunny treek?*'

The audience was clapping again, egging him on with jovial catcalls. Mugabo nodded his head, the turban flopping back and forth. His deep voice was scathing. 'All right. I geev you your *bunny treek.*' He stalked over to the table, gave one glance back over his shoulder at the curtain, then grinned as he rolled back his sleeves. 'Here,' he said. 'I am Mugabo ze mighty mystic . . . or sometheeng. I will dedicate zis treek to zat fuckpig of a clown. Zis *all* for him.'

He reached into the hat and, as Jamie expected, out came a pair of long soft white ears. The rabbit kicked its legs at the air. There was a brief round of polite applause. 'Yes, you like ze bunny?' Mugabo crooned. 'How nice! They like ze bunny. So . . . how do you like . . . *ZIS!*' Mugabo's face ruptured into a scowl. He jerked his fist and the rabbit towards the audience. The rabbit flopped around for a moment or two, little legs pumping the air, before it exploded in a white and red cloud. There was a sound like fruit being squashed. Blood and shreds of rabbit meat splattered over the first two rows of the audience. A small pile of gore spilled at the magician's feet.

'HA HA!' Mugabo yelled. He bent over at the waist, thumping his fist on the table, shrieking something between a laugh and a howl. The audience went completely silent.

Two figures burst through the curtains. Jamie recognised one of them—it was Doopy the clown, who Jamie understood to be an old acquaintance from somewhere just out of memory. The other was a burly dwarf wearing an eye patch. 'All part of the show, folks,' said the dwarf as he threw himself at Mugabo, tackling him around the ankles. Then Droopy and the dwarf wrestled the kicking, flailing magician off the stage.

The show appeared to be over. The audience clapped uncertainly. Jamie picked some white fur from his shirt and wiped blood from his face. A baby in the arms of the woman beside him had its face covered in rabbit blood; she didn't seem to mind, or even to notice. She and her husband stood, waiting for a path to clear to the exits.

There was a faint sound Jamie recognised, like marbles clinking together. It came from below his feet. Looking down, he saw tiny little crystals scattered thinly through the grass. Where had he seen these before? He couldn't remember. He knew this much: the crystals had not been on the ground when they entered the tent. Now they gleamed around people's feet as they made their way down the aisle to the exit, like coins dropping from their pockets.

As they left the magic show, the curtain behind the stage was jerking in accompaniment to the sounds of slaps, grunts, cracks. There was a thud as a body hit the floor. All part of the show.


Outside, through the smell of buttered-popcorn came something stronger, the scent of incense like an invisible finger beckoning him with a long manicured nail. Without a word he followed the scent, Steve on his heels. In the crowd he saw others from the magic show passing by, oblivious to the smears of rabbit blood on their shirts and faces as they chatted and laughed. Steve promptly announced he was going to Sideshow Alley and ran off, shouldering his way through the crowd and nearly bowling people over. Jamie let him go without a care, for he was distracted by erotic visions promised in the sweet scent coiling around him like caressing fingers. Behind his eyes dark-skinned women like Egyptian princesses ran ahead of him, naked bodies in full flight, gesturing for him to follow. Punch-drunk, he did, down a path where the crowd thinned, the background music faded, and the air was cooler.

A pair of dwarfs wrestling in the dirt beside the path froze as Jamie approached, scowled at him, then ran off. Suddenly the teasing erotic visions vanished and he found himself standing before a small hut with hanging beads for an entrance. He shook himself and looked around in confusion, startled to see there was no one else around. Hesitantly he parted the beads which clicked together like marbles. It seemed to be a fortune-teller's hut, but somebody was already visiting.

'Sorry,' Jamie said as the man in the hut turned around.

Something cold crept over Jamie's skin. A voice inside told him to run away, very fast, right now. But as that passed he realised the man's face must be covered in makeup, that's all—that's why his eyes blazed with that insane light from beneath a lump of bony brow as dark as a thundercloud; that's why every contour from forehead to jaw was so wolf-like the man would not have looked out of place howling at the moon, despite the fact he wore a business suit; that's why he was well over seven feet tall, with hands far too large and yellow nails as long as talons.

The monster looked down at him from a full foot above. 'Oh, I *do* like apologies,' he said in a deep, civilised voice. 'But, no problem. I was just on my way out. Enjoy your fortunes.'

He stepped past Jamie with the utmost courtesy. A smile came to his thick lips which seemed almost kindly, perhaps the way a werewolf smiles at a cub. Jamie looked away from him, shivering, and for a second there was none of the intoxicated good cheer left in him, only cold fear of a world made of traps and snags and dark places people stumble into.

The huge man pushed through the rattling beads, stooping beneath the top of the doorframe, and was gone. The chill passed.

What had been an almost overpowering smell of sandalwood outside the hut was merely a mild flavour in the air inside it. The atmosphere was different from the rowdy good cheer outside; cooler and quieter, like sleep. A gypsy woman sat at a round table, fingering a deck of tarot cards and gazing up at Jamie with a hint of a smile. She had smooth light-brown skin, sparkling eyes and straight black hair falling from her head in silky waves. Behind her there were bookshelves stacked with nameless tomes, and charts of bright stars hung from the walls, filling the air before them with a faint white glow. A glass ball sat on the table before her, balanced upon a small wooden base shaped like a claw. 'Don't worry about him,' the fortune-teller said, nodding after the monster. 'He is harmless. That is Kurt Pilo. He owns the circus.'

'He doesn't *look* harmless,' said Jamie.

'That is true,' said the fortune-teller. 'When angered he looks like harm itself.' She stared into the distance for a moment, the smile fading from her lips. 'But it takes a good deal to anger him, and if you tried he would probably only find reason to be amused. Please, be seated.'

Something about the sound of her voice made Jamie think of rich colourful liqueurs being poured into crystal glasses. He sat on the wooden crate beside the table. 'I am in something of a hurry today,' she said, 'I have half a dozen visitors who need their fortunes read, so I must make this brief. Your hand, please?'

Jamie held out his hand and she traced her finger lightly over his palm. Her fingers were cool and sent little shivers through him wherever they touched. 'Look into my eyes, Jamie,' she said quietly. He did, and grunted in surprise; it appeared her irises were changing size, one growing while the other shrank, then vice versa. 'Don't be afraid,' she said, 'just watch my eyes dance. Aren't they pretty, Jamie? Can't you feel yourself walking down a long dark tunnel, through my eyes? You can feel my cool finger on your palm, guiding you, drawing a map to find the pathways through my eyes. Just my eyes, Jamie . . . Just watch my eyes . . .'

The voice slipped inside him like a drug, the sweet voice telling him secrets, words he could hear but not understand, and before he knew it his eyes had glazed over and closed.

*She's hypnotising me*, was his last thought before he succumbed.

A voice hammered as hard as a rock into his head.

*Tomorrow afternoon. You are going to go out, leaving the house at exactly twenty past three, but you will leave your watch at home. You will go to this address: 344 Edward Street. You will wait outside the pub there. On the footpath you will see a blonde woman pushing a pram, waiting to cross the street. You will ask her what time it is. You are going to scratch your wrist nervously as she says something flirtatious.*

Jamie's drowsy head nodded.

You will say, 'Thanks a ton.' Then you will come straight home. You will not remember her face afterwards. You will not think back on the incident in any way.'

'Why?' Jamie murmured like someone talking in his sleep. 'Can't . . . leave me . . . 'lone?'

There was a pause, and the feeling of eyes pressing into him, huge and painful like twin suns. Jamie squirmed and moaned. *Don't question me,* said the voice. *How are you able to question me? Did you . . . Have you swallowed some of the dust?*

Jamie nodded.

*Oh, for crying out—Who gave you the dust?*

'Just . . . picked it up.' Jamie murmured. Talking was so hard each word almost hurt him. His head was slumped down onto his chest and he only wanted the voice not to be angry.

*Was it one of the clowns?* it demanded.

'Yes.'

*Which clown? Where? When?*

'Goshy. Think his name's Goshy. 'Bout a week ago. Fell out . . . his pocket.'

A wave of anger like warm air brushed over him and he cowered, whimpering. There was a pause and the sound of fingernails drumming the tabletop before the voice said, *Okay. Wake up now, Jamie. Come back to me. Wake up.*

He filtered back into consciousness, lured by a wave of perfume and two sparkling eyes. At first he thought he was staring at a pair of diamonds glinting in candlelight; the fortune-teller's face appeared as a fuzzy outline around the jewels, and it seemed to take hours to resume its clarity and shape. 'Pleasant trip?' said Shalice the fortune-teller.

Jamie tried to remember the last few minutes, but it felt like he was thinking through fog. 'What happened? Was there something about a blonde woman?'

'No, I don't think so,' Shalice said. She started packing things away with rapid movements, preoccupied and clearly annoyed about something. 'Well, Jamie, thank you for stopping by. If you'll excuse me I have something to take care of.'

'Yeah, sure,' Jamie said and stood to go. Shalice brushed past him in a hurry, stepping through the beads and outside. Soon she was lost from sight. Jamie stared at the crystal ball for a moment, now hidden beneath a cloth cover, then left the hut.

Outside the dark fragrant little place, the world's colours and sounds seemed an assault. It took a moment to get his bearings: he could remember almost nothing since the magic show, and even that was hazy. Behind him, the glass beads at the hut's entrance rattled in the breeze. What precisely had gone on in there?

Again that soft, insistent voice: *Nothing it's your place to worry about. Enjoy the show.*

He was powerless to argue. The light-headed euphoria returned on a gust of breeze smelling of popcorn, and within a few deep breaths he felt giddy. He wandered slowly back to the more crowded pathways, browsing gypsy stalls as the afternoon grew dark.


Evening fell and the sky over Sideshow Alley was alight with multicoloured streaks. Jamie veered instinctively away from the colours and came to a wooden building with a crimson glow around it and orange tongues of flame bursting from its open door like dragon's breath: the funhouse.

There were few patrons around—most seemed to be heading towards the giant marquees in the middle of the showgrounds, where the gypsy stallholders informed passers-by, the acrobats and clowns were soon to perform. Only two people waited by the funhouse steps: a young couple who stood completely still, staring directly ahead. Beside them was a robed figure holding a staff with a skull at its tip. A black hood concealed his face. From within the funhouse came the expected noises: bestial howls, women's screams, a sound like giant teeth grinding together. Expected sounds, but by God they sounded real.

A cart suddenly burst through the door, sparks flashing around its wheels as it scraped along the metal rail. It squealed to a halt. The robed figure waved his staff. Without a word the young couple climbed into the cart.

Jamie glanced from them to the guardian, then headed for the steps. But the guardian barred the way with his staff. 'What's up?' Jamie asked him.

No answer. There was a horrible squealing that made him jump as the cart plunged ahead on its rail. The couple's heads wobbled like rag dolls. A flash of orange flame burst out from the doors as they went in, then they were gone from view.

Disappointed, Jamie waited for the next cart to wheel its way out. He glanced sidelong at the guardian, trying to make out the face beneath the hood. From inside the funhouse the sound of howling and screams kicked into a crescendo, trailing off into laughter like howling sexual ecstasy, drowning all distant carnival sounds before an abrupt silence fell.

*That* was a bit much. Jamie backed away from the funhouse and turned to go. Then he heard the cart squealing to a halt. He looked back over his shoulder. The couple was nowhere to be seen; the cart was empty.

He found he was hurrying away in a jog, as though his legs sensed danger his mind couldn't. *All part of the show*, the voice inside assured him. Of course. What wasn't?

Set away from the rest of the attractions, he saw a huge tent with only a few small shanties around it—these seemed to be homes of the dwarfs and gypsies. Occasionally luminous pairs of eyes would peer balefully from cracks in curtains as he walked past. The dwarfs had come out in numbers since nightfall, foul-tempered little things who broke off their conversations when patrons came near, then resumed in heated angry voices. They carried small bags and could be seen picking through the grass with steel tweezers. Jamie at first thought they were after spare change, but as he came near a pair of them at work he saw they were picking up the tiny gleaming crystals he'd noticed on the floor of the magician's show. The dwarfs scowled at him with such ferocity he backed away in fright.

When he neared the lonely tent he discovered it housed the freak show, and he hesitated before going in. The sick and weird held no appeal for him, but the eyes at the shanty windows were making him nervous, and getting out of sight seemed wise.

The only light inside the freak show tent came from yellow bulbs illuminating the glass display cases. On the floor were more gleaming little points of light—more of those powder crystals, far more here than there'd been on the floor of Mugabo's tent.

To Jamie's surprise, in front of one of the glass cases he saw Steve, who was staring avidly at something inside a tall fish tank. Steve spotted him and waved him over. 'Have a look at this,' Steve said.

The label on the tank read: *This is Tallow. His every living moment is hellish.*

A pair of human eyes stared mournfully out of a face that looked to be melting. Skin was running like candle wax, bubbling and dripping to the ground in pools before hardening into flesh-coloured lumps on the glass floor.

'Every few minutes he picks up the bits that have melted off and puts them back on himself,' Steve whispered with relish. Tallow watched them both sadly as a flesh-coloured bubble burst on its neck, dribbling and running down its chest. Jamie grimaced and turned away.

'Jamie, look! He's doing it!' said Steve, sounding damn near aroused.

'Let's get out of here,' Jamie said. 'That's sick. Come on.'

'No way. You gotta see this place. Come and check out this guy.' Steve dragged him by the arm to an exhibit not confined in a glass case. They stood before what may have once been human until nature played a very cruel joke. From the neck down he was fine, five feet or so of humanity dressed in a grey suit and tie. The thing's head was where the trouble began—it was covered in scales, too large for its body, and had catfish whiskers growing from gills in the neck. Its mouth was very wide like a shark and packed with vicious teeth. When the mouth opened and spoke Jamie almost screamed.

'Hello. I am Fishboy, curator of the freak show.'

'This is my friend Jamie,' said Steve. 'Jamie, this is Fishboy. He can breathe under water, he says.'

'Pleased to meet you, Jamie,' said Fishboy. His voice was high-pitched as if he'd inhaled helium. There was something obscene about his friendliness.

'I hope you enjoy our exhibits as much as Steve does. Yeti will be doing a glass-eating show in fifteen minutes. I guarantee it's the furriest, bloodiest performance in the whole circus!'

'Oh man, we gotta see the glass show,' Steve said.

Jamie shook his head. 'See you later,' he said.

'Why? Where you going?' Steve demanded.

'*Anywhere*. Jesus. Maybe I'll go wait for the clown show.'

'Ah yes,' Fishboy piped up. 'The clown show is perhaps our most celebrated attraction. Please, feel free to sign the guest book on your way out.'

Jamie cringed away from the perfectly civil shark-toothed smile; he'd have felt more at ease if Fishboy were growling and gnashing at them. He backed out of the freak show tent, trying not to look at the glass cases to either side as the exhibits moaned and hissed. Steve didn't follow him.

Back out in the warm night air, the good cheer had taken a sick, giddy turn. A faint nausea and sense of foreboding wormed into him. *I think I'm in deep tr*——but the thought was never allowed to finish.

And . . . he decided he preferred it that way.


By now large crowds had gathered by the two giant marquees. All present had faintly troubled looks on their faces, glancing about uneasily as though double-checking they were actually here.

The bigger of the two marquees had a sign out front that read:

RANDOLPH'S DEATH DEFYING, HIGH FLYING
ACROBATIC EXTRAVAGANZA

Out front of the other was a chalkboard that said:

GONKO'S FANTABULOUS CLOWN SHOW——COME GET YOUR CHUCKLES

Jamie stared at the chalkboard. Gonko . . . Where did he know that name from? He almost had it when he was shouldered by the crowd who, prompted by some signal he didn't catch, were now trickling into the marquees. There was something resigned about them, like lost souls caught in a storm, gathering under the only shelter in sight. Though much larger, the acrobat marquee filled up first.

Feeling more disoriented than he had since waking that morning and seeing Steve alive and well, with memories shuffling around in his head like cards—there one moment, gone the next—Jamie fell in line with the stream of people heading into the clown show. He sat in the back row of plastic seats, all facing a stage illuminated by bright spotlights, and waited quietly with the rest of the crowd.

*Gonko.* It was so close to his grasp.

When the clown show began, whatever influence had been steering his thoughts the rest of the day suddenly let go its hold, and at once it all came back to him. He looked around wildly for the exits, but they were blocked by people watching the stage, their faces blank. There was nowhere to run. He shrank back in his seat.


Gonko strolled across the stage, hands in his pockets. There was applause, though he scowled at the crowd like he would have happily sliced every throat in the room. He wore ludicrously large striped pants which enveloped his thin waist like a hoop, held up by suspenders. His face was painted white and he sported a red plastic nose. He wore a puffy hat similar to the magician's turban and a tiny bow-tie around his neck.

Stumbling out after him was Goshy, who looked around at the audience with boggling eyes, peering the way a baby does at a room full of confounding things. *What are these creatures?* But there was still that reptilian, calculating edge, suggesting that deep down Goshy knew very well *he* was the abnormality, and revelled in it.

In Goshy's hand was a daisy. His arms were locked stubbornly at his sides. He stumbled forward to a young woman in the front row. Without bending his elbow he offered her the daisy in one abrupt movement. She smiled at him and hesitated a second before she took it.

Goshy stared at her, blinking; he seemed to be waiting for something. Then, suddenly displeased for reasons all his own, he let fly with a slap. Her head rocked sideways with a rustle of blonde hair. Some in the audience laughed, perhaps assuming she was an actor planted for the gag.

Goshy stared around wildly as a murmur broke out in the crowd, his hands up over his ears, his mouth flapping without sound. He staggered backwards up the steps onto the stage. Gonko watched all this unfold with a look of exasperation: this was not how the script was meant to run, but by the way he threw his arms up in exasperation, he'd been half expecting this.

The show degenerated further. Goshy fell onto his back like a man shot and rolled from side to side, gesturing frantically at Gonko with his elbows for help, his hands still stuck over his ears. Then came the kettle sound Jamie knew all too well, loud as a siren: '*HMMMMMM! HMMMMM!*'

From backstage another clown rushed into the spotlight. It was Doopy. He ran to his brother and tried to coax him from the stage. Goshy wouldn't go. He stopped making the kettle noise and pointed at the woman in the front row, who was rubbing her face with a look of astonishment. Goshy's mouth flapped again. 'I know,' Doopy cried, 'she did *bad*, Goshy, she did *reeeeal bad*. But come *on*! It's a *show*! You're gonna be in so much *trouble* . . .'

Gonko sat cross-legged on the stage and massaged his temples. His voice carried over the confused babble of the audience, who didn't know now whether to laugh or not. 'I fucking knew it,' he said. 'Blown the whole gig, and it took less than a minute. Let's get this farce over with. RUFSHOD! Get out here. Bring the apprentice.' Gonko gave this order with violent false cheer. A thin crazed-looking clown ran onto the stage, dragging another clown with him.

The apprentice stood sourly under the spotlight, shoulders slumped. Gonko glared up at him. 'Say, Goshy,' Gonko cried. 'Take a look at the apprentice. What's that he's got in his pocket?'

Goshy had been propped back onto his feet. He turned slowly and waddled over to the apprentice. Rufshod, meanwhile, reached into the apprentice's pockets and pulled out what looked like a fern leaf. For some reason the leaf had a profound effect on Goshy. He stared at it with wide-eyed horror, the most human emotion yet to appear on his face, and once again came the kettle noise: '*HMMMMM! HMMMMM!*'

A look of fear dawned on the apprentice's face. Goshy squealed at him from close range and then with a stiff arm slapped the apprentice hard, as he had the woman in the front row. Doopy made one half-hearted attempt to calm his brother, crying, 'Goshy, stop!', but to no avail. Goshy slapped him again. The apprentice tried to dodge it, then glanced around at Rufshod, who stood blocking his escape. Goshy wound up for another slap. The apprentice gave him a shove. Doopy sprang into action. 'Hey hey hey *HEY HEYYYY!*' he screamed, building momentum like an avalanche. He flew at the apprentice, evidently with some notion of defending his brother. Though he looked the most harmless of the clowns, Doopy's charge had the force of a small bull. The apprentice was flattened, and rolled around at the feet of the other three trying to ward off the kicks, punches, head-butts, elbows and knees. Goshy backed out of the fray with his hands around his ears again. The audience was silent.

Gonko sat back and watched this unfold with a stony face, though the tilt of his lips suggested cold satisfaction with the beating. He turned to the crowd and muttered, 'Show's over. Get the fuck out.' There was a scatter of confused applause as the crowd stood and headed for the exits. Onstage the beating was slowing down and the apprentice, out cold, was dragged away by his feet. A thick trail of blood and face paint followed him.

When the audience had cleared out, Jamie waited in the back row, not sure where to go or what to do. Memories of the last few days rushed at him from all sides—the audition, the stalking, the destruction of his house. Things made less sense than ever.

From the stage Gonko looked directly at him. 'JJ,' he called out. 'Get over here.'

Jamie pointed at himself: *Who, me?*

'Yes you,' Gonko snarled. He stood at the edge of the stage, beckoning with one finger. Jamie stood and walked towards him slowly. *This is it,* he thought. *I'm about to die.*

He was mistaken. 'Welcome to your new home,' said Gonko as Jamie passed the front row of seats. The spotlight sent shadows sliding down the clown leader's face like bloody cuts. He said, 'Looks like they turned the funny gas off you later than I asked 'em to. I wanted you watching us from backstage—but never mind. Plenty more shows to come, my pretty, and no mistake. As you can see, the act's a bit rusty.' Gonko spat.

Jamie stared back at him. 'Would you please,' he said, 'tell me what the hell is going on? Please?'

Gonko squinted at him and answered slowly. 'That's a reasonable request. I don't see why not. What's going on is you're a clown now. Ever heard news that good? Nothin' but chuckles from here on out, with the odd giggle for good measure. Does it get any better? The fuck it does. Come with me, young JJ.'

CHAPTER 7

# CRYSTAL BALLS AND ACROBATS

GONKO led Jamie behind the stage to an area filled with boxes of props, uniforms and spotlight bulbs. There the apprentice lay, his face a pulpy mess, a sheen of blood and face paint still trickling off him. His eyes were closed. Goshy was staring down at him in a startled way without blinking, and Doopy was patting his shoulder, presumably to rouse him. When Gonko and Jamie appeared, Doopy stood, his wet lips working, hands twisting about each other nervously. Doopy no longer looked capable of the violence he'd inflicted onstage; he was once more a diminutive bumblebee of a man, pawing at his own shirt, his whole appearance a profuse apology.

'Nice job, Doops,' said Gonko, eyeing the bloody ruin at his feet.

'Gee, I'm sorry, Gonko, but he punched on Goshy!' Doopy cried. 'He punched on Goshy, right in the face, and I *gotta* look after Goshy. I just *gotta!*'

Gonko leaned over the prostrate figure and his mouth tilted sideways. 'I said nice job. You don't need to make excuses when the boss pats you on the back, Doops. Save that for your whoopsies.' Gonko poked the apprentice with the toe of his boot, then turned to Jamie. 'JJ, meet the crew. This is Goshy.'

Goshy had his back turned and was making low, quiet whistles. He was holding the fern leaf to his face and appeared to be kissing it.

'He knows what he likes,' Gonko muttered. 'And this is Doopy, who I believe you have seen before, destroying the shit out of your bedroom with yours truly.' Doopy stammered through a 'how do you do', while continuing to plead his case to Gonko. Gonko ignored him. 'This is Rufshod,' he said. The thin crazed-looking clown gave Jamie a wave that was like an electrocuted twitch. Rufshod looked to be the youngest of the clowns, perhaps Jamie's age. 'And this sad critter is the apprentice,' said Gonko. 'Now he's basically meat with eyeballs, and not for long, mark my words. And guess what sport? You got his job, in case you were wondering where that piece of the jigsaw puzzle goes.'

Jamie stared down and tried not to envisage his own face beaten as badly out of shape as the one oozing at his feet. He had no idea how to respond to any of this. He supposed the best plan was to keep his mouth shut and wait for the whole situation to make some kind of sense. Any minute now, surely, someone would tell him he was on *Candid Camera*, the victim of a high-budget radio stunt, a subject in a sociological experiment, *anything*.

Gonko led the clowns out of the tent, leaving the apprentice bleeding in the dirt. 'You lot,' said Gonko to the other clowns, 'that was just disgraceful. Doopy, get it through your brother's melon, do *not* slap the audience. Got it? They are *not* part of the fucking act. Do not slap the audience, poke the audience, throw at the audience, kick the audience. They are not props. They just watch the goddam show. You dig? It ain't brain science. *They just watch the fucking show.*'

'Geez, I'm sorry, Gonko,' Doopy stammered, 'but Goshy gets confused sometimes, and—'

'He knew damn well what he was doing tonight,' said Gonko. 'Look at the standard we set for the new guy. Show lasted less than two minutes. Why'd he slap that bint?'

'She took his flower, Gonko, she—'

'He gave her the flower, idiot. It was part of the script.'

'But she shouldn'ta oughtn'ta taken it, Gonko! She shouldn'ta, oughtn'ta, and he can't help it, he—he—'

'See what I have to put up with JJ?' said Gonko with a rueful smile. Jamie shrugged and nodded and tried not to be noticed.

Out in the showgrounds all the patrons had gone. The only sound was the odd clang and thump of stalls being packed up. A few dwarfs hung around in the shadows, muttering amongst themselves and glaring as the clowns passed. The clowns ignored them. They passed the magician's tent, the fortune-teller's hut, and came to a tent Jamie recognised as the place he'd woken in that morning. It was far larger than any surrounding dwellings.

Goshy made a quiet beeping sound and stood still. The others turned to him. Doopy seemed to interpret the sound—he held a finger to his lips and said, 'Shhh.'

There were murmuring voices nearby, too muffled to make out any words. Jamie glanced at each of the clowns, wondering what was next on the nasty surprise agenda. Something violent, he soon saw, for Gonko reached into his pocket and pulled out a long silver blade. Jamie goggled at it, wondering how it had fit in the clown leader's pocket.

Gonko gathered the clowns together in a huddle. Jamie tried to step away but the crazed-looking clown, Rufshod, grabbed him in a headlock and herded him into their midst. The sweaty reek of Goshy at close range was almost too much to bear. 'Acrobats,' Gonko whispered. 'I'll do the talking. And the stabbing. But if it's on, everyone in. That means you, Goshy. Don't stand around staring like last time when that bastard Randolph clocked me. You too, JJ. You look like yer made of elbows and gristle, but you swing them chicken-arms like you're trying to break 'em.'

The huddle broke apart and Gonko prowled ahead, twirling the blade expertly on his palm. The others followed. Three men were waiting for them at the tent's entrance, all dressed in white tights. They fell silent and bristled as the clowns approached.

As first impressions went Jamie found looking at the acrobats almost hypnotic. Their bodies were lithe, their features elfish and finely carved, and Jamie couldn't help but admire the workmanship of whoever had made them. The clowns clearly did not feel the same way. Both parties locked eyes for a moment, the acrobats regarding Jamie suspiciously, before one of them said, 'Mmm, mmm! Heard you boys had quite a show. Five whole minutes, I heard.'

'More like two,' said another.

'Two minutes!' said the first in mock sympathy. 'Shocking, la! Sven, what will Mr Pilo have to say about this?'

'I'm not sure. Maybe he'll suggest the poor dears need some time off doing other jobs, like scrubbing the gypsy shitters, to help them focus on their act. But, of course, we can only ask him.'

'But he won't be impressed, Sven, will he?'

'I don't think so, Randolph, not the teeniest bit impressed.'

Gonko had looked almost eager for confrontation moments before, but it seemed the trashing of the night's show was stinging him. 'Fuck off,' he growled, the arm holding the knife shaking with rage.

'Oh, *touché*!' cried the nearest acrobat. 'Fuck off indeed! This is why I turn to *you* for a battle of wits, Gonko. Your sophistication, la! They don't make 'em like you anymore.'

Quick as a snake Gonko lunged at the acrobat who'd spoken, but the acrobat pirouetted out of the way with ease. Jamie winced, sure the brawl was on. But no—Gonko stepped back, twirling the blade on his palm again, and the acrobats seemed to decide the encounter was over. They smiled contemptuously as they walked away, heaping on more insults for good measure.

'Faggots,' Gonko yelled after them.

The acrobats stopped and turned back. 'What did he call us?'

'He called us faggots!'

'*Touché* again. You know what they say: a male who humps a male is a double male.'

'That's just what I was about to tell him.'

'At least we know who's on top.'

They laughed as they strode out of sight. Doopy turned to Gonko and said, 'I don't *like* those guys, Gonko. I don't *like* them!'

'Well maybe you could convince your brother not to ruin our show,' said Gonko. 'That way, Doops, we got a tent full of giggly tricks and they got nothing on us. You see? It ain't brain science.' Gonko slid the blade back into his pocket. 'And,' he said, 'for the record, if I'd wanted to knife that bastard, I would have. But the way you lazy shits performed tonight, I wouldn't trust you in a scrap if it came to that.'

He led them inside the tent. Goshy marched directly through a canvas door at the back of the room leading to some hidden quarters; the other clowns collapsed on couches pushed up against the walls. Jamie gazed around the chaotic lantern-lit mess, which looked like a nursery for oversized children. Props, clown pants and boxes of trinkets lay strewn everywhere. He recognised the suit of armour with its crayon graffiti. On the opposite wall were wooden statues of what looked like Amazonian gods, propped against each other as though rutting. In the mouth of one of these someone had stuffed a rubber chicken.

His eyes settled on the body bag he'd woken in that morning. 'How'd you like that one, JJ?' said Gonko, slapping him on the back. 'Comfy in there? Ha ha! Rise and shine, my lovely! Anyway, JJ, this is our private space. No one comes in here without our say-so. Anyone does, we can do what we want to 'em, even if it means the circus is looking for new staff come morning. Dig? Best remember that applies to everyone else, too, so tread careful. Gypsies bring chow at nine, one and six. Wet hot dogs or noodles that taste like salty plastic, mainly. Get bored of that, it's candied apples and juice pops.' Gonko spat and muttered, 'Yeah, chow ain't the best part of the circus . . .' before continuing, 'we each got a bunker out back. Show days vary, sometimes two days in a row, sometimes none for weeks. Depends on what shows are happening outside. A competition thing, you dig? Here's where we rehearse.' He pointed at the one space of clear grassy floor.

'Right,' Jamie said. 'Um, I don't quite know how to put this . . .'

'You're among friends, young JJ,' said Gonko. 'Speak from the heart.'

Jamie took a deep breath. 'Who are you people? *What* are you people? What am I doing here? What the hell is going on?'

Gonko peered at him through narrowed eyes. 'You *still* want to know all that?' Jamie didn't quite know how to reply. 'Fine,' said Gonko. 'Come with me. We'll pop over to the fortune-teller and clear up all them little posers. Off we go, li'l JJ and Papa Gonko.'

Gonko led him through the dark showgrounds. The dwarfs were out in swarms now, squatting in alleys playing dice games, or crouching up on rooftops with bottles in their hands, spewing profanities at one another. A pair of them tussled in a doorway over what looked like a ham bone. One combatant stumbled in front of Gonko, who booted him away like a football without breaking stride. The dwarf flew six feet in the air and crashed into a gypsy's door, which opened, a hand reaching out to grab the dwarf by the hair, dragging it inside. Whatever happened in there resulted in much screaming and banging. The other dwarfs fell silent as they watched this unfold, staring after Gonko with quiet malice. He didn't appear to notice.

They came to Shalice's hut, though Jamie barely recognised it from his dim memories of the day. Only the rattling beads seemed familiar. Incense still laced the air, though it was faint. A large white caravan, presumably the fortune-teller's home, was parked a little way behind the hut. There was light shining from both buildings. Gonko marched to the hut and gave the wall a solitary thump with his boot. A hand parted the beads and there was the darkly beautiful woman with playful eyes—though for the moment she scowled. 'Look who it is,' she said. 'Nice one, Gonko. Why didn't you tell me this one was a recruit?'

Gonko raised his eyebrows. 'What's your problem?' He brushed past her and took a seat on the wooden crate, squinting up at Shalice, who watched him icily.

'I did him a reading,' she said. 'As if he were a regular trick. *You know*. And he resisted me. It could have ended very badly. You could have lost your man. There are reasons I need to know these things.'

'Ah, get off my case,' said Gonko, though now he looked faintly amused. 'What were the odds of him stumbling in here?'

Shalice bared her teeth. 'Pretty good, as it turns out.'

Gonko shrugged. 'Well, shucks, guess I figured you would have foreseen it, being the one with the spooky powers and such.'

'I foresee it will not happen again,' Shalice replied, 'for I had a word to Kurt about it.'

Gonko sprang to his feet and looked like he was about to strike her. 'You fucking scag!'

She smiled and stepped towards him, her dark eyes flashing. 'Uh-uh, settle down, precious. *You* know better than that. Behave yourself.'

Gonko ran a hand down his face; his fingers twitched. 'We'll talk about it later,' he said. 'For now, JJ here needs some answers.'

Shalice glanced at Jamie. 'The usual?'

'Yeah, the usual,' said Gonko. 'Who are you why am I here what's going on mama I'm frightened blah blah blah.' Gonko lashed at the wooden crate with his boot, breaking one of its boards. 'No, really, thanks for squealing on me, you fucking——that's two piles of stink I have to clean up now.'

He stormed out of the hut, swiping at the beads as he went. Shalice watched him go, muttered something under her breath, then turned to Jamie. She looked him up and down. 'So. You want to know why you are here and why you should stay. You want to know who we are and what we do. Is that right?'

Jamie nodded. 'That would be a start, I suppose. Then maybe you can tell me where I can call a cab to take me home. I promise not to sue anybody. I'll sign an affidavit. Whatever you want.'

'I think you will see that is not one of our concerns,' she said. She sat down behind the crystal ball and plucked off its cloth veil, then watched him in silence for a moment. 'I will put it to you like this,' she said. 'You are not strictly *in* the world anymore, Jamie. Though of course it is not far away. You are here because you have been given a second chance. You see, you were meant to die young, and before you died you were to live miserably.'

Jamie rubbed the corners of his eyes. 'And how exactly do you know that?'

'Because you are *here*,' she said. 'No one comes here unless they were headed for such an end. Everyone here was saved from death. That is why they stay. They owe something to the show——you, I, everyone else here. Whether we are better off, I could not tell you . . . I have never died. But I can show you what your life would be if we had not found you.' She gave him an appraising look. 'There is magic in the world, Jamie. You have seen enough today to know that. There is magic—it is rare, but most of it is right here in these showgrounds. The very air you breathe is thick with it. Yes, you see? You felt it today, did you not? The circus breathing its will into your lungs?'

Jamie couldn't answer. Shalice nodded, and said, 'The magic is here for a reason. It is not safe loose in the world. Neither are we. And the clowns, in their wisdom, have seen something in you they can use, that the show can use. You are fortunate.'

She traced a finger over the glass orb and said quietly, 'Look.'

The surface flickered white. Jamie stared at the glow and could soon discern shapes. Suddenly there he was in the glass, like a character on a silent TV show. Before him was a familiar scene: he was in his bedroom getting ready for work at the Wentworth Club, in the midst of the usual frantic search for his shoes and socks. He was flailing his arms around, swearing and crying to the heavens. Shalice said, 'This is you, one month ago. Time shows me some of her secrets, you see. Just here and there, like wind blowing back a curtain from a window. Sometimes, when I ask her nicely, she shows me what I need to see. Now, if she will oblige, we will see what would have become of you, Jamie, had we not brought you to us.'

Jamie's mouth hung open, his eyes locked on the glass ball, mesmerised by the fortune-teller's silky voice. He was just aware enough to see himself going through the motions of everyday life, though it seemed already like years before. And as he watched himself running around, desperate to get to work on time, it struck him that he looked ridiculous; what a strange *purpose* to have in life, what a strange thing to take so seriously.

Shalice whispered something he didn't catch, and the picture changed. At first he had to do a double-take, for he thought he was staring right at his father. The resemblance was almost exact, down to the stress lines, the thinning hair, the stubble. But no, it was Jamie, perhaps in his late forties, sitting in an office. There was a beer gut ballooning beneath his shirt and tie, sagging over his belt, absurd on his slender frame.

'Look,' said Shalice. 'This is just twelve years away. You got a dead-end government job. You swore off alcohol in your twenties, but now you are as alcoholic as they come. There are times when you sneak into the bathroom for a swig of bourbon. Your co-workers laugh about it often. See that picture?' She pointed to a framed photograph on his desk that he couldn't quite make out. 'You never married, but you have a son. He was born retarded, so your child support is not cheap. It is where most of your salary goes. You are earning enough for a nice place, but every night you go home to a roach-infested apartment, alone. The other men in the office talk of their vacations and their entertainment systems, but you? You have nothing. Despite twelve years of hard labour, Jamie. It has taken its toll on you. See that twitch below your left eye? That is permanent.'

Jamie watched the hollow-eyed scarecrow with dizzy horror. Throughout life his father had seemed an almost melancholy figure, overworked and trapped in a loveless marriage, but the wreck before him now surpassed anything his father had been. 'The mother of your child was your first girlfriend,' the fortune-teller went on. 'You were together two years. Protestant girl, very pretty. She wanted to be married but you didn't. She stopped taking birth control pills in secret, knowing you would do the honourable thing. You were wrapped around her finger. But it fell apart after your son was born that way. She blamed *you*. Keep watching.'

At his desk, the wreck Jamie had become was staring at a huge pile of folders and sheets. A clerk of some kind waddled over and dumped another stack beside the first. Older Jamie buried his face in his hands.

'It never ends,' Shalice said. 'Decades of this, Jamie. No reward. No way out. Inside you grows a tumour of cynicism and bitterness. Look at yourself. This is what fifteen years of study and twelve years of work have brought you.'

Older Jamie snapped out of his morbid trance with a start to answer the phone on his desk. His resemblance to his father in that moment was so vivid Jamie had to look away, and his mind went back to the morning his father took the phone call telling them Jamie's uncle had hung himself. His father's body had slumped like a sack of loose bones, and he'd burst into tears. It was the first time Jamie had seen the man cry, and for some reason the sight had struck an obscure nerve of pleasure inside him which he'd never felt since. Nor did he want to.

'This phone call will be important,' Shalice said, drawing him back from the reverie he had been slipping into. Her eyes flickered constantly from Jamie to the ball, back and forth in a flash. 'This call is from the mother of your child. She's threatening to take you to court for more money. Your son needs minders, medication, equipment, special ed. Her pill collection is not cheap, either.'

Jamie's throat was dry and he swallowed what felt like a mouthful of lint. Opposite him Shalice was nodding. 'You discovered six months before this phone call that you were entrapped. Your child's mother and sister had a nasty falling out, and her sister told you out of spite. So now, every time you think of the mother of your child, you just want to kill someone. There is no respite from your anger. You want to wrap your hands around somebody's neck and squeeze. That is what goes through your head, nowadays.'

Jamie shut his eyes. His voice came out as little more than a croak: 'What's so special about this phone call?'

'This is the call that drives you over the edge,' the fortune-teller replied. 'Watch.'

In the crystal ball, older Jamie hung up the phone, gently, calmly, then sat back in his chair. He stared into the distance as another clerk came to dump more folders on his desk. Older Jamie didn't seem to notice; he just stared into space, then calmly, gently, picked up his briefcase and strolled out of the office, to the lift, through the lobby, out the building's front door.

'Where's he going?' said Jamie. 'Why are you showing me this?'

The look in her eyes answered him, and a cold chill raced up his spine. 'There, there,' she said. 'It is not a particularly unusual thing to happen. Most murders run to this script. Love gone wrong. A shame, but not unusual.'

'I don't want to see the rest,' said Jamie, for he felt nauseous. 'Turn it off. Please.'

'A little more,' she said softly. 'You need to see it all, Jamie. I show you this for a reason.'

In the glowing ball, Jamie was now walking up a flight of steps. The building looked like an inner city apartment block, a little rundown and in need of new paint. There was a slump in his shoulders, like a great weight hung from his neck, and a slow dreamlike rhythm to his footsteps. The door opened and a woman stood in the doorway, a thirty-something brunette with a bathrobe tied at the waist and sedated eyes. The look on her face said she'd been neither expecting nor hoping for a visit from older Jamie. The pair of them exchanged words for a minute, then she tossed her hands up in exasperation, stepping aside to let him in.

Once inside she went to the kitchen and put on the kettle. Older Jamie watched her with a blank look on his face. With that same blank look he walked to the kitchen and stood directly behind her. She seemed not to have heard him as she reached to take two coffee cups from a shelf. Older Jamie raised his hands and placed them, calmly, gently, around her neck.

She tensed and wheeled about, tried to shove him away, shouted something, and that seemed to break older Jamie out of his blankness. He grabbed her fiercely and threw her to the floor. She fell hard. Her robe came undone and parted, showing legs as white as wax kicking at the linoleum floor as she tried to back away. He took a knife from the rack, his face strangely expressionless as he fell on top of her and, without pausing, rammed it into her guts, again and again and again and again . . .

Blood poured, coating his hands and wrists like another skin. Finally she stopped struggling and curled into foetal position, face gripped in a spasm of pain as her killer stepped away to let her die.

Jamie watched all this and felt sickness rise in the back of his throat. He swallowed and kept it down for a moment, then stumbled out of the hut, bent over and threw up in the grass. Down on all fours, panting and sweating, he tried to swab his mind of what he'd just seen, to think of absolutely nothing.

Across the path, two dwarfs eyed him with suspicion. One muttered something to the other behind the back of its hand.

'Come back,' Shalice called from inside the hut. 'It's almost finished.'

Legs rubbery, he somehow made it back inside and sat on the crate. 'Enough,' he said. 'No more. Please.'

'Just a little,' she whispered. 'The worst is over.'

It took effort to focus again on the glass ball, but he did it. He watched his older self in the bathroom, before the mirror, staring at his reflection. Older Jamie seemed to have washed the blood from his hands, and there were little specks of it over the mirror and sink. He held his hands together and said what looked like a prayer. His face still had that blank look he'd worn when stabbing the mother of his child to death. He retained that blank look as he walked through the apartment, passing the body on the floor without giving it a glance. He opened the sliding glass door and stepped onto the balcony. Impassively, without hesitation, he stepped over the rail and dropped from sight.

The pictures in the ball faded and its light went out. Shalice replaced the cloth cover. 'I know that was hard for you to watch,' she said sympathetically, 'but you had to see it. That is what you were spared by coming here. That is what awaits you, out there.'

'I can avoid——'

'No. You cannot. You would forget about us. We would arrange it. The clowns would knock you out, the appropriate rituals would be performed, you would be taken back to your room in the dead of night, left there, and you would wake thinking you'd had a very strange dream, though the details would escape you. Your present and this future would at some point coalesce. And you would be finished.'

Jamie stood. 'Okay . . . I need to go. I need to . . . think about this. Okay?'

'Yes, Jamie.' She reached for his hand and held it. Her fingers were cool and smooth. 'It is better this way,' she said, looking him in the eyes. 'Much better.'

He swallowed, nodded, and staggered from the hut. Shalice watched him go, then gave the ball a quick rub with its cloth cover.

Gonko came in a moment later. She didn't look up at him. 'Did he buy it?' Gonko murmured.

'Of course,' the fortune-teller replied. 'Some of us are masters of our craft. Now get out of my hut.'

# CHAPTER 8

# WINSTON THE CLOWN

JAMIE found his way back to the clowns' tent and sat outside on a log. From Sideshow Alley came the final distant sounds of carnies packing up for the night. Overhead the sky spread out like a vast black lake, with no sign of the stars or moon.

He was trying, without luck, to put the day into perspective. The show as he'd seen it came back in blurred, disconnected snapshots. The fortune-teller's story had shaken him badly, but he'd already seen so many things that should not be real, there was no reason not to believe what he'd seen. And it stung to think it could end that way; he'd never had grand ambitions, would have settled for the standard package: job, house, wife, 2.3 kids. Enough holiday time to see some of the world, the odd game of golf. It wasn't too much to ask, and he'd been willing to work for it.

So, this was a second chance? Maybe, but she had not really answered any of his original questions. Who, what, why, where, how—those pesky little details.

He turned at the sound of footsteps and saw Gonko squinting down at him. 'Get some rest,' said Gonko. 'Not a good idea to be out alone after dark. Not here.'

'Why not?' said Jamie despondently.

Gonko peered around into the gloom. 'Stay and find out if you want to. Them dwarfs ain't too fond of anyone who ain't a dwarf. Or anyone who is. And they ain't the only thing that comes out at night. Come on. Up. Inside.'

Jamie sighed. He stood and followed Gonko into the tent. Shadows cast by kerosene lanterns flickered on the walls; the body bag still lay in the corner. Jamie and Gonko sat down at the card table, where Doopy and Rufshod were in the middle of a round of poker. Goshy and the apprentice were nowhere to be seen. 'Deal JJ in next round,' said Gonko, dropping a handful of odd copper coins in front of him. The clowns glanced at Jamie for a moment but took no further notice of him, and he was glad. He sat back quietly to wallow in his confusion.

'What's with your brother?' Gonko said to Doopy, who flicked cards around the table. 'Really, no bullshit now. I want to know why we can't get through a single act these days. Kurt'll put us on notice if we don't get through a show sooner or later.'

Doopy glanced over his shoulder to make sure he wasn't overheard. 'Well, Goshy . . . He's got a problem. With his girlfriend. With his *girlfriend*, Gonko.'

'I'm listening,' said Gonko.

'He . . .' Doopy glanced over his shoulder again. 'He pooped the question, Gonko.'

'Popped?'

'Yeah, that's what he done. Goshy done went and pooped the question.'

'Right. And?'

'And he's blue, 'cause she didn't give him no answer. She didn't say nothin', Gonko! Nothin' at all. She gone all quiet. She just sat there, Gonko, you shoulda seen it.'

Gonko took his cards. 'Doops,' he said, 'she's a fucking plant. How's she supposed to answer?'

Jamie sat forward. 'She's a what?'

'She's a fern,' said Gonko. 'Goshy's in love with a fern. He's probably in his room with it right now, whispering sweet nothings. God knows.'

Jamie remembered the first night he'd seen the clowns, the sickening thud Goshy made as he slammed headfirst into the pavement outside the . . . Yes, the gardening supply store. He gave a startled laugh in spite of himself. 'Really?'

'Yeah, but . . .' Gonko made a hush-hush gesture. 'That's the problem, huh?' he said to Doopy. 'He's ruining our act because the goddamn fern didn't say yes?'

'Yeah, Gonko!' Doopy cried. 'I'm mad at her, y'know. She coulda oughta said somethin'. She shoulda oughta said *yes*, is what she shoulda said.'

'Well,' said Gonko, leaning back in his chair, 'we'll have to get him an answer, somehow.'

'The MM,' Rufshod said, tossing down two cards and picking up two from the deck. 'We could make him, you know, change the plant. So it can talk.'

'No,' said Gonko, slamming his fist on the tabletop. 'That creepy shit ain't coming in here.' He turned to Jamie. 'You see the freak show today?'

Jamie nodded.

'The MM is the matter manipulator,' said Gonko. 'Flesh sculptor. Old forgotten art form practised by certain sick fucks in the Middle Ages, only back then they usually used dead bodies. The MM made the freaks what they are. Nasty shit. Small guy, shifty eyes, wears a hat. Lives in the funhouse, which between you and me ain't no fun house, and hardly ever comes out, except when someone's been actin' up and the boss wants to scare 'em straight. Got a nasty dog he takes with him everywhere to protect him. Few gypsies have lost relatives, you see, though if they attacked him they'd be next in his studio. Don't go near him, I don't care how righteously mad you might be. Been known to grab stray carnies for practice.'

'I'll kill that dog of his,' Rufshod said. 'Look at the bite he gave me.' He lifted his calf onto the table and pulled back his pants. A long thick purple scar ran from ankle to knee.

'That's a burn mark,' said Gonko. 'You did that, not the dog.'

'I had to, you know, burn the bite. So it wouldn't get infected.'

'That looks ouch, Ruf,' said Doopy. 'It looks *ouch*! Hey, Ruf, remember when I told you it looks ouch? Remember when——'

'Ruf doesn't mind a little pain,' Gonko said to Jamie. 'Do you Ruf?'

Rufshod's eyes gleamed. 'I don't *mind* it,' he agreed. 'Here.' He held his hand flat on the table and produced a knife from somewhere. He handed it to Jamie. 'Cut me,' he said.

Jamie stared at the knife. 'I don't think . . .'

'Come on,' said Rufshod. 'Cut me. Do it.'

'Why don't you cut yourself?' said Jamie.

'Not the same if I do it. Stab me. Cut me. *Do* something.'

'One thing you're going to have to become accustomed to,' said Gonko, pulling a steel hatchet from one of his seemingly bottomless pockets, 'is a little violence, here and there. It's good for you. Bracing, like cold showers.' He span the hatchet on his hand as he had the knife, earlier. 'You'll get used to a little violence,' he said. 'Or, like Rufshod, you'll get a little *too* used to it. But different strokes, right, Ruf?'

In one smooth motion Gonko held the hatchet up, closed his fingers around the handle and smashed the blunt end down on Rufshod's knobbly battle-scarred hand. There was a loud fleshy sound of bones being crunched to powder. Rufshod screamed, clutched his wrist, and fell from his seat, the bells on his hat tinkling. He rolled around under the table, kicking it as he wailed.

'There, genuine slapstick,' said Gonko, putting the hatchet away. 'That'll keep him happy for weeks. STOP BUMPING THE FUCKING TABLE! Now, where was I? The MM. Stay away from him. He can *change* people. Could take your arm and add something to it. Feathers, say. Could give you wings if he wanted to. You seen Fishboy?'

Jamie nodded.

'Fishboy looks like that thanks to the MM,' said Gonko. 'Disgusting, ain't it?'

'Yeah,' Jamie said. 'He seemed . . . friendly, though.'

'Fishboy's a good feller. Nicest sonofabitch in the whole show.'

Jamie sat upright in his seat and sucked in a sharp breath. Gonko eyed him. 'What's up?' he said.

'Steve,' said Jamie. 'I left him there, at the freak show . . . Oh no . . .'

He got up and ran out of the tent, down the battered path, hoping he was going the right way. Up ahead the funhouse was an orange glow in the darkness—now he remembered, the freak show was nearby. He sprinted off, ignoring the dwarfs crowding in the alleys and the eyes peering from parting curtains.

Behind him, Gonko followed at a brisk walk, hands in his pockets. As Jamie paused to catch his breath, Gonko tapped him on the shoulder. 'Easy feller,' he said.

'I've got to find my roommate,' Jamie said. 'He was at the freak show.'

'Yeah, all right,' said Gonko. 'We'll take a look, but we'll be quick about it. Follow.' Gonko led him off the main path and threaded his way between shanties and some closed-down stalls. They stopped a few metres from the freak show tent and Gonko held a finger to his lips. '*Shhh.*'

Through the tent's door they could see nothing but the dim yellow light of incubators. The sound of pained moaning came from within—Jamie couldn't tell from this distance whether or not the voice was Steve's. A shadowy figure passed through the doorway, heading towards the funhouse. Walking ahead of him was a large black dog on a leash. The dog turned its head towards Jamie and Gonko and growled, but its owner didn't look their way.

'That's him,' Gonko whispered. 'Don't get no closer to him than this.' Soon the matter manipulator disappeared from view. Gonko said, 'If *he's* been in the neighbourhood, your friend probably ain't having a good day. I recall the boss saying we needed more freaks. Hope you weren't too attached to your chum. Hold onto your guts. Here we go.'

The moaning got louder as they neared the door. The freak show exhibits seemed to be asleep. A severed head in a fish bowl stared straight ahead without blinking.

Then Jamie spotted him—Steve was alive and seemingly unharmed. The moaning came from Yeti, who lay on his back, his giant furry body flecked with blood that was rushing from his gums. Steve was wiping his fur with a wet rag which he squeezed out into a plastic bucket. Fishboy crouched beside him, stroking Yeti's head like a nurse.

'Good Yeti,' said Fishboy in his helium-voice, '*good* Yeti. The pains will fade; I'll prepare some powder for you.' Fishboy turned to Steve. 'He'll recover fast, always does. Some days he can get away without eating the glass, but today Mr Pilo was watching. Oh, and Tallow's cage will need to be mopped every two hours on show days when we have the heat on. I imagine they'll have you helping carnies in Sideshow Alley, but try to do that work in the morning——I'll need you here in the afternoons . . .' Fishboy trailed off and glanced through the doors to where Jamie and Gonko waited, watching.

Gonko pulled at Jamie's sleeve. He followed the clown leader away. '*That* feller lucked out,' said Gonko with a chuckle. 'So far, at least. Being errand boy for carnies he'll never pack any clout around here. But by hell it could've been worse.'

Jamie swallowed and nodded his head, surprised at the relief he felt that Steve, of all people, was okay.


Back at their tent, Gonko announced that Rufshod was to quit his bitching and show Jamie around his new home. The clowns' tent was bigger than it appeared from the outside; past the parlour, through a draped canvas doorway, a hall skirted around in a wide semicircle, branching off into several rooms. Jamie had been allocated the apprentice's room, a cramped space not much bigger than a closet. There was a decaying wooden cupboard, and what looked like a medic's stretcher as his new bed. All floor space was taken up by boxes and crates of clown uniforms and broken practical joke parts. He saw a palm-buzzer, a squirting flower, a rotating bow-tie, and some less innocent——knives, spent cartridges, dildos, syringes. There were dozens of broken plastic noses and a couple of plaster casts with dried blood hardened into rust-coloured shells.

The apprentice himself lay asleep on the medic's stretcher. He'd smoothed a thick layer of greasy white face paint over the fractured mess of his face.

At the sight of him, Rufshod ran off and returned with Gonko, who squinted at the sleeping apprentice and bared his teeth. He crouched down next to the stretcher, took a box of matches from his pocket and struck one. 'JJ,' he said, 'don't think this is how we treat all new recruits.' He set the match to the apprentice's pants. A lick of flame crawled over the flower-printed fabric, sending up thin ribbons of black smoke. Gonko stood in the doorway and watched with a smile. The apprentice stirred and rolled around as the fire spread to his shirt, then his eyes flickered and shot open. He let out a wheezing strangulated croak before bolting up and out into the night. Gonko stuck out a boot and tripped him as he passed. The apprentice got to his feet and staggered away, the fire blazing across his shoulders. His screams soon faded in the distance.

'All yours, JJ,' said Gonko, wiping his hands, and he stalked off with Rufshod following.

Jamie lay down on the stretcher, glad to be left alone to speculate on how much trouble he was in. If the fortune-teller's words were true——*You are not strictly* in *the world anymore*——escaping might not be a matter of jumping the fence and running.

It did occur to him that getting on Gonko's bad side was always an option if he wanted a *real* ticket out of the circus.

Next morning the hammering of tent pegs and the distant babble of coarse voices woke him, and Jamie sat up, surprised to find he'd slept. The stretcher was surprisingly comfortable, and his dreams had been vivid and hallucinogenic.

He rubbed his eyes and gave a startled cry——someone was in the room with him.

'Shh,' the stranger said. 'Keep it down.' It was an old clown, one Jamie hadn't seen before, his face impressively aged with stress lines and crow's-feet and sagging bags under the eyes. His body had clearly once been of bullish strength, and was still quite solid beneath his clown uniform of bow-tie, striped shirt, oversized shoes and pants. Thin strings of white hair hung from his head; he wore no face paint. His wet red eyes regarded Jamie sadly. 'So, they got another one,' he said, sighing. 'Another one joins the show.'

Jamie glanced around for a weapon; his eyes fell on a rusty knife within arm's reach in the mess. 'Who are you?' he said, edging away from the stranger and making the stretcher creak.

'Name's Winston,' said the clown in a slow mournful voice. 'And you must be JJ. JJ the clown.'

'Jamie, actually. And yes, I guess I am.'

'Didn't mean to startle you,' said Winston, fiddling with the bowler hat in his hands, 'but I didn't want to wake you either. You looked pretty peaceful just now . . . Suppose I figured you'd need what peace you can find from here on.' Winston scratched his neck absently, setting in motion many flaps of wrinkled skin. 'Don't recall when they got me,' he said, sighing. 'Was a while back. Was minding my own damn business is all I know for sure.'

Jamie wondered what the purpose of this visit was, though he could think of no polite way to ask. The old clown seemed to follow his train of thought. 'I s'pose,' he said, 'I'm here to offer my condolences. You went and landed yourself in the stew this time, son. One mighty pot of bother. I did too, for what it's worth.'

There was a silence as Winston gazed off into space. Jamie looked past him to the door, wondering if he could possibly lock it in future. 'I didn't see you perform yesterday,' he said to break the silence.

'Eh? Oh, Gonko let me have the night off,' said Winston. 'Told 'im my back was playing up. Sounds like the boys were in fine form again——ruined every show for the last month. But never mind that. I should probably give you what lowdown I can. Maybe help you get a feel of the carnival, prevent you getting yourself killed or worse.'

'Worse, huh?'

'Oh yes,' said Winston, looking him in the eye, and he said it so solemnly that a shiver went down Jamie's spine.

'Well, how about the lowdown on this,' Jamie said after a brief silence. 'What am I supposed to do here? I'm not a clown. I don't know why they recruited me. How am I supposed to behave?'

'That'll come,' said Winston. 'There's ways to bring out the clown in you.'

'Wonderful.' Jamie ran a hand through his hair and muttered, 'What the hell have I gotten myself into?'

'Oh, damn it, I'm sorry, son,' said Winston, his voice suddenly breaking and tears appearing in his eyes. Jamie was taken aback. *Hey, it's not your fault*, he wanted to say.

Winston ran a palm over his face and got himself under control. Then he leaned forward and dropped his voice to a whisper: 'All right, I'll tell you this much. At night, take off your face paint. Put it on when you have to, but for God's sake take it off sometimes. You'll want to remember who you were before you came here. If you forget that, you lose *everything*, and you won't ever know it happened.' Winston had grabbed Jamie's arm during this outpouring and his grip became tight.

'What's the face paint got to do with anything?' said Jamie.

'You'll see. You're going to be walking a tightrope over the coming days . . . Just take it off whenever you can, understand?'

'No,' Jamie said, pulling his arm free. 'I don't. But fine, I'll take it off.'

'Good lad. What else should I tell you?' Winston mused, scratching his head. 'Damn it, my head's scrambled these days.'

Jamie shrugged. 'Maybe you could tell me about the other clowns. How come you're so . . . normal, compared to them?'

'I'm not normal, son,' Winston said with a mirthless laugh. 'Not normal. Closer to it than the rest of 'em, that's all. That's why I told you to take the paint off sometimes. You don't want to end up like them, forget what you used to be. Far as anyone knows, they always been what they are now. Goshy and Doopy, you seen 'em. Look at 'em, for God's sake! Lost it for good, the pair of 'em.'

'Goshy,' Jamie said, and shuddered. 'He acts so fucking creepy.'

'It's no act. Goshy don't even know what's going on in Goshy's head anymore. Steer clear of him, Jamie, at least until he gets to know you. Doopy's not so bad, as a rule, but he can flip his lid too.'

Jamie nodded, the scene from yesterday echoing in his ears: *Hey hey hey HEY HEYYYY!* Smack, crack, thud. He said, 'What about Rufshod? He seems okay.'

Winston nodded. 'Usually all right. But he gets himself, and us, into trouble. Plays pranks all over the showgrounds. He's the one put the powder in Goshy's pants then set him loose outside. If he ever says, *Come with me I got an idea*, don't go.'

'And Gonko?'

Winston glanced over his shoulder. 'You seen enough of Gonko,' he whispered. 'He's fine, if you're a clown. Hard to know what makes him tick sometimes. If you don't give him real reason to blow up at you, he won't. There's that much to be said for him. There's worse here than him, believe me.'

From outside Jamie's little room came the sound of voices. 'Keep it down now,' Winston said. 'The boys are awake.'

'But . . . what *is* this place anyway?' Jamie said. 'What's the powder for? Where do those people come from, the crowds I saw yesterday?'

'Tricks. That's what we call 'em. Tricks are just regular folk who never find out they took a wrong turn. They don't remember us, they never come back. The powder, the tricks, what we're really doing . . . I can't tell you all that yet. Too much too soon, when most of it you have to see to believe anyway. I'll just tell you how to survive, this early on. Too much too soon might . . .' He trailed off.

Suddenly the door burst open and Rufshod's crazed bug-eyed head popped into view. 'Conspiracy!' he screamed, and Jamie's heart leapt to his throat. Winston turned around and lashed out, clipping Rufshod's ear. 'Get out, you fuggin' upstart,' he snarled.

Rufshod cackled and vanished. Jamie let out a long slow breath.

'Don't sweat it,' Winston said, standing to leave. 'They don't suspect me of nothin'.' He winced as though he'd let something slip, and added hastily, 'O' course, I never done nothin'. Best head off now. Remember what I said about the face paint.'

Winston the clown ambled away. Jamie sat, pondering what little he'd been told. He wondered if he could trust the old guy, then wondered what he had to lose by gambling that he could.

Out in the parlour the clowns were all gathered at the card table, hunched over in murmuring conversation, and Jamie was hit by a sudden paranoid certainty that he and Winston had broken some rule, that his face was about to become a pulped broken mess like the apprentice's.

Gonko glanced up at Jamie and barked an order at Rufshod to fetch a uniform.

*Why do I get that feeling about the conversation?* Jamie wondered. *The old guy hates the circus . . . Hates it. The others don't.*

Rufshod returned and tossed a bundle of material at Jamie. 'Don't just chuck it, you filthy flyblown shit,' Gonko screamed, slamming a fist on the table. 'That's the uniform. Show some pride!'

Doing his best to show pride himself, Jamie took the clothes back to his room and put them on. They were far too big for him, but they hugged around the chest and waist tight enough not to slip off. He felt ridiculous—his pants had pictures of puppy dogs chasing red balls; his shirt was so frilly and loudly coloured it almost hurt the eye to look at, and his oversized shoes made it impossible to walk normally, forcing him to clomp around in a side-on waddle. Once dressed he hobbled back out to the parlour and the clowns broke into applause.

Doopy stood and approached him, staring with childlike fascination at Jamie's shirt, pants and shoes. 'Gosh . . . He looks like a clown,' said Doopy, utterly astonished. 'He looks like a *clown*, Gonko!'

'Very astute, Doops,' said Gonko. 'He sure does. I was right about you, JJ.'

Everyone stared at Jamie expectantly. He fidgeted and wondered what to do; maybe they wanted some kind of speech. He glanced from one pair of eyes to the next, each sunk into thick layers of greasy white paint, each gleaming with its own brand of insane light. Jamie's heart beat painfully and he wanted to run away. He cleared his throat and said, 'Thanks for . . .'

Goshy's eyes were half open, his left blinking first, then the right. The silence stretched out like a long dark tunnel. They just kept peering, their eyes boring in, drilling . . . For God's sake, what did they *want* from him?

'Would you fucking stop that?' Jamie screamed, unable to take it any more.

Before he had time to regret it, the clowns were applauding with gusto. Goshy alone didn't join in, his arms locked stubbornly at his sides. 'Nice to have you aboard, JJ,' said Gonko. 'Now, everyone, wipe the fucking smiles off. Time for a meeting and I'm pissed at every one of you. Bad news. We've been put on notice.'

The table erupted in moans and complaints which went on for several minutes, veering wildly off topic like Chinese whispers. Gonko patiently waited for it to run its course. '. . . And they said Goshy went poking,' Doopy was saying, 'but he didn't, I seen him all the time, he didn't do *nothin'* wrong, it was just a lake he fell into, a big red lake, and she asked for a poking, but he, he . . .' Doopy finished uncertainly when he realised he was the only one still talking.

Gonko spat over his shoulder and resumed. 'This ain't the first time we've been on notice, as you know, but it's the first time in a long time. I'm guessing it's 'cause of that scag fortune-teller ratting on us. And that accountant Kurt's gone and hired.'

'You want to fill in the background a little there for Jamie, Gonk?' said Winston.

'Eh? Ah, why not. JJ, a while back Kurt kept a stray trick he found amusing and made him his accountant. The guy suggested some bullshit to Kurt about the circus working better if each of us was in competition with the other. So they put the lion tamer on at the same time as Mugabo, they put the woodchoppers on at the same time as the freak show's daily feature, and they put us on at the same time as the acrobats.'

'I don't *like* put us on at the same time as the acrobats . . .' Doopy wailed.

'Now,' said Gonko, 'this is nothing permanent. I'd say Kurt's just entertained by the ruckus it's causing. The accountant, I'd be surprised if he lasts another six months before Kurt gets bored with him and eats his fucking face. The competition crap is just a phase. So, everyone play along, pretend like you give a shit, and we'll be just dandy. But the next show's gonna be a good one. I mean it. Foot's down, you fucks.'

'What are you gonna do about *her?*' said Winston.

'Shalice? Not much we can do,' said Gonko. 'Tart has that crystal ball, you know. She'd see it coming with her spooky future empathy bullshits. And of course, it'd be against Kurt's rules if I were to, say, put a bounty on her head . . .' Gonko glanced sidelong at Rufshod. 'A bounty of, say, one full bag . . .' He kept looking sidelong at Rufshod. 'Yeah, against rules, even if it would let a certain sonofabitch redeem himself . . .'

'Get her good, Rufshod!' Doopy cried. 'Get her real good!'

'Shut up, you bastard,' Gonko hissed. '*Not a word* spoken about this. She's a tricksy one, we must watch our steps. She could be watching us right now. That part of the conversation is over.'

Goshy stirred into motion for the first time that morning. He waddled urgently over to the window and peeked out between the curtains. Doopy got up and watched him intently, as though great prophetic importance hung on Goshy's every move. But Goshy stayed still as a mannequin.

Gonko said, 'That leaves one thing. Pay day.'

Winston caught Jamie's eye and nodded. Gonko reached down behind his feet and picked up a small sack, rummaged around inside it and pulled out a small velvet pouch, similar to the one Jamie had picked up that night after it had fallen from Goshy's pocket. Gonko tossed a pouch to each clown, tossing Goshy's pouch to Doopy. A tiny clinking-glass sound came from the bags.

Gonko glanced at Jamie and said, 'This is an advance. Consider it a welcome to the circus, JJ. But don't think I'm Santy Claus—you got to earn the next one.'

He threw the pouch to Jamie. *This is the salary?* Jamie thought. *What the hell's it for? I already swallowed the stuff* . . . He thought back through yesterday's dim memories, seeing grains of the powder littering the floor of Mugabo's show, and the dwarfs collecting them at night.

'All right, you shits, meeting's over,' Gonko barked suddenly. 'Ten minutes free time, then back here for rehearsal. Put on fresh paint, all of you. Winston, you're the most grandpa-like. You wanna paint up JJ?'

Winston nodded. He motioned for Jamie to follow and they headed off to Winston's room. Goshy stayed by the window, motionless as a tree, not making a sound, not blinking once.

# CHAPTER 9

# JJ THE CLOWN

'NOT much different from a cell,' said Winston. His room was a deal more spacious than Jamie's, with a proper bed and cupboards filled with trinkets and collectibles, chiefly puzzle games to pass the time. A goldfish swam in a bowl by the window, two pet mice ran around in a glass cage. 'Frank and Simon,' Winston said, reaching into the tank and picking up one of the white mice in his gnarled old hands. 'The fish ain't got a name yet, but I can't figure what use a fish has for a name. Still, some of the most civil company to be had around here. This is Jamie,' he said to the mouse, stroking it with one finger while it sniffed the air, then placing it carefully back in the cage.

On the bedside table was a black and white picture of a woman holding a baby. Judging by her clothes, the photograph had been taken before the turn of the twentieth century. Winston followed his gaze. 'My wife and daughter. Well . . . that ain't *them*,' he said, scratching the back of his head nervously. 'Didn't get a chance to pack a photo when they brought me here, found that one in Sideshow Alley. It just reminds me I had a wife and daughter. Both be long gone by now.'

Jamie nodded, privately concluding the old guy was harmless, but insane. Over the floor were newspapers, some laminated to preserve them. Jamie checked the date on the nearest: 9 October 1947. 'You collect old papers?' he said.

'Nope. I collect papers the day they're printed,' said Winston. 'One of the only ways to keep track of what goes on out there. I hang on to some of 'em, sort of like keeping a journal.'

'How do you get hold of them?'

'Well, sometimes we get sent on missions back in the world. Get used to seeing it change mighty fast out there, young Jamie. Next thing you know, we'll get sent out to fetch something for the boss and there'll be flying scooters all over the damn place.'

*Get used to it? Jamie thought. I don't think so. You can 'paint me up', whatever that means, then I'm going to use my ten minutes of free time finding the front gate and running the hell away, no matter what that fortune-teller says about it. Why that plan never occurred to you, old guy, I cannot quite fathom.*

Winston dug around in the top shelf of a cupboard, making a grumbling muttering sound under his breath he didn't seem aware of. 'Ah, here we are,' he said, pulling out a small plastic tub and sitting down on the bed. 'Effects are pretty drastic, early on especially. You'll be a little erratic, oh, I'm guessing for the first two years at least. Takes time for the personalities to . . . meld, I suppose. Odds are, a very different fellow will be walking out the door to the one who walked in a few minutes ago.' Winston sighed. 'Let's get this over with. Close your eyes.'

He did. Winston dipped his hand into the tub and Jamie felt the cool muddy face paint being rubbed onto his cheeks, nose, forehead and chin. It smelled like an unpleasant mix of sunscreen and petrol. 'All done,' said Winston after putting a red plastic nose on him.

Jamie opened his eyes. 'I don't feel any different.'

'Go take a look at yourself in the mirror. Over by the door there.'

Jamie found a hand mirror and picked it up. He peered at his reflection, at the thick greasy coat of white over his face. Almost straight away he did feel different. It began in his belly, a feeling of fingers tickling and poking him. The muscles in his legs coiled like tight springs. Blood rushed to his head, making his face prickle with heat, and little white spots danced behind his vision. His mind went blank as though all thought had been paused like an audio tape . . . And when 'play' was pressed again, the thoughts were not his own.

Back on the bed, Winston said, 'Pass the mirror, would you?'

JJ turned, and it felt like he'd snapped from a dream, broken contact with hypnotic eyes, his own. He took a step towards the bed and found he was leering at the old clown. 'You want the mirror, Winston?' he said in a too-friendly voice. 'I can give you the mirror, Winston.'

'Hand it over then,' said Winston, watching him warily.

JJ held the mirror on his palm and tossed it towards Winston. It fell short, crashing to the ground and shattering. He stared at the shards for a moment, leered at Winston again, wondering whether or not he should slap the old man, then turned and ran from the room, lifting his oversized shoes in a knee-bending stomp.

Winston sighed. 'Nicer the man, meaner the clown,' he muttered as he picked up the bits of glass. That seemed to be the way of things.


Damian the funhouse guardian pushed a wheelbarrow full of tubs of face paint into the clowns' parlour. Gonko took eleven tubs and stacked them in the corner without a word to Damian, who left, marching as slowly as a walking corpse.

Gonko had laid a gym mat over the floor. Erect as a drill sergeant, he stood on it as the clowns gathered around sullenly.

'Hey!' Gonko screamed at them. 'Show a little fucking *enthusiasm!*'

The clowns looked at each other uncertainly. Hesitantly Doopy clapped his hands together. Rufshod joined in. Goshy finally wandered away from sentry duty at the window, observed the others closely, and began clapping without bending his elbows, eyes boggling wide as he watched his own hands move with fascination, mouth gaping. Gonko raised his hands to quiet them but they kept going, so he sighed and sat down, waiting for the outburst to run its course. It was too early in the day to be wielding the iron fist.

Out of the corner of his eye he saw JJ, tiptoeing through the parlour. Trying to skip rehearsal, perhaps. Gonko squinted at him with interest, wondering precisely what type of clown they had on their hands now that he'd been painted up. 'JJ!' he called. 'Over here and line up.' JJ stood perfectly still, lips pursed like a drag queen. 'Come on. Over here.' Gonko repeated. JJ took one step towards the gym mat. 'That's the way,' said Gonko, like he was trying to coax a shy pet. 'Come on. Line up, JJ. Got to rehearse. There's a good feller. Over here now.'

JJ took one more step. Gonko sighed—he could see this going on all fucking day, breathe in, breathe out. He stood, intending to drag the bastard over by the ear. JJ took a frightened step backwards. *He's gonna bolt*, Gonko thought. 'Oh no you fucking don't!' he yelled.

The other clowns grew bored with their applauding and turned to watch. JJ took one more backwards step and Gonko's patience ran out; he charged, and JJ broke into a sprint, shrieking like a tropical parrot as he ran away. Gonko threw up his arms in exasperation and let him run. He knew the type, all right. 'One of *those*,' he muttered in disgust.


Once certain Gonko was not pursuing, JJ relaxed. He had no intention of sucking up to teacher just because they'd beaten hell out of the last apprentice.

Around him, a group of colourfully dressed gypsy types ran around on errands. 'Carnie rats,' JJ mused, passing a pair of old women. 'Out of my way!' he yelled at them. 'Clown coming through. Fuck yourself. Hear me?'

And to JJ's pleasant surprise they flinched back to let him pass. They were wide-eyed, respectful . . . Sure, there was a hint of pure hatred there, too, but what the hell. 'Could get used to this,' said JJ. 'Yeah, you respect me, carnie rats. Stay back, slimy shits!' They stayed back. *They know who's boss*, he thought. *Nice deal!* He marched straight through a group of them, ordering them out of his way, knocking boxes from their hands and tripping their feet.

Once bored with this, he walked aimlessly until he came to Sideshow Alley. Through the wooden archway he went. Before him stretched a long dirt road with game stalls on either side. Up ahead were the rides, including the Ferris wheel, merry-go-round and some mechanical-dealie where cars whirled around on what looked like a giant spinning top. Over in the distance was a large shanty town of rundown houses, and he could make out gypsy women smoking cigarettes in the doorways, chatting to each other. JJ noted with delight the effort the carnie rats made to steer clear of him as he strolled past, snapping his thumbs on his suspenders. Around him stalls were being repaired and cleaned: shoot a duck, win a prize; the drunken sailor ring toss; the juggling jukebox. He stopped before five rotating plaster clown heads, mouths open wide. An elderly carnie rat with weary eyes was wiping the prize shelf behind them with a rag. He turned and grimaced as JJ cleared his throat, undid his fly, and stuck his penis in the mouth of the middle clown. 'No, *señor!*' the carnie rat wailed. '*Debo mantener este limpio!*'

JJ sported an apologetic smile, as if this were completely beyond his control, while orange piss trickled down the plaster clown's throat into the number box. To JJ's immense pleasure the carnie rat did nothing but moan. He zipped up, said 'Bless you, sir,' and strolled down the road, peering at the game stalls and the carnies inside, all of them rushing to appear busy. He paused beside the 'test your strength' stand, where a huge mallet leaned against the bell tower. Behind it a bald carnie rat with a thick moustache stood on a foot ladder, polishing the brass bell. JJ squinted up at him. 'Hey!' he yelled.

The carnie dropped his rag and nearly fell from the ladder. In a Spanish accent he said, 'What? What you want?'

'Can I have a go at this, mister?' said JJ in a cutesy-pooh voice. 'I gotta see how strong I am.'

'You look plenty strong,' said the carnie. 'Leave me alone.'

JJ picked up the mallet. It was heavy in his hands. 'Here we go!' he hollered jovially. 'Ready up there?'

The carnie climbed down his ladder, muttering under his breath. 'On three!' JJ cried. 'One. Two. Three!' On three, he spun and hurled the hammer off into the distance; it sailed out of sight, spinning end on end over the rooftops. The carnie stared at him with his mouth open. 'What?' JJ said. 'Isn't that how it works?' Laughing, he strode to the next stall.

JJ amused himself in similar fashion for the next hour, harassing carnies, kicking their stalls, stealing game prizes, spitting at them, screaming for someone to bring him a beer. He was lord of the manor and it was the best fun he could imagine—until he came across the acrobats.

Ahead, looking resplendent in their tights, were three lithe bodies clad in shining white lycra. They stood chatting to a middle-aged female carnie rat, one of them leaning on a pole next to a hot dog stand. There was something shameless in the way their codpieces bulged beneath the latex, and JJ snarled. He remembered last night's face-off.

With an air of determination, of doing his duty for the clown tribe, JJ pulled up his breeches and ambled toward them like a cowboy, boots crunching in the dirt. He got close enough to hear their voices. They were swapping *pancake recipes* for chrissakes! He scooped up two handfuls of thick black mud from the puddle at his feet, cried, 'JJ! JJ the clown!' and threw both handfuls at the nearest acrobat.

'Guh!' the acrobat spluttered as his head rocked back. JJ had picked his moment well—the acrobat had his mouth open wide on impact. JJ laughed uproariously. The spattered one wiped mud from his eyes, spitting and coughing. 'Oh, you think tha'ss funny?' one of them said.

'He does,' said another. 'He thinks he's a laff riot. This is their new boy.'

'Are you following orders, new boy? Or is this all your bright idea?'

The acrobats appeared so stunned with outrage they were asking this only to verify what they thought they'd just seen. Still laughing, JJ scooped up another fistful of reeking muck and prepared to throw.

'I would *not* be doing that,' warned the nearest acrobat. 'Uh-uh.'

'That's why you would never make it as a clown,' JJ explained, and hurled the new handful. It found its mark, striking the acrobat who'd spoken in the neck. He fell back, wheezing.

JJ closed his eyes and howled with glee, so he never saw what hit him. Something smashed into his face and sent him sprawling to the ground. Dazed, he looked up and saw two acrobats coming for him. The third was hanging back, swinging his leg above his head to stretch the muscles—apparently it had been a kick. It had felt like a sledgehammer.

JJ was astonished; they'd fought back! He scrambled to his feet. Did *he* know how to fight? He wasn't sure. 'Oh yeah?' he bellowed. 'Put 'em up!' He held up his gawky, uncoordinated fists.

'Tha's more like it,' said an acrobat as they closed in around him. 'Want to see how high we can kick, little clown?'

The acrobat gave him a demonstration; his boot lashed past JJ's face in a white blur. He felt the wind brush his cheek. 'Not bad, Sven?'

'Not bad, Randolph. But I know how *high* we can kick. There must be something else we can find out.'

'How about . . . *how many times* we can kick?'

'Oh Tuskan, tha's perfect! We can set a record. What was the last? A thousand times, wasn't it?'

'*About* that. Each, that is.'

'You don't scare me,' JJ yelled as he turned tail and bolted. Shrieking with panic, he ran through the crowds of carnie rats who stumbled out of his path. He could hear the acrobats close behind him and his panic spiralled into a terror so pure it almost blinded him. As he ran he yanked carnies to the ground behind him to block his path. He heard an acrobat curse as he tripped over, and risked a glance over his shoulder—two still chased. Blubbering, he bolted back through the wooden archway and veered right, hopefully headed for the clown tent and sanctuary. But in his terror he lost his bearings and instead found he was over by the funhouse. He dashed past the guardian in his deathly robes, crouched down in an alley between two shanties, and waited, trying to quiet his breathing and his crying. After a minute two acrobats with mud stains on their shirts strolled by, still on the hunt. They looked his way and he ducked out of sight, whimpering almost loud enough to give himself away at the unfairness of it all. Why hadn't anyone warned him of the dangers? Why hadn't the carnie rats seen the situation unfolding and given him a heads-up? It struck him as so grossly unfair he burst into loud heaving sobs, too distraught to keep the noise down.

A miserable hour passed in the alley as JJ tried to console himself. When he emerged his tears had dug rivulets in the face paint, and white spatters dripped down his chest. He cocked his head and listened, but heard only the distant wooden *thock-thock-thock* of the woodchoppers rehearsing. Casting worried glances behind him, he headed down the main path and wondered where he could go, still truant from rehearsal after all.

Someone called his name. 'JJ? Jamie?'

He almost broke down on the spot, but it wasn't the acrobats. It was Winston. 'Oh, thank God!' JJ cried, so relieved he dropped to his knees. 'It's only you.'

Winston jogged over, puffing. 'Yeah? Who were you expecting?'

'No one. I resent your accusation. I did not throw that mud.'

'That explains the mud on your hands, you damn fool,' Winston said. He sighed. 'At least I know what happened now. Want to give me your side of the story?'

'No.'

Winston grabbed him by the shoulder and hauled him into a nearby tent. His voice was sharp. 'Now listen to me. You got your paint on for the first time, so I understand you ain't completely responsible for whatever you're doin', but the fun's over. Get yourself under control.'

JJ was in tears again.

'Cut it out,' Winston snapped. 'That's just what I'm talking about.' He pulled out a handkerchief and began wiping the paint from JJ's face, but JJ pushed him away. 'Not yet,' he said. 'I'm still trying to, you know, vibe it for a while.'

'All right,' said Winston. 'But you ain't leaving my sight for the rest of the day. Got that? Now tell me what happened with the acrobats. You threw mud at 'em? That's it?'

JJ nodded and tried to hold in a giggle; it came out anyway but he turned it into a pained sob. 'Self-defence,' he said. 'They insulted me. There I was, swapping pancake recipes in Sideshow Alley. Out of nowhere, they surrounded me. The rest is a blur. I believe I was shoved in the back. Twice. When I fell, I must have inadvertently scraped my hands in a puddle. I proceeded to stand up, and upon standing moved my hands thusly—' he demonstrated—'to ward off their onslaught. Some of the mud must have flicked onto them. That's all it took. They chased me through the circus. They're *insane*, Winston.'

Winston regarded him with a stony face and sighed. 'One thing I can be glad of, that's saved more'n a few lives, is that Doopy and Goshy don't have a brain between them. Rufshod's got about half and he does more than enough damage with that. You got a whole one, son—or just enough of one for serious trouble. If you want to get yourself hurt, get yourself hurt. Leave the rest of us out of it. You've started some drama today that'll come back on all of us.'

JJ nodded his head, playing the attentive grandson. 'Did the acrobats give you a different version of events?' he said.

'Nope. They popped into our tent though, so we knew somethin' was up. They don't go near us when we rehearse. We don't normally bother their rehearsals either. Kind of a truce we made, because things were getting nasty a while back, murderous nasty. But, today, in the middle of a routine we were workin' on, they came in, wished us luck with our next show, and that was that.'

'Sounds *awful*,' said JJ.

'They're sending us a message, you fool. It's on again. Was just words up till now. Figured you were the one to start it. They mentioned you. Said, *That new guy of yours is going to work out great.* Said you'd be a real superstar. We been wondering what you did. Rufshod can't wait to hear all about it.'

An uncomfortabnle thought intruded on JJ's glee. 'Ah . . . what about the boss?'

'Gonko was kinda quiet about it. Just told me to come find you.' Winston ran a hand over his face. 'You just threw some mud? That was it?'

'I swear.'

'Right. Then it may not be too bad. We'll see.' He strolled out of the tent and JJ followed. 'Guess no one's given you a proper look around yet,' said Winston with a sigh. 'That might as well fall on me. Every other bloody thing does.'

# CHAPTER 10

# KURT PILO

JJ let Winston lead him around, pointing out this and that, offering wheezy commentary and trivia. He pretended to take it all with timid respect, he was for now JJ the shy, vulnerable, overwhelmed new clown. He jumped at shadows, clung to Winston's shirt, pleaded with him not to walk so fast, because by gosh he'd hate to get lost. Winston appeared to buy the act and offered words of comfort, told him not to worry, damn it, stop acting like a pansy.

'What else can I show you, then?' Winston muttered. They'd stopped for a breather by the funhouse, having done a circuit of the woodchoppers' pit and the lion tamer's ring, and made a trip to Sideshow Alley for a hot dog. JJ had played nice around the carnies in front of Winston, but there was no disguising the loathing glances they sent his way. 'I want to meet the boss,' JJ said. 'This "Kurt" I keep hearing about.'

Winston considered this very carefully. 'Might be a good idea,' he said. 'Generally you don't want to be near either of the Pilos, if you get my drift. If they come lookin' for you chances are you're in the stew, which'll happen to you soon enough, the way you're carryin' on. Maybe we can at least make the first impression a good one. Come on.'

Winston led him down a narrow path he hadn't ventured down before, where the grass was dry and yellow. A few dilapidated wooden cabins sat beside it, abandoned like old headstones. Winston lowered his voice to keep the passing carnies from overhearing. 'Kurt Pilo is pretty hard to gauge, 'cause you never know what'll offend him this week as opposed to the last. Just act natural. If he makes a joke, make damn sure you laugh at it.'

'So Kurt's in charge of the whole shindig, huh?' said JJ.

'Kurt and George Pilo are who we take orders from,' said Winston. 'That's all you need to know. The MM's up there with them, but he's stuck in the funhouse most of the time, sculpting or making the face paint we use, and God knows what else he does. There's a few others like him, comers and goers doin' whatever they do away from the rest of us.'

They came to the western edge of the showgrounds, a place free of attractions, with a quiet and stillness in the air which would tell any stray tricks they had taken a wrong turn. Ahead was a tiny white caravan propped up on cinder blocks, covered in chipped white paint, sitting alongside a tall wooden fence.

'Hey, what's on the other side of that?' JJ said, pointing at the fence.

'Nothing worth seeing, and I wouldn't try and climb it, just between you and me. That caravan's Kurt Pilo's home, if you ever need to know. Here's hoping you won't.'

'This little shit box?' JJ cried. 'The *boss* lives here? Our tent's better than this!'

'Never mind that, just remember what I told you. Seen and not heard.'

They walked up the tin steps and Winston rapped on the door. From within a very deep voice called: 'Hmmm?'

Winston opened the door, which creaked like a coffin lid, and they went in. The trailer walls were covered in faded daisy-patterned wallpaper, and crucifixes hung over them at all angles. The floor was a cluttered mess of manila folders, clipped-together bundles of paper and, to JJ's surprise, dozens of Bibles lying in neat stacks or splayed open face down as though cast aside over the reader's shoulder. At the back of the caravan, half-buried in paperwork, was a wooden desk, behind which sat Kurt Pilo with a ballpoint pen in his hand.

JJ's heart seemed to go still; it was the monster Jamie had seen at the fortune-teller's hut. Jamie had nearly wet himself, and with good reason. Staring up at JJ were two unnaturally bright eyes framed by thick bony sockets: wolf's eyes. Kurt Pilo's head was bald and glistening, his face was far too long from crown to jaw, and his lips were thick and blue like a fish's, twisted up into a smile that seemed docile. A predatory energy seemed to radiate from him, as palpable as heat, yet when he spoke it was in a cultured, civilised almost silken tone. 'Hello, Winston. Who's this you've brought along? Someone new? Someone borrowed, someone blue?' Kurt's fish lips stretched at the corners. 'My little joke,' he said. 'Do you think you'll use that in the act, Winston?'

'Maybe so, sir,' said Winston. His voice was unsteady. JJ watched him swallow, set his jaw and pretend to feel no fear. 'I'd have to put it to Gonko, Mr Pilo, but it's a fine gag.'

'Hm,' said Kurt in a satisfied way.

'This here,' said Winston, 'is young Jamie. Or JJ, I suppose. He's our newest employee. Newest clown.'

'Oh, splendid!' said Kurt, who turned his full attention to JJ. 'Come closer. Let's shake hands.'

JJ's legs felt weak. He approached the desk, almost tripped over a Book of Mormons, and held a hand out for Kurt to grasp. Kurt's eyes sparkled with white light as his giant hand enveloped JJ's. JJ could feel the crushing power in those fingers, and he glanced down to assure himself the vise was not about to close, for he couldn't maintain eye contact while Kurt's eyes were glittering with that light. It did his nerves no good at all——he saw talons and fur encasing his hand, and it was all he could do to stop himself from yanking it back.

Finally Kurt released his grip, which had actually been quite gentle. JJ stepped back from the desk, mumbling awkwardly, 'Pleased to meetcha, howd'ya do . . .'

Kurt's fish lips stretched wider—surely they were about to snap like elastic. 'Tell me, JJ,' he said, 'do you believe in Jesus?'

JJ took a glance at the crucifixes and stacks of Bibles and wondered if it was a trick question. Yes or no? Damn it, he was caught. 'Sometimes,' he ventured.

For an instant he thought he'd blown it, but Kurt actually seemed pleased. He said, 'I like that! What a lovely answer. Do you find it odd that we pay homage to the device used to torture and kill him?' Kurt plucked a crucifix from his desk and held it in his giant hand. 'It's a beautiful artefact. You could whip a god . . . all day long.'

Feeling encouraged now that Kurt's gaze wasn't fixed on him, JJ said, 'Yes sir, they knew how to treat a criminal in those days.'

He heard Winston take in a sharp breath. Perhaps JJ was skating on thin ice here, but the newfound clown in him *wanted* to test Kurt Pilo, by God. He wanted to push him, see what he could get away with before the big goon snapped. It was almost an independent reflex and he could barely control it. *Spit on his desk!* a part of him screamed. *Get your dick out! Fuck with him, let's see what he's made of!*

But Kurt rocked back in his chair and started to laugh. It was a deep laugh and made the trailer walls shake. He put a finger to his face and wiped away a tear. JJ winced as a talon scraped at the corner of Kurt's eye and drew a trickle of black blood. Kurt didn't appear to notice. 'Thank you, JJ,' he said. 'I needed that. Lifted my spirits. I've been having trouble with my brother George—old family spat, you know how these things go. I tried to kill him last Wednesday, and he seems upset that I did it while he was defecating, you see . . . Long story. But yes, it brings me to something I've been pondering. Don't you find it odd that Satan acts as God's policeman?'

JJ nodded, his eyes following the thick drop of blood sliding down Kurt's cheek.

'So do I,' Kurt went on. 'The strangest thing, isn't it? Satan only gets his way with those who break the rules. He never gets to . . . *pluck* people off the street and have his way with them.' The blood reached the corner of Kurt's lips. 'Ah well, enough of that for now. Welcome to the circus. We've a fine tradition to uphold, I suppose. That seems the sort of thing a proprietor might say . . .' Kurt reached under his desk. When he straightened he held a dead tabby cat in his giant hands. 'If you'll excuse me gentlemen, all work and no play . . .'

'How's the collection coming along, boss?' said Winston timidly.

'Good, good,' said Kurt. 'I've got plenty from kittens, but no full grown cats at the moment. I run through them so fast, you know.' Kurt laid the dead animal across his desk, then opened a drawer and produced a set of pliers.

'Well, good afternoon to you, sir,' said Winston, pulling JJ out by the shoulder.

'And to you,' Kurt said distractedly. 'Thanks for bringing the new one. Nice to have a hands-on . . . thingy . . . with the staff . . .'

JJ's last look at Kurt Pilo as the trailer door swung closed showed the huge man's eyes lighting up as he opened the cat's mouth and got a grip on its teeth with the pliers. As they headed down the tin steps they heard Kurt say, 'Ah, there we go . . .'

JJ said, 'What's he——'

'Collects teeth,' Winston muttered. 'All kinds.'

They walked back down the narrow path, Winston sighing with relief.

'What was that he said about trying to kill his brother?' said JJ.

'It's not a new thing. Those two are at it all the time, as long as I can remember. One of them dies, the other runs the show. The whole show. Something to do with Pilo Senior's will, but no one knows the details.' Winston considered. 'No way in hell George is going to get the drop on Kurt. It might work the other way around, but still, they both survived a long time already. Both too cunning.'

'Winston, ever seen Kurt Pilo mad? Really mad? Ever seen him really tee off on someone?'

Winston had a distant look in his eyes, and when he answered, JJ thought he was lying. 'I don't think so. Not that I'd want to. Nor would you. Understand?'

'Sure, I'd hate to see that,' said JJ the clown.

With a couple of hours to kill before sunset, Winston took him to the freak show. Fishboy greeted JJ warmly, and took all his attempts at provocation with such good humour and diplomacy that JJ had trouble maintaining the effort. Fishboy saw the funny side when JJ squirted him in the eye with water, pinched his gills, even when he made a crack about pissing in his spawning pond. Fishboy had the manners of a British gentleman, agreeing with the derogatory remarks even as they became more caustic and heartfelt. 'Face like a smashed crab, you say? I'd defend my honour, but you are one hundred per cent correct!'

JJ lapsed into sullen silence and let Fishboy show him the exhibits. He allowed JJ to feed Nugget, the severed head, by dropping protein flakes into the chin-deep water. He arm-wrestled Yeti and lost convincingly. He gloated while Steve scrubbed the dried fleshy ooze at the bottom of Tallow's glass case. JJ left the freak show in high spirits, and couldn't help agreeing with Gonko: Fishboy was a grand feller, a stand-up guy and a fine curator.

Afternoon became evening as they retired to their tent. The other clowns were playing poker and chatting about the day's rehearsal. JJ remembered then that he'd skipped it—he very quickly took the strut from his walk and replaced it with meek old-lady stutters. Time once again for Mr Timid, Mr Please Don't Hurt Me.

Winston muttered something under his breath and wandered off to his room. Goshy's head happened to be pointed in JJ's direction as he walked in, and he made a noise like a hooting barn owl. Doopy turned about. 'Hey, it's the new guy. Gonko, the new guy's back. Gonko, look!'

Gonko turned and squinted up at him. 'Why, hello young JJ,' he said.

JJ flinched backwards as though he'd been struck.

'Come on in, feller,' Gonko said in a gentle coaxing voice. ''Atta boy. We won't hurt ya. Rufshod might, but we'll hurt him back. Come on, sit down here, feller.'

JJ made his hands tremble and lips pucker with fright. He crept slowly to the table and sat between Rufshod and Doopy. The apprentice was nowhere to be seen.

'Good news, feller,' said Gonko. 'Rehearsal was spotless. We're gonna sit Goshy out for now. He's still a bit scrambled thanks to his lady troubles. Women, huh Gosh?'

Goshy made a low gurgling sound.

'But the rest of us, bang on, dead sharp, well-oiled machine and all that shit. We'll blow them acrofucks out of the water. Which reminds me . . .' Gonko's voice lost its brightness. 'What did you do to 'em?'

JJ didn't feel like having this conversation again. He stood as though startled by the question, turned on his heel and ran, sobbing like an affronted soap actress. No one followed.

In his room, he lay back and pondered the day's events. He pondered Winston, and wondered how he could use the guy's kindness for his own ends. If JJ was to climb the clown hierarchy, it was time to step on a rung.

And now . . .

And now, what? Take off the face paint? What the hell. JJ fumbled around for a rag. It was getting dark so he lit a candle, sending shadows scurrying over the enclosed little space. The sight of his surrounds filled him with a sudden fondness for his new job, his new life. 'Yeah,' he whispered. 'This is just dandy.'

He wiped his face clean. The paint came off with ease thanks to a day's worth of sweat and tears. He dropped the greasy rag and lay back, instantly asleep.


Sleep was filled with a nightmare; a line of chained people stood docile as cattle while Kurt Pilo walked past, sucking blood from the neck of each one. Jamie was puncturing their necks for him with a finger turned into a thin blade as Kurt made pleasant small talk between sucks.

Jamie woke and sat up, and the instant he moved his body clenched in nausea. He moaned, whimpered, pleaded for God to stop the pain. It felt like a swarm of insects was eating him from inside. He had never felt pain this bad.

Soon he wondered why he was trying not to scream; scream he did, and it trailed off pitifully. There was a commotion outside and mumbling voices. Soon Winston came in. 'Ah, yep,' the old clown said. 'Forgot about this. After-effects of the face paint. Sorry, Jamie, I should have remembered.'

'It's okay,' Jamie gasped, 'just, how do I make it stop?'

'Right. You got that little bag Gonko gave you? Your salary? You know, the powder?'

Jamie tried to remember through the latest spasm in his gut. He bunched into a foetal ball and felt the bag in his pocket pressing against his thigh. He dug it out and handed it to Winston, who had a small clay bowl in his hands.

'I heard how you came to be here,' said Winston, opening the bag. 'About how you accidentally swallowed some o' this stuff. I'm guessing the accident part, because what kind of lunatic would swallow some weird lookin', weird smellin', weird *sounding* powder he just picked up off the ground from out of a clown's pocket?'

Winston shook a tiny amount of the powder into the clay bowl as he spoke. It tinkled like glass. 'Anyway, having it in you was enough to bring you to the show's attention. But you wouldn't have noticed much when you swallowed it. Wasn't prepared right, see? This stuff is good for what ails you, and I mean *whatever* ails you. You gotta cook it up, though. Watch . . .'

Winston flipped open a silver cigarette lighter and made a small flame tickle the bottom of the bowl. 'Got to be a flame,' he said. 'Can't boil it, steam it, put it in the sun. Got to be flame.'

In the bowl the thick round crystals gave off a thin bluish smoke as they popped and cracked. The smell was foul. For a moment Jamie thought he could hear a tiny sound, not unlike human wailing. Soon the powder had melted to a silvery liquid. 'Now,' said Winston, 'make a wish.'

'What?' Jamie gasped.

'I said make a wish. I'm not yankin' yer chain, hurry up, make a wish, swallow this, and you'll be fine. Hurry now.'

Jamie wiped sweat from his face and said, 'I wish this—ohh, Jesus—pain would stop.'

'That'll do it. Swallow. Quickly.'

Jamie took the bowl and nearly spilled it over the blanket. He got it to his lips and slurped the liquid down. It left a strange, unpleasant taste in his mouth. Almost instantly the pain was snuffed out like a smothered candle. There were no lingering echoes of it, no gradual ebbing—it was gone, just like that. He patted himself all over in disbelief and stared at Winston, who said, 'There we are, all better.' He stood to leave.

'Wait a minute,' said Jamie, feeling his midriff in amazement. 'That's our salary? Painkiller?'

'Not just painkiller,' said Winston, heaving a sigh as he sat back down. 'The powder gets you whatever you want, within reason. Wish dust is what some call it. It's . . . expensive, I guess. The most expensive stuff going around. Worth more than anything else in the world.'

Jamie squeezed the small velvet bag in his hand. 'What do you mean? I ask for something, it appears?'

'Doesn't quite work like *that*,' said Winston. 'Look, whatever you ask for has to be approved by . . . Damn it, how do I put it?' He slapped his forehead then leaned close, dropped his voice to a whisper. 'Has to be approved by the highest authority in the show. Higher than Kurt Pilo, higher than anyone we've ever met. I can't say no more, don't want to and just plain can't, all right? Leave it at that. There's rules, and if you ask for somethin' against the rules, then you wasted your wages. Those don't come cheap.'

'How do I know what to ask for, then, and what not to?'

'Start low key. Small things, like we just did. Don't wish harm on anyone else in the show. Chances are it won't work, but apart from that, it's not how we settle scores here. Use the powder sparingly, save it up. Never know when you'll have to get yourself out of a jam. Or wake up in worse pain than you were in just now.'

Winston stood and his manner said he had pressing business elsewhere. He paused in the doorway. 'Consider it,' he said, without turning to face Jamie, 'like having a teensy prayer answered with a certain "yes". Just don't get carried away. And don't worry, those pains'll be gone in maybe three days. That face paint is pretty heavy stuff, as you'd know.'

Winston left. 'Face paint?' Jamie said, and then it hit him. 'Holy shit . . . Winston!' he yelled. 'What the hell happened yesterday?' But Winston didn't return.

What had happened? After Winston had applied his face paint, the day was mostly blurred pictures. He remembered vividly the *mood*— wickedness, gleeful wickedness, completely at the mercy of any impulse. *I became someone else*, he thought, and it chilled him so much he pulled the blanket up around his shoulders. *I did, too. I completely lost control.*

Next came the memory of Kurt Pilo, the way his eyes had glittered with light below a brow like a storm cloud. Jamie closed his eyes and groaned; suddenly he felt sick.

*I am in . . . so . . . much . . . fucking . . . trouble . . .*

And it was worse than that. Gone now were any lingering doubts about what the fortune-teller had told him, about any of the impossible things he'd been asked to believe. It was all real. After yesterday, he could not doubt it if he tried. He was part of the circus.

Now might be a good time, he supposed, to use some more powder. Hands shaking, he tipped a little of it out onto the clay bowl, which Winston had left lying by the stretcher. He found a box of matches, melted the crystals into silvery liquid. 'Please, let me get some more sleep,' he whispered. He swallowed, set down the bowl, and barely had time to lie back before his prayer was answered.

# CHAPTER 11

# THE BREAK-IN

THE day passed him by, and whether or not it was the work of the dust no one tried to wake him until dark, when a hand impatiently tugged at his shoulder. Groggy and barely able to string two thoughts together, he peered up at the silhouette of a three-pronged hat with silver bells, which tinkled quietly by his bed. It was a clown, and for a blissful instant he was back in New Farm wondering what a clown was doing in his bedroom. The instant ticked by. 'Hey, JJ,' said Rufshod in an excited whisper. 'Wakey wakey!'

Jamie sat up and rubbed his eyes. 'Huh? I'm 'wake.'

'Come with me. This is gonna be great. Put your face paint on. You're probably too chicken shit without it.'

Harsh but true. Jamie remembered Winston's warning about joining Rufshod for any adventures, but so close to sleep he didn't have the wits to argue. He heard Rufshod rummaging around in the darkness. 'Aha!' he said, and sat on Jamie's chest, pushing him back down. He quickly rubbed a palmful of greasy white paint over Jamie's cheeks.

'Hold on a second,' said Jamie. 'Get off me for chrissakes. I'll put it on myself.'

Rufshod sprang off him like a jack-in-the-box. He fetched a hand mirror and a lighter, lit it, and presented Jamie with his own reflection. His face was half painted, but that was enough. The feeling of giddiness hit him instantly, and all fear left him.

JJ grabbed Rufshod by the collar and pulled him close. 'You come in here and wake me up again,' he whispered slowly, 'and I'll fucking kill ya. You got me? I'll *fucking kill* ya.'

Rufshod grinned and rubbed a finger along Jamie's forehead. 'Missed a spot,' he said. JJ got up and lunged for him. Rufshod dodged him easily and kicked him in the belly. 'Missed a spot!'

'All right, that's *enough*!' JJ screamed.

'Shhhhh . . .' Rufshod grimaced. 'Quiet! We're breaking the rules. It's show day tomorrow. No high jinks on show day eve. That's the rule. Come on, you awake yet?'

'Where we going?' JJ said, regaining his composure and making careful note that he 'owed' Rufshod 'one'. Rufshod leaned close and grinned. 'You know the fortune-teller?'

JJ nodded.

'We're gonna fix her. We're gonna get her good. And right before show day!' Rufshod giggled. 'She's gonna be so pissed at us.'

JJ considered this and decided he liked the idea. The fortune-teller had come across a tad lofty for his liking, now that he thought about it.

Rufshod picked up something he'd set on the floor when waking Jamie. He held it carefully to his chest now, motioning for JJ to follow. They stole through the tent to the parlour, where Rufshod paused, making a hush gesture, pointing at the table where Doopy lay sleeping with an empty bottle sitting loosely on his chest. As they tiptoed past him Doopy mumbled in his sleep: 'No . . . Don't poke her, Goshy . . . s'not *funny* . . .'

JJ paused to listen. 'Goshy been poking . . . all over town . . . twice more in the sore spot . . . ate her up in the sore spot, Goshy . . .'

*Fucking space cadets,* JJ thought, disgusted though not sure why. He ran to catch up with Rufshod, and the pair of them crept across the grassy lanes, threading a path through the carnie dwellings. The showgrounds were silent as a tomb, and JJ found that when his mind was set to it, he could move with complete stealth, not betrayed by a single popped joint or rustle of his pants.

The fortune-teller's hut was soon in sight. Her caravan had no lights on. Rufshod kneeled down and removed the cloth from his bundle, held up a lighter and showed JJ what he had—a glass ball. JJ crouched beside him. 'What's that?'

'Shh. Watch.' Rufshod held a hand over it, the same way the fortune-teller did with her crystal ball. In the light of the tiny flame an image appeared on the glass: a scrotum, packing two nuts. 'They're mine,' Rufshod explained. 'This is all she's gonna be able to see, all day.' He started giggling but managed to hold it in. 'We're gonna take hers. Replace it with this.'

JJ looked up and down the path. No one was around, but the very first dawn light was creeping into the gloom. 'Asleep in there,' Rufshod whispered, pointing to the caravan. 'Go watch her door. If she comes out, make a noise like an owl. Okay? Then run.'

JJ nodded. He crept to the caravan door and waited, crouching down by its front steps. He could hear Rufshod spluttering as he tried to contain his laughter. There was a minute of total silence, rudely broken by the sound of wood being ripped, obscenely loud in the still night. JJ listened intently for signs of life inside the caravan, his heart pounding. It seemed they'd gotten away with it . . . Then the sound of tearing wood was repeated.

*What's the dumb bastard doing?* JJ thought, shaking with adrenaline and biting his knuckle so as not to laugh. He very faintly heard the beads rattling at the hut's entrance. There was a moment in which everything seemed to hold its breath and wait—the night air, the buildings around them, the grass underfoot. Then came a giant noise as something crashed to the floor; glass broke, the earth thudded.

JJ heard a female voice murmuring, as though in sleep, inside the caravan.

*Hurry up, you idiot!* he thought giddily. *Jesus, man, hurry up!*

If there were no more loud noises, they'd be okay, he thought . . . And right on cue came the loudest yet, a noise like a cabinet of glass statues being toppled. From Shalice's caravan came a voice no longer clouded by sleep. 'Who's there?' she asked sharply.

There were footsteps in the caravan. JJ stood up and ran. He forgot to make the owl noise. As he rounded the fortune-teller's hut he saw Rufshod sprinting through the doorway, sending beads clattering like rattlesnake tails. He held a bundle to his chest. Mission accomplished. The pair of them sprinted away, giggling madly. When they were at a safe distance they paused to watch the lights coming on in the hut. 'Oh shit, run!' Rufshod whispered. They raced back to their tent.

Doopy was still asleep at the card table. Still high on adrenaline, JJ grabbed the bottle from Doopy's chest and smashed it on the wood next to his head. The sound of shattering glass exploded through the parlour, and they bolted for the safety of JJ's room. Doopy gave a snort but didn't stir.

Rufshod lit two candles and carefully placed the bundle on JJ's pillow. The candlelight gleamed on the glass ball like two yellow eyes. Rufshod waved his hand over the ball. 'What was all the noise?' JJ asked him.

'Didn't know she boards the place up at night,' said Rufshod, tapping the glass with his thumb. 'Had to rip off the planks. Think I knocked over a couple of shelves. How do you turn this thing on?' He held both palms over the ball, and suddenly it glowed with white light. 'There we go. Ha! Look at her. She's awake . . .'

Rufshod giggled madly. In the glass the fortune-teller was examining the wreckage of her hut, a gas lantern in hand. Wooden planks lay on the ground by the door. Visible through the doorway were broken ornaments and books scattered over the floor. The fortune-teller's face was wooden. She plucked the cloth veil from the replica crystal ball and seemed to sense nothing amiss. She replaced the cloth. JJ and Rufshod exchanged a glance of pure glee.

JJ figured he and Ruf could become fine friends indeed.

'Wait till she has her bath,' Rufshod whispered. 'We'll see that bush of hers. Wow. Should've stolen this thing a long time ago.'

JJ *knew* he and Ruf could become fine friends indeed.

They watched her as the sun came up, the crystal ball bathing Jamie's little room in its flickering light. Shalice had set about clearing the damage from her hut, her rage evident in the deliberate calm of her movements. 'Been awhile since she's had her comeuppance,' Rufshod explained. 'She's not used to it. Looks like she forgot what it feels like. Been getting too big for her boots, last few years. Knows too much about everyone, what people get up to. Watches it all in this ball, you know. Thinks the Pilos need her more than anyone else, just 'cause of her outside jobs. We fixed her now! It's show day, and she's gonna be looking at my nuts all day!'

When it seemed Shalice wasn't likely to look into the prank crystal ball any time soon, Rufshod got up to leave. 'Can I borrow this?' said JJ.

'Yeah, why not, since you helped. But if she gets naked, you come and get me, okay?'

'Can do, buddy.' JJ watched the fortune-teller for a while longer as a burly gypsy came to help her tidy the hut. He put the ball under his blanket when he heard the other clowns up and about in the parlour.

Stepping out of his room, JJ had to stifle a scream; Goshy was standing right outside the door, marsupial eyes peering directly into his own. First the left blinked, then the right. There was something menacing and surreal about the moment that JJ didn't care for at all and he cringed away.

Goshy turned to the right and stared at something down the hallway. JJ watched him for a second then carefully stepped around him.

*What the hell was that about?* he wondered, then he remembered smashing the bottle beside Doopy's head. Was it some kind of warning? He wasn't sure. And looking back over his shoulder at Goshy, still staring fixedly at a patch of bare wall, it occurred to him Goshy wasn't sure either.

# CHAPTER 12

# SHOW DAY

ONCE the morning was a little older the clowns gathered for one last pre-show rehearsal. Gonko began with a pep talk to get everyone's head in the right frame, but the heads he was working with were bent into odd shapes, and the frame was stretched, cracked and coming apart. He managed to get the clowns paying attention, itself no mean feat. They were all here bar the apprentice, whom Gonko didn't expect to see any time soon. Setting him alight should have gotten the point across . . . *You're fired, fucker*. He was presumably lurking somewhere in Sideshow Alley, but sacked performers didn't tend to last long. Whatever the circus decided to do with him was not Gonko's concern.

He checked his pocket watch; an hour till the tricks started coming in. Small crowd today. From New South Wales this time, some regional fair or other, one of those deals where people wander around smelling cow shit, having their wallets stolen, looking at preschool finger paintings. Highlight of their calendar, sad fucks. They'd be entertained today, and no fooling.

Gonko squinted at his troops. The new guy, JJ, was hiding at the back of the group trying to look inconspicuous. He seemed timid and frightened, overawed. No doubt he expected to get away with all kinds of trouble while he was new, and that was fine: Gonko was glad to see some personality emerging. As long as JJ was compatible with the group, no problem. The apprentice had been useless both as a performer and comrade in arms, the latter only marginally less important—factional spats in the circus were no joke.

Earlier Gonko had taken a casual morning stroll past Shalice's hut, observing the carnage and her distress with satisfaction. Rufshod had done something, which was just dandy, but most importantly Gonko didn't know what that something was. Shalice was a tricky one to lie to, with her psychic mumbo jumbo and such like. She'd spotted him as he walked past and ran over demanding answers. Luckily she'd been too worked up to point her questions shrewdly.

Gonko took Rufshod aside before the pep talk, got the lowdown, and was pleased to hear JJ was into the swing of things. He upped the bounty to two bags, and Ruf split the loot with the new guy. Heart-warming stuff.

Down to business. 'Listen up. Shut your fuck flaps!' he barked at the clowns. Doopy was cleaning out Goshy's ear with a cotton bud while Goshy made chirping sounds, but they seemed to be listening. 'Tonight,' said Gonko, 'is an important show. Don't forget, we're still on notice. Like I said yesterday, pretend like you give a shit and put on a good one. Never know, ol' Kurt might just decide to make an example of us if we blow it again. I don't like getting sneered at by the acrofucks either. DOOPY PAY ATTENTION!'

'Sorry Gonko, I just, I—'

'Now line up. JJ, you're not ready for a spot onstage yet, since you been dodging rehearsal like you're Goldilocks and I'm the big bad wolf.' JJ looked shamefaced and cowered behind Winston's shoulders. Gonko decided to keep pretending he was falling for the act, and softened his tone. 'It's okay. You're new here. You'll get the hang of things, sooner or later. It's a big adjustment. We've all been there, new and confused, once upon a time.' JJ cowered even further, as though he'd been reproached. 'But, JJ, stick around and watch. You might learn something. All right?'

'Yes sir,' JJ stammered.

''Atta boy. All right, my pretties, into it. Go!'

Doopy coaxed his brother onto the mat and the clowns went through their routine. Gonko watched with an appraising eye; the act was shaping up okay. Goshy was copping bats to the head with the right look of surprise on his face—probably because he *was* surprised—and his skull made the right sounds when Rufshod whacked it with a hammer. *Pop!* Ruf, for his part, was easily dodging the hatchets Gonko threw, and Doopy's pants-down routine came off without a hitch. Winston looked a little off-colour, a little tired. Maybe he was under some kind of strain. Gonko frowned; whatever it was, the powder should be able to fix it, and the old guy was getting more than his fair cut.

Not thrilled, but satisfied the act wouldn't be a repeat of the other night's disgrace, Gonko called out, 'That's a wrap.' The clowns dispersed. Gonko turned to have a word with JJ about some of the finer points of the routine, but JJ had gone.

JJ hadn't watched any of the rehearsal, having snuck off as soon as Gonko's back was turned. He felt pretty sure that as long as his eyes were moist and his voice trembled he could do whatever he liked. For now he wanted another look into the crystal ball, which he'd decided was a godsend. No wonder the fortune-teller was so snooty—she must know everything about everyone, probably had a century's worth of blackmail options stored away in her head. JJ wanted in on that action.

There also remained many unanswered questions about the show. He was curious for his own sake, and for Jamie's, since he seemed a bit more stressed out about the whole deal. First, he wanted to see more of Kurt Pilo. Very much. He wanted to know what the big monster was capable of, when mad enough. Then there was the matter of the tricks. Where did they come from? They seemed to be regular people, the type who eat pies, watch football and breed. They turned up here in their hundreds. JJ made a brief sift through Jamie's memories, searching for mention of the Pilo Family Circus. He found none. But a show like this would be noticed; how could so many people come here every few days, go home, and keep it a secret? It wasn't like all visitors were . . . ha ha, get this . . . *killed* at the end of the night.

Was it?

Hm . . . no. No, he didn't think so. Not killed, but . . . *something* happened when they were here. What did the circus gain by putting on the show? Surely not just the price of tickets.

In any event, he'd made his plan for the day: watching the carnival in action from start to finish in the crystal ball.

Back in his room for a change of clothes, he saw a fine new pair of pants laid out on his bed, much like those Gonko wore. He frowned and put them on, ignoring a quiet little suspicion that there was something odd about finding them there. Once dressed he strolled down the main street. A few tricks were arriving already, just a handful of families and old folks who roamed down the path in a slow march, eyes glazed.

What JJ needed was a secluded spot from which to peer behind the scenes. He squinted up at the roof of the clowns' tent, standing tall over the surrounding attractions and gypsy homes. Up there would do nicely. He ran back to his room and grabbed the crystal ball, wrapping it in a pillow case. As he was about to dash outside a noise stopped him dead in his tracks. At first he thought it was a siren or alarm, one long note, rising and falling at an absurdly high pitch: 'EEEEEEEEEEEEE-*EEEEEEEEEEEEE*-EEEEEEEEE!'

It was the eeriest thing he'd ever heard. As the sound trailed off it began again, a dog's howl and a fire engine, coming from somewhere inside the tent. JJ held his hands over his ears—by Christ it was loud. On it went, mercilessly.

'EEEEEEEEEEEEE-*EEEEEEEEEEEEE*-EEEEEEEEE!'

Terrified but curious, he headed towards the sound and saw Doopy burst out into the hallway. 'Guys!' he cried. 'Guys, come look! Come look, guys! Oh, gosh, he's so *happy!*'

'JESUS!' JJ screamed, unable to take it anymore. 'What the hell is it?'

'Come on, JJ,' said Doopy, bounding over and tugging at his sleeve. 'It's Goshy. It's Goshy and she said yes. JJ, she said yes! I just knew she would JJ, I just knew it!'

Goshy? She said yes? What was this nonsense? Doopy dragged him by the shirt to Goshy's bedroom. What he saw sent a chill to his heart. Goshy stood in the middle of the room wearing a look not meant for a human face. His eyes were so wide they seemed about to burst; his lips were pulled back unnaturally far over the gums to reveal small sharp white animal's teeth; skin was bunched around his forehead, cheeks, neck and ears like waves of dough, as though someone had tried to peel it off by massage. The ungodly eyes turned to JJ in what he could only guess was a look of rapture. Then came another wail.

Averting his eyes from that monstrosity, JJ saw what this was all about. On a small table there sat a fern in a black pot. It had thin yellow-green leaves that feathered out from the stems. On one of the thicker stems there was a gold diamond ring. Goshy's fiancée. Doopy pawed the back of JJ's shirt. 'Ain't it grand?' he whispered. 'Ain't it just super?'

JJ couldn't find the strength to disagree. His knees felt weak. Beside him Goshy wailed and wailed and wailed. JJ backed away slowly.


Once all was quiet, he went outside with the crystal ball hidden behind his back and looked for a way onto the tent's roof. He tapped the wall with his knuckles and was surprised to find it hard like wood, or a carapace. But when he tried to climb he could find no foothold and get no grip. As he pondered the steep wall his hand absently strayed to his pocket. He was surprised to feel something hard and cold in there. He pulled it out—it was a steel pick, the kind used by rock climbers. Frowning, he shifted the crystal ball to his armpit and reached into his other pocket. There was another one.

He was quite sure these weren't in his pants when he put them on. 'How 'bout that,' he said, and swung the picks into the wall with a loud *thunk*. Placing the crystal ball down the front of his enormous pants, he hauled himself up the side of the tent, and found the muscles in his arms not the least bit strained by the effort. Whatever this face paint did to a person's head, it was rocket fuel for the body.

Once on the roof he indulged in his first bird's-eye view of the showgrounds. The place looked bigger from up here than it seemed on ground level. There were crowds on the move below, all walking at that same dazed pace as they trickled into various tents and stalls. Off to the south was Sideshow Alley, the gypsy hive with its one long road of attractions and rides, with the shanty town behind it. JJ could just make out carnie rats swarming around down there doing last-minute work on their stalls and games.

Turning north he could see the gleam of sunlight reflecting off the roof of Kurt's trailer. It looked innocent and inconspicuous out there on its own, by all appearances no more than a janitor's hut full of mops and brooms. As he watched he saw the trailer door open and shut as someone exited. Hard to tell from this distance, but he had a feeling it was the fortune-teller, perhaps reporting last night's raid to the boss. JJ then tried to look over the tall wooden fence behind Kurt's trailer, and noticed something strange: he could see nothing but a misty white light. After a moment he had to look away from it—it hurt the eyes. 'Ain't that the damndest,' he muttered. He could only guess the circus was in a deep valley somewhere, with lots of fog.

Ah well, Jamie could worry about that. Down to business—other people's. He removed the ball from his crotch, took it out of the pillow case and sat cross-legged on the roof with his back against the vertical support pole. He did what Rufshod had done, tapping the glass, waving his hand over it, and soon an image appeared.

After a few minutes he had the hang of it. By moving his fingers over the glass, left, right, up, down, he could pan in any direction, even through rooftops and walls. The vision could be shifted from one end of the showgrounds to the other with one sweep of the hand. Shown in the ball now was the minute but crystal clear image of a bunch of tricks from overhead as they marched like zombies down the main dirt road. Some had cameras, but none took photos. He swept the image off towards Sideshow Alley, the direction they seemed to be coming from. Following the line of people he came to a place where the main path simply ended. There was a dead-end alleyway; no gate, no door. There was a booth where a fat old carnie, looking bored and sick of life, sat scratching his thigh. JJ frowned and zoomed in on the booth. Painted on it was the word TICKETS.

*Well that explains sweet fuck all,* he thought. He was about to pan back and look elsewhere when two tricks, a young couple, appeared out of nowhere and stood in a daze by the old carnie's booth. One moment there had been a patch of trampled grass, the next, two people . . . No flashing lights or vortexes, at least none he could see. Just blink and you missed it, there they were. And as he blinked, there were two more people, granny types, one with a walking brace, standing a little to the right of the others.

He pushed the vision along a little further afield to the magician's tent. He'd almost forgotten about that crazy sucker—*I do your bunny treek—splat!* He pressed his fingers down on the glass, panning through Mugabo's roof. No tricks were yet assembled for the magic show, all the plastic seats were empty. Up on stage was the magician, looking ten feet tall in that turban, skin dark as midnight. Mugabo was clearly lost in some private grief, face buried in his hands. After a moment he moved his hands and JJ saw Mugabo wasn't crying, but enraged. He was talking to himself—no, shouting, head wrenching around, veins in his neck straining, teeth gnashing. Mugabo tried to calm himself with steadying breaths, massaging the back of his neck, smoothing his long cream-coloured gown. He didn't succeed—five seconds later he was screaming again. He kicked at a chair in the front row and JJ grunted with surprise as a small shower of sparks lit up when the magician's foot connected with the plastic.

JJ rubbed his chin and pondered. This guy was indeed a formidable customer. Maybe that was just it—mighty powers, but he was stuck pulling bunnies from hats and reels of handkerchief from his sleeve. He wondered what would happen if Mugabo simply refused to perform. Who got the job of sorting him out?

That question was answered immediately as Gonko strolled into the magician's tent. The clown leader smiled as he strode casually to the stage, hands in his pockets. Mugabo bared his teeth, body hunching over like a wildcat about to spring, fingers clawing at the air. He pointed an accusing finger at Gonko and yelled something, teeth bared. 'Wanna be careful there, Gonks,' JJ whispered. But Gonko didn't seem in the least concerned. There was contempt, almost pity, in his gaze. With one lithe jump he was onstage. Mugabo backed towards the wall until Gonko had him cornered. Then the magician moved sideways, tripped on something, and Gonko towered over him, nodding his head with a sympathetic smile, hands still in his pockets. Mugabo crawled backwards away from him, propelling himself with his feet. Gonko took a hand from his pocket and pointed at the upside down top hat, and with a few choice words sent Mugabo into a spiralling rage. The magician was about to attack, JJ could see it in his face, but Gonko just kept at him, sneering. *C'mon, I dare you . . .*

A lot happened in the next few seconds. First, Mugabo snapped and took the bait. He was suddenly on his feet, hands raised overhead like guns ready to fire.

Just as quickly, Gonko leapt backwards and pulled his hands from his pockets. He seemed to be reaching for a weapon, but found only a handful of lint. He stared down at his hands with a look of dismay. JJ missed whatever happened next, for the crystal ball lit up with a blinding flash of white light. In the distance he could faintly hear a *crack* ringing through the air, like a car backfiring. Once the light in the ball had faded, JJ saw Gonko hightailing it out of the tent, running for his life. Behind him, Mugabo chased for a few paces, hands still raised, shouting something. JJ could faintly hear his voice screaming over the background noise. Mugabo gave up the chase, calmed himself and strutted back to the stage, triumphant.

JJ took his eyes from the ball for a moment, trying to work out what had just happened. He remembered that Gonko's hands had been in his pockets the whole time, as though he'd expected to find something in them to defend himself. Exhibit B, the rock-climbing picks. He'd had nothing in his pockets when he put these pants on, he was certain of it. He then thought back to all the things he'd seen Gonko whipping out of his pockets: hatchets, blades, and so on.

About the time he connected those dots, he heard someone directly below him screaming at the very top of his lungs. It was Gonko.

*'If I find the motherfucker who took my pants*—I DON'T CARE WHO YOU ARE: CLOWN, ACROBAT, BELOVED FRIEND OR RELATIVE, AN *INANIMATE OBJECT* . . . AN *ASTRAL BODY* . . . *ME MYSELF* . . . *A ROCK OR A BOWL OF PICKLES* . . . SOMETHING *UTTERLY IMPOSSIBLE TO KILL,* LISTEN UP: I'LL *FUCKING KILL YOU.* I'LL FIND A WAY, IF IT TAKES ME A HUNDRED YEARS . . . *I'LL FIND . . . A . . . WAAAAAY!'*

Each pause in speech was filled with smashing and banging—Gonko was, it seemed, killing a few things impossible to kill right now: tables and chairs and windows, and anything else within reach, anything at all.

Around then JJ crooked a thumb in his waistband and pulled it out until he could read a little white tag within: Gonko.

Minutes passed. Below, Gonko's shouts had degenerated into incoherent screams issued through clenched teeth, punctuated with the occasional splintering of wood, crunching, smashing and banging. There was a thunderous rattle, which ever so slightly shook the very roof he sat on. Perhaps the card table had been hurled against the wall . . . Not a bad show of strength, that. JJ lay back waiting for peace and quiet. He fought back the urge to yell *shut up.* He grinned, thinking of how frightened Jamie would be when he looked back on this later.

He drew his finger across the ball, taking it away from Mugabo and towards some kind of commotion that had broken out on the main street below. A few tricks within earshot of Gonko stood, disoriented, like sleeping people disturbed by some noise outside. A few carnie rats gathered by the roadside, peering towards the clown tent, wondering what the commotion was. Bustling through, shoving them aside, was someone JJ hadn't seen before. Still, he looked oddly familiar—in fact, there was a touch of Kurt Pilo about him, mainly in the eyes, brow and lips.

It clicked: *George Pilo! Ahh, this is the other big boss type, Kurt's brother.*

The resemblance to Kurt ended at the face. George was *tiny*—he would barely clock four feet. For all that—maybe because of that—he was one angry customer. He headed for the clown tent, where Gonko was still making guttural howls and kicking things. As George rounded a bend in the road for the entrance, Gonko stormed outside, narrowly escaping his notice. George went inside and JJ could hear him cry shrilly, 'Who's upsetting the tricks? Is that Gonko?' A muffled voice—it sounded like Winston's—answered. George spat a rapid-fire burst of obscenity then marched off, his voice trailing away until it was lost in the bustle of the circus coming to life.

For three more hours JJ watched the exchanges between carnies and tricks, trying to figure it all out. The tricks laughed at the funnies, bought trinkets and souvenirs from the stalls, behaved themselves like sheep on Ritalin. The gypsies took their money but seemed uninterested in it—twice he saw them drop coins and notes on the ground without bothering to pick them up. He spent some time watching the acrobats rehearse and, despite recent events, he had to admit they had a slick routine. They bounded and flipped, walked fearlessly across the tightrope, flew through the air without looking for a moment like losing balance. He noted how easily one piece of sabotaged equipment would spell a death sentence.

He watched Mugabo's magic show, too, and the magician performed the bunny trick with cheerful gusto, his gestures sweeping and flourishing— letting off some steam had done him the world of good. JJ also spied on his fellow clowns. He saw Goshy sitting in his room, staring at the plant and not moving a muscle. Doopy was cheating in a game of solitaire and checking over his shoulder to make sure no one caught him. Rufshod lay beside his bed, dead to the world after knocking himself out by slamming his head into the wall.

The one thing JJ had been delaying, pleasantly afraid of what might happen, was a look in on Kurt Pilo. Now he shifted the image across the showgrounds, towards that abandoned northern quarter. As usual, only a few carnie rats were out that way, all walking quickly with their eyes down. He zoomed in on the little trailer, through the roof, and from overhead he saw the owner and proprietor sitting at his desk. Kurt leaned forward with his shining bald head bent over a Bible. In his monstrous hand was a highlighter pen—it seemed he was colouring in his favourite passages. His trout lips were twisted upwards into the smile that seemed his stock expression. On the desk beside him was a large bowl of what JJ at first thought was popcorn. On closer inspection he saw the tiny white objects were teeth; big ones, small ones, pearly whites of all description. Kurt reached into the bowl and popped one of them into his mouth, sucking on it like a lolly. JJ winced as his jaw crunched down, then he swallowed.

'You're one creepy sonofabitch,' JJ whispered as Kurt turned the Bible's pages gently. As JJ said this Kurt's head came up and he appeared to be listening for something. He peered directly ahead, frowning in puzzlement, though the smile still lay on his lips like something dead. Then he slowly and ominously tilted his head upwards until he was gazing right back at JJ through the glass. Kurt's eyes widened. So did the corners of his lips. JJ's heart missed a beat and his breath caught in his throat. Slowly, Kurt raised a hand over his head and gave a little wave.

JJ quickly jerked his hand sideways over the glass, away from the trailer. He let the image rest on the funhouse, where an empty cart sat on the rail.

*Don't sweat it,* he thought as his heartbeat gradually slowed.

Down below he could hear Gonko wandering around, still worked up but no longer erupting. JJ supposed it was time to get down there and hide the pants. He ran to the edge of the tent and surveyed the drop— far enough to break something, quite likely, but he was in a hurry. He dropped to his backside, braced himself for pain and slid down the steep wall clutching the crystal ball in one arm. He was right not to worry; the pockets of his pants ballooned out, puffing into two small parachutes which caught the wind and slowed his descent. Once down, the pockets folded themselves back into the pants.

He ran inside. The ruined debris from Gonko's rampage was absolute. Back in his room JJ wrapped the ball in an old towel, stiff with sweat and blood stains. Off came the pants, folded into a neat bundle. Back out in the parlour he slid them under one of the larger pieces of wreckage. With a little luck, Gonks would think they'd been there all along.

He looked at his watch—one o'clock. From memory, Yeti would be doing his glass-eating show now. JJ sprinted through the showgrounds in his boxers, past the tricks and carnie rats, resisting the powerful urge to swat and spit at them. At the freak show tent a crowd was milling around Yeti, who sat sadly on the floor, a group of colourful glass ornaments spread before him. Steve stood beside him with a syringe and towels in hand, and he nodded in greeting as JJ pushed his way through the onlookers. Steve looked attentive and proud to be of service to the show—JJ had to hand it to him, the guy had more spine than Jamie.

After a moment Yeti slowly lifted a blue glass penguin to his mouth, closed his eyes and chewed, moaning as blood gushed down his chin. JJ burst out laughing.

Steve frowned at him as he kneeled to wipe at the blood with his towel. The onlookers murmured, and some cringed and turned away from the spectacle. Tears streamed from Yeti's eyes as he fumbled for a bright green glass tiger. 'Chow down!' JJ yelled happily. '*Bon appetit*, ya big hairy fuck!'

Yeti's eyes fixed on him sadly—then anger sparked in his face when he saw it was a performer taunting him, not a trick. He bared his teeth and got to his feet, growling. 'What?' said JJ, looking at Steve, who stood by shaking his head. JJ turned to the onlookers. 'That's his job, right? It's a show, I can say what the hell I want! You think I won't get heckled when I'm up on stage clowning?'

Yeti took an unsteady shambling step towards him. A hand yanked JJ's shoulder back through the crowd. Winston and Fishboy shepherded him out the door. 'Wait a sec!' said JJ. 'I wanna see the rest of the show.'

'I don't think so,' Fishboy said sharply.

JJ raised his eyebrows. 'Aw, come on!' he said.

'No. I think Winston's ready to escort you back to your tent.'

'What?'

'Come on, JJ,' said Winston, pushing through the crowd of tricks. 'It's Fishboy's show. His rules. Let's go.'

'What's his problem?' said JJ as he and Winston made their way to the clown tent.

'You gotta understand, Fishboy actually cares about his freaks,' said Winston. 'He's not like Gonko. Fishboy's got a bit of compassion in him. Think you upset him, the way you were laughing at that poor bastard.'

'Poor bastard?' JJ cried. 'What about me? What about *my* rights?'

Winston grabbed him by the shoulder, surprising him into silence. 'Poor bastard is right. Spare a thought for him. He used to be a normal person. Now he's gotta do that every show day. Understand? Every show day, for years and years and years. You're damn lucky I pulled you away from him—he would've taken about a second to tear your stupid head off.'

Winston let him go and kept walking. JJ tried to get his drift, sympathy-wise, but he simply couldn't. It still struck him as hilarious—more so now. Thinking about it, he had to battle not to laugh. Winston looked at him sidelong in disgust.

They came to the clown tent and Winston paused to stare at the destruction. He whistled low and said, 'Wouldn't wanna be whoever took them pants.'

'Yeah, me either,' said JJ, waxing innocent like a pro. Then, 'Hold on. What? What do you mean?' Winston walked off. JJ raced over to block his path. 'What do you mean by that, Winston? Why the I-gots-a-secret vibe?'

The old clown stared at him for a moment, then nodded towards JJ's bedroom. They went in. JJ sat on the bed, trying to read Winston's expression. 'You get a feel for types of clowns,' said Winston. 'And for types of people. I seen 'em all before. Some are dangerous to know, like Gonko. Some aren't dangerous to *know*, but they're dangerous to trust.' Winston looked him in the eye. 'I'm neither type, just so you know. I don't know about you though, JJ.'

*Winston planted those pants in here!* JJ thought with sudden certainty. *This BASTARD put those pants in here. On purpose.*

'There's been clowns like you before,' Winston went on. 'I have seen it *all*, young JJ, believe you me. I know what happens when the likes of you run around unchecked. Now. You might see some things, some things about me and certain others I associate with. These things, if known, may just land me in a sling. I wouldn't doubt for a second that you, JJ, would spill any beans you came across, if it suited you. So . . . it never hurts to be careful. Never hurts for a man to have himself insured.' Winston stood to go. 'I've spoken to you straight,' he said. 'Means you can trust me.'

He left. JJ sat staring after the old guy with his mouth open in shock.

He spent the next hour thinking long and hard. Winston was right—JJ would have stabbed him in the back just for chuckles—had in fact been searching for a way to do it. He supposed the old guy was off-limits for now, whatever he got up to in his spare time.

Of course, JJ would endeavour to find out precisely what that was.

# CHAPTER 13

# SHOW NIGHT

DAY became night and the showgrounds were bathed in gloom, broken here and there by bursts of flashing light over Sideshow Alley, some so bright the colours flickered through the window in the clowns' parlour.

Around seven the other clowns became nervous and jittery about the coming show. Doopy was complaining about anything and everything. Rufshod seemed to be in competition with Doopy to get on everyone's nerves. Goshy drifted about the place with a look of vacant alarm on his face, whistling like a budgerigar. Winston kept to himself, stretching his hamstrings in the corner, avoiding eye contact with JJ when their paths crossed.

Out in the parlour JJ saw Gonko for the first time since that morning's eruption. The clown boss was in a foul mood; he'd collared Doopy and was threatening him for some infraction or other. There was a giant scorch mark on the back of Gonko's shirt, part of which had been burned away, leaving a hellish purple stretch of blistered skin.

Gonko turned and saw him. 'JJ!' he snapped. 'Just where the hell have you been all day?'

JJ held his hands up and hunched his shoulders in fright, invoking Mr Don't Hurt Me; there was some conviction in the act this time.

'Cut the horse shit!' Gonko roared. 'It's an hour till show time. You're going to watch it, you're going to like it, you're going to learn something. No more sneaking off or I will staple your balls to the floor. Where's Rufshod?'

Rufshod bounded into the parlour, marched up to Gonko and said, 'I took your pants, boss. It was me.'

Gonko stared at him sourly.

'Hit me,' said Rufshod, dropping to his knees. 'Please . . .'

Gonko turned away, shaking his head in disgust. Doopy took it upon himself to do the honours. He made a fat round fist and threw a clumsy punch which looked, perhaps, the way the Queen might throw a right cross, but it did the job; Rufshod fell back on the ground with his nose gushing blood. 'Gee, I'm real sorry Ruf,' said Doopy. 'I didn't mean ta, wasn't s'pose ta, I just, I——'

'LISTEN UP!' Gonko screamed. The clowns listened up. Gonko gave everyone in the room a look of revulsion. 'All right. Tonight, it's going to come off right, or some of us will be very badly hurt—by me. I am undergoing some executive stress. It would give me great joy to stomp the shit out of any one of you. Great joy. Bear that in mind before you fuck everything up again. Let's go.'

Doopy shuffled over to Gonko and whispered something in his ear. Gonko nodded and said, 'Yeah. Also, congrats to Goshy, who's gonna be married soon. Don't let it change you, Goshy.'

The other clowns patted Goshy on the back, and he peered at each of them with curious eyes, as though he'd never seen them before in his life. In a mood of sombre determination the clowns departed for their stage tent.

They passed the acrobats' stage tent, which had had extra rows of seats brought in during the day, removed from the clowns' stage tent. Gonko struggled visibly to control his rage. The acrobat show had already begun, and they could hear *oohs* and *ahhs* from the audience as the acrobats defied death high above the ground.

Backstage in their own tent, the clowns were accosted by George Pilo. This was JJ's first sight of him up close, and he felt an instinctive dislike that was a far cry from the awe he'd felt for Kurt. From the height of Doopy's navel George's eyes glared while his mouth smiled. Gonko stiffened and his shoulders twitched, but his voice was gentle when he said, 'Why, hello there, George. Come to watch us? Maybe have a laugh or two?'

'No,' George replied, and his voice was at once condescending, whiny and sneering. 'I've come to remind you you're still on notice, and you're due for a *perfect* show tonight. Nothing less whatsoever. Did you notice what's been done with the seating? With the *amount* of seating?'

'Yes, George, we noticed,' said Gonko.

'I took three rows from your tent and put 'em in the acrobats' tent,' George pointed out anyway. 'They've got a bigger audience. They've earned it.'

'Thank you, George, for bringing that to my attention,' said Gonko. 'Tell me, George——'

'What's more,' said George, taking obvious pleasure in interrupting, 'I've been looking for you all day, Gonko. I could hear your little spat halfway across the showgrounds. You upset the tricks. You distracted them.'

'George, there was an incident with the magician—'

'If I have to put you personally on notice, don't think I won't do it. I know you're in bed with Kurt, but *I* don't like you, Gonko.'

'I had no idea, George.'

'I don't like any of you,' George cried, waving his arm around like a chimp. He shuffled closer to Gonko, so close his face pressed into Gonko's belly, and his voice became muffled. Gonko stared down into the pair of wet white eyes glaring up at him without blinking. 'Things are changing around here,' said George. 'Changing. You hear me? For some of us, the party is over. For some of us.'

'Thank you for the advice, George,' Gonko whispered.

George Pilo glared up at him for a moment, then abruptly stormed off, lashing his arms at anything in his path.

'I don't *like* George, Gonko. I don't *like* him!'

'Shut your fucking word hole,' Gonko snapped.

A loud burst of applause broke out from the acrobats' tent next door. 'Show time,' Winston murmured.

Their own audience could be heard talking quietly and JJ felt excitement ripple through him; the thought of being up there in front of a bunch of strangers, making an idiot of himself, almost made him wish he hadn't skipped rehearsal.

Gonko motioned for everyone to gather around. 'Get your heads on,' he said. 'Like we rehearsed, lead with Doops then Ruf. Start with the stealing his hanky routine. I'll come out and play copper. Milk the first three minutes for all it's worth, but it was piss-weak in rehearsal, and if they ain't giggling I'm coming out early. Out comes Goshy when I clap the cuffs on Doops—Winston give him a push up the steps to make sure he goes when he's meant to. Doops, if he blows it tonight I'll give him something to whistle about. JJ, you watch, pay attention, and if you sneak off I will break your fucking skull. All right. GO.'

Doopy stumbled up the steps and onto the stage as the lights came on, flooding the stage in heat. Whatever he did out there drew a brief laugh, and JJ climbed up on a crate to watch. Rufshod took a huffing breath and bounded onto the stage, all his mania uncoiling like a spring, each step a leap taking him high into the air. The audience seemed to draw breath at the bouncing cartoonish apparition, a blur of bright colours flashing through the air. Doopy put on a look of sorrow at losing their attention, gazing mournfully at Rufshod, waving his arms, trying to get the spotlight back. Rufshod mocked him, pointing in triumph at the audience—*ha ha, they're watching me*. A forlorn figure, Doopy shuffled to the back of the stage, then paused as though struck with an idea. He pulled down his pants and stood in his striped boxers, arms held out like a composer. The spotlight beam switched back to him and Rufshod stopped still, mortified, as Doopy blew kisses at the crowd. Striding over to Doopy, Rufshod plucked the handkerchief from his shirt pocket in revenge. Doopy waxed indignant, pants still around his ankles. He put up his dukes clumsily and drew a laugh. Turning to them, Doopy bowed, forgetting all about the fight and, while his attention was diverted, Rufshod kicked him in the backside.

Backstage, Gonko muttered, 'Rusty as shit, but it'll do.' He'd slipped into a British copper's uniform, with a sheriff's badge and billy club. In a bizarre goosestep he strutted onstage, pulled a whistle from his pocket and blew it. Then everything went wrong.

As the whistle rang out shrill and loud there was a popping sound from the rafters above, followed by a hissing as smoke began to billow from the floor. A thick grey cloud soon enveloped Rufshod and Doopy. Gonko stopped dead and stared around in alarm.

JJ turned to Winston. 'Is this part of—'

'No. It isn't,' said Winston grimly. 'It's sabotage.'

Winston motioned to Goshy and the pair of them stepped onstage. Goshy's arms were locked stiff at his sides. He wandered towards his brother and was soon lost in the smoke cloud. JJ last saw Winston kneeling on the floor, pawing through the smoke to find its source. The cloud got thicker and before long the audience was coughing as smoke wafted over the rows of seats. JJ's eyes watered and he felt a rough tickle in his throat. Onstage, Goshy began the kettle noise in his distress: '*HMMMMMM! HMMMMMMM!*'

There was a muffled: 'It's not . . . *funny* . . .'

Gonko bellowed at the top of his lungs: '*If I find . . . the dirty mother-fucker . . .*' but he had to stop there, caught by a coughing fit. The audience, too, were hacking up a storm. There were panicked confused shouts, then the sound of people climbing over plastic seats and stampeding to the exits. The clowns staggered off the stage, spluttering and hacking, except Goshy, who kept up the kettle noise. The group of them made for the door and stood outside, gasping for air. Still squealing, Goshy looked about in alarm, his face doing the same grotesque contortions JJ had seen earlier that day, all the flesh peeled back into thick rings. '*Goshhhh-eeeee,*' said Doopy, stumbling over to his brother and holding him by the shoulders. 'They smoked us out, Goshy. They gone and did it . . . They smoked us all out!' Doopy embraced his brother, trying to calm him, but the kettle noise just wouldn't stop.

Next door, the acrobats were enjoying thunderous applause.


The clowns sat quietly around their new card table, which Rufshod had stolen from the woodchoppers. Quietly was not what JJ had expected—he'd expected fireworks from Gonko at least. Instead, Gonko leaned back in his chair with a speculative look on his face. Winston was doing the talking. 'Smoke bombs. Can get 'em from the joke stall in Sideshow Alley. They'd give you a hundred for a few grains o' powder.' He held one between his thumb and forefinger, a small object like a black ping-pong ball. 'They burst open and puke up smoke if you whack 'em. Must've dropped a few dozen from the roof onto the stage.'

'How'd they get 'em to go off when Gonko blew his whistle?' said Rufshod.

'That I'm not sure. May have just been coincidence. Maybe someone had a carnie up there on the rafters with a bag full of 'em. Have to ask that gypsy who does the spotlights if he saw anything.'

'Whoever did it, they're fucked,' Gonko said. His voice was tranquil. 'I mean to the hilt. They'll need a mop and a band-aid, I kid you not.'

'Any way we can find out?' said Rufshod. 'I know! We'll just look in the—'

JJ cut him off with a violent coughing fit and a pointed glance. Rufshod got the message. Winston watched the pair of them closely and lapsed into thoughtful silence.

'Look where, Ruf?' said Doopy. 'Look in the where?'

'Ah, we'll . . . look in their tents,' said Rufshod.

'Whose tent, Ruf?' said Doopy.

'Whoever done it.'

Doopy pondered this carefully then cried, 'Yeah! Yeah that's a swell idea. Let's do that, Gonko, let's look in whoever done its tent and see who—'

'We all know who it was,' said Gonko. 'They wear tights. They wished us a good show yesterday. JJ threw mud at them, God bless his little heart. And do not fear, there shall be comeuppance. But all of you listen and listen good. No revenge attacks yet. No lines to read between, I mean it. For now, we play nice as custard and pie.' Gonko squinted around at each of them. 'None of us is going to forget tonight any time soon. There is *no* hurry. For now we take it on the chin—and they fucked us pretty good, you gotta hand it to 'em. But we'll fuck 'em back. This will be a steady campaign of fuckery, but we gotta do it just right. Coming up now is the foreplay. Nice and slow.'

'Knock knock!' came a voice from the door.

'Ah, here we go,' Gonko muttered.

George Pilo marched in with someone at his heels, a fat man with eyes so close together it looked like they were sharing a socket—it appeared the matter manipulator had decorated his face. This, JJ guessed by the suit and tie, was the Pilo's pet accountant, and orchestrator of the clown-versus-acrobat competition policy. Beside him, George looked absolutely gleeful. 'Gonko!' he cried. 'Let's have what you might call an open dialogue about tonight's show. Do you feel you lived up to your own expectations, first off?'

'A little rusty, to be honest, George,' said Gonko serenely.

'A little rusty!' George echoed, beaming. 'I like that. No wonder you're in charge of this crew, you're a funny guy. Roger and I were just doing some sums, what you might call a cost-benefit analysis of your show. Tonight, Gonko, your show cost us the lives of nine tricks. Nine whole unharvested tricks, dead in the stampede. Now, most crowds boo when they don't like a show, so I suppose a suicidal stampede indicates "a little rusty" is dead on the money. What does nine tricks equal in powder, Roger?'

Roger the accountant dropped his briefcase in the furious rush to pull a calculator from his pocket. He punched in some numbers and said, 'Nine bags, Mr Pilo.'

'Nine bags!' cried George, grinning his head off. 'Nine bags, Gonko. Roger, what were we going to pay the clowns for tonight's performance?'

The accountant punched in more numbers. 'Nine bags,' he said.

'Right!' said George. 'And what is nine minus nine?'

Roger did the maths. 'It's, ah, zero, Mr Pilo.'

'Right you are! A nice round number. What do you think of that, Gonko?'

Gonko opened his mouth to speak and shut it again as George slapped a piece of paper down on the table. He gave it a disinterested glance and said, 'What might that be, George?'

'Notice of suspension!' George cried.

Gonko sighed. 'What if I were to tell you our act was sabotaged?'

George feigned a judicious look and rocked back and forth on his heels. 'If you were to tell me *that*, I would ask you to bring forth the mountain of evidence you presumably have on hand to prove beyond doubt your wild allegation.' Gonko held up the smoke bomb. 'Bear in mind that what constitutes doubt,' said George, and Gonko threw the smoke bomb away. 'I'd then remind you that each performer is solely responsible for their act, including upkeep of their performance facility and, or, if applicable, their stage. That's what I'd say, hypothetically, if you were to, hypothetically, make such a claim. An appeal could of course be made to a manager, but said manager's ruling would be final and binding. And said manager would be . . . me, Gonko.'

'Thanks for clearing that up, George.'

'Not at all. My pleasure! And thank *you* for respecting due process. That's exactly what I told the fortune-teller when her crystal ball went missing. So, your act is suspended indefinitely. Don't worry, though, I have other duties for you.'

'I don't *like* other duties,' Doopy moaned. 'I don't *like* it!'

'Quiet, Doops,' said Gonko.

'Report to my trailer next Friday night for outside jobs,' said George. 'You'll be working directly for me. Aren't we both lucky?' George turned on his heel and marched off without another word. The accountant bustled out after him.

Back at the table, Gonko flicked the notice to the floor, then stood and left. JJ turned to Winston. 'What's *outside jobs* supposed to mean?'

'What does it sound like?' said Winston. 'Jobs off the showgrounds. Back where we came from. Before we ended up *here*.'

In his bedroom JJ wondered how Jamie would react to the day's events. It was a big day for the pair of them, many a narrow course threaded through the minefield, so to speak . . . Hell, JJ could have gotten them both killed a few times over.

*I'll do the guy a favour,* JJ thought. *I'll leave the paint on. Yeah, he'll thank me for it.*

With that, JJ the clown lay down to sleep. But his considerate gesture was foiled by his pillow and sheet. Dreams are vivid in the circus, and with the tossing, turning and sweating, the face paint rubbed off after just a couple of hours.

# CHAPTER 14

# THE MORNING AFTER

JAMIE woke.

His hands seemed to be acting on their own as, shaking, they reached for the little velvet bag. As he moved the pain set in and his first thought for the morning was that the pain would kill him.

Slow, deliberate movements ... Rushing might mean spilling the powder and starting all over again. Into the clay bowl it went, then he struck a match, managed somehow to keep his hand steady as he melted the grains into a silvery pool of liquid, croaked 'Make this pain stop,' drank it and sank back. It may have been the laying of blessed hands; he sighed and thanked God, savouring the feeling of being whole, in one piece, without every nerve set alight.

As the minutes ticked by his mind emerged from its slumber. The thoughts being connected in there were unwelcome ones, dim memories of yesterday, when a stranger was in charge of his body. His mind went through a routine which would become very familiar upon waking: *This can't be happening, but it is. This is impossible, but here I am. I no longer have control of myself most of the time. A lunatic is at the helm, and I am completely in his hands. If he wanted to get me killed, I wouldn't be able to stop him. I attacked the acrobats. I have stolen property which, if discovered in my possession, will probably get me killed. I have the resident psychopath—the psychopath who is now my leader—out for somebody's blood, and it's only a matter of time until he realises that somebody is me.*

Next he remembered the death of nine tricks, which to some meant human beings. With dull horror Jamie realised that he—JJ—hadn't given that a moment's reflection. Not a thought.

'Oh man,' Jamie whispered. Every time he donned the face paint and surrendered himself to that lunatic, he was going to wake to more mornings like this.

What now, then? What could he do about all this? The answer seemed obvious: he had no idea *at all*. But there had to be something. There had to be a way out of here.

Sure, and if he found it, they'd find him. Just like last time. They'd follow him to his job, appear in his bedroom late at night, stalk him wherever he went. They'd bring him back or kill him. He was stuck and had better get used to it. No one back in the real world could help him, or even believe him. All that rang so true he cried, burying his face in his pillow like an ostrich in the sand, until he heard someone enter the room. Winston.

The old clown sighed as he sat down beside the bed. 'Don't worry about it, son,' he said quietly. 'You'll be okay.'

Hearing a human voice offer such badly needed comfort evoked such a burst of gratitude that Jamie reached for the old man. Winston held him and patted his cheeks with a handkerchief. 'Shh. You'll be okay,' he said.

'Nasty business, being in the show,' said Winston after Jamie had calmed down. 'Nasty, nasty business. What we do here is worse than you'd believe, even if I told you.'

'I'd probably give you a fair hearing,' said Jamie, wiping the dampness from his cheeks.

'No doubt, yep. You'll see in time. I'm in no rush to tell you. And don't worry about Gonko's pants. I didn't do it to blackmail you. I'm covering myself from JJ, is all. I wouldn't trust him runnin' loose without a reason not to do harm. He ain't exactly predictable. Seems to like watchin' people suffer.'

Jamie nodded and sighed. 'Is this it, then? Am I trapped here until I die?'

Winston took a while to answer. 'Maybe. But . . . maybe not.'

Jamie blinked, then seized on this, and found his hands clutching at Winston's arm. 'There's a way out of here?' he said. 'How?'

But Winston looked reluctant to say more. He scratched his head for a moment, then with a grimace leaned over and whispered: 'Look. I'll tell you one thing, one word. It won't make any sense yet, but when the time comes, you'll understand. That word is *freedom*. Don't ask me any more about it, not now, when I don't know what you'll say or do when you put your face paint on.'

'I won't put it on again,' said Jamie. 'Never again.'

'You're going to have to,' said Winston.

'No.'

'*Yes*. You will have to. You don't know the lay of the land nearly well enough to get by on your own. You can't act like JJ when you're Jamie. You couldn't do it, they'd eat you up. They'd kill you by accident, in ways the paint would protect you from. And you'd crack up. I know damn well. Do you think you could look Kurt Pilo in the eye the way JJ could? JJ who's too stupid to be afraid of anyone?'

Jamie's face paled when he thought of JJ's introduction to Kurt, and he shivered. 'No. I don't think I could.'

Winston nodded. 'Just remember that word. Freedom. You'll see what I'm driving at soon enough, I'm guessing. And when you're JJ, you remember the pants, and what Gonko would like to do to you. Only when you're JJ.'

Winston left him.


Winston had private business to attend to. It was private indeed, the type that could land him in the stew, cut to pieces and pureed by the Pilo brothers if they learned of it. He would be made an addition to the freak show if he was lucky. If he was unlucky the matter manipulator would be given complete licence, and would twist him into shapes unable to die, only to suffer. But the secret had been kept for a long time.

It was early and the circus was still mostly asleep; things were usually subdued the day after show day. Winston strolled down the main street, past the fortune-teller's hut and acrobat tent. A few carnies were up and about cleaning and restocking their stalls with trinkets. Most averted their gaze from him, wary of the clowns as always.

Nine dead tricks. Quite a stir that would cause on the outside. Winston sighed with a sadness that reached his bones. He knew well enough how cheap human life was around here, but the show insisted on reminding him.

He came to the freak show tent, confident he was unobserved by prying eyes, and confident no prying minds were wondering why he spent so much time here chatting with Fishboy. Neither of them gave much reason to wonder; they were careful. Inside, Fishboy was in conversation with the severed head, known as Nugget to his friends. Yeti had been allowed out back to eat grass by the fence—it helped soothe the hideous wounds in his gums after the glass-eating shows.

'Winston!' said Fishboy, hustling over to slap him jovially on the arm. The pair of them exchanged small talk about the weather, about yesterday's show, chit chat just to deflect the interest of any prying ears. After a few minutes, Winston lowered his voice. 'Our show last night . . .?' and he finished the question with a raised eyebrow.

Fishboy answered with his own eyes, thin slits set very far apart on his face. *No, it wasn't our doing,* his eyes said.

Winston nodded. 'Didn't think so. Just wanted to be sure. Got news for you, though.'

Fishboy leaned close, an intimacy that would cause those unused to him to cringe away. Winston whispered, 'I was right about Shalice's ball. It's in the new guy's room, JJ's room. Wrapped in a pillow case. And what's more, George knows it's missing!'

Fishboy raised his eyebrows at this. *Are you sure?* he said with facial expressions Winston had learned to interpret.

Winston nodded. 'It's safe,' he said. 'Used powder . . . keep it hidden from her.' Fishboy nodded; his nod indicated he would use some of his own supply for the same purpose. Winston wasn't fluent enough in body language to pick up on that, but he assumed it would be the case, and assumed many other interested parties would be taking similar precautions. *Keep JJ's secrets hidden* was all they'd need to say, and with a dozen of them blocking the secret from the fortune-teller's psychic probes, the crystal ball was as safe as JJ made it.

They finished off with more small talk then Winston left. He was glad to have eyes which missed very little . . . Without them, he wouldn't have spotted the round bulge at the foot of Jamie's bed this morning, confirming the suspicions formed last night. 'We'll just look in the . . .' Rufshod had said, and Winston hadn't missed that either. His visit to Jamie, whilst humanitarian, had confirmed his suspicions. Rufshod's raid on the fortune-teller could prove to be a bigger blow than Winston had first realised, though it was early days yet.

Taking a casual detour through the showgrounds, paying visits here and there, Winston gave some other interested parties the news, which would then spread to all who needed to know. With the ball out of Shalice's hands, the two keenest prying eyes were now blind. But prying eyes never close completely . . . That should never be forgotten.


Jamie found Steve in the freak show tent, cheerfully pretending to to be busy cleaning empty cages while the freaks were out getting some exercise. Steve had taken to the circumstances with such ease that Jamie almost found himself admiring the guy.

'Man, this is the life,' said Steve as Jamie sat down with his back against a glass case. 'You know those dwarfs? I'm going to dinner with one of the females. Her name's Loretta. Met her when I was oiling some gears on the Ferris wheel.'

Jamie looked up at him in disbelief. 'Wait a minute—you're not just coping, you're *happy* here?'

Steve looked at him like he was crazy. 'Sure, why the hell not? You *seen* the kind of shit you can do with that powder? Tell you what, if Marshall was here, he'd be into that stuff around the clock.' Steve beckoned him closer and dropped his voice to a whisper. 'Like, imagine if you wished to hump, say, Pamela. For an hour or so, you're actually *in* the room, doing it. When it ends you wake up like you had a dream. Trust me, I tried it.'

Jamie shook his head. 'But . . . our *lives* . . . Are you just going to accept our lives are over?'

Steve laughed. 'Bullshit they're over! What's over is where you have to do the nine to five, pay a mortgage and get old. You get that part? No rent, no bills to pay, and we get to see some crazy shit most people never dream of. You know how long these guys have been around, the acrobats and that? They've been here *hundreds of years*, Jamie. They don't die! They look as young as they did when they joined.'

Jamie didn't have the heart to point out how broken and battered most carnies looked from the endless labours of the show—those who, like Steve, weren't performers. 'We'll never see our families again,' said Jamie, and there was a catch in his voice. again. You don't care about that?'

'I haven't got much family anyway,' said Steve, shrugging. 'Never knew Dad, Mum never wanted me around. Used to send me money each week to keep me away from her, I reckon. Who cares? Make a new family. Anyway, how do you know you won't see 'em again? They might end up here one day, or maybe you'll get a holiday out there. Just keep your head down and stay out of trouble . . . Some of these dudes *hate* each other. Seen the clowns and acrobats go at it? You would've, huh? You're a clown, right? Damn, you got lucky. Hey—what's Gonko like in private?'

Jamie sighed. 'He's mean as hell. Don't go near him.'

'He looks hardcore,' said Steve with admiration. 'They're scared to death of Gonko, over in the Alley. They keep a watch for him, and if he comes through they scatter. Dwarfs want to kill him but none of 'em's got the balls to actually try.'

There was a silence as Steve polished the iron bars of a cage. After a while Jamie said, 'Hey, about the clowns and acrobats. Do you know what that's about? Why do they fight like that?'

'Yeah, I heard a thing or two. You should talk to some of the old guys in Sideshow Alley . . . No, wait, they hate your guts. You shouldn't've pissed in the plaster clown's mouth, man.' Jamie winced. 'But yeah,' Steve went on, 'some of those old guys, they seen it all, watched it for years and years. All these fights started over *nothing*. You get a bunch of psychos like this in a closed space, one little thing sets 'em off.'

'Like what?'

'Like in Chopper Read's book, how he says the big gang war started over a plate of sausages? The first clown and acrobat fight started over who got to use the stage first for a show. Over fucking *nothing*. Then it was on forever. Heaps of these psychos got killed. It comes and goes in waves, according to the old guys. No one forgets a thing either. Plus everyone's bored.'

'There's got to be more to it than that,' said Jamie.

'Yeah. They're freaks, plain and simple. Just mental cases. They don't need a reason to go off. The bosses don't help. Kurt likes to start fights. The carnies reckon he watches it like sport.'

Jamie nodded, not in the least reassured by what he was hearing, but somehow glad to hear it all discussed so casually, accepted so readily. It lent an air of normality to the place and he didn't want Steve to stop talking. 'What do you make of the bosses?' said Jamie. 'The Pilo brothers?'

Steve whistled. 'Scary. Fishboy says to avoid 'em, do exactly what you're told and to suck up if you come near 'em. Just like a normal boss. Fishboy's pretty cool to work for. Hey—why were you such a prick yesterday?'

Jamie grimaced.

'It's true,' Steve went on, missing the subtleties as usual. 'You laughed your head off at Yeti. He wanted to kill you. Me and Fishboy had to calm him down after the show. You're probably safe now, but don't laugh at him when he eats glass. He doesn't like that.'

'It's not me,' Jamie said, wondering how to explain it. 'You know the face paint? When I put it on it does something to me. I can't control it.'

'Nah, man, it was *you*, I saw you!' Steve said, throwing his rag down in anger. 'Same tall skinny redheaded wanker. Can't believe you laughed at him. You ever tried eating glass? You're such a prick, man, I swear.'

Jamie smiled ruefully and got up to leave. 'Good luck on your date,' he said.

'What? Oh yeah, Loretta. She's all right—kinda short though. Hey, come get me next time you rehearse, okay? I wanna watch.'

Jamie nodded to prevent an argument and left.


In their tent the clowns felt the morning after in full. Only Goshy seemed free of the lethargy; from his room came an occasional loud coo, sliding like alien fingers into the ears of anyone in range. Gonko and Rufshod sat at the card table, both looking glum. Gonko's hoard of loot made the loss of nine bags a triviality, but he was still livid about the whole business. *No one* sabotaged the clowns. He and Rufshod were talking tactics to help ease the post-show blues. 'We'll start,' said Gonko, 'by acting like we're beat. We treat the acrobats like they won, got our nuts in their handbags. We'll be so sweet they just wanna puke whenever they see us. If we act hot and bothered, they'll know we got nothing on 'em. If we act beat, they'll see right through it and know something's coming. So we wish 'em a happy rehearsal, every day. Happy performance, every show day. They'll get to a point where they're too scared to rehearse at all, thinking someone cut a wire on their equipment. They won't even wanna leave their tent alone.'

Rufshod nodded solemnly then asked Gonko to hit him, just this once.

'Not till you've earned it, snookums.'

Jamie came through the door. 'Mornin', JJ,' said Gonko.

'Morning,' said Jamie.

Gonko peered at him, not caring for the timidity in his voice. It wasn't JJ's play-acting; the guy was scared. He either had something to hide or he was chickenshit. The latter could be solved by a little camaraderie. 'What's the matter, JJ? Got a case of the mummy-I'm-scareds?'

Jamie flinched and shook his head. 'Nothing's the matter . . . just homesick, I guess.'

'Ah well, don't worry about that,' said Gonko. Diagnosis: chickenshit. 'You're home now. Why be homesick? Don't tell me you miss that fucking cesspool outside?'

'Yeah, Gonko,' Jamie said quietly. 'That could be it.'

'Don't you worry, my sweet. We got our own cesspool right here. Come on in, the water's fine. Besides, soon we'll be right back out there, thanks to last night. Thanks to little Georgie too.' Gonko spat. 'I fucking hate outside jobs. We can swing by your joint if you want. What do you say? Got a girlfriend out there? Wanna pay a visit to yer parents? We can do that. I'll play nice around 'em. I won't kill nobody. And if I do, it'll be real fast. What do you say, young JJ? Christ! What's his problem? Running off like I stole his lollipop! What'd I say?'


Shalice was in her caravan with her lover, a muscular gypsy man who lay beside her covered in a sheen of sweat. She had brought him to the show long ago, arranged his escape from prison and then ensnared him in her own webs, not a *slave* to her, but neither an equal nor friend. She felt little for him and did not need his help to survive. His body was all that interested her, and he did not burden her emotions; those had become numb over the years, blunted by the knowledge of so much pain and death, much of it channelled through her own hands at the Pilos' orders. She lay with her eyes half-closed and distant, pulling at her bottom lip with her thumb and forefinger, a pose she adopted when troubled by unwelcome reflections on her position in the circus.

She and her lover rarely talked, having said what little they needed to say long before: he had no insight to offer and they would just be repeating themselves. Today, though, he did observe: 'Something's upset you.'

She gave a start, as though she'd forgotten he was there. 'Yes,' she replied. 'I had thought after many harsh lessons the rest of the show had learned to leave me be. It seems they must be taught again.'

'Is it the clowns?' he said.

'It could be.' She sighed. 'When age and death are not likely to trouble people, they have no need to acquire wisdom. They are unafraid to play with fire.'

The gypsy grunted and rolled on his side away from her, rocking the bed with his weight. His huge tattooed shoulders lay like a wall between her and the window, over which blue curtains were drawn, filtering the dim light. He knew she would not expect him to offer his help. A few minutes passed and he began snoring. *That habit is one of the things I should have foreseen before bringing him to me,* Shalice thought, not for the first time. Then she turned her mind back to the problem at hand.

While the crystal ball was her most important asset, it was not her only one. She was certain the thief would be revealed. It might come to her in a vision, flashing into her mind sudden and unbidden. For some reason that escaped her completely, the powder was telling her nothing and she looked forward to finding out why. Suddenly there seemed more mysteries afoot than she had supposed.

Who had she crossed swords with of late? Gonko for one. Being friendly with Kurt, he seemed to believe he was invincible, he and his band of creeps. Not long ago, against every rule in the book, he had taken a trick girl back to his room and fed her some powder, though what he'd made her use it for was anyone's guess. Shalice had intended to use the girl as a domino which, carefully placed, would culminate in a business empire toppling. The term for such magic was *Fortuna Imperium*, or fate-steering. Practitioners could be found amongst the kings, queens and emperors of times past.

It worked like this: Man raises his middle finger at a passing car; the driver ponders it, wondering what he'd done to offend the stranger, misses his route home while distracted, and collides with a van, killing the driver who was the real target of the exercise. The simplest of scenarios, but the setups could be so elaborate and huge they shaped the course of history; wars could be started or finished.

Shalice's programming of JJ the clown on his first day would, according to Kurt's orders, have resulted in a shooting massacre in New Zealand next year. The clown's interference may well have caused any number of variations to the final result, possibly including bloodshed on a global scale.

Often she could steer the less tasteful chains of events like these off course and get away with it, but every so often such orders had to be carried out; it was imperative the Pilos trusted her. She would not deny that she enjoyed the power, nor could she stand the thought of such power being entrusted to someone else. The way she saw it, the world had already been spared many hurts for the price of just a few. In the girl's case, Gonko's disruption had made the first domino topple the wrong way. Things had been frosty between them since. But the clowns had other enemies, who would delight in starting a feud between Shalice and Gonko. On the off-chance this was the case, she would not be firing any shots until she was certain.

Who else was there? Mugabo, of course. She'd been given the unenviable task of coaxing him to perform earlier this month. Whoever did so was in for an interesting morning, and destined for Mugabo's bad books for a long time. He had the magical skill to pull off the fake crystal ball. It didn't seem likely to her, but he was unpredictable; another one to watch.

Then there were the woodchoppers. Her feud with them had been constant since they joined the show sixty-two years ago. In their eyes, she was the only decent piece of tail on the showgrounds, and every time she passed them they'd holler their moronic innuendoes and wolf-whistle. There had been one attempted rape, decades back, and after a string of cruel 'accidents' the perpetrator had not witnessed his next birthday. They'd had more than their share of bad luck over the years; there'd been collisions with runaway wagons, electrocutions, mystery illnesses . . . Every grain of powder they earned was spent on pain relief and cures. Perhaps they'd cottoned on to her at last and sought revenge. Again, unlikely, but bigger surprises had been sprung on her before.

That covered the list of suspects. The freaks, gypsies and dwarfs she had no quarrels with, as far as she knew. Already she almost pitied the fool who'd crossed her.

In his trailer Kurt Pilo was sucking on a wolf fang and setting aside a Bible. He'd found it a highly entertaining read and had marked in his favourite passages with a highlighter pen, which amounted to every single word.

Intuition told him his brother George was due to make an assassination attempt. Kurt wondered with pleasant curiosity what the poor fellow would try this time. He also wondered with pleasant curiosity whether or not George would succeed, though he doubted it. Kurt supposed it was George who had the fortune-teller's ball—he'd felt himself being watched yesterday. It had to be George; who else would dare do such a thing? If anyone were *that* suicidal, surely they would choose a quicker means of death than annoying Kurt Pilo. 'George, George, George,' said Kurt. 'Why do we have such hate for the ones we love?'

His jaw clenched, crushing the wolf's fang into powder with a sound like cracking knuckles. He swallowed and reached into the bowl, dug around for a while, then picked out a deer's tooth. He held it between his thumb and forefinger, gazing at it with a serene smile before setting it on his tongue.

His eyes fell on the calendar on the wall, where 9 March was circled, and he sighed happily. What would the employees do for his birthday this time around? They were probably already making plans. The competition over gifts was fierce, with everyone out to curry his favour or avoid his wrath. *What a lovely thing it is to be in charge,* he thought.

Back in his room, Jamie sat staring at the wall, a look of tiredness on his face. Before him lay a dangerous and narrow range of choices. In fact, there were only two: stay or go. The latter seemed impossible, and pointless in any event—they'd find him as they had before. That meant staying here without a fuss, which seemed to mean kissing himself goodbye and surrendering entirely to JJ. Maybe he should try to accept it, even embrace it the way Steve had. No more visits to his parents' place for Christmas. No more posting on his Internet forums. No more computer games . . . no more *Sim City*. No more David Bowie or Devo records on vinyl. No more scheming to get a date with Svetlana the Russian girl who served drinks at the Wentworth. No more rainy nights reading Stephen King in the lamplight. No more anything.

In a way, he supposed he was dead. He reached for the tub of face paint, so he wouldn't have to care for a while.

# PART 3

JAMIE
VERSUS JJ

*Love and blood begin to meld, you've lost the self you once held*
*Merry go round your head—awake, alseep, alive, or dead*

CAROUSEL

# KURT'S PRAYER MEETING

FOUR days had passed since the show day that saw nine tricks trampled to death and the clowns relegated to odd jobs outside the showgrounds. George Pilo was to hand them their first assignment that night and the clowns were tense.

Later that afternoon (much to everyone's chagrin, not just the clowns') one of Kurt's 'prayer meetings' was scheduled, a new bimonthly tradition inspired by Kurt's recent interest in all things biblical. All circus employees of note, which excluded only the gypsy and dwarf masses and the shadowy beings lurking in the funhouse, good-naturedly gathered to hear Kurt give a speech, offer encouragement to his charges, strut and make tasteful jokes. Prayer meetings were ostensibly designed to foster some sense of community in the show, but Kurt's good intentions were, as usual, well off the mark.

Meanwhile, it was now important that JJ keep the crystal ball hidden from the other clowns. He'd told Rufshod he no longer had it, that the ball had simply vanished, presumably stolen. Rufshod bought the story and had been moping sulkily around the tent since. As for Jamie, he didn't last five minutes each morning without rushing for the face paint. He'd take one look around, reel like a man who'd woken into a nightmare after pleasant dreams, and JJ would find himself in charge.

His concern lately had been trying to work out precisely what he could do with the wish powder. There seemed strict limits—for instance, he'd swallowed a small amount and wished death upon all the acrobats. After making the wish he'd almost felt the words sitting somewhere in limbo, like a line cast out over the water and yet to fall. When he opened his eyes and ran excitedly to the acrobat tent, he was disappointed—they were all still kicking. Back in his room he'd made the wish again with a larger dose of powder, but again no luck. That spelled Tantrum—he'd kicked the walls and choked back tears for an hour. Sullenly he made another wish, this time wanting just to see Rufshod trip up on his own feet. Out in the parlour he saw Rufshod's pants snag on the corner of the card table, sending him head over heels.

At that point JJ realised he was wasting his whole stash, and asked Gonko what the limits were. 'Anything goes, as long as it doesn't upset the balance of things,' said Gonko. Asked what he meant by the balance of things, Gonko had snapped: 'Look, anything that doesn't directly harm the show. Within reason. The more you use for a wish, the more likely you'll get it.'

JJ spent the rest of his leisure time tormenting the carnie rats. He threw things at them, tipped over their stalls, kicked the women in front of their husbands, spat in the men's faces, stole their wares by the armful and dumped them in the latrines, threw the 'test your strength' hammer over the distant rooftops every few hours, helped himself to their food and generally made an absolute menace of himself. The carnies patiently endured him, tried to avoid him and waited for his interest in them to fade, but that wasn't going to happen any time soon; they were the best fun JJ could find. Sometimes the rats ran and fetched the acrobats for protection, and the three of them would stride into Sideshow Alley in their tights and bulging codpieces, stalking him through the showgrounds, forcing him to hide, sobbing quietly until they left. When they left he would resume the harassment, beginning with whoever had squealed on him.

JJ was in his room polishing Shalice's crystal ball with a rag when a deep voice boomed cheerfully from the parlour, 'Knock kno-*ock!*'

Kurt! JJ gasped and dashed out into the parlour. Kurt stood in the doorway, a jovial smile on his dead lips. Gonko emerged from his room and called to Kurt, 'We don't want any,' as though he were a wandering salesman. Kurt chuckled appreciatively. 'Come in, boss,' said Gonko. Kurt entered, gazing around the tent with that serene smile. His cheeks glowed with good humour, and he seemed to find quaint amusement wherever he looked—only his brow suggested that what was so amusing was the thought of everything around him drowning in a river of blood.

Gonko strolled over with a smile that seemed at odds with his face, as though nature had never intended the muscles to pull that way. Kurt clapped him gaily on the shoulder. JJ watched Gonko closely, trying to work out how the clown boss was able to endear himself to Kurt so easily; what it came down to, he supposed, was a lack of fear. Nonetheless, Gonko was minding his manners. 'Prayer meeting today, right, boss?' said Gonko.

'Yes,' said Kurt with a happy sigh. 'Oh, and I am sorry to hear about that odd jobs business. But I know you boys are up to it.'

'Yeah, well, good with the bad, you know, boss.'

'Good man.' Kurt clapped Gonko's shoulder again. 'Actually I just stopped by to borrow an umbrella. You know the ones, the small ones that deflect things from above. Things larger and heavier than rain.'

'Yeah, no probs, boss. RUFSHOD!'

Rufshod emerged from somewhere and Gonko barked an order to fetch him one of the 'funny umbrellas', then he fell into quiet conversation with Kurt. JJ tried to eavesdrop, sneaking as close to them as he dared on the pretext of searching for something or other, but they went quiet when he drew too near. Rufshod soon returned with a small green umbrella. Kurt took it. It looked minuscule in his giant hand. 'Thank you *so* much,' he said. 'I'll return this after the prayer meeting. I shouldn't need it after that. Toodle-oo, clowns.' Kurt loped away.

Gonko went to the card table and dealt a hand of poker to the empty chairs, which soon filled with clowns. 'Hey, Gonko,' said Doopy. 'What happened to the 'prentice, Gonko? Gonko? What happened to—'

'Ah, *him*. I had a little encounter with him over by the woodchoppers' pit yesterday,' said Gonko, spitting over his shoulder. 'He should be just about parboiled by now. Other than that, Doops, I'm sure he's faring well.'

'He punched on Goshy!' Doopy cried. 'He shouldn'ta oughtn'ta punched on Goshy.'

'You always were the high-minded type, Doops,' said Gonko. 'Now, listen up, you fucks. It's an insult, odd jobs, but we're gonna take it on the chin and keep rehearsing. Kurt's birthday is coming up, so all we gotta do is outdo everyone else, gift-wise, and we get our show back. It ain't brain science, people.'

'Whatcha got planned there, Gonko?' said Winston.

'Still working on it. What's Kurt's latest fad? I ain't been paying much attention. Religion right?'

'Yup. Christianity,' said Winston.

'Oh yeah. Gotta be easier to shop for than the Muslim phase.' Gonko rubbed his chin in thought. 'Well, I dunno. Piece of Noah's ark, maybe? A Bible signed by Jesus? A nun's tit? Whatever. I'm open to suggestions.'

JJ saw movement by the door as George Pilo scuttled in without invitation.

'Hello there, George,' said Gonko. 'How's life?'

Ignoring him, George pointed at JJ and Rufshod and barked: 'You two, come with me.' He about-faced and marched out as quickly as he'd entered. Rufshod groaned as he and JJ followed. George led them inside the acrobat stage tent, where they stood at the edge of the stage before the rows and rows of empty seats. Certain this excursion was to be some kind of punishment for stealing the crystal ball, JJ began to blubber, on the brink of explosive tears.

Rufshod looked at him in disbelief. 'What the hell's wrong with you?' he whispered. 'You're cracking up.'

'I'm scared,' said JJ. He turned to George Pilo and cried, 'I didn't do it!'

Pilo turned, stomped over and pressed his face into JJ's belly, peering up with malicious shining eyes. JJ could feel George's lips moving on his stomach as he said, 'I couldn't be less interested in what you did or didn't do if it was spoken in your bitch mother's eulogy. Today's prayer meeting. You're helping me set up. You can cry if you like, but you work while you're crying. Got it?'

'Yes sir,' said JJ, sniffling and wiping away tears.

George disengaged and stomped back across the stage, head tilted back as he examined the rafters. Along them were hooks, pulleys and ropes fixing the stage lights in place. There were two tall platforms at each side of the stage to hold the tightrope, which was presently not tied. The acrobats used no safety net—below the high-flying apparatus was nothing but the wooden stage.

George stared up appraisingly for a minute. 'Right,' he said at last and pointed to a spot behind the stage, where several wooden crates sat. 'See those?'

'Yes sir,' said JJ meekly. 'We see them.'

'Good. Put 'em up on the rafters. All of 'em. Up there next to that stage light with the X painted on it. Tie 'em in place with a rope that'll come undone with a hard pull.'

'How the hell are we supposed to do that?' wailed Rufshod.

'I don't care,' said George. 'But if it's not done in two hours, you'll be selling pies in Sideshow Alley for the rest of your lives. The Sacked Clown pie shop, just what this circus needs. Now get cracking.'

George grinned, savouring their dismay for a moment before he stalked off. Rufshod examined the crates and threw his arms up. 'How the hell are we meant to . . . Look at these fucking boxes! They're full of sandbags for chrissakes. What the hell's he want 'em up there for? Can't even lift them!'

'I know,' said JJ. 'You know that, um, whatchacallit? Trampoline? The acrobats use it. Why don't you climb up there and I'll bounce the boxes up to you?'

'Man, why do I always get these jobs?' Rufshod muttered.

'Where's the trampoline?'

'Probably in the acrobats' home tent.'

'Oh no!' JJ cried.

'Oh yeah. And since I gotta risk death and climb up there, you can go ask 'em if we can borrow it.'

'NO.'

'Yes.'

'*NOOOOOO!*' This went on until Rufshod pointed out their two hours were now down to an hour and forty. JJ had a vision of working alongside the carnie rats, screamed, and made his way to the acrobats' tent. When he got there he was treated to half an hour of mockery and taunting while he tried everything he could to win their cooperation. He grovelled, flattered them, tried reverse psychology, threatened a hunger strike, gave them the silent treatment, played hard to get, offered to spy on the other clowns, played the race card . . . Finally he threw a rock at Sven, which brought them to their feet, inviting him to do it again. At that point JJ cowered and lay sprawled in the dirt, whimpering, which did the trick; they told him he made them sick, to take it and go away. Sobbing, he hauled the bulky trampoline out of their tent, while they assured him that for every scratch they found on it he would suffer three broken bones. JJ believed them and cried harder as he made his way back to the stage tent, pushing the trampoline along on its side like a hexagonal wheel. Carnie rats smirked at him as he passed, tears and face paint running thick down his cheeks. He screamed at them to get away or they'd pay, did they hear him? They'd all pay!

Back at the stage tent Rufshod was perched dangerously on the rafter beams. 'What took you so long?' he bellowed, and almost slipped.

'Don't take that tone,' said JJ. 'You have no idea what I've been through.' He dragged the trampoline onto the stage, and with much complaint hauled the crates beside it. 'This was a stupid idea,' he said. 'How am I supposed to get enough bounce?'

'This is acrobat show gear,' said Rufshod. 'It isn't for decoration. Their gear is where their act comes from. This stuff *works*.'

JJ tipped one of the crates up onto the trampoline, expecting the wood to tear the canvas, but it held firm, bouncing and creaking the springs. He jumped on the crate, trying to get some momentum. To his surprise the crate was soon airborne and rising higher with each bounce, an ominous sight as it spun end over end, but its course stayed perfectly straight. 'Told you their stuff works,' Rufshod called down. 'Don't know how I'm meant to catch it, but we'll see.'

There were only a few seconds in which to work it out because the crate was soon cartwheeling in the air beside him. Rufshod made a grab for it as it hit its peak height and just managed to get it resting on the rafter before wrapping thick ropes around it and tying it in place. They got the second up there without too much trouble and to Rufshod's delight his toes were crushed under it as it landed on the rafter beam.

George Pilo had wandered in and was watching them work. They didn't spot him until the last crate was on its way. As Rufshod made a grab for it, George announced himself by bellowing, 'Wasn't so hard, was it?'

This distracted Rufshod just enough for him to lose his balance and fall from the rafter. He plunged to the ground one second before the crate, which landed on top of him with a crunch like a giant egg shattering. Rufshod made one loud wheezing sound then lay motionless.

JJ gaped at George, whose face showed nothing as he reached into his pocket and pulled out two velvet bags. 'Two crates'll be enough,' he said. 'For your troubles.' He tossed one bag to JJ and another towards Rufshod, then bustled off without another word.

JJ heard a moan from beneath the crate and ran over as Rufshod's legs twitched. Somehow he was still ticking. 'Can you hear me?' JJ said. Rufshod made a gurgling sound; a blood bubble poked out one nostril and burst.

JJ considered his options, one of which was finishing off the only person capable of ratting him out for his part in the crystal ball theft. He settled on swiping Rufshod's velvet bag and bolted for the clowns' tent. The others were playing poker as he entered—except Goshy, who was lying on the ground beside the table making chirping sounds. JJ stood panting in the doorway.

'What did George want?' said Gonko.

'Rufshod . . . He's DEAD!' JJ cried in the tone he had mentally rehearsed on the way over. He burst into tears, then added, 'almost.'

Gonko didn't even look up from his hand. 'Joke?' he said.

'No sir!'

'Inconsiderate shit!' Gonko yelled, throwing down his cards. 'I'm on a straight draw here.' The group of them headed over to the acrobats' stage tent, though no one seemed in much of a hurry. They found Rufshod twitching beneath the wooden crate, a pool of blood slowly leaking onto the grass. He was moaning quietly in pleasure, if JJ was not mistaken.

'Ah, JJ, you got my hopes up,' said Gonko, poking Rufshod with his boot. 'This is nothing. This is a fix for Ruf, probably the highlight of the week for the sick fuck. Takes more than this to kill a clown, my lovely. Clowns take some killing, make no mistake.'

Gonko lashed at the crate with his boot, cracking the wood; it rolled sideways to reveal Rufshod's blood-soaked shirt and a chest horribly flattened and lumpy. 'Right,' said Gonko. 'JJ and Winston, you two are the girliest, most nurse-like pair we got. Peel him off the ground and get him back to the tent. If you kill him en route I'm docking your pay.'

They carted Rufshod back to their tent and tossed him onto his bed, where he lay with his eyes bulging and face soaked in sweat. JJ, who'd felt entitled to a share of the attention, sulked until five o'clock, when Gonko summoned the clowns together and they made their way to Kurt's prayer meeting.


The acrobats waylaid them. Two nearby carnies scuttled out of the way as they sprang out of an alley, blocking the clowns' path. 'YOU!' said the one called Sven, pointing at JJ. 'Where's our trampoline?'

'It's where I left it, you dumb fairy,' said JJ, who was taking no lip from these guys when the other clowns were here to do the fighting for him.

'So fuck off!' he added.

'What did we tell you, little man?' said the one called Randolph, squaring his shoulders and stepping towards JJ. 'If you didn't bring it back, we'd break you in half. I think tha'ss wha' we said.'

'Yes, sounds about right, love,' said Sven.

'So then,' said Randolph, flexing his leg slowly and levelling his heel with JJ's face. 'The rest of you, stand back. This will be quick and painful.'

Gonko sighed. 'Come on, fellas. We copped your little smoke bomb prank on the chin. Let poor li'l JJ off the hook, what do you say? We'll call it even.'

'Smoke bomb?' said Randolph. 'Don't know wha' you're talking about. Don't blame us when your show falls apart. Bunch of amateurs wouldn't know entertainment if it kicked you in the face. Watch!' Randolph made a graceful flying leap towards JJ with his heel raised to strike. It was so graceful JJ found himself admiring the body in motion rather than getting out of the way. Gonko, however, wasn't similarly enthralled; he leaped between Randolph and JJ, whipped an iron bar from his pockets, and clobbered the acrobat in the ribs with a dull musical thud. Randolph flew through the air, spinning around like a high diver before landing roughly in the grass.

The other acrobats watched their comrade's body come to rest and turned to Gonko, surrounding him with an air of intimidation JJ wouldn't have thought possible for men wearing tights. Gonko rounded on them and held the iron bar aloft, his teeth bared, his head nodding. Then something unexpected happened: Goshy saved the day. All present, probably everyone on the showgrounds, clapped their hands over their ears as an unbearable noise attacked the air, shriller than an air raid siren, loud as an explosion. The clowns and acrobats dropped to the ground, heads buried in their arms. Then the acrobats scrambled to their feet and ran.

JJ had been first to hit the ground. He glanced sidelong at Goshy, whose face was pulled back taut into those doughy ripples around his mouth and neck. What JJ found strangest was that Goshy faced away from the rest of them, and had his eyes fixed intently on the tent peg of a nearby gypsy stall. It was impossible to believe he'd been keeping track of the confrontation, or that his outburst had been designed to end it; it was quite likely something he'd been going to do anyway. A drop of blood leaked from his ear.

Finally the shriek subsided. Doopy ran to his brother. 'Goshy!' he said in an awed whisper. 'You done *goood*. You done *real* good, Goshy!'

Goshy's arms were locked stiff at his sides. He turned to face Doopy with three shuffling steps, stared at him as though he'd never seen him before, and uttered a low whistle. Gonko removed the ear plugs he'd pulled from his pockets and slapped Goshy on the shoulder. JJ shuddered as Doopy wiped the blood from his brother's ear.

The clowns went on their way. Carnies peered from windows as they passed, wondering what the hell had made that noise. All others on the showgrounds wondered the same thing. Even Goshy.

A patch of Rufshod's blood still coloured the grass by the stage. The clowns were second to arrive. First were the acrobats, who stared daggers at them from across the room. Gonko blew them a kiss. The other performers soon arrived to delay, if not ease, the tension. Among them were the woodchoppers, burly denim-clad musclemen who, judging by their manner, didn't need the muscles to support a great weight of brain matter. They scratched themselves and stared about vacantly. There were a few members of the freak show present, including Yeti, seven or so feet covered in long hair, a profoundly mournful and gentle face. Fishboy wheeled the severed head in a shopping cart. The freaks settled at the back of the room and Fishboy cast friendly waves around at everyone. He seemed the only one without any enemies, and JJ wondered how he managed it.

Mugabo stumbled in as though by accident and sat at the far left of the room, looking confused. Shalice came next, her eyes smouldering as she peered around to take everyone's measure. JJ ducked behind Doopy to avoid her gaze. George Pilo stormed in after her, four feet of bitter rage, and stood some distance behind the podium, not sparing a glance at anyone else. He was looking intently at the crates tied to the rafters. Another rope had been added, presumably by George himself. It ran down the trapeze support beam and its tip lay at George's feet.

JJ suddenly noticed that the crates were perched directly above where George had put the podium, and he went pale beneath his face paint as he realised what they were for. George was about to assassinate Kurt—and he, JJ, had helped set it up! Fear flooded through him like ice water, and he squirmed in his seat. Maybe there was time to go warn the boss . . .

In he came, strolling down the aisle between the rows of seats, hands in his pockets, gazing around at his employees with that smile. He went straight to the podium and raised his hands as though to quiet the audience, though no one spoke. JJ cringed lower in his seat, afraid to watch.

'Good afternoon,' said Kurt in a rich deep voice. 'How are we all? How am I? Fine, I suppose. Nothing has killed me since last we spoke, and the same could be said of you, which is lovely. We've had a busy week. Two shows. That's busy indeed, and you are to be commended. Almost everyone lived up to the high standard of entertainment that the Pilo Family Circus expects of its performers. It is our aim to provide an experience of unforgettable entertainment to anyone who visits our show. That is how you survive so long in this business, folks. You *entertain*. Everyone deserves entertainment.'

This banal spiel continued for several minutes, and the performers' eyes wandered anywhere but the podium. JJ watched Kurt nervously as he towered over all present, his huge hands rending the air around him with civilised gestures, like a lion with table manners. 'Now, I have some unpleasant business.' Kurt's smile turned to the good-natured frown of a patient schoolmarm. 'Seventeen people have taken the Lord's name in vain. Shalice did it twice, while copulating, so I suppose that could be forgiven . . . Though Shalice, begging the saviour to fuck you is a little much. There is only so much we can ask of him. Nugget of the freaks did it once, while talking in his sleep—nice work, Fishboy, you run a tight ship. Of the clowns, Rufshod did it six times, Gonko ten, Winston twice, and JJ thirty-two times. My dear brother George did it eleven times. Now, there will be no breach notices delivered this time around, but please keep it tasteful. There are *so* many words. Why use the Lord's? Let's bear that in mind.'

At the mention of George, JJ scanned the stage, but George had vanished from sight. Then a movement caught his eye and he saw something tugging at the rope which ran across the roof and up the trapeze tower. Up above, one of the crates gave a tiny jerk, tipped sideways, and both crates fell.

Down below, Kurt didn't miss a beat of his speech, even as both crates thudded into the stage to either side of him. In his hand was the umbrella the clowns had loaned him, raised just above his head a split second before the crates would have hammered into his bald skull. The performers snapped back to attention at the cannon-blast of the crates hitting the wooden stage, where they broke on impact, the ripped sandbags spilling their contents with a faint *hissss*.

Kurt didn't even glance at the fallen crates. Behind him, George's face was turning red, his arms were flailing around like a chimp having a seizure. Kurt calmly folded the umbrella and put it aside as he reminded his charges it wasn't a matter of asking what Jesus could do for them, but what they could do for Jesus.

JJ bit his nails. Nothing was happening. Gonko and Winston looked only mildly interested in the attempted murder. 'Winston!' JJ whispered. 'I put those crates up there!'

'So?' said Winston.

'SO? Are you fucking dense?'

'Quiet, please,' said Kurt from the podium. JJ yelped in fright before he could stop himself. Winston leaned across to JJ and said, 'This is nothin' we ain't seen a thousand times already. Doesn't matter if you helped George. Kurt'll probably ask you to help him bump off George next week. Just do what you're told and keep your mouth shut.'

Kurt was winding up his speech. George made a quiet exit, tripping over his own feet, his body shaking with rage. 'Looks like George thought he was in with a chance that time,' said Winston.

'Gonna be fun taking orders from that shit tonight,' said Gonko. He spat.

Kurt concluded by urging people not to go overboard with birthday gifts this year, though they could go a little overboard if they really wanted to. The performers stirred, all of them relieved the meeting's end was in sight.

Suddenly there was a creaking sound, a loud one. It seemed to come from the rafters. JJ looked up, startled, as the whole tent seemed to sway. The trapeze towers wobbled and a hush passed through the audience. Winston immediately ducked down under his seat. Even Kurt paused and gave a slow curious look around. At that moment the support beams toppled forward like falling trees, and there was a ruffling sound like a flag being unfurled in strong wind. A banner opened across the horizontal rafters, tied to the same rafter beam Rufshod had been perched on earlier. It was a white sheet, and painted on it in red was one word: FREEDOM.

Then the tent collapsed. The support beams went down, the rafters fell inward and there was a huge ripping noise. A shriek went up outside the tent as the whole thing caved in on itself, burying everyone under thick canvas. There were great thuds as the wooden and metal supports broke and slammed into the rows of seats. JJ just had time to hide under his seat as a pole landed next to him. The ground quivered with its impact

From the podium, Kurt Pilo's voice carried through the wreckage. He sounded mildly amused. 'Well,' he said, 'I wasn't expecting that.'


The apparent sabotage would be the source of much talk over the following days. It was strange that no one had been killed in what amounted to an attempt on every performer's life. Vandalism on a smaller scale was never uncommon—someone always had it in for someone else, and most in the show had seen far too much for their own good, an aphrodisiac for random violence. Of course the banner had ruled out the possibility of an accident. Freedom? A pretty word, but no one knew what to make of it.

The first accusations were levelled at George, behind his back of course. His sneaking out of the tent had been awfully convenient. If George was the culprit, that raised serious questions about how he was to be brought to account; he was, after all, second in command, and Kurt wanted him dead already. But there was no case for George to answer. Everyone in the show would have loved to see him squirm for the pleasure of it, but none thought he'd actually done it. The chaotic nature of the attack, leaving so much to chance, lacked the signature of a control freak like George . . . It simply wasn't his style.

The worst off were the acrobats. Their stage was in ruins and their act relegated to the smaller alternative: the clowns' stage tent. Once that was announced, the clowns became the worst off, and the acrobats saw a great big silver lining. Nonetheless, their show was reduced to basic stunts on a gym mat until their stage was rebuilt, which would take some doing, with no one exactly sure of how to treat the machinery to give it the magical effects required.

The freaks were also aggrieved, as Fishboy had been seriously hurt; his head had been flattened beneath a support post. A visit to the matter manipulator was all that had saved him. Meanwhile Mugabo, panicking, had unleashed a small firestorm, melting some of the otherwise repairable apparatus. He was now vowing never to perform again, and refusing to let anyone near enough to tend to the burns he'd inflicted on himself.

The rest of the injuries were minor. JJ had no more than a bump on the shoulder and a dark wet patch down the front of his pants from a combination of fright and too many juice pops. Some others had ringing ears, thanks to Goshy, whose outbursts and screams amidst the calamity had helped no one at all. He'd been hyperactive for hours afterwards, until finally the kettle noise became the budgerigar noise and everyone was able to relax.

'Well,' said Gonko as they took their places at the card table, 'wasn't that something.'

'Who done it, Gonko?' said Doopy. 'Who done it? They shouldn'ta oughtn'ta done it, Gonko. *They scared Goshy*, Gonko, they scared *Goshy*!'

'Scared li'l JJ too by the looks of things,' said Gonko. 'Might wanna change them pantaloons, baby cakes.'

'It's just sweat,' said JJ, crossing his legs to hide the stain.

'Looks like Fishboy was hurt pretty bad,' said Winston as he dealt a round of blackjack.

'That's fucking rotten,' said Gonko, thumping his fist on the table. 'Fishboy never hurt a fly. Whoever done it, I will slice 'em eight ways from Sunday.'

'Who done it, Gonko?' said Doopy. 'Who was it what done did it, Gonko? Who was what done did it was what do——'

'No idea, Doops. Good question, though—you always were the inquisitive type. Who'd wanna kill . . . *everyone*? And what was that "freedom" horse shit?'

Something clicked in JJ's head. *Just remember that word. Freedom.* Winston! Why hadn't he remembered it before? His head turned to Winston with the deliberation of the clown game in Sideshow Alley, and his mouth was gaping just as wide. Winston gave him the merest glance and said, 'Odd, wasn't it? Hate to be in the pants——I mean, shoes, of whoever hung up that banner.'

JJ took the hint, but his mouth still hung open. Winston gave him another flashing glance and yelled, 'JJ, are you going to ante up or sit there blowing the invisible man all night?'

This got a chuckle from Gonko, and JJ shut his trap. 'You're wound up,' said Gonko to Winston. 'I never once heard you talk that dirty.'

'Yeah, well, we're going to be some time getting our show back now, aren't we?' said Winston. 'You hear what George said? The acrobats got our stage. How long's it gonna take to rebuild theirs?'

'Oh Christ, you're right!' Gonko wailed.

JJ decided it was time to leave, for he couldn't stop gaping in disbelief at Winston. 'Hey!' Gonko roared as he slunk away from the table. 'Where the fuck are you going? What kind of poker can you play with three players?' JJ whimpered and ran. 'No one buys that play-acting shit,' Gonko called after him. 'I know *you*, matey, I know you well.'

Back in his room JJ sat on his bed and tried to think things over. Winston still had him by the balls—but did he have Winston by the balls too? Freedom. What did it mean? Why had he said it to Jamie in a moment of sentimental mush? What, did he think there was some chance for Jamie to get out of the show? Was that the old guy's caper?

'I think,' JJ whispered, 'that maybe, yeah, that's his caper.'

He lay back, thinking, and his head bumped against something round and hard. A grin spread over his face as he patted the glass ball. He knew how he'd be spending his day tomorrow. He took the crystal ball from its cover, caressed it and said, 'You and me against the world, baby.'

# CHAPTER 16

# INCRIMINATING JJ

JAMIE woke and went through the usual: vertigo, nausea, terror, doomed helplessness. On the plus side, physical pain was no longer part of the ritual. As usual, he remembered he'd narrowly escaped death the day before, via falling support beams this time. One had slammed down right next to his—or JJ's, rather—face. And how had JJ reacted to all this? Once he was free of the carnage, he hadn't given it a second thought. The guy didn't care one bit what happened to the body they shared. *I am going to die here,* Jamie thought with absolute calm certainty. *Any day now.*

This was what Jamie had woken to every morning, and this was why he usually rushed for the face paint straight away. Not this morning, though. He had to think. Something big had happened yesterday, something at odds with how the place operated. Someone had attacked everyone in the show—all who mattered, at least. They hadn't been fucking around, they'd been after scalps. That banner: FREEDOM. The word Winston had told him to remember. *Winston was in on it!* Had to be.

He thought of Winston, the one shoulder he had to lean on.

*Freedom.*

Or perhaps there were many shoulders.

He regarded the small tub of face paint with a look of disgust. Today he would face this place as himself.



The rest of the carnival was waking up and Jamie could hear the clean-up of the acrobats' stage tent getting under way. He suited up with shoes, red nose, a puffy striped shirt, bright pink spotted pants. He double-checked the pockets and found nothing but lint. Once dressed he sat on his bed, listening to the clowns out in the parlour. It seemed quiet out there. He got up and opened his door, then had to choke back a scream; Goshy stood once again just outside, and God alone knew how long he'd been there staring at the door panels. All night?

Jamie's hand squeezed tight on the door handle. 'Good morning,' he managed.

Goshy peered at him without change of expression. Jamie saw something green on his top lip, like a grass stain. 'Morning, Goshy,' Jamie repeated. Goshy answered with a blink: right eye first, then left. He gave a low chortling whistle and turned around to face down the hallway. Jamie, deciding it probably wasn't safe to ask him to move, slipped through the narrow gap between Goshy's shoulder and the door, doing all he could to avoid contact.

He looked nervously up and down the hallway, trying to remember which was Winston's room. At the door he knocked, and from within heard the old clown's voice saying, 'Huh? Who's that?'

'Jamie.'

There was a sound of bed springs creaking. 'JJ?'

'Jamie.'

'Jamie? Come in.'

He went in and sat on the one clear patch of floor beside Winston's bed. Winston sat up yawning. 'Haven't seen you for a while,' he said.

'Yeah. Listen . . . I don't want to wear the paint today.'

Winston scratched his chin and picked his ear with a cotton bud. 'You picked a bad day,' he said. 'We rehearse today. You're going to be made part of the act. We gotta keep the act in shape in case they put us back on.'

'Why can't I do that as I am now?'

'You might get hurt. Maybe killed. The paint does more than turn you into a backstabbin' cretin, remember.' Jamie's eyes dropped. 'Look, I'm sorry,' said Winston, 'and we both know it ain't your fault, but it's the truth. Let's have it out in the open.' The old clown sat back and heaved a sigh. 'Quite a fix you're in, ain't it? I can't tell you nothin', because when you put the paint on you'll blab it to everyone.'

'What about the pants?' said Jamie. 'JJ thinks you've got him by the balls. He doesn't want to cross you.'

'Well and good, but if JJ learned all there was to know, he'd have the goods on *me*, let me tell you. And it's safe to say this, because it's just my word against his. Been here longer than him, they'd believe me.' Winston went quiet and shook his head. 'I don't know what to do with you, Jamie. No idea at all.'

'What if—what if I were to arrange it so you had more dirt on JJ than he could ever have on you? What then?'

Winston raised his eyebrows. 'Go on.'

Jamie leaned forward. 'If I did something today, something really incriminating, and got away with it but somehow gave you proof, you'd have it all over JJ. Maybe you'd be safe enough to tell me what that freedom thing meant.'

Winston's eyes darted to the door and back. 'Shh. For God's sake Jamie, keep it down.'

Jamie grimaced. 'Sorry.'

Winston sat back on his bed, thinking. 'I suppose,' he said, 'that arrangement could work. But you know what sort of risk you're taking? If you got caught . . . Won't be fun and games, son. You don't want to know what they can do to you.'

'You're right, I probably don't,' Jamie sighed. 'I'm just sick of waking up like this, feeling like this. I can't keep it up much longer.'

Winston nodded. 'Desperate times and all that, eh? Well, we'd better work out what high jinks you're gonna get up to.'

'Winston, something I've been meaning to ask you.'

'What's that?'

'Why don't you change? When you put on the face paint?'

Winston smiled the ghost of a smile. 'I don't wear it,' he said, and reached under his bed for a small box. 'This is regular old face paint. From outside. Not the stuff they make in the funhouse. No one notices any difference. I just act surly. Ain't hard. My stage personality ain't much different to my real one. Guess I lucked out there.'

'But how do you manage to perform?'

'Make sure the parts I get ain't dangerous. Not easy, mind you. I tell Gonko my back hurts too much for the hard routines. I still get plenty of bruises, and sometimes just have to take my chances with dangerous stunts. And for you, JJ, should you look back on this little talk, remember I could put the real face paint on any time I like and break your goddamn neck.'

Jamie blinked, surprised by the sudden viciousness in Winston's voice.

'Now you get out of here, Jamie. I'll give some thought to what we can get you to do—if you're sure this is the way to go?'

'I don't see any other. I honestly don't.'

Winston shrugged. 'Me either, now that you mention it.'

Jamie went back to his room and waited, trying to calm his heartbeat and trying not to think. After half an hour Gonko poked his head through the door to bark: 'Rehearsal at one. Odd jobs at eleven tonight. Life's a bitch then you just keep on fucking living.'


It was an agonising wait as Winston hatched a plan. Jamie longed for JJ's contempt for death; unrealistic maybe, but effective. When Winston finally came in he carried a knapsack. He held his ear to the door to make sure they were alone, then opened the bag and produced a folded white sheet. It was a smaller version of the banner that had unfurled before the tent collapse, with FREEDOM in red paint. Winston's voice was a whisper. 'Here's what you do. Hang this inside the freak show tent. There'll be a ladder in there. Climb to the top rafters, tie it. When you're done, there'll be a note stuck on the inside of the front door. Take it off, read what it says, then swallow it.'

'What if I get seen?'

'You'll just have to make sure that doesn't happen. You're friends with Fishboy's new assistant, right? What's his name, Steve? You visit him sometimes?'

'Yeah.'

'There's your alibi. Now go, quickly.'

'Won't the freaks see me?'

Winston shook his head and left without another word, and Jamie wondered what made him so sure. He checked the pocket watch JJ had stolen from Sideshow Alley: two hours till rehearsal. Sighing, he picked up the banner and stuffed it under his shirt, which was puffy enough to conceal the bulge. As he passed through the parlour and down the main path he tried to walk like JJ, overly bending his knees, adjusting his crotch, scowling at the gypsies he passed. He felt like an idiot. Soon he came to the funhouse, where Damian the guardian stood out front as normal, hooded and motionless; he never seemed to budge at all. Jamie thought he saw something move at a high window, a curtain falling back into place, but he couldn't be sure.

Past the funhouse was a scattering of little shanties with decaying wood and chipped paint, gypsy homes. He headed through these trying not to be seen, and he felt he was safe on that front; the distant babble indicated most carnies were over by the wreckage of the acrobats' stage tent, cleaning up. The rear of the freak show was in shadow. That mysterious wooden fence ran around behind it. Jamie put his eye between two boards, thinking of escape for the first time in a good while, but he could see nothing out there—just that white mistiness JJ had seen from the rooftop. He held his ear to the scratchy wood and was surprised to hear a sound not unlike holding his ear to a seashell; the ocean from far away.

He was tempted to climb the fence, but a noise from the nearby gypsy hut snapped him out of it. There was a loud crash followed by angry voices shouting in Spanish; one male, one female. He ran to the freak show tent and found a gap in the canvas. He paused as the gypsies' squabble became explosive; there was a shrill scream from the woman, then ominous silence. A burly fifty-something man kicked open the hut's back door, an olive-skinned beer gut spilling over his pants. Over his shoulder was the limp body of a middle-aged woman, the back of her head cracked open and dripping red. The gypsy tossed her to the ground by the fence. Jamie winced and ducked inside the freak show.

Just a murder. These things happen.

'Come on,' he whispered, trying to calm his nerves—he felt dangerously close to falling apart on the spot. He bit his knuckle until it hurt, counted to ten, and got himself under control. *Worse things than that happen here,* he imagined Winston's voice saying to him. *Worse will happen to you. Get on with the job.*

Around him the freak show was dark, as it usually was, except for the yellow light bulbs of the incubators, gleaming over their atrocities. Now the incubators were empty and the light itself seemed obscene, the kind of light one might expect to find shining in a serial killer's basement, illuminating an operating table, soundproof walls, red stains and sharp objects.

The only exhibit still here was Nugget, the severed head. Nugget was chin-deep in water and had his eyes closed. The tin ladder was lying flat on the ground by the wall. Jamie raised it against a support beam and kicked off his clown shoes. The rungs dug hard into his feet as he climbed until his head was bent against the roof. He wrapped the banner around the rafters, legs feeling suddenly weak as he tried not to picture himself falling.

As he coaxed the banner along the rafter a bright light went off below with a popping noise. He had to fight for balance from the start it gave him, and stared around wildly, heart pounding. Someone was ducking out the freak show entrance. Winston. What the hell was that noise? A camera? He cursed Winston for not warning him about that part of the plan. Well, he was sure as hell incriminated now. Jesus, he hoped he could trust the old guy.

He climbed down the ladder and saw with annoyance that the banner was upside down. He ran to the front door, pausing to check the severed head was still sleeping, and pawed around on the canvas for the note he was supposed to find . . . There it was. He tore it from the wall and ran to one of the incubators to read it in the yellow light:

*Tip the head over. Do that last. First smash the glass displays. Head is sedated, won't hear. Then get out. Take detour back to clown tent, out back of this tent, run along the fence line. Don't get seen.*

'Oh man,' Jamie whispered. He looked around for a way to smash the glass cabinets and his eye caught something leaning against Yeti's cage— an iron bar. Winston had thought of everything. He picked it up and ran to Nugget's bowl, where he coughed and snapped his fingers, tapped the glass—no reaction. *Here goes*, he thought. The tall glass incubator was first; one blow bent the glass and made a patch of spiderweb cracks. Two more swings and the whole thing shattered into small chips of glass, scattering over the ground like confetti with a storm of rattling sounds. Tallow's booth was next; one swing left a jagged hole in the left wall, another finished it off. Glass sprayed over the floor, over the disgusting dried-flesh-coloured ooze. Next was the case shaped like a glass coffin. One solid blow and the whole thing shattered.

Suddenly he heard someone shouting in the distance—it sounded like George Pilo. If he could hear George, George could hear him; he had to hurry. He glanced at the other exhibits—Yeti's cage was iron, not much he could do there. That left the severed head in his bowl. Jamie ran over and kicked the stand. It wobbled and fell, sending Nugget splashing to the floor and skidding to a halt against the ladder, spinning around on his bald spot.

Time to run. He made it to the shadows at the back of the freak show and had half his body out the same slit he came in through as George Pilo stormed through the front door, four enraged feet of him. 'Who's there?' George screamed. 'Who's there?'

Jamie sprinted along the fence line, behind the funhouse, and paused as movement caught his eye. Behind him the gypsy man was hauling the dead woman up over his shoulder, her body flopping around like a big doll. Jamie ran on, pausing to look back only once as the gypsy stood up on a garbage bin, throwing the body up over the fence. Her dress caught on the top of it for a moment, her lifeless head bobbing about, hair swaying, before the dress tore and she dropped down to whatever lay on the other side.

Jamie ran all the way back to the clowns' tent, so he could panic in the safety of his own room.

It had all gone off without a hitch, as far as he knew, but the minutes that ticked by were excruciating. Any second now, George Pilo's voice would ring out shrilly from the parlour: *'Get JJ out here! He's going to ride the funhouse, he's got himself a free ticket . . .'*

Sure enough, a commotion could soon be heard out there. Doopy's voice hollered: 'GUYS! GUYS! THEY PUNCHED ON THE FREAK SHOW, GUYS! THEY DONE IT AGAIN, THEY GONE AND DONE DID IT, THEY DID DOGGONE DONE DO'D IT!'

'What the fuck are you talking about?' Gonko screamed from his room.

'THEY PUNCHED ON THE FREAK SHOW, GONKO! GONKO, THEY BROKE THE FREAK SHOW!'

'Who did?' Gonko screamed.

'I DON'T KNOW WHO DONE IT, GONKO! WHO DONE IT, GONKO?'

'You're a dull one, Doops. *CLOWNS!* Everyone out here now. Head count!'

Jamie ran out there before he could think about how easily Gonko would spot his guilt . . . It was all over him, had to be. Oozing from his pores, he reeked of it. One look in his eyes and it would all be over . . .

'Head count,' Gonko yelled again. 'Come on, something went down. No one's hanging this on us, not if I can help it. Everyone out here pronto. Don't make Gonko go all ragey.'

Jamie paused in the hallway. There were little glass slivers on his pants. He ran back to his room, kicked off the pants, paused . . . He couldn't do it, couldn't face them. He'd get himself killed in two minutes. He went to his cupboard, grabbed the face paint, slopped it on his cheeks, grabbed the hand mirror, took a look at himself, and—

JJ stood perfectly still. He was speechless. The last hour replayed quickly before his disbelieving mind's eye.

'GOSHY AND JJ GET OUT HERE *NOOOOOOW!*' Gonko screamed.

JJ started and ran out to the parlour. The other clowns were all there, including Winston. JJ snarled and bared his teeth.

'Fine, we're all here,' said Gonko. 'Never seen a more innocent bunch of motherfucks in my life. Boy, it's sweet, couldn't hurt a puppy with a chainsaw. JJ, put some pants on and make it the last time I ever have to give you that particular instruction.'

'Yes boss,' said JJ in a cooing, gentle voice. He stared daggers at Winston, who looked back at him mildly. After he'd changed, Gonko led the clowns over to the freak show. JJ sidled up beside Winston and grabbed him by the shoulder, pulling him out of earshot of the others. 'That was a low, low bit of work,' he whispered.

Winston gave him that mild look again and said, 'Wouldn't know. I wasn't the one doin' it.'

'Oh, you'll get *yours*,' JJ snarled. He was shivering with anger.

'That photograph will look just fine in a nice big frame, hung up on Kurt's trailer door. Really captured your good looks.'

JJ sucked in the ramifications and decided to change tact. 'You won't tell, will you? It's not me I'm worried about . . . It's Jamie. Poor Jamie didn't ask for any of this . . . He just . . . He . . .' JJ made his voice choke with tender emotion. Winston merely shook his head in disgust and jogged to catch up with the others.

'Bastard,' JJ spat. How could Jamie fall for that kindly grandpa act? How *could* he? 'Oh, Jamie, you'll get *yours* too,' he said. And he meant it.

A crowd had gathered inside the freak show, quietly observing the shattered incubators and the banner, which still hung upside down from the rafters. Kurt Pilo had wandered over to see what the fuss was about. JJ watched him closely; Kurt's fish lips were twisted in that good-natured grin, but his brow was clenched like a fist. The sum effect was a puzzled frown, like a man in a room full of laughing people, suspecting but not certain the joke is on him. Gonko sidled up to Kurt—Gonko was, JJ noticed, the only one who dared approach Kurt at this juncture. The pair of them exchanged a few words. Kurt's voice was mellow and calm. Gonko came back to the clowns and gave a low whistle. 'He's *not* happy,' he said.

Doopy pawed at Gonko's shirt. '*Gonko*. Who done it, Gonko?'

'Shh. Later.'

Kurt loped over to the freak show entrance and cleared his throat. 'Friends,' he said, 'we have suffered more mischief. I do believe this was no accident.'

'You don't say, Kurt,' Gonko murmured.

'It hurts me to think,' Kurt went on, 'that amongst my beloved employees . . . and friends . . . the perpetrator is hiding and feasting on the hurt he has inflicted on our beloved freaks. Feasting on hurt is *expressly* forbidden——how many times must I say it? Let's remember, we are family here. I am the Pilo, you are the family, this is the circus. This kind of violence is fine amongst friends, but not *family*. I will conduct interviews in the coming days with each team leader.'

Kurt said all this in a voice that was almost gentle while his bestial eyes roamed over the crowd's faces. JJ could feel the sweep of his gaze like a beam of hot light, but the fish lips still curved upwards, the cheeks were still red with cheer. 'Two other things,' said Kurt. 'Whoever has Shalice's crystal ball, we'd like it back, please. Anyone who knows where it is . . . There'll be a reward, I suppose.' As an afterthought: 'Oh, a reward *if* you tell me where it is. And lastly . . .' Kurt's smile widened, and for a moment the fire left his eyes. 'Although my brother George was first on the scene, and although he was, shall we say, *lurking* in the area during the crime—before *and* during the crime—in fact, *standing at this very spot as the crime occurred*—and even though he couldn't name a culprit, though it was broad daylight, I would prefer to hear no gossip suggesting that he himself did it. In fact, I would prefer it if his slanderous, intimate *proximity* to the crime were not known at all, much less talked about. God bless!'

Gonko and Winston traded an amused glance. JJ breathed a little easier. Now he could busy himself with refraining from murder every time he looked at Winston. It wasn't going to be easy.

The clowns were due to rehearse, and JJ was cornered and dragged to the gym mat before he could escape. He was told of his first routine: the rolling pin gag. 'Just like in your bedroom that time,' said Gonko. 'Classic. You came down the stairs like a grumpy housewife with sand in her pussy. Remember?'

'Yeah, yeah,' JJ said bitterly.

'I got that very same rolling pin. Swiped it that night, along with your driver's licence. Those come in handy once in a while. Here ya go.' Gonko tossed the rolling pin. JJ caught it with a pout on his face. 'Now,' said Gonko, 'Goshy, stand opposite. Hold that face, that's perfect. JJ, throw it at Goshy.'

Goshy's surprised left eye blinked; the right one seemed to narrow . . . *I dare you.*

JJ's face crumpled. Tears were coming. 'I . . . don't wanna . . .'

'*JJ!*' Gonko roared. '*THROW THE FUCKING ROLLING PIN!*'

JJ whimpered and threw. Goshy gave a surprised toot as the rolling pin struck his belly and bounced off, sailing up at JJ's head. He ducked aside in time but it was a near thing. Goshy's mouth flapped mutely; both eyes locked on JJ.

'I'm sorry,' JJ gasped, dropping to the floor at Goshy's feet. 'I'm *sorry*. Following orders. Didn't want to . . . He made me . . .'

Goshy peered down at him without blinking. 'Come off it, JJ,' said Gonko. He sounded disgusted. 'Goshy's a professional. This ain't personal. Jesus. I been kicked in the balls onstage by Ruf almost every show. Never fazed me. Get up and throw it again.'

So he threw the rolling pin, over and over, ducking aside each time, each time a near miss. Goshy's belly seemed to be aiming for him, directing the pin towards where he'd ducked the previous throw. Tears streamed down his face and he whispered apologies all the while, but there was no telling if Goshy even understood them. His right eye didn't blink, never leaving JJ's face, while the left followed the movement of the rolling pin.

When rehearsal finally ended JJ calmed his nerves by watching the crystal ball, which he was beginning to love more than life itself. He scouted around for clues to this 'freedom' thing. He watched Fishboy climbing up the ladder to take the banner down, his head still bandaged from the stage tent collapse. The freak show floor was littered with broken glass. Suddenly Kurt Pilo ambled into the tent, and JJ hurriedly panned away. When a look at Winston didn't reveal the whereabouts of the damning photograph, he spied on Goshy and Doopy, both in Goshy's room with the plant which still had its engagement ring stuffed on a stem. It was hard to tell, but it looked like Goshy and the plant were having some kind of lover's tiff, and Doopy seemed to be playing mediator. 'Sick *bastards*,' JJ whispered and panned over to the woodchoppers. They were crowding around one of their comrades, who seemed to have fallen from a great height and now had an arm bent at an odd angle. JJ shook his head——they had to be the unluckiest sons-of-bitches in the whole show. Every time he checked in on them, someone was tripping, catching fire, or getting brained by a flying axe head.

He sighed—just not a lot going on today. Even Mugabo was fairly placid in his potion lab, concocting brews. It was only when the ball's vision swung past the funhouse that something caught his interest. A figure was creeping out the front door over the cart tracks, on all fours. JJ zoomed in close and grunted in surprise—it was the apprentice, last seen fleeing the tent with his clothes aflame. Damian the funhouse guardian didn't move a muscle as the apprentice passed him in a shuddering crawl. He looked like he'd just escaped a concentration camp; thin and starved, clothes hanging off withered limbs. His skin was blackened and burnt, peeling from his face. His eyes, once shifty and full of sullen malice, were now wide, unblinking and terrified. Smoke drifted from his clothes in white puffs. He dragged himself to a spot of shade and sat there, shivering.

JJ whistled. So this was what happened when you crossed Gonko. That begged the question: What happened when you crossed JJ?

# CHAPTER 17

# OUTSIDE JOBS

AS predicted, George Pilo was in a foul temper when it came time to hand the clowns the night's assignments. It wasn't that George had expected the assassination attempt on Kurt to succeed—what got to him was the lazy ease with which Kurt had seen it coming and repelled it. Merely seeing him in some kind of distress would have been a triumph for George; seeing that dopey fish-lipped smile waver in front of the performers would have kept him as happy as a clam for months.

The sabotage of the whole *tent*, now that had come as a surprise. When the surprise wore off, George was livid—but then, he was always livid. Since Kurt Senior's will had left 70 per cent of the show to Kurt Junior some 470 years ago, the wounds ripped open had never stopped bleeding. Half an hour after making that will, Kurt had bitten Papa's face in half like a piece of fruit.

As for the sabotage, the idea of someone striking against his show was so utterly insufferable that George felt anger oozing through his skin, evaporating in heated waves and fouling the air around him. And this afternoon, what do you know—sabotage number two. George had seen it coming, or more accurately Shalice had. She'd had one of those future empathy bullshits and warned him straight away. He'd been loitering by the freak show, saw Fishboy and his troupe go walkabout, saw Winston pop in and out, saw nothing was going to happen, then set off to give the fortune-teller a hiding for wasting his time. Then he heard the glass breaking.

Those were the ingredients of George's bad mood. When the clowns showed up at his trailer door at eleven, he slammed it open so hard the carnies in Sideshow Alley thought they'd heard a gunshot. 'What do you want?' he screamed at the clowns, momentarily forgetting in his rage they were here on his orders.

'Only to serve, George,' said Gonko, bowing low, a twinkle of good humour in his eye. George remembered the odd jobs, scowled bitterly and went to fetch the instructions.

On the doorstep, Gonko turned to his troops and made a hush-hush gesture. 'Georgie's had a bad day,' he whispered. 'I'll handle him. Everyone be nice.'

George returned, slamming the door behind him with the same violence, and saw the clowns smiling at him sympathetically. He made a noise of disgust in the back of his throat. 'Simple job,' he snapped. 'Get out there, burn down the house at this address.' George threw an envelope at Gonko. It bounced off his forehead into his hands. 'Then beat up the man you see walking down this street at the time listed.' He threw a second envelope at Gonko's forehead, but Gonko caught it in midair. 'Then steal this car. Trash it, come back. Three jobs. Simple.' He tossed the last envelope after a baulk and it hit Gonko on the chin. 'Got that, you useless cunts?'

'Yes, George, clear as day,' said Gonko pleasantly.

George slammed his door.

Gonko cleared his throat. 'George?'

'WHAT?'

'The pass-outs would no doubt prove helpful.'

The door opened and shut again in a flash, during which a small bag was tossed out, hitting Gonko in the chest. He rifled around inside it and pulled out a bunch of plastic cards, each connected to a loop of string. There was one for each clown. 'Pass-outs,' said Gonko as he handed one to JJ. 'Can't pass out without a pass-out. Put it on and if you lose it I skin you. Let's go.'

'I don't *like* going, Gonko. I don't *like* it!'

'That pygmy is the exact reason you should never give short people authority,' said Gonko, jerking his thumb at George's trailer. He led the clowns——Rufshod alone was absent, still nursing his crushed ribs—— through the deserted games and stalls of Sideshow Alley. Taking paths JJ hadn't yet explored, they came to a network of dark streets that resembled a London slum. There was no carnival glitter here; it stank and it was filthy, and broken glass crunched under their feet. Dwarfs with mean faces peered at them from windows and alleys. JJ scowled at them, and they scowled back; he'd earned a little infamy in these circles, and none dared get close.

They came to a small outdoor latrine in a dark narrow alley. Gonko opened the door. There was a small slit by the back wall. He swiped his pass-out card through it and a small red light flashed. The other clowns did the same. JJ went in last, pressed uncomfortably against Goshy, whose breath smelled like rotting fruit. Gonko pulled a lever on the roof which looked like a gearstick, setting it against a notch marked 'City 4'. There was a creaking sound from above as the lift rose. The ascent was long, and JJ didn't know how much longer he could stand it——Goshy's breath was getting worse by the second, creeping like snails into his nostrils. When finally they came to a halt he pushed open the door, stumbling out into the night air, hacking and spitting.

He blinked and looked around—they were in the middle of a construction yard, and he was astonished to find he recognised the surrounding streets. This was Brisbane, not one mile from the place Jamie had called home. Around them were cement mixers and heavy machinery, still as fossils of mechanical animals around a half-grown apartment building. 'Here we are,' said Gonko, stepping out into the yard, gravel crunching under his shoes. 'Good ol' Brisbane,' he muttered. 'Festering stink hole. Thinks she's grown up now into a city. Horse shit. Nowhere near enough murders here to call this a city. First job's here, next two jobs are in Sydney. The larger festering stink hole.'

JJ followed Gonko as he marched to the fence, and to JJ's alarm Goshy was following *him*, marching right behind him with shuffling steps in hot pursuit, close enough to head-butt. JJ squealed in panic and nearly wet himself. Doopy spotted the trouble and ran over, grabbing his brother by the shoulders. 'No, Goshy . . . It's *JJ*, Goshy, it's *JJ*. He does the *rolling pin*, Goshy. He does the *pin*.'

Goshy regarded Jamie with alien coldness. His mouth flapped. JJ shuddered and thought, *He's either King of the Headgames or the dumbest bastard on the planet.*

'He's a *clown*, Goshy,' Doopy assured his brother. 'Now c'mon, we got stuff to do.'

Gonko was by the fence, reading George's instructions by the flame of a cigarette lighter. Once Goshy was a safe distance away, JJ looked back at the latrine sitting inconspicuously behind a bulldozer. He pointed to it and said, 'Gonko, is that how tricks get into the show?'

Gonko glanced up. 'Huh? No one told you how we get tricks in the show? No, not through the lift. What do you think, a hundred people simultaneously walk into a goddamn portapotty? Winston, you tell him.'

'Ticket collectors bring in the tricks,' said Winston. 'They find circuses happening here in the real world, like those once-a-year bashes they have in the capital cities. They set up their gate in there, in a spot where no one would notice anything amiss—sometimes in the places of the actual entrance. The gates are like spider's webs. The tricks just wander through into our show.'

'How's that work?' said JJ.

'The gates? I don't know how they work. They were part of the gadgets Pilo Senior collected in his worldly travels. Some say he robbed the pyramids of a lot of stuff. That'd be the least he did, let me tell you.

Collected all kinds of arcane stuff, Pilo did. Would've had to, to make the show the way it is today. Probably the biggest thief the world's ever known. But I don't know how the gates work any more'n I know how the face paint works. Tricks walk through, they end up in the show. They don't even notice. Maybe it ain't even their actual bodies that come to the show, you know? Just . . . that part of 'em that makes 'em tick, makes 'em alive. The mechanics of the circus are strange.'

'Why don't they just set up the ticket gates in a city then?' said JJ. 'In a busy street. Tricks'd walk through all day.'

'Secrecy,' said Winston. 'We get tricks already on their way to a show. They go out to see a carnival, so that's what they see. Pilo Senior was paranoid about discovery, which is why he made us rehearse the language of our host country whenever we moved base. Pointless if you ask me, but I don't make the rules. The tricks come home from the circus with foggy memories, but not knowin' what's up. Probably only wonder why they didn't take any pictures. Now, if people off the *street* have foggy memories of going to a carnival, when they thought they'd spent the day at work, and if thousands said the same thing, well, probably wouldn't change a whole lot, if it came to it. But that's how it's always been run and it ain't changin'.'

'Shut it, you two. Let's go,' said Gonko, stuffing George's instructions back in his pocket. He rocked back on his heels and with one lunge leapt to the top of the fence and over it, making the wire rattle. Doopy shoved Goshy into the fence and ducked down, poking his head and shoulders under Goshy's legs. With much complaining he climbed up for the pair of them, his brother straddling his shoulders and making confused whistles. Winston was last over, puffing and panting.

The city was quiet except for the honking of traffic a few blocks away. The night sky above the CBD was a pink-white glow on the belly of thick clouds. The clowns jogged through the dark streets, passing only the odd drunk wandering home. On those occasions Gonko signalled everyone to stay in the shadows, something the clowns had down to a fine art despite their bright colours; they blended into the dark as though a light had been switched off around their bodies and they were never seen. 'What's this place we're doing?' Winston asked Gonko as the clowns paused to check their location.

'Interesting one, this one,' said Gonko. 'This house has a one-month-old baby inside named Louis Chan. This baby, according to Shalice, will grow up to be a researcher of some kind, who will discover some miracle cures. Georgie doesn't want that shit to go down. So here we are.'

'And we're burning the house down?' said Winston, and JJ heard a hard dark edge to his voice; he was outraged and trying not to show it. JJ sneered.

'Yes we are, Winston,' Gonko said cheerfully. 'We are going to burn down the house, with fire and flame and cinder and ash and whatnot. Three blocks from here, step lively, you shits.'

The clowns came to a house at the bottom of a hilly street, two storeys, half brick, half wood. In the front yard the crown of a mango tree hid them from the streetlight. Gonko dug into his pockets and pulled out a small glass bottle filled with petrol. He produced half a dozen of these and passed them around. Winston was grave-faced, and JJ was strongly tempted to provoke him into some kind of emotional outburst. He sidled up to him and said, 'I'm scared, Winston. I've never smelled cooked baby before. I—'

Winston eyes flashed in a way JJ hadn't seen before; he backed up a step, sensing he was about to be struck, and fell silent.

'On three,' said Gonko. 'Three. Go!' Gonko ran down the side of the house, leaping the fence. A German shepherd emerged from the shadows, growling fiercely. With a kick Gonko sent its head jerking at a grotesque angle and there was a *crack* as its neck broke. He poured petrol over the side of the house, digging more bottles from his pockets. Doopy ran down the other side, doing the same. Goshy peered at his bottle, standing perfectly still. JJ poured his petrol over the porch, adrenaline rushing through him. He had to fight not to whoop and laugh. Gonko vanished under the house, dousing the supports. While down there he lit the first flame.

Winston threw his bottle at the house and it crashed into the window, loudly smashing it.

'Who threw that?' said Gonko, emerging from below the house.

'Me. Sorry, Gonks,' said Winston.

'Hope it didn't wake 'em up,' said Gonko, wiping his hands on his pants. 'Ah well, not my problem. Back to the lift. Go, go, go!'

The clowns rushed back through the dark streets, their footfalls smacking the pavement and arousing a chorus of barking from neighbourhood dogs. Behind them the orange glow of the fire was spreading. JJ paused at the top of the street to admire the flames embracing the house like a demon's arms; *I did that*, he thought giddily as a sense of power rushed through him. Suddenly he felt like he was onstage being applauded by a huge crowd, praising him, chanting his name . . . Or booing, what did it matter? Inside, he kicked up his heels, strutting, laughing maniacally. It felt sublime.

Winston had paused to catch his breath just ahead. JJ passed him and gave him a beaming smile. The old clown stared straight ahead, hot tears in his eyes.

*You'll get yours,* JJ thought, and a shiver ran down his spine. *You'll get it real nice. It's coming.*

Back at the construction yard they sprang over the fence and ran to the lift as the first sirens wailed. Goshy paused at the door, staring off in the distance as though he'd heard the cry of some kindred spirit. 'Come *on*, Goshy!' said Doopy, pointing to the portaloo door. Goshy turned a full circle and let out a low whistle, a look of childish excitement on his face. He stared meaningfully at his brother and pointed back over his shoulder as more sirens sounded from another direction. 'I *know*, Goshy,' said Doopy, holding him by the shoulders, staring into his eyes. 'I heard it too, I really did!'

JJ squirmed against the door as the lift descended, and finally could hold it in no longer. 'What fucking *planet* are you two from?' he cried.

Doopy and Goshy answered him with silence.

The clowns completed the rest of their duties in Sydney. Gonko set the lever inside the lift to 'City 2', making it lurch for seven minutes. When it stopped they found themselves in another construction yard in a city with cooler, more polluted air. They began by beating up the pedestrian on his way home, a nightclub bouncer with organised crime connections. They'd really laid into him, silhouettes lashing and kicking at a writhing shape in the dark by the roadside to the backdrop of passing headlights. According to the fortune-teller, this beating would be the first blow in what would become a major gang war, complete with public shootings, car bombings and civilians caught in the crossfire. JJ asked why George wanted the gang war started, but Gonko shrugged and warned him not to ask that question again, as George was probably following orders himself.

Stealing the car came next, a flashy BMW they'd taken for a spin out in western Sydney. They smashed it up nicely and ran it into a house. The car belonged to an up-and-coming ALP man, one day destined for parliament. Gonko wasn't told what the purpose of it was, only that it was part of a far longer chain of events, the results of which wouldn't manifest themselves for more than a decade. 'We're just doing that skag's work for her,' Gonko said as the clowns went back home. 'No tricks around? Give it to the clowns. Fucking sickens me.'

JJ didn't mind the chance to stretch his legs back in the real world. He'd snatched a newspaper from the ALP man's front lawn. Back in the clown tent he unrolled it and saw the headline:

### Penrith Show Death Inquest

Police are no closer to answers about the freak accident that killed nine people at the Penrith annual fair in February. The bodies were found at the close of the fair, apparently trampled to death. No witnesses to the accident have yet come forward. No date has been set for the coroner's report, but relatives are considering legal action against the show's organisers, a source revealed. Police are understood to be conducting further interviews with those who attended the fair.

The case has attracted international media attention around the world, including the USA and Britain.

'I'll be,' said JJ. 'Guys! We're famous. We made the papers.'

JJ showed Gonko the article. 'Thought they might notice that,' said Gonko. 'Nine dead tricks. Dead ones are better off, if you ask me.'

'What do you mean?'

Gonko gave him a smug look. 'Tricks are like cows, JJ. They come in here, we milk 'em. Only difference is they can't get their milk back. You dig?'

'No. What the fuck are you talking about? What do we milk them for?'

'You should know, my pet. I give you a small bag of the stuff every week.'

JJ fell silent and Gonko dealt out a hand of poker. 'But this isn't fame, JJ,' he said. 'We've been involved in shit *wa-a-ay* bigger than nine dead tricks. Try fifty fucking million dead tricks. Try that on for size, JJ. That's famous. That'll get you the front page. More than once.'

'*What?*'

Gonko squinted at him with a thin smile. 'Let's put it this way. A failed Austrian painter owes his political success to Kurt Pilo. He wasn't known for his paintings, but you have most certainly heard of him.'

JJ was tired of this conversation. He went to his room and opened one of the velvet bags—he had three, as George had reluctantly paid the clowns when they returned tonight—and tipped some grains onto his palm, staring as the light glinted off them in tiny rainbow flashes. 'What *is* this shit?' he muttered.

Soon the other clowns went to bed and the showgrounds were silent. JJ took out the crystal ball, not expecting to see anything at this time of night. He figured he'd check out the dwarfs to see what they got up to when they emerged at lights-out. After a few minutes of watching them squabble on the rooftops he swept the ball through the parlour and was surprised to see something else: a figure blending with the shadows was creeping into the tent. JJ panned in as close as he could, but whoever this invader was, he could sneak in the darkness as well as the clowns; JJ saw only an outline with slumped shoulders and a bad limp. Suddenly he knew who it was—he'd seen this same wretched figure crawling out of the funhouse earlier today, skin charred and body spewing smoke. As the apprentice passed a lantern in the parlour JJ saw his face, pink, white and purple with burns. There was steel in his gaze, the look of a man whose last straw has been well and truly snapped. In his hand was a lead pipe.

Fear clawed at JJ as he understood he was the target; after all, it was he filling the apprentice's shoes, taking his wages, occupying his room. Whimpering, he propped a chair next to the door to buy himself an extra second or two. His hands were already shaking. He rummaged around in the boxes for a weapon and found the rolling pin, then went back to the ball and watched closely. The apprentice stumbled forward with clumsy but relentless steps.

JJ tried to hold the rolling pin steady as he cocked back his arm. He would throw it with everything he had; his aim was spot-on, and with a good wind-up he could break the bastard's face. Eyes flickering from the ball to the door, the apprentice came into view . . . But he passed JJ's door without giving it a glance.

JJ switched emotions like he was changing socks—all fear left him. Suddenly eager for bloodshed, he set the rolling pin down and crept out the door. The apprentice staggered up ahead like a zombie fresh from the grave. JJ followed. Movement caught the tail of his eye; he turned and saw Doopy creeping up the hallway. They locked eyes for a moment then both moved without a sound.

Four feet ahead the apprentice's neck was a scorched, blistered patch of seething purple. His clothes were sooty, speckled with white ash, with patches burned away to reveal hideous weeping wounds. Only a single printed daisy remained visible on his shirt.

The apprentice paused at Gonko's door, unaware of his audience. He swayed on his feet. JJ wondered whether or not to warn the boss; he felt no concern for Gonko. Asleep or not, any leader who couldn't repel an attack by this wretched wounded figure should probably not be leading.

The apprentice reached a mauled blistered hand to Gonko's door, wrapped his fingers around the handle, splitting the skin on his knuckles.

JJ heard him hiss through his teeth, then he opened the door and went in. Doopy and JJ rushed up behind him and stood in the doorway.

A single candle burned in Gonko's room, the tiny flame almost extinguished in a pool of red wax. The clown leader lay under a sheet, breathing deeply in his sleep, his shins and clown shoes hanging over the end of the bed, the blanket over his chest and face. The apprentice raised the lead pipe and stepped close, one step, two steps, his fingers tightening around the weapon. Then he stood, gazing down at his helpless enemy, either working up the nerve or savouring the moment.

There was a sudden loud ringing noise, and it came from Gonko. Rather, it came from one of his pockets, where an alarm clock was going off violently in his pocket. The apprentice froze as Gonko whipped off his blanket and his eyes shot open. In one violent wrench he was on his feet, rolling backwards, putting the bed between himself and his enemy. He glanced at the apprentice and at the lead pipe and his lip curled up. Though Gonko's face was the same rough mask, to JJ's eye he looked delighted.

The apprentice recovered from his surprise and raised the pipe, crouching down as though to leap onto the bed. Gonko's eyes narrowed. He reached into his pocket and pulled out the alarm clock, still ringing shrilly, clicked it off with his thumb and tossed it aside. His eyes flickered past the apprentice's shoulder to JJ and Doopy. He reached into his pocket again and in his hand was what looked like a rolled-up sock. Like a baseball pitcher he drew his hand back and threw it; the apprentice ducked aside and it landed in Doopy's hands. JJ caught a whiff of something chemical. As though he'd been instructed by Gonko's glance, Doopy crept behind the apprentice and pressed the cloth roll to his face. The apprentice snorted, dropped his pipe and swooned to the ground.

Gonko strolled over to the prostrate figure, picked up the lead pipe and pulled another rolled-up sock from his pants. He waved it under the apprentice's nose, and again JJ caught a hint of chemicals. With a spluttering cough the apprentice opened his eyes, waking to the sight of Gonko standing over him, tall as a god, the lead pipe in one hand.

a smile on his face which was almost fatherly. The clown leader blew the apprentice a kiss then raised the pipe over his head, and slammed it down, raised it, slammed it down, raised it, slammed it down. Each blow sang out a dull chiming note, singing in sick harmony with the crunching of bone. Doopy watched with a look of mild curiosity as blood spattered up onto Gonko's shins, spouting in a ring on the ground around the dying clown.

JJ watched his master strike at the thrashing and utterly defenceless body below. The sights and sounds of murder touched him, titillated him in a spot no sexual craving could, though the feeling was not dissimilar. His mouth hung open, his eyes sucked in every spatter of red, every dent. The lead pipe thundered down steadily long after the limbs had ceased thrashing.

Gonko finally stopped swinging. He muttered, 'Clowns take some killing, JJ. Clowns don't die easy.' He tossed the lead pipe aside and folded his arms, nodding once towards the corpse. As though part of a long-rehearsed drill, Doopy kneeled down and grasped it by the feet. JJ crouched down and took it by the shoulders, badly dented and soft in his hands. The broken ruin that had been the apprentice's sullen face rested against JJ's chest as he and Doopy carried the body out into the night, through the deathly silent showgrounds to the tall wooden fence, gravel crunching under their shoes. They swung the body to and fro, gaining momentum and heaving it over the fence. A streak of red drops splashed against the fence in a vertical line as the corpse fell to the other side.

Without speaking the two clowns returned to their tent. Eyes peered from curtain cracks as they passed the gypsy huts. Death was never far away; it paid to peer through the curtains on nights like this when footsteps crunched by on the gravel paths. It paid to lock the door.


The night was not over yet.

In bed JJ's mind replayed each swing of the lead pipe, not missing a detail. He saw clearly each speck of blood flying, heard each sound of breaking bone and the dull metallic chime ringing to the steady beat of Gonko's swings, and discovered something new—a new emotion.

Almost without thinking JJ rose from his bed. He distantly remembered Jamie, remembered the attack on the freak show and the fat carnie Jamie had seen as he fled. Any excuse would do; this would certainly do. JJ had forgotten why Jamie betrayed him, but it didn't matter. What mattered was teaching him not to do it again. What mattered was covering his tracks.

Out he went again, not bothering to quiet his footsteps on the gravel. In the quiet stillness of night the sound was large and lamplights flickered on in the gypsy slums as he passed. Death was never far, and the new clown had learned how to make it. He found an axe leaning by a woodpile. He picked it up and kissed it.


Jamie woke around midday, his face paint rubbed over the pillow as usual. His bed felt hot and stuffy and stank of sweat. Sweat, and some other smell, not dissimilar. There was something sticky on his fingers so he held them up to his bleary wet eyes. At the sight of blood his heart kicked into gear before his mind understood what he saw. Blood covered his hand, coating every finger, down to the wrist.

The dim grisly memories returned like a nightmare: kicking open the hut door. Lighting a lantern while the gypsy man lay sleeping with an empty flask at his feet, beer gut hanging over his pants, dripping with sweat like a big glistening pot roast. Lifting the axe, whispering: *Watching, Jamie? This is your mess.*

Up. Down. Up. Down. The flat of the axe into his skull. The calm emotionless ease of the swings, not a moment's hesitation, the small grunt the gypsy made as his skull was crushed. That had been the moment of death but the beginning of JJ's fun. Something had happened while he killed. He'd been clear-thinking, calm, almost detached from the physical act, but his blood had felt heated as it flowed through him. There was an intoxication that was almost sexual. He'd gripped the axe so tight it felt like part of him. After the wounds stopped pumping their blood he'd kept swinging, oh yes, oh fuck yes, up down up down, faster, intending to keep going until he could swing no more but his arms just didn't tire. He'd been panting like a wolf, spattered so thick with blood it was a second skin. Finally he'd slipped in a puddle of it, dropped the axe, and the swinging stopped. He'd dragged the body to the fence, not troubling himself to haul it over. Instead he'd set it upside down, propped on the stump of its neck.

Jamie recalled all this, done with his own hands. He remembered Gonko's pipe work on the apprentice. Nausea flushed through him. He got up from the bed and collapsed. His sheets were drenched in blood; he'd slept in it all night.

*Now that's a wet dream*, his mind babbled sickly. He threw up and retched on his knees, saliva running from his mouth in long strings.

And there was more. JJ had left him a message, painting it in blood with a perfectly calm hand. Up on the cupboard door:

# its coming jamie

It was coming; yes, Jamie remembered now. JJ owed him one. Last night he'd just been tying up loose ends. The party wasn't even started yet.

He forced his head to go blank.

*I'm a killer.*

But only for a moment.

Time passed and the shaking fits and vomiting stopped. Gonko poked his head in to announce a rehearsal at two. He took a look at the blood-soaked sheets, smiled, said 'Hot date, JJ?', then left.

Jamie stood up, the fourth time he'd attempted it this morning, but now there was enough strength in his legs. His head was spinning like he'd smoked too much pot. These thoughts kept repeating: *I killed someone. But it wasn't me in control. But I put the face paint on knowing it wouldn't be me in control. I never asked to be here.* Round and round they went, cutting to images of the kill and that single grunt as the gypsy died. In dizzy shambling steps he made his way to Winston's room and knocked on the door. 'What?' came the muffled answer. Jamie went in. The blood was still on his hands.

'What the hell happened?' said Winston, sitting up and taking him by the shoulders.

He tried to say it, swallowed, then tried again: 'I killed someone.'

Winston's voice was sharp. 'What? Who? Who did you kill?'

'I don't know. A gypsy. The one who lives—Jesus, *lived*—next to the freak show.'

Winston sat back and sighed. 'You had me worried there.'

Jamie gaped at him; he felt like the old guy had sucker-punched him. 'Didn't you hear me? I *killed* someone.'

Winston regarded him gravely but his voice was gentle. 'Jamie, there's plenty worse going on here than killing one lone carnie. That's *nothing*. The Pilos won't even notice one dead carnie. And it wasn't *you*, was it? It was JJ, am I right?'

'Yes, but I was—'

'No but. You are two different people. Understand? Completely different people. Now I want no more talk about that, you got me? Do you know why JJ did it? He have a reason, or was it his idea of a good time?'

'Yeah, I think . . . remember yesterday, the freak show . . .'

'I know damn it, don't say it out loud.'

'Sorry. JJ thought the gypsy might have seen me. A witness.'

'Funny,' Winston said after a moment. 'If he did see you, JJ probably did us a favour.' Winston ran a hand over his face. 'Look, Jamie, I don't know how much I can tell you. I got JJ under wraps, he'll keep his mouth shut if he knows what's good for him. But what I got to tell you . . . I don't know. I want to help you, son. And I want your help too. But I don't know if I can take the chance. It's not just the Pilos I'm worried about. It's the other clowns. Gonko likes being here. He's the king here, you see? He does *not* want *any* mutiny from any of us. You know what he'd do if he thought we were tryin' to pull the rug from under his feet?'

'What am I meant to do, Winston? Last night I—JJ—killed someone. And he's mad at me. He's mad as hell. He's going to get even and he's going to make it hurt. He doesn't know what to do to me yet. He can see everything I do. I can see everything he does. It's like trying to play yourself in a game of chess.' Jamie wiped sweat from his brow then pulled his bloody hand away in disgust. Winston reached for a rag and handed it to him. 'Last night wasn't even the square up,' said Jamie. 'He's going to get me, Winston. He's serious.'

'You sure about that?' said Winston. 'Seems strange he'd do anything to really hurt you. You'n him are renting the same space. Worst he could do is scare you or make you feel bad.'

'But he's insane. He's getting more insane every day. Last night, you saw how he was when we burned down that house. He was crazy. He felt like he was . . . I don't know, possessed by a demon. And he was *glad* about it, on top of the world. Killing a baby . . . Jesus, Winston, what did we *do* last night?'

Winston stood and went to his mouse cage as though he didn't want his face seen. He broke off a small stick of biscuit and poked it between the bars. There was a catch in his voice when he spoke. 'We did what we were told by our bosses. And they do what their bosses tell 'em. No one cares. Everyone does their job, takes their powder . . . Oh, the hell with it, Jamie! I want you to come with me tonight. Try and get through the day if you can, without the face paint. It'll be rough and you might get hurt, but try it. Tonight I'll come get you when it's time. Got something important to show you.'

Winston went to the door, got down on his knees and held his face to the crack between the door and the floor. Satisfied no one was out there, he spoke in a voice barely audible and refused to look at Jamie, as though he had grave reservations about speaking at all. 'There's more of us,' he said. 'We've waited for a long time to do something about the show, but waited long enough. You come meet 'em. Tonight, only if you stay off the paint, just for today. You'll see what freedom means . . . Who freedom is.'

Jamie found he was speechless for a moment or two; the thought of organised resistance thrilled him as much as it scared him. 'One more thing,' said Winston, now looking him in the eye, 'really important you keep the crystal ball secret.'

Jamie raised his eyebrows. 'How did you . . .'

'Saw it a few days ago in your room. Whatever you do, don't return it to the Pilos or let anyone know you got it. Do you think JJ would hand it in?'

'Not a chance. He likes it too much, it's his favourite toy.'

Winston still looked troubled. 'All right,' he said, 'only if you're certain.'

# CHAPTER 18

# FREEDOM MEET

JAMIE was still hiding out in his room, waiting for the moment to make an appearance in the parlour. Tensions seemed high out there at the moment—Doopy and Rufshod could still be heard squabbling over their card game. It had been going on all morning; at some stage Rufshod had gotten on Goshy's bad side and there'd been an outbreak of high-pitched squawking, followed by Rufshod's enraged screams and Doopy's whiny pleas for Gonko to *come save little Gosh-Gosh*. Eventually Jamie went out there, played cards with the others, kept his mouth shut. The clowns paid him no special attention. Rehearsal came and went, and though it racked every nerve he had, he got through it. Goshy was already riled up, thanks to Rufshod, and the rolling pin rebounded at Jamie with murderous speed; he'd stood as far back for the throws as Gonko had let him. Gonko told Jamie that during a show he was to let the pin collide with his face or, if he could arrange it, his crotch. When they finished up Goshy followed Jamie at close range as he walked off the gym mat; Jamie screamed. Doopy rushed over to restrain his brother, saying something that chilled Jamie's blood: 'No, not *yet* Goshy, not *yet!*'

Jamie fled to his room and sat there taking deep breaths. *Not yet?* What the hell was that supposed to mean? He hoped it was just the clowns sensing a 'straight' in their midst—they seemed to have a knack for that. Maybe JJ would defend them both if the need arose. It was strange that they were comrades in arms as much as enemies. All he could do for now was try to get by in five-minute chunks . . . Still ticking? Fine, on to the next five, try not to count how many hours still remained in the day. Sweet Jesus, it was going to be a long day.

At around six Gonko called the clowns into the parlour. He was laughing his head off. They took their places at the card table. 'You guys gotta hear this,' said Gonko, wiping his eye as if a tear of mirth had sprung there, though his face was dry as sandpaper. 'First off, no odd jobs tonight. George is too mad.'

'What happened, Gonko?' said Doopy. 'Goshy wants to know, you just *gotta* tell him, Gonko, you just *gotta!*'

'Never seen George so steamed up,' said Gonko. 'He actually took a swing at me, can you believe that? Goddamn! Short people. What can you do?'

'What's his problem?' said Winston. His voice was casual, but Jamie had the impression that none of Winston's remarks were casual, and that he was taking careful note of all he heard.

'Kurt got his own back,' Gonko said gleefully. 'He took a shot at George, but the way he did it . . . Ah, fantastic. He rigged up George's bed with electric wires, hooked up to a generator he put on the roof of George's trailer. At the flick of a switch, a thousand volts go through George's bed. He waits for George to go to sleep, then knocks out a support block from under his trailer, so the whole thing gives a lurch. George gets out of bed, and he thinks he's pissed off *now*, but he needs about twenty seconds more to know what pissed off is. He opens his door, screams at whoever's out there, then goes back to his bed ready to snooze. This is the thing—he's been in bed two hours, and Kurt could've flicked the switch any time. But the beauty part is, he let George live. He waits till George gets near the bed, then pulls the switch: BOOM! Fucking bed lights up. George runs screaming into the night, and when he's got time to think it over, realises Kurt was playing with him. Could've knocked him off with the touch of a button, but he let him live, just to fuck with him!'

Rufshod fell off his chair, seized up with laughter.

Gonko said, 'Kurt even went to the trouble of leaving a Bible open on George's desk, with *Thou shalt not kill* highlighted. Ah, sibling rivalry.'

'What's sibling ribaldry, Gonko? Goshy wants to know, and you just gotta——'

'What's on tonight, then, Gonks?' said Winston.

'Tonight we're birthday shopping for Kurt, that's what. Who wants in?'

'Me,' said Rufshod.

'No one else? Fine. Two of us should be plenty.'

'What're you getting him?' said Winston.

'You'll see,' said Gonko, smiling. 'This might just get us our act back, boys. Kurt is just gonna love us to death.'


Gonko and Rufshod departed on their private mission soon after. Gonko was in high spirits now that he'd settled on a gift idea, and there was something ominous about that. Jamie just hoped none of his friends or relatives crossed the clown leader's path out there.

The other clowns went about their business. Goshy was having a romantic night in with the missus-to-be. Doopy was playing solitaire, cheating, and telling anyone who walked past he wasn't cheating, *nuh-uh, no way, honest, just ask Goshy*. Around nine the parlour was quiet. Winston came in and motioned for Jamie to follow. The pair of them headed through the dark paths towards Sideshow Alley, and Jamie had the distinct feeling of *eyes*, peering from dark places and missing nothing. Shalice came up the path towards them and Winston grabbed Jamie by the shoulder, dragging him behind a small caravan and pulling him to the ground. They waited for her to pass. She bristled as she came level with them, glanced back over her shoulder, tightened her hood and was soon gone. 'You want to be careful of her,' Winston whispered. 'She's probably more dangerous than any other performer.'

'More than Gonko?' said Jamie.

'Oh yes. She's got more tricks up her sleeve than him. A lot more.'

Winston led him through another of Sideshow Alley's seemingly endless nooks. Around them were the night-time sounds of gypsy life, conversations in Spanish, strange music, old women cackling like crones and the slightly noxious smell of food cooking. They came to a place where the tall wooden perimeter fence appeared at the end of a dead-end lane, behind a broken wagon. Winston pressed his hands against the fence, pushing on it with all his weight, his shoulders trembling with effort. With a small creak the plank moved, falling back but not hitting the ground, caught instead by a loop of rope rigged on the other side. 'Took us a long time to find a way through the fence,' Winston said, panting slightly. 'Thing was stuck tighter'n all hell.' He glanced behind them up the alley, frowned, then climbed through the gap in the fence, sucking in his belly to make himself fit. Once on the other side he motioned Jamie to follow. 'Watch your step,' said Winston, 'and I mean really watch it.'

Before destruction of the freak show, when Jamie held his ear to the fence he'd heard the faint hiss of the ocean. The sound was magnified now, but all he could see through the fence was night, a giant black canvas without a cloud or star visible. When he stepped through the gap, underfoot was only a thin shelf of ground hugging the fence, and beyond that . . . oblivion. It was as though the showgrounds were on a small island floating in its own dark cellar of the universe—only where were the stars? Before he'd stepped through the fence, there had been a moon in the sky. Out here the sightless void above and at his feet was absolute beyond the narrow shelf of turf. Jamie's knees buckled at the sight. Winston gripped his shoulder hard, pinching it and calling his name sharply. The pain brought him back, but by God he'd come close to fainting and falling off the edge. Down, forever, dropping until he starved. 'Hurry up and get used to it,' Winston said. 'I've got to fix the fence. Never know who might wander past.'

'Okay,' Jamie said, swallowing. 'I'm okay.'

'Take my hand,' Winston said after shoving the board back in place with his shoulder. 'Path gets thicker a little further around.' They had about two feet of walking room. Jamie closed his eyes and kept his body against the wood, scraping him as he went. Though it didn't feel like it, it must have been only a minute before Winston said, 'Okay, going's easier now.'

The shelf jutted out twenty feet or so; bare, dusty sand-coloured turf. 'Where is this place?' said Jamie.

'No need to whisper,' said Winston. 'They can't hear us. Or see us, or know about us. That's why we come out here. As for where we are——right next to hell. In a little pocket of the world reserved just for the show. Leased, I guess you'd say. Kurt's bosses arranged this strange real estate. He probably forgets he has bosses, but he does. His daddy made lots of friends. Masters, of course, is the truth of it. As for what they are, I do not rightly know.'

Jamie felt dizzy; with an ocean of black infinity ten paces away, this talk was unnerving. They walked abreast as they circled the outer side of the perimeter fence. 'Scary, first time out here,' said Winston. 'There just ain't another place where we can all meet up and be sure we ain't heard. Others should be out here by now.'

Sure enough they could soon hear voices in conversation just ahead. They rounded a bend in the fence where the ground stretched out to a thicker platform the size of a basketball court. The side of the cliff, a slab of amber rock, stretched down beyond sight. There were people gathered on the platform, and Jamie recognised many of them. He saw Randolph of the acrobats; Fishboy of the freaks, and the rest of the freak show minus only Nugget; Stu the lion tamer; a handful of dwarfs; a dozen dirty-faced gypsies, including the one who operated the 'test your strength' bell. When he saw Jamie coming his face curdled into a look of menace and exasperation.

That look was mirrored on every other face, too, and Jamie understood his invitation tonight had come as a surprise to most. The group fell silent and watched the clowns approach.

'Well, I think some of you know Jamie,' said Winston. 'And I think *all* of you know JJ.'

'How's it going?' Jamie mumbled to the cold silence.

'Jamie, this is the freedom movement,' said Winston.

Randolph broke the silence. 'Winston, what were you thinking? This one cannot be trusted. He is clown, through and through.'

'He's Gonko, only dumber and more of a coward,' said one of the carnies. Jamie recognised him as one JJ had often singled out for special attention in Sideshow Alley.

'I got reason to trust him,' said Winston. 'You can trust *Jamie*. Maybe not when he puts the face paint on. But even then, I don't expect trouble from JJ either.'

'He's right,' said Fishboy, though there was still dislike on his face, and on Fishboy's face dislike was a particularly unpleasant thing. 'JJ won't be telling. We have evidence it was JJ who attacked the freak show. And hung the freedom banner.'

'What evidence?' Randolph demanded.

Winston reached into his pocket and took out the photograph. In it Jamie stood on the ladder, tying an end of the banner to the rafters. Randolph took a close look with the help of a lit match then passed it around. The group seemed to relax, just a notch. 'Ah, tha's more like it,' said Randolph. 'I trust there's more copies of this picture?'

'There are,' said Winston. 'Safely hidden. A few others here know about it too, in case JJ gets any ideas about bumping me off. Now, let's welcome Jamie aboard. God knows an extra pair of hands won't go astray. And who knows, even JJ may come in useful. He's the one who took the crystal ball.'

'You'd better keep it hidden,' Randolph said to Jamie. 'If they get it back . . .'

'It's over, yup,' said Winston, looking pointedly at Jamie. 'Never know when the fortune-teller will be looking over our shoulders. She's dangerous enough without the ball. Bloody miracle the Pilos haven't done anything much to get it back. If we'd known they'd sit on their hands, we would have taken it a long time ago.'

'I don't think he should be left with it,' said one of the gypsies. 'We should take it out here and throw it over the edge.'

'Maybe you're right,' said Fishboy. 'Jamie, are you certain you can keep it safe? Are you certain JJ will too?'

Jamie nodded. 'JJ loves it. He wouldn't trade it for anything.'

'I'm still not comfortable with that, but we can work it out later,' said Fishboy. 'For now, your mission is to protect it. If JJ gets any ideas, don't think we wouldn't rat him out, even if it costs you your life, my friend. You aren't the only one with something to lose, understand?'

'I'm not the one you need to convince,' Jamie said, and he felt a flush creeping into his face. He was tiring of the sidelong looks of disgust the others were giving him, and couldn't remember volunteering to be a clown.

Winston cleared his throat. 'Come on everyone, let's not spend our time coming down on Jamie. He's here, we can trust him. Fishboy, you wanna tell him the background about us?'

'Certainly.' Fishboy stood and everyone else sat down. He cleared his throat, making the gills puff out on the side of his neck. 'Jamie, there are some things you need to know, such as why the circus must be shut down. It's not merely to save our lives or the lives of people who wind up here from outside. This place is a tumour in the world that will *never* be detected. I'm sure you've heard a little about that, and seen enough with your own eyes by now.'

Gonko's voice filtered through JJ's memories: *Try fifty fucking million dead tricks . . .*

'We began meeting,' Fishboy went on, 'when it became clear to us that our suffering was never going to end. We freaks were the first to consider rebellion, and you can see why. All of us walked in here functional, healthy human beings. Look at us now. They have warped us, taken our humanity away, mutilated and ruined us. Look at Tallow. Could you live like that?'

Jamie looked at Tallow, whose skin was running in rivulets and dripping off his fingers, forming a flesh-coloured pool which was hardening at his feet. 'You get used to it,' said Tallow in a voice like someone gargling water.

'And Yeti,' said Fishboy, 'turned into a beast on display, an ape in a zoo, forced to eat glass every show day. There have been other freaks who could stand the torment no longer, and finished themselves.' Fishboy waved an arm at the abyss, and a chill went down Jamie's spine. 'How would you deal with such agony?' Fishboy continued. 'Nor have we suffered for a noble cause, Jamie. We've suffered for evil. Do you know what the circus does with its "tricks"?'

'No,' said Jamie. 'I know about the fortune-teller, I think. Subliminal commands, or whatever you'd call it. She tried it on me the first day.'

'Yes, you see what she does. Do you know the results of her commands? Around the world, disasters, murders, crimes and suffering. Shalice could start a war, if she was ordered to. I do not doubt she has.'

'What about the rest of us?' said Jamie. 'You, me, the acrobats. What do we do? What are we *for*?'

'We are thieves, Jamie. We steal something more precious than life. If only it were as simple as killing those who fall into our trap! Each part of the show is designed to part the tricks with the most precious thing they have: the human soul, Jamie. We steal them by the dozen. It began a long time ago. Kurt Pilo Senior established the circus as a farm for human souls, and that is what it remains. During his travels, Kurt Senior stole many forbidden things, artefacts and tomes kept hidden from the world, hidden for good reason. In a couple of decades, he tracked down the world's deepest secrets, guided by an intuition too astute to be his own. No doubt he was being used, not that he knew it. He travelled across the world on his thieving treasure hunt, the world's most vile pirate, yet a complete unknown in human history. He traversed paths of black magic never traversed before. With each new secret unveiled, his powers grew and he opened lines of communication with forces long banished from the world. They were banished to make way for humankind. They have the bodies of ultimate reptile predators and power that seems godlike to us. They would devour us if they had the chance. We are a delicacy to them, Jamie, an exquisite treat. They are addicted to us.

'No one knows who expelled these beasts from the human world. It may have been God, if God exists . . . May have been shamans in tribes long lost to time, may have been Mother Nature herself. In this dark little realm the demon bastards lay, longing for the world they once ran rampant through. They starved and waited for a very long time, and for a very long time none knew their secrets. None knew they existed.

'In their prison the rules of the outside world did not apply, and because those rules were unable to hold them, laws beyond the natural laws were required. And they banged on the walls of their cell until someone heard. That someone was Kurt Pilo Senior. He found in his studies a way to reach these beings in their prison. They bargained with him. They lured him towards them. He agreed to bring them what they craved, what they were unable to go forth and take for themselves. They helped him cheat mortality, he and all who work for him. The powder helps us do this. If Kurt Junior had not become impatient to run the circus himself, Pilo Senior would still be here.

'Once human beings are lured here, they are as good as gone. Unfamiliar with the dimensions and boundaries that lock in these feasting predators, any human is easy enough prey; robbing souls is as simple as hypnotising someone and ordering them to shed their clothes. And this is where we come in. We each play a different part in persuading the tricks to part with what is most precious. We are paid with some of what we steal; the dust. It is the human soul shattered into pieces like some glass statue and discarded, for here, where the natural laws are not quite the same, the soul can be translated into something physical, tangible, almost as flesh. Some call it wish dust, prayer dust—but it is soul dust.

'For a human to part with their soul, he or she must be persuaded, deceived. Just as a person has a breaking point where he will decide living is unbearable and will choose death, a person has a breaking point where they will part with the force *behind* their physical life. For some, greed is enough. Those lose themselves in Sideshow Alley. Step right up, win a prize. The greedy ones play for baubles and trinkets, while under the carnival's spell they gamble and lose more than they know. Little diamond crystals fall to the ground like beads of sweat. The dwarfs collect them at night.

'The acrobats appeal to vanity. Beautiful creatures, they dazzle all who watch their movements: the vain and insecure covet them. Silently whispering in their ears is the voice of the circus, the demon bastards, stripping them with promises. *This beauty could be yours. What would you do with such power, such grace?* Little diamond crystals fall to the floor. The dwarfs collect them at night.

'So on for each of us. Mugabo's show appeals to those who crave power, though Mugabo doesn't know it. While he does his paltry tricks, whispering in the audience's ears just beyond hearing is: *this power could be yours. What would you do with such power?* The woodchoppers, similarly, appeal to the frail and weak and downtrodden. The clowns appeal to the rebellious, the cruel, the naturally wicked—everyone has the capacity for wickedness. The clown show always includes an authority figure being usurped. Have you noticed?'

Jamie thought back to the show he'd seen, with Gonko strolling onstage in a British copper's uniform.

'Do you see a pattern here, Jamie?' Fishboy continued in his strange high-pitched voice. 'Every human weakness is catered to by some part of the show. Everyone has a pressure point, and like moths to flame they are drawn to whatever attraction will best be able to milk them. Despite that, some resist, clinging to their souls with rare tenacity. Which is where we freaks come in. Our hideous bodies pulverise that strength, horrifying the strong into letting go.'

'How do you know all this?' Jamie said, shaking his head.

'We've been here a long time, Jamie,' Fishboy replied. 'Anyone with keen eyes and ears can see the process in action, if they watch and listen long enough. Listen to the tricks talk as they walk around: listen to what they say. Listen to Kurt when he's in a boisterous mood, boasting about the trailblazing pioneer his father was. All the answers are here . . . Just don't look like you're trying to find them. Like us, you may survive.'

'One more thing,' Jamie said. 'The fortune-teller. If she doesn't steal people's—I don't know . . . souls, what does she do?'

'The people who walk in whole leave as living shells. But that is not enough for the Pilos. They want to inflict as much havoc and pain on the outside world as possible. To this end, Shalice sets off series of events like dominos toppling, which finish in disasters. Each trick she commands is the first domino to fall. It is revenge, we theorise, from those banished to this prison. Perhaps they want to cause so much pain their jailer will be forced to bargain with them. No one knows.'

Winston cleared his throat. 'Fishboy, I think we've maybe spent enough time on explanations. Jamie's got the gist of it, right, Jamie? We should really get on with things.'

'Right you are, Winston,' said Fishboy. 'People, welcome Jamie to our ranks. We've said enough about the show. Now, onto what we can do about it.

'Right, now as I've mentioned, the carnival cannot see us work,' said Fishboy. He was speaking quickly; time had gotten away from them a little and the night was wearing on. 'For the first time we can operate unseen, thanks to Jamie and the crystal ball. These are uncharted waters for us. This is our first, perhaps our last shot at putting a stop to it all. The strike on the acrobats' stage tent was the first open act of rebellion, and has created uncertainty amongst those in charge. Yeti and I arranged the collapse ourselves in one week's intense labour, sneaking out at night while everyone else slept. Jamie's follow-up attack on our show was intended to absolve us from suspicion. Next, we must provoke tensions that already exist. The clowns and acrobats must be brought to daggers drawn. We must turn Mugabo against Shalice. Must turn the Pilos against everyone, somehow. If they come down hard on everyone, who knows? Rebellion may just have a shot.

'You all know who hates who, what old scores are still unsettled. I want you to think about how you can exacerbate that hatred, play on existing rivalries, create new ones. Be bold, but be careful.'

Hearing all this, Jamie felt excitement building within him slowly. The idea of the show being undone and reclaiming his old life fired something within him, a spark of hope where there had been only ashes. There was deadly fear there too; JJ would soon be privy to every word spoken, would know the name and face of each rebel.

'There is enough instability in the circus to bring it down,' Fishboy was saying. 'The competition between attractions that management has been promoting will help us no end. Play on every rivalry! Agitate everyone! We must turn the show into a small war zone, get it fraying at the seams. Sabotage the attractions. Spare no one—*especially* each other. Anyone who remains unscathed will be the first suspect.'

'Can I ask,' said Jamie, 'what all this would achieve, precisely?'

Fishboy looked him in the eye. '*Something* will happen, Jamie. The powers running this show are unstable at the best of times—a barrel of explosive chemicals that has never been struck hard, never shaken. Kurt has never had his bluff called, never had underlings rebel, never been challenged other than by his brother. There have been breaches of edicts, yes, punished so severely none would dare rebel further, and God help us if they catch us at it. But put that out of your minds. We are targeting the whole show, but we are really targeting Kurt. If he grows angry enough, anything is possible—even total collapse.'

*In short, the answer is you don't know*, Jamie thought.

Winston interrupted again to remind Fishboy time was getting on. Fishboy finished the meeting, calling several individuals aside to talk privately about specific plans. Jamie waited with Winston by the fence. Randolph and some others were filing back around the narrow shelf of turf towards the entrance to the showgrounds. Against the backdrop of complete blackness they looked minuscule, like insects marching along some finger of earth. The sound of a distant roaring ocean seemed ready to swallow them all with one crashing black wave. Finally Fishboy approached Jamie and gave him an appraising look. His gills fluttered, something that seemed to happen when he was distressed. 'Jamie,' he said, 'there's something I don't like saying but which needs to be said. And I am really talking to JJ here, and JJ, I know you're listening. I want you to know that if you move against us, we will not hesitate to kill you. There is too much at stake here for games. You remember that well, JJ. I advise you to enjoy what time the circus has left. Enjoy your privileges while you can. Join the fun, if you like. Attack the gypsies. Sabotage the woodchoppers. Torment the acrobats. Whatever you do, though, *leave us alone*. If you manage that, we will leave you alone.'

The intensity left Fishboy's gaze and voice. 'Remember that, Jamie. He needs to hear it.'

Jamie swallowed and nodded. Winston clapped him on the back. 'Let's go,' he said. 'Been out here too long.'

'Yes,' said Fishboy. 'I shouldn't have waffled on so much. See you around, Winston. Jamie.' Fishboy ran off ahead, and Jamie held his breath to see the freak show curator sprint so quickly along the narrow path. He and Winston followed at a brisk walk, with Winston's hands on Jamie's shoulders to guide him.

*One push would do it,* Jamie couldn't help thinking. *I'm a liability here. One push to the left. Long way down.*

They came finally to the fence paling, pried it loose and were back in the showgrounds. Jamie had never felt so glad to be there, though he didn't expect the feeling to last.

# CHAPTER 19

# KURT'S GIFT

WINSTON led him back to the clown tent via a long detour so no one would see all the 'freedom' personnel moving in one large group across the showgrounds. Doopy was asleep on the card table again as they came in, his face pressed into a hand of solitaire. The place was quiet. Gonko and Rufshod weren't home yet, something Winston had fretted over on their walk back. Jamie went to his room and lay down, suddenly elated he had gotten through the day unscathed; if he could make it through one day, he could make it through another.

A moment later he heard Gonko and Rufshod returning from their mission. He got up and took the crystal ball from its covering and focused it on the parlour, where he saw the pair creeping in with a body bag squirming in their arms. They disappeared with their burden to Gonko's room. Another victim. Jamie sighed, his elation gone and a weary sadness in its place.

He lay back and waited for sleep. Someone knocked on his door. Thinking it was Winston, Jamie sat up and said, 'Come in.'

It was Gonko. He stood in the doorway, arms folded across his chest, the dim light behind him sending a long shadow over the threshold of the door. Jamie's heart skipped a beat. 'JJ, do me a favour,' said Gonko.

'Uh, sure, Gonko. What's up?'

Gonko smiled, as though something had just confirmed a suspicion he'd held. 'Make sure you wear your face paint tomorrow. What do you say?'

Jamie's heart skipped another beat; his mouth was suddenly dry. 'Sure thing, Gonko,' he said. Gonko's lip curved at the corners. He shut the door.

Jamie stared at the wall for a long while. Then he reached under his bed and picked up one of the small velvet bags. He would have to use some powder if he wanted sleep tonight. He tossed the bag up and down on his palm, trying to ward off the sense that it was all about to come undone, that by tomorrow he would betray everyone as soon as JJ made an appearance, stab Winston in the back out of sheer spite, no matter what the consequences.

The small glassy beads chimed faintly in his hand. Suddenly he had an idea.

His sleep was deep that night, so deep that he didn't notice Rufshod sneaking into his room in the early morning. Nor did he hear him take the tub of face paint from his cupboard, crouch down beside him and begin smearing it over his cheeks, nose, forehead and chin. Rufshod lit a match, held a small hand mirror before the flame, and screamed in Jamie's ear the words: '*I FUCKED YOUR MOTHER.*'

Jamie thrashed around and sat bolt upright, caught a glimpse of himself in the mirror, and JJ snarled, 'You son of a . . .' He cocked back a fist, then paused, came to himself and said, 'Hey! You did good. That bastard's been hogging the body. He had it all day yesterday.' JJ was about to thank Rufshod profusely but noticed what Rufshod was using as a seat: the pillow case inside of which he'd wrapped the crystal ball. 'Get out!' JJ shrieked. 'Leave me be! I don't want you to see me like this!'

'Don't blame you,' said Rufshod. JJ chased him out of the room then propped a heavy box against the door.

Jamie. What had the guy been up to yesterday? JJ couldn't recall offhand. He lay back and tried to sift through yesterday's memories. Let's see, he'd woken, had his usual hissy fits—*Please don't hurt me, baby Jesus* and all that. After that . . . After that . . .

It was all blank. JJ frowned. Why would that be? *Something* must have gone down; Jamie had used the body all day.

He got up and put on his shoes. This blankness of mind was making him uneasy . . . very uneasy. He could remember all the childhood crap, computer games, sketching buildings on rainy afternoons and such, getting beaten up waiting for the bus after school, but nothing about yesterday.

As he tied his laces he saw the small velvet bag on the floor. Picking it up he was startled to feel it was empty. He grabbed around under the bed for the other bags; *those* were empty. Every last grain, gone. 'What the hell?' he yelled. 'MY STASH!'

He let out half a scream, half a sob. His hands shook with rage. 'Too far this time,' he whispered, delighted by the menace in his voice, wishing only there was an audience to see him. 'Way too far now, Jamie.' He crushed the bags in his palm and tossed them away. He had a feeling that the missing powder and the missing memories had something in common, perhaps a cause-and-effect relationship. How could Jamie *do* such a thing? To JJ of all people . . . he tried to fight back the tears but it was no good; he bawled into his pillow.

Someone opened the door. JJ peered through the tears and saw Gonko, who smiled and said, 'Good to have you back, JJ.'

'GO *AWAY!*' JJ screamed. Gonko smiled wider and left.

After a while he stopped crying and tried to work out the hows and whys of it all. One name sprang instantly to mind: Winston. At once JJ got up and stormed over to Winston's room. Outside the door, arms locked at his sides *à la* Goshy, fists bunched and shaking, he fought to keep his voice as polite as possible. 'Oh, say, Winston old bean?'

'Who's that?' said a sleepy voice.

'Might I pop in for a chin wag?'

'Jamie?'

'More or less.'

Winston groaned. 'JJ. What do you want?'

JJ had to quell an explosion of anger. 'You know very well,' he said in a hoarse whisper.

'No, I don't. Just open the damn door would you?'

JJ flung it back and stood in the doorway, trying to look threatening. He judged he succeeded, even if the old clown was hiding his fear. 'You!' he cried.

Winston watched him carefully. 'Get in here and shut the door if you got something . . . *personal* to discuss.'

JJ slammed the door behind him and stood watching Winston, licking his lips.

'Well then,' said Winston. 'I see you have something on your mind.'

'Actually, no, I don't. That's the problem,' JJ replied. 'What would you know about *that*, buddy?'

Winston frowned, his eyes never leaving JJ's. 'You ain't making much sense. Want to slow down there and tell me plain what the problem is?'

JJ spluttered: 'I can't remember——' Then he stopped as his mind did a few very quick sums. Winston didn't know what he was talking about, which meant as far as Winston knew, JJ knew everything, whatever dirty secrets Jamie had wiped from the files. Maybe he could ad lib a little, glean some of the missing info . . .

'Out with it,' said Winston. 'You come in here, wake me up, now what's the story?'

'You,' said JJ, changing tack from menacing to hurt and sad. 'How could you do that, yesterday?'

Winston blinked. 'Go on.'

'You know what I'm talking about. Yesterday. The stuff. What's the deal?'

'What specific part of yesterday got you upset?'

'How could you involve me in all that stuff? How could you put Jamie at such a risk?'

'You're being mighty vague there, young feller,' said Winston, sitting back. 'And it's a little early to be caring about games like this. How about you haul your arse back to your own room—'

'No! Something happened yesterday. We both know it. What was it? Why can't I remember any of it?'

'Ah, I see.' A faint smile touched Winston's lips. 'What happened, you woke up with a blank head?'

'Yes! Was that your idea?'

'Nope. I'd say Jamie had that idea before bedtime. Not sure why he did it, he had nothing to hide, really. Waste of powder, if you ask me.'

JJ scowled and took a step towards the old clown. He lowered his voice to a harsh whisper. 'It must have been big, whatever it was. Oh yes, I'll find out. And I'll tell. You hear me? I'll squeal. Just to get square. Even if I go down with you, I'll make sure you are *in the fucking stew*, Winston. You got me?'

Winston raised his eyebrows. 'I get your drift, but I don't know what beans you'd spill. Only one around here with beans to spill is . . . well, me. But I know how to keep my mouth shut. How about you?'

JJ stood caught between words for a moment, glaring at the baggy eyes and crow's-feet and smile lines he so detested. Finally he turned to leave, searching desperately for a venomous parting shot, but he came up empty. He slammed the door behind him.


Winston watched the door rattle on its hinges, then sat back, deep in thought. Jamie had been right about one thing—JJ was changing. He was more aggressive and getting bolder. Winston understood what must have happened last night: Jamie would have looked in the eye all that could go wrong if JJ really wanted to play dirty. Must have used the powder to blank out the day's events from his mind . . . Good thinking, although

Winston was a little surprised the request had worked. It was risky as hell for one thing, and that it worked only meant 'the demon bastards', as Fishboy would call them, weren't paying much attention to their charges these days. There were times past when the oppressive *presence*, intense but undefined, was very real and inescapable. Memories from those times had often kept Winston from using his powder, just in case the higher powers ever had cause to wonder about him, just in case they looked at him a little closer.

And Winston had discovered something new: he was pretty damn scared of JJ. He would not show it; it would be curtains for him if JJ knew. But there it was—Winston was scared as hell.

Another nasty thought occurred: what happened when JJ got his hands on more powder and started making requests of his own?

That brought a sinking feeling to Winston's gut and he cursed himself for giving in to his soft side, taking Jamie under his wing in the first place. Life at the show was hard enough without dangerous enemies under his own roof. His eyes fell on the door with its weak little chain lock, and he wondered if he'd have time to wake and arm himself should someone boot it down during the night.


JJ threw a tantrum in the parlour, kicking things and thrashing his fists in the air. He remembered Gonko's tantrum, which had destroyed all the furniture out here, but try as he might JJ didn't have the same in him. Eventually Gonko heard the fuss and came out. 'What's new, JJ?' he said.

'Oh, nothing,' JJ replied, invoking Mr Don't Hurt Me from force of habit.

'Someone put a bee in your bonnet,' said Gonko. 'Got something that might cheer you up. Want to see what we got for Kurt's birthday?'

JJ did want to see that. He followed Gonko to one of the storage rooms. Some boxes had been pulled out into the hall to make way for the body bag, which lay on the floor. The lumpy bag gave a twitch. JJ poked it with his boot. A quiet moan came from inside. Gonko reached down and unzipped the bag with a noise like metal squealing in pain. Inside it was a barely conscious man in his fifties, balding, fattening around the chin and jowls. He was wearing a black robe with a white collar. 'You got him a priest?' JJ said, amazed.

'Yep.'

'He'll love it!'

'He'd better. Catching him was easy, but making him get dressed before we took him was hassle city.'

The priest's eyes peeled open and he squinted from the sudden light. His voice was thick and confused. 'What's happened? Where are we?'

'Night, night, Father,' said Gonko as he zipped up the bag again. The priest moaned and struggled weakly before lying still.

'Great present!' said JJ.

Gonko winked and shut the storage room door. 'Keep this hush hush, JJ. Don't want the other crews to get wind of it.'

JJ went back to his room feeling a little better about things. A nice long stretch of spying on people would just about heal his wounds.


All seemed to be as normal around the showgrounds. JJ panned in on the acrobat tent and saw Randolph convincing the others to go on an outing. Then, to his surprise, Winston snuck into their tent a minute later. 'Hello hello, what's all this then?' JJ murmured. Winston had a suitcase in hand. He peered around to make sure he was alone then went into one of the back rooms where the acrobats stored their props. The trampoline JJ had borrowed was leaning against a wall. Winston took it down and pulled a knife from his back pocket. He gouged a long rip in the mat. Once done, he moved on to the tightrope, hanging from a hook on the wall in a giant thick coil. He took it down and dropped it to the floor, then pulled from his suitcase a jar of clear liquid. He soaked the tightrope then lit a match, dropped it, and flame soon twisted over the rope. There were some spare sets of tights hanging up on coat hangers, which Winston took down and laid on the fire.

In the suitcase were more bottles of liquid. Yellow liquid—urine. Winston opened one of these bottles and splashed it over the other equipment in there: dumbbells, exercise gear, medicine balls and skipping ropes. He opened a second bottle, drenching everything in sight, before taking the remaining three bottles back to the acrobats' parlour. Next to get a soaking were the suede couches and beanbags. Once Winston emptied the bottles over these, he took one more thing from his suitcase: a red plastic clown nose. To JJ's puzzlement, he placed the plastic clown nose on a urine-soaked cushion. Then he grabbed his suitcase and ran out of the tent with one nervous glance over his shoulder.

JJ suddenly felt very mixed emotions about all this. Maybe Winston wasn't all bad. Yet there was something fishy about the whole deal, something he couldn't quite put his finger on. Had Gonko given Winston secret orders for this attack?

JJ decided to find out. Covering the ball, he went in search of Gonko. He found him kneeling by the body bag, splashing the unconscious priest's face with water from a bottle. Gonko glanced around at JJ, dropped the bottle inside the bag and zipped it up.

'Say, Gonks,' said JJ, 'when are we gonna get square with them acrobats?'

'They'll get theirs, like I told you,' said Gonko. 'Don't do anything yet. Wait till I give the word. I ain't forgotten *them*, my sweet, you believe it. They'll get it, and good. Now ain't the time, what with all these mystery vandals running around.'

'Sure thing,' said JJ, frowning.

'JJ, in three hours come back and give this guy more water. Don't want him dead before tomorrow.'

'Yeah, why not?' JJ went back to his room, wondering what to think. Winston was disobeying Gonko's orders—but he supposed he was a little proud of the old guy. Why should they wait for payback? The acrobats had had it too good for too long.

........................................

As he made his way back to the clown tent, Winston was confident no one who mattered had seen him. Then he saw JJ waiting by his bedroom door and his heart thumped reluctantly. *Oh great. What now?* he wondered, his nerves already worn out from the raid.

'Hi, Winston,' said JJ, smirking.

Winston had decided casual nonchalance was the best bet with JJ: be unafraid, but don't challenge him. He said, 'What do you want, JJ?'

'Nothing, nothing. Nice job. That's all I wanted to say.'

*Nice job?* Winston thought, then he realised: the ball. Of course. 'Yeah well,' he said. 'They had it comin'. Now excuse me, JJ, gotta have a rest.'

'Sure, sure. Hey, Winston. Sorry about this morning. Didn't mean to come across as . . . you know. Pushy.'

'No problem, JJ. But wanna keep this just between us?'

JJ's face darkened, yet his voice held the same jocular tone. 'Sure. Wouldn't want to spill any beans, would I? Neither would you.' JJ left.

Winston shut his door and fastened the chain. He sighed. No way could he let JJ keep the crystal ball, no way at all. Having JJ aware that *something* was going on was dangerous enough, let alone making him Big Brother. And maybe, just maybe, Fishboy's hardline stance on JJ would have to be acted on, though it sickened Winston to think so. Until now they'd supposed it was better the devil they knew——bump off Jamie and who knew what kind of replacement would be brought into the show? But the devil they knew was getting out of hand. There might be no way around it: Jamie might have to die to kill JJ.

CHAPTER 20

# LIGHTING FIRES

WINSTON wasn't the only one busy on the sabotage front. Around the showgrounds, several performers were discovering nasty surprises in their homes.

Mugabo had just been to visit Kurt Pilo. Kurt intimidated and infuriated him; when the magician lay awake at night, most of his time was spent picturing Kurt as a giant mound of steaming ash, for it was Kurt who sent instructions as to what degrading stunts were to be performed each show. The bunny trick, pulling coins from behind the ears of children in the front row, the connecting and disconnecting of silver rings, the ten feet of bright fabric pulled from his sleeves . . . All done on Kurt's orders. Those who enforced Kurt's orders were just as bad, and Mugabo made confused, muddled vows of revenge against each one: Gonko, Shalice, the woodchoppers, even Fishboy—although Fishboy had been decidedly more polite to him than the others.

That afternoon he'd meant to give Kurt a nice big glowing-red piece of his mind, and he'd kept his rage burning long enough for a brazen knock on the trailer door. When Kurt's gentle answer came from within, 'Hmmm?', Mugabo's hands tensed into rigid sticks, his lip quavered, and his rage fled him. Had Mugabo an undamaged mind, he would have remembered the same thing happening scores of times before.

In the trailer Kurt had heard him out, although Mugabo hadn't been able to make much of a case for himself. Under Kurt's gaze he became a shivering mess. 'Can't do ze bunny treek,' he'd stammered. 'Can do ze f-fire treek?'

'Ah, Mugabo,' said Kurt, cheerful as ever, 'we've discussed this before, haven't we? Your act isn't changing. Those are lovely tricks, the ones you do. If we let you do the fire trick, you will scare the audience. It would be coming on far too strong, mmm yes. They need but a hint of your mighty powers. Just a taste.'

'My tricks are . . .' Mugabo made a spitting noise. It was as close as he dared come to arguing with Mr Pilo.

'No, you are too hard on yourself,' said Kurt, his fish lips frozen in that grin. '*Far* too hard. Dangerously so. There's a reason we make you do the bunny trick. You are to woo and seduce the audience with wonder and amusement. You aren't to frighten and overwhelm them with pyrotechnics.'

Mugabo wanted desperately to disagree, but Kurt was standing up from behind his desk. Kurt was approaching him. Mugabo tried to square his shoulders, hold his gaze level, but to no avail. Kurt popped something small and white into his mouth; there was a crunch as he chewed and swallowed. 'Mm. Speaking of bunnies . . . lovely mandibles . . . mm. Lovely. Where were we?' His eyes had misted over. 'Ah yes. I'll tell you what, Mugabo. How would it suit you to do a private show for the carnival staff? Then you could do whatever tricks you like. How does that sound?'

To Mugabo it sounded repugnant—he hated nearly everyone, and had no desire to be put on display for their amusement and catcalls and jeers. But Kurt was towering over him . . . 'That be okay,' he whispered, defeated yet again.

'Lovely!' said Kurt, clapping him on the back with one giant paw. 'I'll schedule it for one week's time. Now off you go and get your act ready. Show day approaches and you must pluck the bunny from your hat! Pluck like there's no tomorrow. The adorable little bunny, Mugabo. Good man, good man. Off you go, God bless.'

On the walk back home each step raised Mugabo's rage one notch. Soon he'd be blind with it, unable to see for the hazy white-hot glare behind his eyes. *Think he so big*, Mugabo thought bitterly. Problem was he was right—Kurt *was* so big.

His hands were shaking when he got back home. Behind his stage was a small laboratory where he spent his leisure hours dabbling in potions and medicines. It saddened him greatly that no one came and asked for a draught once in a while, for he had something to cure everything—or so he assumed. Right now he felt a tonic was in order to calm his nerves, so he could get through the afternoon without exploding. The bubbling purple batch could well be the ticket—if it wasn't a nerve tonic, he had no idea what it was.

He scowled at the vacant plastic seats as he walked past them, but stopped cold when he got to the stage. Over the floor, someone had written in white paint: CALL USEFUL MAGICIAN? DO BUNNY TRICK U SCUM.

Stammering, Mugabo fell to his knees as he read then reread the writing. From the back of his throat came a rasping cry. Here was the proof in block letters: the world was against him, laughing behind his back. The only thing he couldn't work out was whether the vandal was calling him names because he *did* the bunny trick, or because he didn't do the bunny trick very well?

Not that it mattered. He held an arm over the paint and with the same rasping cry shot fire at the message, his palm acting as a hose for a jet of orange flame. The words blackened and smoked and were soon an illegible burnt patch of floor. With massive effort he checked himself before he torched the whole stage. He picked up one of the many sacks he kept on hand and beat out the flames.

It would be some time yet before Mugabo headed out back to find his potion lab in ruins, with bottles smashed, potions spilled and written formulas ripped to shreds. The same message was written on the walls in there— CALL USEFUL MAGICIAN? along with, U CANT EVEN TELL FUTURE U SCUM.

In her bath, Shalice was quite aware she was being gazed at through the stolen crystal ball. As could Kurt, she was able to feel its presence, like a cold shadow from above.

She was still patiently waiting for the thief to slip up. The Pilos seemed unaware of how rare and precious a thing the ball was, for both Kurt and George had ignored her requests for help. Perhaps another attack by the mystery vandals would stir the venerable Pilo siblings into action. Perhaps she should arrange such an attack herself.

She lifted her leg above the suds, letting hot water run down her shin. Her eyes were closed and a lazy smile played on her face. 'Keep watching, you pig,' she whispered. 'I'll find you.'

As she lay back, trying to decide what she'd do with the thief when she found him—God knew her options were extensive—something came to her. It was a powerful vision indeed, an image clear and urgent. It was Mugabo, entering her hut with his eyes and hands ablaze. She saw herself turning to face him just as a stream of orange flame poured over her.

Her heart raced and she had to fight the urge to get up right now, bolt the doors, switch off the lights. She had to wait, capture as much of the vision as she could for clues. Finally it faded; the last glimpse was of Mugabo standing over her burning body, teeth bared, screaming. Once the vision was gone she rose from her bath, towelled herself off, alert for the sound of footsteps outside. She ran to her hut, locked her door and sat, thinking hard. Then she took her charts from the wall, her tarot cards too, and headed for the home of her lover to hide out. It was going to be a busy night.

The resounding BOOM from the direction of Mugabo's hut some time later turned many heads. They saw a pillar of fire shoot skyward, as though a comet had landed on a gigantic trampoline. A wave of hot wind swept through the showgrounds.

The fire occurred two minutes after Mugabo wandered into his potion lab and saw what had become of his sanctuary. He'd held off until he'd made it onto the roof, where he now lay unconscious, all his energies spent.

Kurt Pilo peered out the window of his trailer as the last flames dissipated. He raised his eyebrows then sat back at his desk. The magician was obviously rehearsing for his private show—a stroke of managerial brilliance, that. Whereas Pa would have skinned the magician, sodomised him, then fed them to the funhouse creatures one spoonful at a time, Kurt Junior met the performers halfway. That was what good management was made of, yes sir. 'Going to be quite a show,' Kurt said to no one.


The acrobats had spent the day in Sideshow Alley, charming the womenfolk and chumming it up with the men. They returned late to discover the vandalism of their equipment and furniture, and there was unanimous consent: the clowns were going to be pissing blood and shitting their own teeth over the coming days.

'No no no,' said Randolph, 'we should play it cool, let them sweat for a while, wonder wha'ss coming.'

'Maybe,' Sven replied, 'but whatever we do is going to settle this bullshit, once and for all.'

'Once and for all? Only way to settle it is to take them all out,' said Tuskan.

'Then maybe tha'ss what we should do,' said Sven.

'You don't mean kill them all?' said Randolph.

'At least one or two,' said Sven.

'Which ones?'

'That old bastard. How about him?'

'Winston?' said Randolph. 'No, he's hardly the worst of them. Someone else.'

'Who, then?'

'That new guy,' Randolph suggested. 'That redhead, the one who's been hassling the gypsies. Wha'ss-his-name.'

His name was JJ and Randolph didn't trust him for a second. The others agreed he'd make a fine example for the other clowns.


JJ put the ball away and lay back, wondering if there was any way to prevent the face paint getting rubbed off in the night by the pillow. He was about to go ask Rufshod to paint him up come morning when his hands felt something under the pillow, a folded piece of paper. He unfolded it and saw it was a letter from Jamie. Presumably he had been meant to find it first thing that morning. It read:

> Dear JJ,
>
> I'm sorry I used so much of the powder, but there was no other way for me to get to sleep, waking up with blood all over me like that. I know we've had our differences, but I would like to propose a truce. Apparently after a few years of using the paint I'll be gone altogether. In the meantime, let me be, I'll let you be. What do you say?

JJ crumpled the paper in his fist and threw it away. A grin spread over his face. 'Here's what I say, chumbo.'


Past the lion tamer's hut and under the wooden gates of Sideshow Alley crept a figure through the shadows. Only the keenest eyes could have seen him, JJ the clown stalking like a scarecrow with an axe in his hands, sometimes twirling it around like a walking stick, sometimes propped on his shoulder like a parasol. Just faintly there came the sound of him whistling 'Que Sera, Sera'.

None heard him gently prying open the door of the shack behind the 'shoot a duck, win a prize' stall. Inside lived—for the moment—a gypsy woman who made necklaces from seashells. She was the oldest carnie in the show, had been around before Kurt Junior inherited the circus, and could remember the furious sounds of Pilo Senior's voice railing against his underlings, could recall what happened back in those days to gypsy girls who made the mistake of being born pretty.

Some heard the sharp scream she made as her time in the show came to an end, some heard the dull thud of the axe head striking, *thump, thump, thump.* None got up to investigate, for this was nothing new. The carnies did what they always did when something went bump in the night: double-checked their doors and windows were bolted, crossed themselves and went back to bed, wondering whose turn it was this time.

JJ was still grinning when he inscribed Jamie's reply on the cupboard door with a bloody finger. He left a second message in pencil on the wall outside in case Rufshod came to paint him up come morning, telling him to leave him be this time. JJ wanted Jamie to see this.

Jamie saw it. He woke to the babble of the circus preparing itself for the coming show day and overcame a moment's surprise—he hadn't expected use of the body again for a good while.

His eyes strayed to the cupboard door and with despair he remembered last night's killing. In blood on the door were the words:

# it's a deal

He pushed a box in front of the door, hoping for some uninterrupted time to think. The plan had worked, and the plan had been to get another day as himself; JJ had taken the bait. He'd outsmarted his clown incarnation. If it could be done once, it could be done again. But somehow he had to keep it up, provoking more payback jabs and somehow blank out his mind when it came time to put on the face paint.

He went to Winston's room and knocked on the door. A sleepy voice answered, 'Aww, what now? Can't I sleep in for one bloody morning?'

Jamie went in and told him what had happened from the point Rufshod painted him up yesterday, and explained his need for more powder. Winston listened, nodding his head like he'd figured most of it out already. 'I'll do you a deal, Jamie,' he said. 'I have enough powder to keep your memories hidden from him, probably for as long as we'll need to. I hardly ever use the stuff, gives me the creeps and makes me feel plain wrong. So, if you come to me as Jamie, I'll spot you for however much you need. If you come as JJ, I'll tell you to take a hike. But in return, I want something from you.'

'Sure, anything.'

'Give me the crystal ball. I didn't want to take it, cause it's puttin' me at risk of more trouble I can do without. But I thought it over. It's too risky for JJ to hold onto it. Far too risky. Could live without him seein' our every move.'

Jamie sighed as he imagined how angry this would make JJ, but he was in no position to argue. He nodded.

'Good lad,' said Winston. 'I'll put it somewhere safe and you'll understand if I don't tell you where. Now, get yourself ready for the day. It's Kurt's birthday. Put on your best poker face. In fact if I were you, I'd use some powder straight away and paint yourself up. Better *you* decide when JJ appears than to have Rufshod bring him out when you ain't ready. If he catches you unawares and you haven't cleared your head, we'll——'

Winston stopped and cocked his head; there was a commotion out in the parlour, shouts and the sound of something breaking. 'What's this?' Winston said with a groan. 'Hell with it, they can sort it out. I'm gettin' some more sleep.'

Winston tossed him a velvet bag then threw himself back on the bed with a storm of creaking springs. Jamie thanked him and left. As he passed the parlour he heard a wooden *crack* ring out like a shot, and saw an acrobat fly through the air, landing roughly on the ground. Jamie paused to watch, keeping most of his body hidden in the hallway and poking only his head around the corner. Gonko stood near the acrobat with a two-by-four in his hands. Goshy, Doopy and Rufshod were beside him; it seemed the end of a very brief fight. 'He was doin' somethin', Gonko, I swear he was!' Doopy cried. 'Look what he had in his hand, Gonko, just look!'

Gonko bent down and picked up something from the ground, a syringe full of clear liquid. 'Right as usual, Doops,' he said. 'You always were the perceptive type. He *was* doing somethin'. He sure was.'

The acrobat was trying to get to his feet but his knee was bent at an odd angle. Gonko strolled over and gently prodded him so he fell onto his back. 'This ain't a tetanus booster, Sven, I think it's safe to say. What's the deal? What's with the whole slinking into our tent thing?'

The acrobat tried to stand again and Gonko kicked him in the chest, not so gently this time. 'You'd better let me go,' Sven spat. 'I'll have you on odd jobs the rest of your life. You'll never do another show.'

'You know the rules,' said Gonko. 'You're in our tent without our say-so. We can do whatever the fuck we like to you. Spit it out. What have you got against JJ?'

Jamie's eyes went wide.

'You know what you did,' said Sven. 'You brought it on yourselves. We owe you.'

Gonko looked around at the other clowns, confusion on his face. The acrobat tried to crawl away. Goshy began making the kettle noise. Gonko raised the two-by-four like a golfer preparing to swing, but he was interrupted by George Pilo. 'Hey!' George screamed from the doorway. 'Just what the hell do you think you're doing?'

'Hullo, George,' said Gonko, the plank still raised above his shoulder. 'I think I'm protecting our premises. Was about to give this guy a . . . what's the opposite of a facelift?'

'Squash smash face,' said Doopy. 'That's what it is, Gonko, I think so, me and Goshy was just talking about it. Squash smash face.'

'Well put, Doops. Yeah, George, this feller was sneaking in here with a murder weapon. What do you make of that?'

'I don't give a damn about your squabbles,' said George, marching to Gonko and putting his face in the position, pressed into Gonko's navel, his wet white eyes gleaming upwards balefully. 'I don't want to see you squabbling with other performers, Gonko. You're a senior member of the show. You're supposed to set an example.'

'I was setting a *kind* of example, George,' said Gonko.

'I'm cutting your pay for tonight's odd jobs,' said George. Gonko twitched, and for a moment looked like he was about to perform a squash-smash-face procedure on George Pilo——but he dropped the two-by-four and smiled pleasantly. 'Tough but fair, George, as usual,' he said.

George turned to the acrobat. 'Look at your leg, you idiot. We have a show coming up and you go and get yourself incapacitated. Drag yourself over to the MM for repairs. I'll let him know you're coming.'

A shadow of fear passed over the acrobat's face and a smirk appeared on Gonko's. George marched off. The acrobat crawled away, leaving the clowns to enjoy a round of backslapping. Jamie made himself scarce, but two minutes later Gonko stood at his door. 'JJ?'

'Yes?' said Jamie. 'I was just going to put the paint on now—'

'You been fucking with the acrobats?' said Gonko.

'No.'

'Then why do they wanna kill you?'

'I didn't know they wanted to kill me.'

'Looks like they do. Doops said this one was sneaking in here early this morning. Doops locked him in the closet then went back to bed. Acrobat got outta there somehow, tried to sneak into your room to give you a shot of something. I don't think they were treating you to a hit of morphine.'

Jamie shrugged. 'Why me?'

'That's just what I wanna know, feller. You didn't do anything to 'em? No throwing mud, anything like that?'

'No. I swear it.'

Gonko watched him closely. 'Maybe you're right, or maybe you're a top-class liar. Either way's fine with me. But don't do anything, not yet. Time'll come and we'll get ours. For now it's all happy love vibes, you got it? Live and let live and all that cutesy-pooh shit. Now is a time we clowns wanna lay low, believe me. Some joker's running around knocking shit over and whatnot. The boss won't put up with it much longer, I'll bet my brightest penny.'

Jamie nodded.

'And paint up,' said Gonko as he shut the door.

# CHAPTER 21

# TROUBLE BREWING

AROUND midday the clowns headed over to their performance tent for Kurt's birthday celebration. There was a spring in JJ's step, for he was glad things had settled down a little with his counterpart: Jamie had put the face paint on first thing this morning, so it looked like the games were over. If it stayed that way, JJ might just ease up on him . . . Little chickenshit hadn't really understood who he was dealing with at first, but he'd learned his lesson. He'd better have.

The clowns were last to arrive at the stage tent, aside from Kurt. Gonko and Rufshod laid the weakly thrashing body bag on the ground beside them. Kurt had pretended not to arrange this gathering by sending gypsies out to do it for him. As he walked in he feigned surprise, clipboard in hand as though he'd wandered in on some regular maintenance check. All on hand had seen it many a time before; as instructed, they let out a chorus of 'Surprise'. Kurt blushed, paws to his cheeks in pretend embarrassment, gushing 'This is too much!' and 'Oh, you!', and making limp-wristed *get outta here!* swishes at the air. He stood just before the stage and gazed around expectantly at everyone.

The competition for gifts had been overshadowed by the recent vandalism and was not as intense as years gone by. The acrobats had taken a safety-first approach and gave him a plastic bag full of teeth, the same gift they'd presented four years back, earning themselves diplomatic immunity in all the squabbles they'd been involved in at the time. It had been acrobats versus the sword-swallower in those days, since they'd shared a tent. The acrobats had won out, the sword-swallower had been relegated to Mugabo's tent until, in a literally heated exchange, Mugabo turned him into a pot roast. But that was in the past, and the acrobats seemed to sense they'd been outdone this time. Their glances towards the clowns, who sat smugly by their writhing body bag, were plain murderous.

The acrobats gave Kurt the teeth first up, and Kurt was pleased. Not *thrilled*, but pleased. 'Got a good feeling about this,' Gonko whispered to his troupe.

Shalice, not terribly happy with either of the Pilos over their handling of the theft of her crystal ball, went to no bother at all; she presented Kurt with an ivory-handled toothbrush—something she'd found in Sideshow Alley—a gift just good enough to avoid any serious recriminations. Kurt was graciously disappointed, sighing as might a wistful schoolgirl at a poster of some famous heartthrob, forever out of reach.

The lion tamer was clearly out of touch with Kurt's present interests, and seemed to think Kurt was into birdwatching, as he'd been a year before. He gave Kurt a caged parrot he'd taught to say 'Happy Birthday'. In the audience, Goshy bristled for some reason when the bird was unveiled, as though he'd spotted a rival. Glancing at him sidelong, JJ knew only that the more he learned about Goshy, the worse off he was.

Kurt wasn't happy with the parrot at all; his fish lips were smiling, but he said not a word of thanks and his brow darkened like storm clouds gathering. The lion tamer walked back to his seat with a tremble in his step, looking much paler than when he'd stood.

The woodchoppers surprised everyone by proving themselves somewhat on the pulse: they gave Kurt a giant crucifix they'd constructed from redwood logs. As the four of them hauled it in Kurt glowed, showering them with praise. Gonko decided the time was ripe. He motioned to Rufshod and the pair of them carried the body bag to the stage, the priest moaning and wriggling like a netted fish inside. Gonko had tied a pink ribbon around the bag at the waist. 'What's this?' said Kurt, already delighted as they laid the bag at his feet.

'Little something we thought you might like, boss,' said Gonko. 'All yours. Enjoy.' Kurt gushed again as he untied the ribbon, guessed at what it might be, joked that he hoped it wasn't another pair of socks—not that anyone had dared give him a first pair—and undid the zipper.

'What's going on?' the priest said in a croak. 'I'm thirsty . . . please . . .' He blinked at the gathered crowd, recoiled from the effusive seven-foot monster bending over him. Kurt's monstrous eyes took in the priest's collar, black robe and crucifix, and he looked like he might well burst with pleasure. 'Oh *my*!' he said. 'Is this the genuine article? Not an imitation?'

'Nothing but the best, boss,' said Gonko, grinning viciously at the crestfallen acrobats. 'No generic brands for you. Swiped him from a parish in Perth. All yours.'

Kurt was overcome. 'Oh my!' was all he could say. He gripped the priest's head in his hands, his fingers engulfing the man's skull easily. He poked a thumb into the priest's mouth, lifting a gum and inspecting the teeth as one might do to a farm dog. 'Oh *my*,' Kurt whispered.

'Since he's here, we figured maybe we could use him at Goshy's wedding,' said Gonko, 'if that's okay with you, boss. Make it official and all.'

'Oh, sure!' said Kurt, hauling the priest—who couldn't stand for cramp—over his shoulder. The priest's limp body seemed tiny so high above the ground. 'You can borrow him, of course. The rest of you, just leave your gifts by the door of my trailer. I simply must play with this one right away.' Kurt loped off and the performers cleared out of the tent.

Gonko was in high spirits as the clowns returned home. 'See the look on his face? We'll have our show back tomorrow, I'll bet my left nut.'

JJ left them to celebrate and went to his room, intent on watching what Kurt got up to with that poor bastard. He propped a barricade against his door, reached under his bed for the pillow case, and—

It was gone. Instantly he knew he'd been betrayed. He let out a scream that scraped his throat. There followed a frantic and fruitless search of his room, then JJ sat down and stared straight ahead, teeth grinding, every so often lashing his fist against his pillow and convulsing with anger. 'Jamie,' he whispered, 'this is war.'

Winston was tired, feeling the full weight of his extended years hitting him. The face paint may have been what kept them all going for as long as they did—he himself had stopped counting the years—but Winston was starting to think just being on the showgrounds was what did it. He'd stopped using the paint long ago, but his body just kept plugging on. He'd heard rumours of tricks who'd visited the show living long miserable existences after they'd been here: soulless creatures, meat and bones whose only claim to life was that their bodies still ticked over. That was certainly how Winston felt right now.

He was trying to meet up with Randolph, a tricky stunt with both clowns and acrobats on full alert against each other. Things hadn't been this tense for a good while, not since the acrobats had lost three of their performers in the last major feud. The clowns had lost two of theirs. Winston was recruited in 1836 to replace Wendell, the legendary obese clown, a 400-kilogram obscenity. Many had said Wendell's stage act— wearing a tutu, gyrating grotesquely—would have been more at home in the freak show. Some time back, that was, when the circus had moved from France to this out-of-the-way prison colony, which went and became a nation right under their feet. Before France it had been Scotland, before Scotland Greece, and before that . . . There the record got a little hazy. Winston could remember the show unpacking after the move right as he joined, after each part of the carnival had been broken to small parts and carried through the ticket gates, piece by piece.

Though Winston wore the body of an old man, he was a relatively new face here. Rufshod was newer than he, Doopy and Goshy had appeared well before him, though their history was long forgotten. They were both too warped to be younger than multiple centuries each. And Gonko? Winston had no idea. He'd heard that Gonko had been chummy with Pilo Senior . . . and Pilo senior was long, long gone.

Winston stood outside the acrobats' tent and gave a loud wolf-whistle, the signal to Randolph that he needed to talk. It got an instant response— two acrobats ran out, yelling threats. Randolph strolled out after them. 'No, he's not worth it,' he said contemptuously, standing between Winston and the others. 'Not this one. Old fogey's about to drop dead without our help, I'd say.'

'Don't come down here,' said Sven, his leg wrapped in thick bandages. 'I'm telling you, if I see you by this door again, I will snap your neck.'

'That goes for your friends, too,' said Randolph. Winston could hear the relief in his voice.

'Don't know what your problem is,' said Winston. 'I always come by here on my way to the freak show.' His eyes met Randolph's for an instant—message sent.

'Get out of our sight,' said Randolph, spitting at Winston's feet and turning on his heel. The other acrobats followed him inside.

A few minutes later they met in the shadows of the freak show.

'What is it?' said Randolph.

'What's going on?' said Winston. 'One of your guys tried to bump off Jamie.'

'Yes. Retaliation.'

'Why Jamie? He's one of us. Why not take out Rufshod, or Doopy?'

'Jamie—no, JJ, is more dangerous than the others, Winston. He knows about us, for God's sake. It was a bad move to bring him to the meeting.'

'We've got that covered. Jamie's found a way to keep his thoughts hidden from JJ. Blocks his memory with the powder. JJ wakes up not knowing a thing.'

'And how do we know this?'

'I live with them. I see JJ every day.'

Randolph looked exasperated. 'And how am I supposed to get the others to change their minds about him?'

'I don't know, maybe you can't. But there's better targets than him, that's all. JJ could come in useful, somehow.'

'He could also get us all fucking *killed*, Winston.'

Winston sighed and rubbed his temples. 'I can't let you do it. Jamie's a good kid. JJ's an utter bastard, but I think Jamie's got him worked out.'

'Jesus, Winston . . .'

'It would take a load off my mind having him dead, believe me. But I have enough on my conscience. He didn't ask to be here, Randolph.'

Randolph said nothing but gave him a look that said plenty: *Neither did I, nor you, nor anyone the hell else who works here, nor any of the visitors lured here, nor the victims of what the fortune-teller does, nor, nor, nor . . .*

Winston sighed again. 'Just . . . I don't know, warn me if they're going to attack. Okay? Some signal. Let me know. I'll save him myself.'

Randolph turned to leave without argument or agreement. Winston watched him go—and came very close to calling him back and telling him to go ahead and do it, go ahead and kill him. Very close.


Around three in the afternoon a letter arrived for each performer, hand-delivered by Doopy. Doopy had a hard time giving the letters to the acrobats and came away with a black eye for his efforts, which he told Gonko he got from 'falling over, honest' (though why he lied he wasn't even sure himself).

The letters were invitations to Goshy's wedding. Gonko had suggested they fast-track the event to tonight, as it was doubtful the priest would be in any shape to read vows much longer. Doopy had a hell of a time convincing Goshy this was the way to go, because (he guessed) Goshy wanted a little longer to bask in anticipation. (He was certainly not getting cold feet.) What Doopy would never tell anyone—never ever in the whole wide world, honest—was that it was *he* who put the ring on her stem.

There wasn't much time to prepare the vows, and Doopy wasn't all that literary-minded, so he asked Kurt Pilo real nice if the priest could do it for him. As Doopy left Kurt's trailer he passed Shalice on her way there, and something about her body language and the smile she shot him worried him more than a black eye ever could.

'It's an I'm gonna get you smile,' Doopy mumbled to himself, scratching his head. Then, straightening up in panic, he cried, '*It's an I'm gonna get you smile!*'

He sprinted back to Kurt's trailer, muttering, 'Uh, gosh, uh, oh, gee, gosh . . .' and stood with his ear to the door. Spying on the boss was a bad idea, but spying on Shalice was just fine, which resulted in an okay idea. He couldn't hear what she was saying, but Kurt's voice carried through the trailer door clearly. 'Are you sure it's him?'

Silence. Then: 'Are you positive?'

Silence. Then: 'Well, I'd never have guessed it would be *him*. I thought it was George. Oh well. We'll have to do something about that, won't we?'

Doopy heard footsteps approach the door and he sprinted away as fast as he could.

*Who's him?* Doopy wondered fretfully. *Him's not me, is he?*

When he got back to the clown tent he heard Goshy making the kettle noise and soon forgot his other troubles—Goshy was upset! He ran to Goshy's bedroom and saw his brother standing still, arms locked at his sides, the skin on his face peeled back in distressed rings. Goshy was about to scream, oh yes he was. 'Goshy!' Doopy whispered. 'What *is* it? What *is* it, Goshy?'

And then he saw: the ring had fallen from his fiancée's stem and lay on the floor. 'Oh, Goshy!' Doopy cried. 'Oh, oh no! Oh noooo!'

'HEEEEEEEE—*EEEEEEEEEE!*' Goshy screamed, 'HEEEEEEEE—*EEEEEEEEE!*'


'What the bleeding Christ is that RACKET?' Gonko roared. In Goshy's room he saw the commotion. 'Oh you fucking morons,' he snapped. 'Here.' He picked the engagement ring up off the floor and stuffed it back on the stem.

'Thanks, Gonko,' Doopy called as Gonko marched off. 'By the way, she's gonna get him, but I don't know who him is, but it could be us.'

'Yeah, great,' Gonko said over his shoulder. 'Ever considered being a writer, Doops? Shakespeare would be jealous.' As Gonko passed the parlour he heard Kurt's voice calling, 'Knock kno-*ock!*'

Shalice was standing beside him at the doorway—how curious. 'Hey boss,' said Gonko, frowning. 'What brings you here?'

'Oh, sad business,' Kurt said, stepping inside. 'I heard from someone—' he nodded none too subtly at Shalice, 'that the crystal ball thief is here in your tent.'

'Crystal ball?' said Gonko. 'What, hers? Who do you think has it?'

'Winston,' said Shalice, giving Gonko a cold stare. 'Your friend Winston.'

'Winston? No way,' said Gonko. 'What the hell makes you think he has it?'

Shalice smiled and tapped her forehead with a long manicured nail. 'My "spooky powers" as you would put it. So tell me, was he acting alone or under someone's instructions?'

Kurt smiled serenely as he looked from one to the other.

'You tell me,' said Gonko, 'use your spooky powers.'

'Which room is his?' Kurt said pleasantly.

Gonko led them to Winston's room. It was locked and Winston wasn't home. Gonko kicked the door in. Shalice brushed past him and started digging through the clothes and boxes. 'It's here somewhere,' she said. 'I saw the old pervert this morning. He has been enjoying free peepshows every day.'

Gonko watched with narrowed eyes as the fortune-teller turned over everything in sight. *Peepshows* did not sound like the Winston he knew. She started tapping on the walls, looking for an echo to reveal some hidden hollow. 'All right, cut the shit,' said Gonko. 'Winston's one of my most trusted performers and—'

'Aha!' Shalice said, a gleam in her eyes. She pried with her nails at a patch of wall painted a slightly lighter colour than the surrounding wall, and with a *crack* it came away. She reached her arm down into the hollow and, grinning, brought the crystal ball out from its hiding place.

Gonko ran a hand over his face and sighed. 'Ah, boss, I'm as shocked as you are.'

Kurt was still smiling serenely, but Gonko knew Kurt and could see the disappointment in his face; and he was glad it was only disappointment. 'Oh, I understand,' said Kurt. 'We'll talk about it after the wedding, though, don't you think?'

'Your call, boss,' said Gonko.

'It is, isn't it?' said Kurt. He loped away. Shalice followed him, not glancing at Gonko as she passed. He watched them go, then slammed his boot into the wall, punching a hole in the plaster. 'Winston . . .' he said with a sigh, and left it unfinished. The rest of it went something like this: *You have some explaining to do, old feller.*


While Shalice was finding the crystal ball, Winston was at Mugabo's tent on George Pilo's instructions. Rumour had it Mugabo was in a bad state, letting no one near his hut, which spelled trouble the day before show day. Winston had no luck getting in there either; the magician was worked up like never before. After calling platitudes through Mugabo's door for an hour Winston gave up and headed home. Now at least two acts were scratched from tomorrow's show, and the afternoon was young——with a little more pandemonium, maybe they could get the whole show day cancelled. It would be the first time a show had been cancelled in Winston's memory.

Just before he stepped through the door to the clowns' tent he was hit by a sudden bad feeling, and a second later saw Gonko sitting at the card table, staring at him through narrowed eyes. He did not look happy. 'Have a seat, Winston,' he said.

A wild fluttering thought flashed through Winston's head: *Something's wrong——JJ told. He remembered everything and he told. It's all over.*

He sat down and it struck him that Gonko looked saddened rather than angry, which seemed more ominous still. Gonko looked him in the eye and said, 'What have you got to say for yourself?'

Winston shifted on his chair and fought to keep a quaver from his voice. 'What do you mean, Gonks?'

'Kurt and Shalice found it,' Gonko said, slowly and quietly. 'In your room. I don't care that you had it, but how could you let them find out? I thought you were smarter than that.'

For a moment Winston was genuinely confused, then a rush of relief came on him. The ball, that was all. The bigger secrets were still secret. 'Ohh,' he said. 'They found it.'

Gonko's eyes flashed. 'Don't sound so damn happy about it.'

'Happy? No, just didn't understand you at first.' Winston tried to think fast. 'I saw the ball lying around, out in the open. Knew it'd be trouble if it got found, so I put it in a safe place. Thought it was a safe place, anyway.'

Gonko nodded; he looked satisfied with that, though it was very hard to read him in situations like this. 'Bad timing, Winston,' he said. 'We needed to cash in on Kurt's birthday, but that's fucked it now. Good and proper.'

'Ah, damn it——I'm sorry, Gonks.'

'Yeah, yeah,' Gonko said, sighing. 'I don't know how they found it; probably she had one of those visions. But that doesn't matter. You don't put a foot wrong too often, so I'll let this one slide. *I* will, but I don't know if Kurt will.'

Winston straightened up in his chair and wiped his brow. 'Kurt? What did Kurt say?'

'He wants a chat with you. Wants me to send you over there right away. He probably sees this as serious shit, after he specifically asked for the ball back. He'd see it as directly disobeying his orders——which it was, actually. And Kurt's not in the best of moods lately, with all this . . . *freedom* stuff.'

'Jesus . . .'

'Nah, don't sweat it too much,' said Gonko. His eyes looked closed, but he was watching Winston very closely. 'Go see him, get it over with, then forget about it. You ain't let me down before . . . I'm guessing you won't do it again.'

Winston nodded and stood but his legs gave from under him and he grabbed the table for support. He left and Gonko's eyes followed him out. The clown boss sat there for a while, lost in thought.

In stunned calm Winston knocked on Kurt's trailer door. He wondered whether Shalice had really had a vision or whether JJ had squealed on him out of spite. 'Hmmm?' Kurt's jovial voice called from within.

Winston managed to keep the stammer from his voice. 'It's me, Mr Pilo.'

'Oh, Winston! Come in.'

He opened the trailer door, stepped inside and froze when he saw Shalice sitting in a chair beside Kurt's desk. *Oh, wonderful,* he thought. This was going to make lying very tricky work, and the excuses he'd come up with on his way to the trailer were now useless.

Kurt clasped his hands together on the desk, resting them on a thick Bible. 'Winston,' he said, 'I wanted to ask you something . . . What was it again? . . . Oh yes. What were you doing with the fortune-teller's crystal ball?'

'Well, boss,' said Winston. 'I don't really know. Can't say what possessed me to keep it in my room after I found it. But I want you to know I'm very sorry.'

Kurt didn't react to this at all. There was a very thick silence, and when Shalice spoke Winston was almost grateful, even though she said: 'You did not *find it.* You are lying. I can see it on your face.'

Winston kept his eyes fixed on Kurt. 'Boss, I'm sorry.'

'Was *thou shalt not steal* one of those, what do you call them?' said Kurt.

Unsure who he was addressing, Winston stayed quiet. After a moment Shalice said, 'Commandments? Yes.'

'Hm,' said Kurt, tapping an index finger on the Bible. 'Then this is a bit serious, isn't it? I don't approve of stealing. And you were spying on me, too. Was that one of those commandments? Don't spy on me?'

'No sir!' Winston said, wondering how JJ could be so unbelievably stupid. 'I never even looked in the thing. Swear to . . . to God. I didn't steal it from the fortune-teller either.' With effort Winston stopped himself from saying more.

Kurt glanced at Shalice and while Kurt's eyes were averted Winston felt like he'd been released from a hard grip. She nodded reluctantly. 'Truth. *This* time.'

'Hmm,' said Kurt. 'It's not so serious then, I suppose. What worries me, Winston, is that since Shalice lost her ball, there's been a number of *incidents*. Do you know the ones I mean?'

This was the moment. Winston summoned what willpower he had left to keep every muscle in his face completely still, his voice even. 'Yes sir. I think so.'

'Hmm.' Kurt tapped on his Bible again with a thick finger, his long sharp nail gouging into the hard cover, *tap tap tap*. 'I'm all for a little sport here and there,' said Kurt. 'Competition helps the show. Would you repeat that for me, Winston?'

Winston swallowed. 'Competition helps the show, sir.'

Kurt nodded. 'That's a very good point, Winston. But the acrobat tent was a very expensive piece of equipment. It's going to take a long time to get it up and running again.'

*Tap tap tap.* The drumming got faster, drilling into Winston's head like Chinese water torture. He tried to concentrate but there was no hiding the quaver in his voice now. 'Yes sir, I imagine so,' he said.

*Tap tap tap.* Two monstrous eyes bored into Winston like hot white lights, and he felt he was about to scream. One more second of that glare and he was going to wet his pants, turn tail and run.

Suddenly Kurt sat back in his chair and unclasped his hands. Winston flinched back at the sudden movement. The Bible on the desk had a hole in its cover as though it had been shot. 'Very good,' Kurt said lightly. 'I'm glad we had this chat, Winston.'

Winston started. Had his ears deceived him? The way Kurt's questions were headed, with a living lie detector by his side, he had been bracing himself for catastrophe. 'Thank you, Mr Pilo,' he said after a moment's silence.

'Hmm,' said Kurt. Then, as though an afterthought, 'Oh, but stop by the funhouse tonight, please. I'd like you to see the matter manipulator. Can't have people thinking I'm a soft touch, I hope you understand.'

Winston's mouth went dry and his knees buckled under him. 'Yes, Mr Pilo,' he whispered.

'Good man,' said Kurt. 'Off you go then. Enjoy the wedding.'


Winston wandered away from the trailer in haunted shambling steps, looking as dazed as the tricks who wandered through on show day. Shalice passed him without a word, feeling justice had been partially served, which was about as much as she could hope for in this charade. But now there were more pressing matters, among them a certain chain of events she had to quickly reconsider. To secure the Pilos' help in retrieving her crystal ball, she'd stressed to George that if she had it she could be monitoring these vandal attacks. To emphasise the point, she'd set about staging an attack of her own. The dominos were toppling already, she could see this as she walked through the showgrounds. Two carnies passed her carrying a crate of fireworks to the funhouse, as per a written order fraudulently signed in George's name by Sven of the acrobats, who intended to use the fireworks in an attack on the clowns. Shalice had set this up the night before by watering a patch of ground on the path outside the acrobats' tent until it was slippery. A dwarf passing the tent had slipped, dropping a glass cabinet he was carrying to the freak show. Investigating the noise, Sven had presumed the clowns were up to something, and conceived the fireworks plot as a shooting star streaked across the sky.

Like the shooting star, the dwarf's role in this had been destined, part of a natural chain of events Shalice had hijacked by watering the ground. It was that complex and that simple, like switching a track lever at a train intersection; all that was needed was a map of the future's landscape to see what went where, and when. It had taken her three hours of meditation, examination of the tarot cards and consultation of her star charts and fate-webbing charts. Had anyone seen her watering that patch of ground, would they have been in any position to accuse her of an untimely explosion?

She probably had time to alter that train of events and stop the conclusion, but now that she thought about it, she owed the Pilos no favours. Besides, she had other fish to fry—or one other at least, and his name was Mugabo. She had some courses of action ready to roll for the magician but she was holding off, waiting for more clues to shed some light on this business. What was his beef, for heaven's sake?

As yet no more visions had come, but no matter—the ball was hers again. She would be watching the magician like a hawk.

Him and, for the moment, no one else. The rest of the circus could burn to the ground for all she cared.

# CHAPTER 22

# THE WEDDING

'NO, Goshy, you can't see the bride before the wedding, you just can't. It ain't *tradition*, Goshy, it ain't *tradition*!'

'*HMMMMM! HMMMMM!*'

He had one hour to wait.

The dwarfs and carnies set up the clowns' stage tent for the wedding, with Doopy overseeing it and making a nuisance of himself by complaining that it wasn't 'purty enough'. But they got it as purty as they could at short notice, and it seemed to satisfy Goshy. He'd acquired a suit from somewhere and his brother led him through the tent, asking his opinions on this and that. He wasn't upset, that was all anyone knew for sure.

Doopy had never seen the bride so radiant. He'd lured Goshy out of his room and convinced him to stare out the parlour window for twenty minutes while he'd decorated her. He'd put on some tinsel, Christmas lights and bulbs.

By midafternoon all were gathered. True to his word Kurt brought the priest, who stood before the plastic seats with wide haunted eyes. He held in his shaking hand the marriage vows. On a table before him Goshy's bride sat in her pot, thin yellow-green fronds swaying gently.

Goshy was coaxed into the tent, waddling like some kind of mutant penguin in his suit. Some bridesmaids had been found among the gypsies, and they stood waiting like everyone else; sullen, staring in silent revulsion at the plant and at Goshy. All who were able to decline their invitations to the wedding had done so, and the acrobats were certainly nowhere to be seen. Fishboy, Gonko, Nugget, Yeti and Kurt Pilo were the only guests who were there voluntarily.

Under the close and affectionate scrutiny of Kurt, the priest—who had parted company with his two front teeth—began reading the vows. From the look on his face it was clear he was holding onto one last thread of hope he'd wake from this nightmare. His voice trembled as he began. 'Dearly beloved, we are gathered here today . . . Ah, to witness the union, ah . . . between . . .'

He shook himself and peered around at everyone. Kurt laid a hand gently on his shoulder as though for moral support. The priest flinched, shut his eyes and with difficulty continued. 'To witness the union between, ah, Gosh . . . Goshy? And . . .' Doopy bustled over and whispered something in the priest's ear. 'And this *Athyrium filix-femina*. Uh, the importance of love is . . . all through God's teachings . . . and, ah . . .' The priest swayed on his feet, about to faint. Kurt whispered something in his other ear, evidently a prompt to cut to the chase. 'If anyone here can see why these . . . these two shouldn't be wed, may he speak now or forever hold his peace.'

The silence was the loudest thing JJ had ever heard.

'I pronounce you . . .' said the priest, 'oh God help us.'

Kurt slapped his paws together in hearty applause. Gradually the rest of the gathering joined in. Doopy nudged Goshy in the ribs. Goshy had seemed confused and startled throughout the ceremony, arms locked at his sides, eyes wide. As the applause wound down everyone held their hands to their ears; a single burst of high-pitched sonic assault shot from Goshy's mouth, a note that rang out for no longer than a second, striking all ears present like a bullet. 'What's that one mean?' said Rufshod as the clowns lowered their hands from their ears.

'I think it means he's happy,' said Gonko, 'but that's a guess.'

The gathering dispersed much quicker than they'd coalesced. JJ ran ahead of the others. He'd broken into Rufshod's room earlier to steal some powder, as he had something in mind for young Jamie. He went into Goshy's room, opened the cupboard, perched his backside on the bag of fertiliser inside and frantically scrubbed off his face paint. He slid the cupboard door shut—it was a tight fit, and his knees were pressed up around his chin. With some difficulty he melted the stolen powder and wished for exactly two hours sleep.

When the bride and groom entered the room, he didn't stir.


Jamie woke right on time in the cramped confines of Goshy's cupboard. He wondered where he was, why he was here, and why he could smell fertiliser. He clutched at his lower back, grimacing. Straight lines of light marked the outline of the closet door. He held his eye to the gap, trying to work out if he was in some kind of immediate danger, but could see nothing outside.

Before he could remember what JJ had been doing up until he slept, he heard a noise close by. Strange noise, too, possibly made by a human throat, but it was hard to tell—a kind of high-pitched chortling, a mix between a whistle and a throat gargling water. There was a papery, rustling sound in the background.

As quietly as he could, Jamie slid the cupboard door open. Lantern light flooded in.

He saw two bulbous fleshy pads, wrinkled and pink, skin that looked like it had never seen sunlight. There was a trail of stubbly hair running down the middle, as was a single drop of sweat. It was a backside, sitting atop two creased fatty thighs, connected to calves, to ankles, around which a pair of clown pants sat in a bunch. The whole package was moving in a grotesque steady rhythm that could only be sexual, were there not something so unearthly about it. Jamie's eyes travelled upwards and he saw that waist high to the apparition was a table with a plant sitting on it, the species *Athyrium filix-femina*, feathery yellow-green leaves. It was decorated with tinsel.

Jamie understood then that JJ had locked him in the honeymoon suite. Payback.

Forward and back Goshy's backside plunged and withdrew. His throat made that horrible gargling whistle sound as the plant's leaves shook with his thrusts. The buttocks loomed over Jamie larger than life. The chirping sounds became more urgent as Goshy upped the pace. *Oh Jesus*, Jamie thought. Shivering, he slid the door back in place. The wood creaked.

Goshy turned around, his face pulled back into fleshy rings, eyes bulging. His penis, six solid purple-pink inches of it encased in a condom, wobbled from side to side. His face flashed with livid alien fury. Then came the screams.

The noise pierced every room in the tent, short jabs of violent sound, each outburst louder than the last. Jamie huddled back in the cupboard, shivering, while above him Goshy loomed, pants still down, erect and wailing. The plant sat mute on the table. Someone pounded at the door. Goshy stopped hollering and seemed to come to some kind of decision. He reached for something on the floor then took a step towards Jamie. It was a wood saw.

'HELP!' Jamie screamed.

'Goshy!' Doopy cried.

Gonko and Doopy kicked down the door and surveyed the scene: Goshy, armed, aroused; Jamie cowering at his feet. Goshy turned to face them and Jamie seized the moment, scurrying out like a rabbit and sprinting through the door, the parlour and out into the showgrounds. He ran till his legs could carry him no further, then he bent over, retching.

After a time, he took in his surrounds and found he was near the fence plank, the exit to that odd space outside the showgrounds. Not knowing where else to go, he pushed on the board until it loosened, then stepped out there.

Back in the clowns' tent Gonko lay on the floor of Goshy's room, mildly concerned. He was concerned he would soon die of laughter.

As directed by the bogus orders, the crate of fireworks was left by the funhouse, where Sven had believed no one would stumble across it since, to his knowledge, hanging around the funhouse was not anyone's idea of a good time. The fireworks were covered by an empty potato sack, and after Sven's visit out here earlier in the day the load included five extra sticks of dynamite. He was considering nuking the entire clown tent in one blast, but he wouldn't get his chance this time around, thanks to Shalice and a carnival employee known as Slimmy the smoking dwarf.

It was Slimmy's habit to sneak out of his house every evening at six and enjoy a cigar in the shadows of the funhouse, away from his enemies amongst the short folk. Slimmy's bad habit included throwing his lit match at the discarded tyre lying on its side four feet from the crate on which he sat. He'd been keeping score—so far he'd dropped the match into the tyre 12566 times, just better than 50 per cent. That afternoon Slimmy's daily routine, which had gone unchanged for sixty years, would prove costly. Slimmy lit up, tossed the match and watched it fly through the air, glance off the tyre's rim, and land just out of sight. Slimmy grunted with annoyance and marked a notch in the *Miss* column in his mind.

The match landed right on top of a fuse trailing out of the box of explosives like a tail. Slimmy heard the faint hissing noise as the fuse burned, but still had time to enjoy three-quarters of his cigar before the blast. He died doing something he liked.

The blast ripped away one of the funhouse walls and roared through the carnival. Every head except Shalice's turned towards the sound. Flying debris shot skyward and fell as lethal missiles onto roofs and paths, ripping holes in tents and smashing windows. Two dwarfs who'd been on the verge of fisticuffs over a game of dice had their dispute settled for them as they were flattened beneath a section of airborne roof.

In the clown tent Gonko sat up, muttered 'Goddamn,' then ran out into the parlour just in time to see a brick land in the doorway. He had a sudden impulse to check up on Winston.

He went round to each of the clowns' rooms, knocking or pressing his ear to the panels and listening. Winston and JJ were both absent.

# PART 4

FREEDOM

*Poly*
*Topsy Turvy*
*Hang upside down*
*Fall to the ground*

CAROUSEL

# CHAPTER 23

# SHOCKWAVES

IT was moonless and starless in the artificial carnival sky, helpful conditions for the freedom rebels sneaking out to their emergency meeting, and in the circumstances one of few blessings they were able to count. Their mood was mournful as they could see their brief and long overdue resistance coming to a close, relegated as they were again to utmost secrecy, never able to know when prying eyes were watching. None of them had expected Jamie to appear tonight, and when he found them, sitting in a mood of grim silence, their glaring looks made him wonder if he'd have been safer taking his chances with Goshy. One push, one push . . .

Randolph stood up. 'And just *what* are you doing here?' he said. 'Come to gloat now that we're all dead?'

'What do you mean?' said Jamie, moving as far as he could from the edge of the chasm.

'It wasn't anyone's fault,' said Fishboy, laying a restraining hand on Randolph's shoulder. 'Have a seat, Jamie.'

Randolph backed off, spitting and cursing under his breath. 'Not anyone's fault, but Randolph is quite right,' said Fishboy. 'We are as good as finished now. The Pilos have their eyes and ears back. There's nothing we can do.'

'We could take it again, couldn't we?' said Jamie. 'We took it once already.'

'Any volunteers?' Fishboy said quietly. 'Winston, show him.'

Without speaking Winston lifted his shirt, and Jamie had to hold back a scream. A burst of glowing red light poured out like blood, and it looked as though the middle of his chest had been dug out and replaced with hot coals. The skin around it was smoking and blackened. There was a smell of cooking meat.

'Hurts,' Winston said in a quiet voice. 'You know, the pain was pretty bad. The matter manipulator said I could come back in a week, get it put back to normal. Used the powder, asked for the pain to stop. Didn't make it stop completely. Less, though, just feels hot now. It's the smell that gets me. The smell's a bit much.'

Jamie felt a sting in the back of his throat; this could so easily have been him. 'I'm sorry,' he said, putting a hand on Winston's shoulder.

'Not your fault,' said Winston. 'I think . . . fortune-teller had a vision, that's all. It's okay, though, she doesn't know about the rest of us.'

'What's next for us?' said one of the dwarfs. 'Show day tomorrow. We can still stop it.'

'No,' said Winston in a distant voice. 'I think maybe we should forget about all that. If you decide to stay in the show, make the best of it, get by. There's worse things than being here. If you want out, you know what to do. Not worth fighting them. World's survived them so far, thousands of years . . . Not worth fighting them.'

Fishboy's strange face was set like stone. 'No one would blame you, Winston, if you chose to bow out. But I won't. Doing nothing would hurt worse than fighting them.'

'Don't be so sure of that,' said Winston. 'They went pretty easy on me. Could've been worse. Should see the sorry bastards he keeps up there in his studio . . .' Winston trailed off and stood to leave. 'See you all later. Need some sleep. Need another dose of powder. It's starting to warm up a bit more.'

They watched him leave in a slow, shuffling stupor. The lion tamer ran after him to help him cross the narrow path safely. When he was out of sight, Fishboy spoke: 'Can anyone here surrender the fight after you've seen what they did to our friend?'

'No,' said isolated voices in the audience—without much conviction, Jamie thought.

'You see what they do to rebels,' said Fishboy. 'We've got to keep pushing. The Pilos have their eyes and ears back but they can't watch everywhere at once. I am willing to risk myself to strike them. Are any here unwilling to do the same?'

'No,' said Jamie. Randolph looked at him with surprise and contempt. Jamie met his gaze. 'I'll do whatever it takes,' he said.

'Prove yourself,' said the acrobat.

'How?'

'Come now, Randolph . . .' said Fishboy.

'What?' said Jamie, and now his temper was kicking in. He stood up, fists clenched. The dwarfs watched him with interest, as though anticipating a fight. 'How can I prove myself?' he said.

'What we have to do,' said Fishboy, talking over the top of him in tones of laboured patience, 'is shock Kurt Pilo to his core. He's never had anything but fawning obedience. We need to make him feel the rug is being pulled, even if it's just an illusion.'

'How?' said Jamie, still eye to eye with the acrobat. 'I'll do whatever you want. The riskiest part of the job. Whatever it is. Name it.'

Fishboy peered at him, gills puffing in and out. 'Are you quite sure?' he said.

'Yes.'

'Very well, Jamie. You can have the job I was going to assign to Randolph: the break-in.'

'A break-in? Okay, fine. Where?'

'Kurt's trailer,' said Randolph, and he smiled. *Here's where you back out,* the smile said. 'Break into the trailer, trash it. The job's all yours.'

Before Jamie could respond, heads turned towards the narrow path; Winston was running towards them. His steps were unsteady and he looked in imminent danger of dropping over the edge; dust and pebbles kicked up by his shoes scattered over the side of the cliff, lost forever. When he made it around the narrow bend many of them sighed with relief. He leaned one arm on the fence and struggled to catch his breath. His eyes were wide.

'What is it?' Fishboy said, jogging over to him. The others followed.

'Something happened,' said Winston. He gulped in some air before continuing, panting between words: 'There's been an attack. On the funhouse . . . explosion. Everyone get back there now, everyone . . . got to account for themselves. Hurry.'

'But this wasn't any of us?' said one of the dwarfs, cocking his bushy eyebrow around at the others. 'Was it?'

'Anyone involved?' said Fishboy. No one raised their hand. Fishboy turned back to Winston. 'Tell us everything you know, and make it quick.'

'Don't know much,' said Winston. 'Just heard from a carnie, half the funhouse, blown apart. Pilos are over there. Kurt's gone strange. He's . . . changing.'

Fishboy went rigid. 'Changing? What do you mean, changing?'

'Changing shape, his face. Talking funny . . . I think this has gotten to him. Think he's cracking up. Come on, *get back in there.* Everyone.'

The group began filing back around the path. Fishboy held up a hand and said, 'Wait!' He paused and looked to be thinking hard, quickly. 'Okay,' he said, 'listen. Everyone step up the attacks! For the rest of the night, forget any dangers and go, full steam ahead. Some of us will be caught, punished and killed—or worse—but never mind that. This could be the last sacrifice we ever have to make. This could be the last night of the circus! Jamie, go through with your mission—now, while Kurt's away from his trailer.'

'What exactly do you want me to do there?' said Jamie, for the first time actually considering what he'd volunteered for.

'Come, use your head,' Fishboy said with annoyance. 'You know what will get to Kurt. Defiance. So *defy* him, Jamie, for heaven's sake. Attack his personal space and make it nasty. Go! If you're not up to it, speak now and I'll send someone else.'

Jamie groaned. As he ran back towards the pathway he heard Fishboy telling Winston to 'execute the Goshy plan, straight away'. Jamie wondered what the hell that meant, and felt vaguely comforted not to have drawn that assignment. He took one last look back and saw Fishboy slapping backs and barking instructions.

Well, if JJ really wanted to see Kurt lose his grip, he might get the chance—if Jamie lived long enough to put on his face paint one more time. He climbed through the gap in the fence, took a deep breath then sprinted off towards Kurt's trailer.

The explosion was an hour old. A considerable crowd had gathered to watch. The side of the funhouse had been peeled back like a scab, and sickly red light poured out into the night air like blood leaking into water. On the upper floor was the matter manipulator, now getting some unwelcome fresh air, in the spotlight for the first time in his shadowy life. The pasty-faced little man stared out at the crowd staring in, his studio around him looking like a hotel room in hell. The back wall was made of flesh, a flat pulsating web of skin and veins. Horrible creations made of human and animal parts lay dying and bleeding, strewn across the room by the explosion, some embedded in the wall. This was where the freaks were made, where rule-breakers were punished, where every so often one or two tricks were donated as playthings for the flesh sculptor. The man himself appeared caught in the headlights, unable to move. Eventually he crawled out of sight behind one of his pulsating statues, leaving the crowd to worry about something that disturbed them more: Kurt Pilo.

Kurt and George had both appeared on the scene almost immediately after the blast, but on seeing his brother's mood George had fled quickly. Kurt's lips were twisted upwards, the anatomy of a smile. His big yellow teeth showed through his parted lips and strange laughter rumbled from the back of his throat, as though his teeth were cage bars trapping in some gleeful lunatic. Hardened carnies who had until now believed they'd seen it all shied away from the proprietor as he prowled through the wreckage, laughing that laugh.

'Oh, ho ho ho ho, ho ho *hoooo*,' Kurt chortled. It appeared he was trying to take this incident as a practical joke at his expense, and was fighting tooth and nail to hang on to a semblance of his normal good cheer. The strain was immense, and showing. As Winston had reported, Kurt's face had indeed undergone a change; his eyes glowed savagely white, the tanned skin on his cheeks was spread thin like it might snap, and it appeared his jaw had lengthened. His teeth were pressing hard against the stretched skin on his cheeks. His hands were clenched and shaking. 'Oh, ho ho *hoooo*,' he said. 'Well now, well now, isn't this something, ho ho ho, someone's having a laugh, there's, ohhhh ho *hoooo*, there's, ho ho, traitors, and I'm . . .' He trailed off with a sound like a crocodile growling from deep primitive depths before the laugh faded back in. He prowled through the mess, plaster and glass crunching under his feet. The crowd began to back away.

Gonko was among them, watching his boss through narrowed eyes. He had seen Kurt stirred up before, a very long time ago. It was not a pretty sight. *He's stirring up now*, Gonko thought. *Actually getting madder by the second. This could get ugly. Might be a fine time to get scarce* . . . Gonko got scarce without further ado.

Kurt's shirt had begun to swell around the shoulders. He let loose a particularly loud burst of laughter and the mystery lump of flesh ripped the back of his shirt, sprouting into a mighty hump. The crowd dispersed completely.


Back in the clown tent, Gonko saw Winston backing away from the front door. Gonko nodded to him, glad to see he was there and out of trouble's way, then he paused—Winston had one hand behind his back, hiding something. 'What's that in your hand, feller?' said Gonko.

'Nothing, Gonks,' said Winston. 'See?' He brought his hand around to the front—it was empty. 'Why the questions?'

'Something heavy's going down,' said Gonko. 'I'm rounding everyone up. Now ain't the time for games.'

'I'll go fetch JJ, if you like,' said Winston.

Gonko nodded. 'You do that.' Gonko gave him a measuring look that said: *I know you're up to something, old guy, but is it something I need to know about, or something I don't want to know about?*

Winston supposed it was the former. Tucked into the back of his pants was a bunch of feathery yellow-green leaves. What Gonko hadn't noticed—thank the stars—was the thin trail stretching from Winston back to Goshy's room. The trail was destined to end at the fortune-teller's hut. Winston took a deep breath and headed that way, ignoring the pain in his chest as the glowing patch there began to heat up.


Meanwhile, over at Kurt's trailer, Jamie was trying to keep himself under control. Adrenaline was making his hands shake. It seemed Kurt would never suspect anyone of possessing the gall to break into his trailer, for the door was not only unlocked but slightly ajar. Jamie took a deep breath, reflected that keeping one's damn mouth shut occasionally could prove a survival advantage, then up the steps and in he went. It smelled like a zoo in the cramped dark trailer, lit only by a small gas lantern on the desk, moths and mosquitoes hovering around it. Jesus looked down at him from half a dozen plastic crucifixes. 'Nice touch, Mr Pilo,' Jamie whispered. 'Thanks for that.'

Here went nothing. He started by ripping up the Bibles piled on the desk. Each page of each book had been coloured in completely with highlighter pen. Jamie dropped the ripped pages and covers on the floor. Was this an adequate mess? He didn't think so. What would JJ do? He would know how to make a scene here. Maybe he'd do something along these lines . . .

Jamie grimaced and dropped his pants. Propping himself on the desk, he unleashed everything he had, bowels and bladder, not easy in the circumstances. He wiped himself with Bible pages and stuck them to the wall. He took a crucifix from the wall and used it to spread the mess over the desk. The piss ran off in rivulets, dribbling to the floor. What the hell else could he do here? The filing cabinet against the back wall, behind the desk . . . He tugged at it and, with a noise that made him wince, it toppled over. The top two drawers came loose, spilling their contents— not paperwork, as Jamie had expected, but thousands of small white lumps that fell and scattered like hail over the floor. Teeth. Thousands and thousands of teeth.

He'd been here no more than a couple of minutes, but figured he'd done enough. As he turned to leave there was a bumping sound from the desk and a low moan. The moment of panic was like an electric shock; he stared at the door, so delirious with terror that he actually saw Kurt standing there, smiling serenely, bestial eyes promising death. He blinked and it was gone. He examined the desk and saw a small lever like a handbrake by the bottom drawer. He tugged at it, not knowing what to expect, and a spring released. There was the sound of wood sliding, and a heavy drawer slid outwards towards the trailer door. There inside a hollowed-out compartment was the priest, Kurt's birthday present, lying shivering with the eyes of a frightened animal.

Jamie reached down and undid the ropes knotted around the priest's wrists. The priest struggled and tried to fight him. 'Shh, I'm letting you out,' Jamie said. 'Don't make a sound, okay?'

'Thank God,' the priest said, though the words came out strangely. Jamie saw why; the man had not a tooth left in his mouth.

'Can you walk?' said Jamie. The priest stood and half-collapsed. Jamie lent him a shoulder and they stumbled out of the trailer.


In her hut, Shalice watched the magician in her crystal ball. She had left the hut in darkness and her caravan lights on so that, should he decide it was time to strike, she would have some extra time to make an escape. Twice he had resolutely stepped out with a gleam in his eyes, and both times paused, thought it over and headed back inside. The rest of the time his mood swung from furious rage to utter depressed stillness and blank stares. During the quiet times he would mutter to himself, gradually working up to one of the towering rages that had him tearing at his hair, shooting sparks from his hands and screaming like an animal. That Shalice was the cause of his rage she didn't doubt—she'd read her name on his lips a dozen times. She had also seen the apparent cause of the trouble: the destruction of his silly laboratory. For some reason he blamed her, which would need some investigating once this had settled down.

For now, she decided she'd seen enough. Mugabo had to go.

As she came to the decision there was a knock at her door. With a deft wave of the hand she panned the ball's vision to outside her hut and saw with some surprise George Pilo standing out there. 'Open up!' he barked.

She went to the door and opened it. 'What is it, George?'

'Don't take that tone with me,' George almost screamed. 'Something's going on here. I want the ball. Hand it over.'

*Oh you little SHIT,* she thought. 'George, please—now is a bad time. Whatever you want looked upon, I will do it.'

'What the hell!' George snapped, face pressed into her belly, eyes peering up like two malicious white lumps of gristle. 'Am I in charge, Shalice?' he said. 'Does that seem to be the basic thread of our interactions? I could be miles off the mark, but what do you think?'

She cringed away from him, disgusted to have him in such close contact. 'Yes, George. You have a share in the leadership, I believe.'

'Very good,' he said, not rising to the bait. 'Then hand it over. With every word you *don't* talk back, you'll get the ball back one day earlier.'

'George—'

'Did I say *day*? I might have meant year.'

'You do not understand,' said Shalice, knowing it was futile, 'my life is in danger—'

'Well,' George cried, 'tell me *all* about it! I'll just let the circus come crashing down while I sit here, your shoulder to cry on. Have I ever told you your feelings are important to me, Shalice? I must have done. Let me set the record straight, you stupid bitch. *Give me the ball.*'

Not looking at him, she handed him the ball. George snatched it, spat over his shoulder and marched out the door as fast as his Napoleonic legs could carry him. Her eyes blazed out after him. 'Your time is coming, little man,' she whispered as she shut the door then locked it.

George looked like a miniature drill sergeant in a film run at double speed for comic purposes as he scuttled back to his trailer, but there was no smile on his dial. He barrelled through everyone who found themselves in his path. There were two deeply conflicting emotions coursing through him: bitter triumph because Kurt's ship was sinking, and disgusted fury that anyone would dare strike out at the show. If George had his way, everyone would be dead except him ... Bitter flavours were all his palate knew.

Once in his trailer he placed the crystal ball on his desk and glared at it. Over by the funhouse Kurt was still prowling around, though no spectators remained. A mighty big hump had grown on his back and his jaw had stretched far longer than normal, rendering him unable to close his lips, which still formed the words *Oh, ho ho hoooo* ...

Moving the ball's vision along towards Kurt's trailer, George saw something that made his eyes go wide. That new clown, J-something, was sneaking down the path with Kurt's priest. George gave a short bark that might have been laughter. He snatched one of the accountant's notepads and jotted on it: *Culprits.* First name on the list: *J the clown.* George panned over to the acrobat tent. Only one of them was home, Randolph, and for some bizarre reason he was emptying a bag of manure over the furniture. *Why the hell is he messing up his OWN STUFF?* George wondered. Randolph then placed a red plastic clown nose on the suede couch, buried in manure, and sprinted away. George shook his head in bewilderment and added Randolph's name to the list.

He spent the next hour gazing into the ball at the strange goings on which, if he didn't know better, looked to be bloody well *organised*. Every so often he'd mutter 'that qualifies', or 'gotcha', and scrawl another name on the notepad. He saw several dwarfs and gypsies he knew by name vandalising this, setting fire to that, tipping over this, covering in excrement that. Before long the list had a dozen names on it. George summoned the accountant, who bumbled and bustled into the trailer. 'Take this to Kurt,' George ordered, handing him the paper. 'I think he's still at the funhouse. If not, try his trailer.' The accountant nodded his head, jowls quivering, and left. George didn't really need his services any more anyway.

Kurt wasn't prowling around the funhouse anymore. He stood in the doorway of his trailer, eyes roaming about slowly, taking in each detail of his defiled office; the spilled teeth, the human waste, ripped-up Bibles, and the open desk drawer with his priest no longer inside. He'd said one thing as he stood there observing it all: a barely audible '*Ohhh, ho ho ho.*'

Even the distant piercing cry, loud as an explosion, as Goshy discovered what had become of his wife, didn't cause Kurt to flinch.

Behind him someone cleared their throat. Kurt gave a start as though roused from a trance and turned around. Had the throat-clearer been privy to the grin on Kurt's face he would have kept quiet, turned and walked away very quickly, for the jolt Kurt had received from the attack on his office had manifested itself physically. Suddenly his face appeared to have been divided into two portions; his forehead and brow were as normal, but his nose was protruding out into a bent knuckle shape, almost like a small spine bulging under the skin. His lips and cheeks were spread thin. His teeth jutted like sharp knuckles of stained ivory. Kurt Pilo no longer resembled a human being—half his face had become a jagged weapon closer to an upside-down shark's jaw than a man's. This face was the last thing Pilo Senior had seen this side of the grave.

The jaw lowered like a drawbridge. Kurt said, 'Hmmm?'

The accountant had about a second in which to turn pale and wet himself before Kurt ripped his head off cleanly. With a thud it dropped to the grass, glasses cracked but still intact. Kurt pulled a handkerchief from his pocket and daintily patted his cheeks. His words were half-formed, but jovial. 'What have we done? Made a mess. Must control myself.'

He reached his hand down—the bones in his fingers had grown longer than the skin—and carefully picked up the note the accountant had dropped to the ground. His eyes flickered across it, though it took his eyes a moment to recognise letters and words again. He knew the names listed, the faces too. The culprits. '*Ohhh* ho ho ho,' Kurt said, stepping out of his trailer and heading for the clowns' tent.



Goshy's face was changing colours from one moment to the next; his skin went blue, yellow, green, black, bright red, then back to its normal sickly pink. He stood motionless in the doorway of his room, like a pile of lard sculpted into a vaguely human shape and painted tacky colours. The black pot lay on the floor before him, soil tossed over the floor in the rough pattern of a giant brown teardrop. Feathery yellow-green leaves lay scattered in a trail leading out the door.

Doopy seemed to sense the mood from afar. He came running from his room, calling out, 'Goshy? G-G-Goshy?' No one in the showgrounds was spared the ear-needling pain of Goshy's shriek. The lamp's light bulb smashed. Blood leaked from Doopy's ear in a thin stream as he stared at the empty pot. 'Oh Goshy,' he said breathlessly. 'Oh Goshy, no!'

Goshy pointed a stiff arm at the trail of leaves and his mouth flapped mutely.

'I know, Goshy,' said his brother, 'we should maybe oughta follow it, should maybe oughta see where it *goes*, Goshy, maybe we gotta! C'mon, Goshy, c'mon . . .'

Mugabo was in a frenzy of paranoid rage. He tried to keep it inside, the fire begging to come out and play, whispering, *Release me! It's dry out there, dry and crispy, we could make it shimmer and turn orange and black, you and me, let's do it, come now, you have your reasons, I have mine, let's burn burn burn burrrrrrrrn . . .*

'No,' he croaked weakly in reply, 'no, must . . . think . . . make sure is . . . really her . . . make . . . certain . . .'

This battle had raged for two nights and Mugabo was losing. The fires spoke louder, relentlessly. *She's so very dry, they all are, like bundles of straw, let's make them crackle and spit and glow . . .*

'Shut up!' Mugabo screamed with some force. The fires quieted down for a moment, giving Mugabo a chance to breathe, calm himself . . .

That's when Goshy's scream jabbed his ears as painfully as darts. *HER!* the fires cried. *LOOK WHAT SHE DID!*

Mugabo lay on the floor, shivering uncontrollably. 'Look what she did,' he whispered.

*LET'S MAKE HER—*

'Glow,' he said, and rose, kicked down the door, stepped out into the night.


After George left, Shalice had consulted her charts and knew the attack was on its way. She had worked furiously in a short time and now her trap was ready. One quick stop-off in Sideshow Alley and the preparations were complete: a word to four gypsies, one subliminal command, and *voila*, all in readiness. She checked her pocket watch—two minutes from now, Mugabo would be finished, out of his misery at long last. Right now the gypsies should have just finished loading a wagon with lumber for the woodchoppers. Four concrete bricks were in place on the road, as directed by the charts. Around the time the wagon passed her hut, it would flip onto its side, veer on one wheel off the road and into her door, where Mugabo would be standing. He'd be crushed like an insect. It was not a perfect plan, and left a few things to chance, but at short notice it was the best she could do.

Someone thumped on the door. Shalice checked her pocket watch in disbelief—he was here early. One minute, forty seconds; her calculations had been wrong. Impossible. She'd set far more elaborate chains of events under way with perfect timing. A minute forty out? It might as well have been years.

*Thump thump thump* again on the door. Years? Maybe not so bad as that—she had to keep him here for seventy more seconds. She stepped away from the door in case he blasted it open and lay down on her belly. 'Who is it?' she said.

'Open the door Shal! You shouldn'ta oughtn'ta done it, you really shouldn'ta!'

'HMMMMM *OOOOOOO* HMMMMMMM *EEEEEEEEEE!*'

Hold on a second . . . 'Who is that?' Shalice said, then, 'Oh shit, get out of the doorway. Move it, I'm telling you now, get away from the door.'

'You dirty rotten, shouldn'ta, never shoulda, we gotta kill you dead, we just *gotta*, good and proper, you oughtn'ta done it, you really shouldn'ta . . .'

Shalice stood and went to the door. 'Listen, you freaks, I don't know or care what your problem is, but—'

'*Beeee-yoooo WIP!*' Goshy screamed.

Shalice winced and held her hands to her ears. 'But if you don't get away from the door—'

Too late. There was a metallic sound, like a chain being struck with an axe, and the sound of hoofs. Shalice jumped away from the door just in time to see it give in as the wagon, right on time, thundered into it. The door fell inward, and stuck to it was a squashed flat mess dressed in bright colours, flower patterns and stripes.

Doopy had borne the impact at the neck. Had it been his torso, he might have made it . . . Clowns took some killing. Goshy was still twitching. He turned his marsupial eyes to Shalice, and his expression hadn't changed from what it had been since Goshy became Goshy. The left eye was wide and surprised to see his brother turned to a soft bag of dead clown, the right was coldly calculating which part of Shalice to remove first once she came within arm's reach.

For her part, Shalice had no idea Goshy was still ticking, biding what remained of his time to strike. She was wondering why her star charts had told her Mugabo was coming, only to have the freak twins appear at her door with some kind of grievance. Two dead clowns was going to take a hell of a lot of explaining come morning.

Suddenly there was a bright flash of white light and an orange tongue of fire as Mugabo launched all he had at Goshy. He'd seen Goshy at the door, making the same noise that drove him from his home minutes before. Now unarmed for this confrontation, Shalice ran to the back of the hut, her heart slamming as she hid under the table, a knuckle gripped in her teeth, counting what she believed would be her last seconds. *What a way to end,* she thought—*and I saw it coming. Trapped like a rat, burned. I had the power of a goddess in my hands and still I could not escape this.*

But Mugabo, his rage spent, stared perplexed at what remained of the two clowns. In the confused recesses of his mind it seemed that Goshy had been the antagonist all along, so he turned away from the fortune-teller's hut, staggering down the pathway, the fires quiet in his head, for now.

The minutes ticked by and Shalice understood she would live. But in the passing minutes another vision came to her, something so clear and vivid she almost believed it had come already. But no—it was coming, fast and deadly, and there was time yet to find her way off the showgrounds. From the pages of a tome on the bookshelf she grabbed a pass-out she'd hidden long ago in case of emergency, then stole her way through the shadows towards Sideshow Alley, and her way out. It was coming—Kurt was coming.

On her way she saw Fishboy's new assistant, Steve, ducking through Sideshow Alley's wooden archway with a hot dog in his hand and grease all over him from tending to the rides. *The boy has about an hour to live,* Shalice thought. She shivered, then she paused mid-step. In her mind she saw Winston, in Kurt's trailer, sweating with fear of the punishment coming to him. *Spared many hurts for the price of a few,* she thought. She grabbed Steve's arm, looked him in the eye and said. 'Come with me. We are leaving.'

'What?' said Steve, frowning. 'Why?'

'Kurt is why. No more questions. Come.'

# CHAPTER 24

# UNMASKED

GONKO heard some of the commotion and figured it was a mess someone else could clean up. He was pulling objects from the pockets of his pants and laying them on the bed: a loaded Glock pistol, a throwing hatchet, a poison dart, an axe. He'd decided his act could spare one performer, so Winston had told his last fib. Gonko had not missed the trail of green leaves. His first impulse had been to gut Winston on the spot, but he held off . . . Such decisions were best made after a little thought. Winston had been faithful for a long time, at least as far as appearances went. Had all else been rosy, Gonko would have given him a hiding and let him live. But all was not rosy; suddenly, from out of nowhere, the showgrounds had the feel of a war zone.

He settled on the axe for aesthetic purposes—to Gonko there seemed something entirely appropriate about a clown killing a clown with an axe. He picked it up, flipped it in the air and caught it by the handle. 'Going to miss you, old feller,' he muttered, testing the edge with his finger, 'but not much.' He stepped out into the parlour, and almost dropped the axe when he saw what was out there waiting for him.

It took a moment for him to recognise it was Kurt, and only the torn remains of Kurt's necktie gave it away, dangling off the hump on his back. The beast had to hunch to get its head through the doorway. Kurt looked closer to dinosaur than man; the top part of his human face was smeared like part of a broken plastic mask to the beast's crown. His legs had burst the fabric of his pants, bulging out into scaled muscular pillars, claws bursting through his shoes and sinking deep into the battered grass. His deep cultured voice was still jovial; the shark jaw contorted with difficulty to form the words: 'Gonko . . . normally when I come knocking . . . you do a little gag. Would you . . . do it now?'

Gonko swallowed, blinked, wiped at his eyes and wondered for a moment what Kurt was on about. Thankfully it came to him. He swallowed again and said, 'Ah, yeah, I can manage that, boss. No thanks, we . . . we don't want any.'

The jaw shook. Each note of Kurt's laughter sounded like it was made with two voices, one deeper than a crocodile's, one his usual unstable cheer, in blood-curdling harmony: 'Ohh, ho ho *hoooo*.'

Gonko wiped his brow and clutched tight at the axe handle, wondering if it would even chip one of Kurt's scales should Kurt come charging at him. He doubted it.

'Gonko, we have trouble,' the monster said.

'Ah, is that right, boss?'

'Yes, Gonko.' A thick purple tongue lolled down between two of the teeth—now more like tusks—and hung loose, flapping against the patch of hellish red gum. 'There's traitors in the show,' came that horrible voice, 'but the show must go on. You see that, don't you, Gonko?'

Gonko's voice was a thick whisper. 'Yeah, boss. I think I do.'

'I thought perhaps . . . George was behind it,' said Kurt Pilo, taking two steps towards him. Gonko fought not to back away, to keep perfectly still. 'That's why,' said Kurt, 'I didn't try to stop the rot before now. But then, it was my brother who made this list.' Kurt held up a hand that looked like another jaw, all bone and scale. Clasped in its grip was a piece of paper. Kurt's eyes bored into Gonko from high above. 'Two of your men are on this list. That's a shame, Gonko. We'll have to talk about that . . . after.'

'Yeah, boss, I hear you,' said Gonko. 'I'm as shocked as you are.'

Kurt spoke very slowly. 'I don't think . . . you're quite *that* shocked. Do you?'

'No, boss,' Gonko whispered.

'Hmmmm. Come then, Gonko. We have work to do.'


With only a door separating Jamie from the nightmares outside, he sat in his room waiting for it all to end. He'd heard something step into the parlour, caught a glimpse of what had become of Kurt Pilo, and had run back here to sit in a foetal position on his bed, shivering. Jamie no longer expected to live through the night; Kurt knew he was in on it, he'd been seen rescuing the priest, seen shepherding him to the loose plank of wood in the fence, pointing him towards the safest spot out there, telling him to come back when it was safe—ha, when it was safe. How did he know Kurt had seen all this? He didn't. Logic had taken a little well-earned holiday from his mind and in its place was a crippling exhaustion. Now he wasn't sure if it mattered that he'd likely be dead before the night's end; it would mean rest.

A memory of the thin pathway came back to him, the way the priest had staggered along it, refusing to look at the abyss to his right. At the time Jamie had thought the priest might be better off falling than staying around to endure whatever Kurt had in store for him. Falling off, or jumping. Jumping. *You know*, he thought, *that's probably a damn fine idea. Probably the logical choice at this point. I've got a hunch I've seen enough.* Still, he sat there a while longer. Out in the showgrounds he heard the deep volcanic roar of Kurt Pilo unmasked.

Jamie stood up and walked calmly through the parlour, without a tremor in his step and with a steady heartbeat. If he made it to the brink before they found him, he supposed it would be some kind of victory. If not—well, what did it matter.

The trail of bodies was piling up fast. Gonko made a point of killing as enthusiastically as he could because the boss was keeping an eye on him. The boss was looking for traitors everywhere, and finding them. The acrobats now lay in bloody ruin. Kurt had told them the show must go on before he tore them up like screaming dolls. Had Gonko been told yesterday that he and Kurt would butcher the acrobats, he'd have thought it too good to be true, but there was something not right about this. The show was *not* going on. It felt like the final curtain call, and Gonko could do nothing but sit tight and hope Kurt came out of this 'mood'.

Kurt stalked to the freak show tent, Gonko at his heels. Fishboy was at the door, waiting for them. He looked minuscule as Kurt towered over, every sharp edge of his body gleaming wet and red. Fishboy stood there, arms folded, somehow meeting Kurt's stare with one of his own. His gills flickered once. Behind Kurt's back Gonko wore a look of disbelief as he gestured for Fishboy to get back, stop blocking the doorway . . . Why the hell was he staring Kurt down?

Behind Fishboy the other exhibits looked on, silent in their glass cages.

'Took your time,' said Fishboy, not even looking at Gonko. 'We've been waiting for this a long time. We would have killed ourselves, if we hadn't thought there was a chance to bring you with us.'

Gonko's jaw dropped. What was Fishboy fucking *talking* about?

Kurt let out a quiet 'Oh, ho *hooo* . . .'

'Fishboy, what——' Gonko began, but he had no need to finish. Kurt swooped down. It was over in a second.

'You see, Gonko?' said Kurt, turning to face him with waterfalls of blood pouring between his teeth, down the side of his face. 'Traitors. Everywhere. Flush them out, Gonko.'

Gonko did as he was told. Minutes later there were no freaks left in the show. Yeti had grappled with Kurt fiercely, bitten at his claws and broken one finger away, but Kurt had merely toyed with him a while before crushing him in one fast squeeze. 'Sideshow Alley,' said Kurt, who was beginning to find speech very difficult. 'Others on the list . . . must be hiding there . . . Show must go on, Gonko.'

'I guess you're right,' said Gonko, then froze as Kurt tilted his head skyward and howled. The sound sent chills down Gonko's spine. On Kurt's breath he could smell the stale reek of swamp land, ancient battlefields for scaled warriors who had lived long before man's time. The monster charged off into the distance, booming footsteps and sending shivers through the ground.

It seemed Gonko's help was no longer needed. He stayed put, gazing around at the ruins of the freak show, wondering if he'd been dreaming when yesterday seemed just another day. Time for a little holiday, he reckoned. Time to round up his crew and get the hell off the showgrounds.


JJ stood and dusted himself off. 'Whoa, shit's getting heavy,' he said, reaching down to help Rufshod to his feet. 'Thanks for that. Owe you one.'

'Thank Gonko, his idea,' said Rufshod. 'Been looking for you for hours.' He cocked his ear, listening to the screams of carnie rats getting offed by whatever was offing them, then dropped the tub of face paint and the hand mirror and bolted back towards the clown tent. 'Come on,' he said over his shoulder. JJ followed him through some obscure back route out of Sideshow Alley.

'OHHHH HO HO HO!' something bellowed. It sounded vaguely like . . . It was Kurt, had to be. JJ paused in his stride, wondering whether or not to go and watch the show. He'd been waiting for this since he first laid eyes on the big goon.

Then everything came back to him; Jamie hadn't had time to clear his mind of memories this time before Rufshod waylaid him. JJ took a quick look at the hidden files—oh, look at that, secret meetings, conspiracy—and he had to admit he didn't blame the guy for hiding it all. Jamie was an enemy of the show, and JJ guilty by association. Through no fault of his own, JJ was an outlaw. 'Son of a fucking tramp!' he screamed.

'JJ?' someone called. He turned and saw Gonko standing with Rufshod. Gonko was spattered thick with blood.

'Wasn't me, boss, swear it. Jamie set me up,' said JJ.

'You still a clown? Then I don't give a damn,' said Gonko. 'We're going. The clowns are out of here. We'll find ourselves a new home till this shit blows over.'

'Going? Where?'

'I don't know. We'll find a hippie commune or start a religious cult. Come on, we're off to Georgie's trailer for some pass-outs. You, me, Ruf and Winston. I'll let bygones be, since we're short on staff all of a sudden. Gosh and Doops seem to have got killed at long last. They'll be back, I reckon, but death'll keep 'em busy for a while. Tonight at least. Let's go.'

'Okay!' said JJ. 'Coming!' He bounded over to Gonko. 'You're not mad about all that stuff, are you boss? About that whole conspiracy-to-make-all-this-happen stuff, are you?'

Gonko squinted at him. 'On your brightest day I don't think you could have planned for Kurt's little tantrum.'

'For sure,' said JJ, nodding emphatically, 'that was the last thing on our minds.'

Across the showgrounds came a roar that seemed to shake the ground. Following it was the sound of something huge, possibly a house, being crushed. 'God*damn* he's ticked off,' Gonko muttered.

'*Who took . . . Lord's name . . . in vain?*' Kurt's voice rolled across the showgrounds like thunder.

'Whoa, here he comes,' said Gonko. 'Step lively!' Gonko, Rufshod and JJ ran for George's trailer. Soon they came across someone standing in their path. Mugabo had blue waves of electricity rippling over his robes and turban. JJ's hair stood on end and the air became thick with the smell of ozone. 'Mugabo!' Gonko cried cheerily. 'How the hell are ya?'

By way of answer Mugabo appeared to grow in size, arching his hands over his head, fingers splayed. 'White man bring da plague,' he growled.

'Oh great,' Gonko muttered, stuffing both hands into his pockets. 'Mugabo, buddy, don't get any ideas just because you zapped me the other——'

Mugabo's hands swept down and two balls of white fire flashed through the air. Gonko leapt sideways, rolled and came to his feet—by that time he'd somehow manoeuvred a thin fire extinguisher from his pockets. He took two hops forward and sprayed foam all over the magician. Mugabo groped blindly and spluttered. Gonko threw the canister at him. It caught Mugabo squarely in the face with a hollow metallic *thunk* and he dropped to the ground. Gonko kicked him as he ran past.

They came to George's trailer and Gonko paused, drawing the clowns into a huddle. 'Now, we'll tell Georgie to hand the passes over, and if he doesn't cough 'em up he's clocking out, courtesy of us. As far as I know, Georgie packs no punch at all apart from a surname and some hot air. Got the plot?'

Rufshod and JJ nodded. Gonko kicked at the trailer door but received no answer. He shrugged and wrenched it open and the clowns charged in. Gonko pulled at the desk drawers, fumbling around until he found the pass-outs. Just as he held them up and said, 'Let's go,' the trailer door slammed shut. Gonko went to it and shoved it with his shoulder. It didn't budge. He kicked it, kicked it again. It still wouldn't budge. 'Well, this is news,' he said.

'I'm scared!' JJ cried, only half faking.

'We're moving,' said Rufshod. 'Look . . .' He tore the curtains from the side window. Outside the landscape crawled along slowly. The trailer shook.

'What in Cleopatra's panties is going on?' Gonko yelled.

What in Cleopatra's panties was going on was George Pilo packing what punch he had—a rat's cunning, if nothing else. Kurt had been so enthralled with the priest he'd been given for his birthday, he'd neglected to make sure the redwood crucifix had been delivered to his trailer. George had spotted it and knew it was likely the only barricade strong enough to hold his intended prisoner—Kurt—inside. Still, he was happy enough to have caught the clowns, who weren't getting out of this alive either, if George could help it. He'd signalled for the woodchoppers to jam the crucifix against the door, held in place with heavy iron rings recently welded to the trailer's front corners, a trap he'd planned for his next assassination attempt. Now he was hauling the trailer along at a slow pace with a small buggy he'd hooked up to it. He could hear the clowns banging and yelling in there and he smiled, tasting one of his life's few bitter victories. Others could well be in store—first he had to get these clowns to the funhouse.

Inside the trailer JJ was crying up a storm, getting reacquainted with his inner coward. He'd been Death's Angel for just a little while as he killed sleeping carnies, but now that danger had looked at him cockeyed he was wiping his nose on the curtains, whining like a puppy. Rufshod seemed completely unconcerned, peering casually out the window and commenting on the trail of bodies they passed. 'Hey, I know him! That's the carnie who sold me that lighter that didn't work. He's fucked up now! Check it out, his head's in three pieces.'

Gonko was pulling from his pockets all manner of things with which to open a door—bolt cutters, dynamite, skeleton keys—but nothing seemed to work. 'Goddamn it!' he snarled after trying to jemmy the lock with a credit card. 'Sometimes I think these pants have a sense of humour.' He wrestled with the handle ferociously, then stopped and sighed. 'Well, boys, I'm guessing it's George who's got us, and he's got us good. If we get out of this trailer, you have my permission to hurt him real bad. Maybe you can throw your tears and snot at him, JJ. You're a good man to have on hand in a crisis.'

'I'm sorry,' JJ blubbered.

'Seen corpses put up more fight than you. Fucking pathetic.'

'Leave me alone!' JJ shrieked.

The trailer came to a halt, bumping hard against something and knocking the clowns off their feet. Gonko crouched. 'Get ready,' he said, 'soon as the door opens.'

They could hear George Pilo outside barking orders. Something heavy banged against the door once, and with an ominous creak the floor tilted. The trailer was being lifted from its rear end and tipped forward. The desk slid across the floor, along with a filing cabinet and a chest of drawers.

The clowns jumped out of the way as the furniture crashed into the door. Suddenly all was still. Gonko frowned, climbed up on the pile of furniture and leaned towards the door, listening hard. He gave it a tentative push then pulled himself back as it swung open. 'What the——' he said. 'Oh fucking hell. We're at the funhouse.'

George had the trailer tilted at a 45-degree angle, trying to tip them out. Before them, like an open mouth, was the gaping wound blasted open in the funhouse explosion. Down below were the bowels of the carnival. The funhouse basement was a hollowed-out cavern with stone walls, ten feet below the floor. In the middle of it was a pit, the mouth of a long tunnel leading down out of sight. An orange glow shone up from the depths, from which came a stench like burning rubber and cooked meat.

JJ took one peek out the trailer door and screamed. 'Oh no, no I don't want to, please don't make me go down there, please . . .'

'You're sounding like Doops now,' said Gonko, disgusted, 'only he would've put up——' He stopped as the trailer shifted again below them. 'Oi!' he screamed.

'Be quiet in there,' said George from close by; the delight in his voice was thick and pure. 'You're still employees. Do what you're told. Jump out. Out of my trailer.'

'Fuck yourself,' Gonko screamed. The trailer shook again. Gonko listened hard. 'Woodchoppers,' he said. 'They're trying to shake us out.' He reached into his pants and pulled a pistol from his pockets, which he threw to Rufshod. 'Take 'em out,' he said.

Rufshod aimed at the back of the trailer and fired twice, punching two small holes in the wall. George yelled an order outside and the trailer shook more violently than ever. All three clowns lost their balance; the pistol flew from Rufshod's hands out the door and clattered to the stone floor in the funhouse basement, narrowly missing the glowing pit. 'Damn it,' Gonko muttered, then changed tack. 'What's this about, George? What do you want from us?'

'Want you to shut up and die,' George said gleefully.

Gonko's body shook with rage. He gave himself a moment to recover then spoke calmly. 'No, really, George. Is this something to do with Kurt? Why don't you let us in on the gag? Maybe we can help.'

'You can get down into the funhouse is what you can do,' said George, his voice petulant. 'Take that J traitor down there with you. Kurt'll be right down.'

Gonko frowned and thought quickly. 'Ahh,' he whispered to the other two, 'he's going to get Kurt down into the basement. But what the hell for?' He paused, then addressed George, 'Is JJ the only one of us you want down there?'

'NO!' JJ screamed. 'PLEASE!'

'Shut *up*,' said Gonko, 'just testing the waters. Trust me. What do you say, George? Just JJ?'

George ignored them and barked more orders at the woodchoppers. The trailer shook again and tipped at a steeper angle. The filing cabinet toppled out the open door, and Gonko missed being barrelled out with it by about a foot. With a crash it fell into the pit below, down the tunnel and out of sight. As it fell a burst of orange fire shot out of the pit's shaft and bloomed like a tiny mushroom cloud. There were dancing shapes in the fire, black shadowy forms like fluttering bats.

Gonko scowled at JJ. 'Motherfucker, if you don't stop your crying . . .'

JJ stopped his crying—something caught his eye. There was a small wooden cabinet embedded in the wall just overhead. He didn't know what it was about it that caught his eye or gave him a sense of faint hope. He planted his foot on the desk in the doorway, ignoring the drop that waited if his shoes slipped, and reached for the cabinet's handle. Gonko turned his attention back to George. 'Come on, I been a good worker, did my job without complaint. Why the whole sacrifice-the-clowns thing?'

'Ha!' was George's answer.

In the distance there was another sound, a distant rumbling, coming closer. Kurt was on his way. George barked a furious order at the woodchoppers and the trailer began shaking again.

JJ reached the cabinet. It was locked. 'Hey, Gonks . . .'

'Don't want to hear it, JJ, shut your trap,' Gonko snapped.

JJ had been about to ask him for something to open the cabinet, but he saw sitting on top of the desk the skeleton key Gonko had pulled from his pocket. He reached down, grasping for it, and as the trailer gave another shake the key flew up into his hand. The trailer was still for a moment then gave another violent spasm; JJ and Gonko held their footing, but Rufshod slipped through the doorway, snatching for a hand-hold, and dropped into the funhouse. JJ watched him with fascination as he dropped like a rag doll, missing the pit and landing on what looked like a sacrificial slab right beside it, square on his back. He lay writhing with agony and joy. Gonko grimaced. 'Hear that, George?' he yelled. 'JJ just fell. He's down there now. Come on, put the trailer down. You got the traitor.'

'Got one of them,' said George.

At this Gonko appeared to lose what remained of his cool. 'Fucker! If I get out of this, George, I am going to kill you very slowly. You dig? Snotty little shit, I have been waiting for the chance for years. I'm going to take *years* to kill you, you hear me?'

'You just blew it. I was about to negotiate,' said George.

'*The fuck you were*! You're a dead dwarf, Georgie, no wonder your Pa didn't trust you to run the show. Once a snivelling shit, always a snivelling shit. Every time you tried to take out Kurt I was there to tell him your plan. It was too much fun watching your face curl up ready to cry.'

'Ha! How's your face looking right now, Gonko?'

Through all this Kurt's thudding footsteps were drawing nearer. JJ put the skeleton key into the lock of the cabinet. He turned the key and the small wooden door swung open. Standing on tiptoe he could see piles of velvet bags. They spilled out of the cabinet and dropped through the trailer door. JJ grabbed one of the bigger ones as it fell, looking around wildly for something to hold the powder. Gonko turned his head and said: 'What the . . . George's stash! Oh, fuck me, that was close. JJ, throw one here.'

'Need a bowl,' said JJ, 'and a lighter.'

'Good, good, cook me up a load.' Gonko drew a bowl and lighter from his pockets. 'I'll keep George interested. Hey, Georgie! Remember back in forty-four when someone killed that pet parrot of yours? What was his name, Reynold? You know, the only friend you ever had? That was me, George. I fucked it to death then fed it to Goshy.'

'When you get to hell you can say hi to the little bastard!' George screamed shrilly. Gonko had finally struck a nerve.

Balancing dangerously on the desk, JJ held the flame under the bowl long enough to melt three small bags worth of grains. Gonko held his hands out to take the bowl. 'Hurry up, JJ, for Christ's sake.'

The air was split with another roar: 'LORD'S NAME . . . IN VAIN!' Kurt was close; Kurt was *here*. There was no time to lose. JJ held the bowl out to Gonko . . . then withdrew it.

*Hold on just a second*, he thought. There was no time to lose, especially not by being Mr Nice Guy, Mr Comrade, Mr Noble Here to Save Somebody at His Own Expense. Had that ever been part of JJ's repertoire? No sir, he didn't think so. Neither had Mr Here Gonko, You Go First.

Without a word of apology he swallowed the liquid.

Gonko gaped at him. 'JJ! WHAT THE HELL ARE YOU—'

'Get me out of here,' JJ whispered, closing his eyes. 'Out of this jam. Out of the trailer, pronto. Please please please.'

JJ opened his eyes and looked around; the trailer gave another shake. Nothing had happened. He stared in horror at Gonko, who was shaking his head, eyes blazing. 'You did it now, you stupid sonofabitch. You did it now . . .'

The trailer gave a sudden almighty heave, as though it had been hit by a truck. Kurt had barrelled into the rear end, and the two clowns fell down into the funhouse basement. JJ got his wish.


Jamie saw the whole thing. He came to as though he'd been jerked from sleep by an earthquake. He lay in the grass, thirty metres from the funhouse, with a perfect side-on view of Kurt, who'd grown *huge*, running headfirst at the trailer for his second charge. The whole rear end caved in and crumpled like a tin can. As the trailer lurched Jamie saw Gonko drop into the funhouse, and he saw someone else drop, too. Someone who looked just like him.

Jamie patted his arms and chest, making sure he was really here, whole and in one piece. He didn't know how, but he was. He was dressed in a clown suit from head to toe, though when he patted his face he felt no face paint, just sweat and skin.

*How?* his mind screamed at him, but there would be time for that later. He picked himself up and ran.

Kurt finished tearing through his brother's trailer and with a wrench of his arms threw it aside. It spun through the air and landed with a crash on top of the woodchoppers, who'd been enjoying a well-earned break over by Slimmy the smoking dwarf's rest spot. Too exhausted to move, they only had time to throw each other one last exasperated glance as the trailer came down.

Meanwhile, Kurt was peering down into the funhouse basement. He was breathing like a dragon in ragged growling gasps. From scaly head to clawed feet he was drenched as though he'd been caught in a storm of blood. George Pilo watched his brother carefully from behind a pile of chopped logs. He stepped from behind the wood pile, taking a calculated risk, and a big one. 'Hey, Kurt!' he called.

Kurt turned his head sideways, narrowing his eyes at his brother.

'Be careful,' said George with perfectly mimed sincerity. 'Gonko's pants . . . dangerous.'

Kurt's lip peeled back, his tusks glistening. 'Thanks, little brother.'

'No problem. Get the traitors, Kurt. Oh look . . . you might want to take that. Defend yourself, you know.' George pointed to the big wooden crucifix, which lay on the ground nearby. Had Kurt's face been capable of human expression, it would have lit up with delight. He snarled, 'Oh, lovely,' and reached for it, cradling it in his arms. He said, 'Fitting, isn't it?'

'Yes, Kurt,' said George, ducking back behind the wood pile. 'Fitting for the traitors. Go get 'em.'

Kurt turned to the funhouse again and leapt down into the basement, his airborne bulk a sight as ominous as a bridge collapsing or a car being carried away in hurricane winds. And the game was over. Checkmate, George Pilo. He rushed to the funhouse. eyes alight with triumph. The folks down below didn't take too kindly to crucifixes, didn't take kindly to them at all.

Kurt Pilo was a runt in the litter compared to what roamed at the end of that fiery tunnel, but in his bestial form, rational thought was almost beyond him. In such company, carrying a crucifix was an unforgivable breach of etiquette, yet he heard the roars erupting from below as camaraderie, cheering him on. Across the showgrounds the survivors who heard those roars would find their nightmares tainted forever by the sounds.

In three blows Kurt clubbed Rufshod to death then turned to Gonko. As savagely as Gonko fought, nothing in his pockets was enough for Kurt unmasked, and he couldn't even bruise the beast before Kurt threw him hard against the wall, knocking him out cold before turning to JJ. Pleading for mercy, JJ died on his knees.

Dropping the crucifix, Kurt reached for Gonko's body, tucking it under his arm and stroking the clown boss's head tenderly, the gently muttered recriminations lost in the primordial growl from his throat. The crucifix dropped down into the mouth of the pit, burning as it fell, spinning and bouncing down the walls of the tunnel.

Exulting as he was, hell's own sword, Kurt noticed nothing amiss even as the flames roared from the pit, and great shadowy arms lifted him and drew him into their midst. He fell amongst his own kind, forever unmasked, Gonko unconscious in his arms.

# CHAPTER 25

# SURVIVORS

AS the roaring from the funhouse faded Jamie rose shakily and stared about himself like a blind man. Nothing seemed to register, none of the bloody ruin around him. Kurt's slaughter had spared no one. Fishboy and the other rebels had won their freedom the only way they could.

Not knowing where to go, Jamie found himself headed for the clown tent. At the card table was an abandoned game of solitaire. He wandered through the rooms where all seemed as it had been before: there was the bed he'd woken in every morning to guilt and tortured memories, and the surprises JJ left for him. He sat there for a minute then got up and wandered in a daze to Winston's room.

Winston was there, sitting on his bed. Jamie rubbed his eyes and blinked to make sure. Slowly Winston turned his head to the door. 'It worked,' he said quietly.

'What . . .' Jamie began. At the foot of Winston's bed were a hundred or more little velvet bags, all of them empty.

'About two years' worth of wages, all in one go,' said Winston. 'Kept swallowing the stuff till I couldn't stand any more. Didn't know if it'd work . . . They don't make many exceptions to the rules. Maybe it was already all finished, and they just didn't care anymore. I've wished myself out of here, that many times—bargained, pleaded, you know. Never answered, that wish. They'll give you anything you want, except—freedom.'

Jamie sat at the foot of the bed. Winston was staring off into space. 'Just kept asking this time,' he said. 'Looks like they let you go.'

Jamie embraced him; tears came to his eyes. 'Knock it off,' said Winston, a hint of a smile on his face. 'What happened out there? Sounded like fun, whatever it was.'

Jamie told him what he could remember, much of it drawn from JJ's memories, stopping at the point of JJ's wish. The late JJ. 'I don't know if Kurt's still . . . out there,' said Jamie.

'Don't think he is,' said Winston. 'Dunno if you heard that godawful screaming match, but it sounded like Kurt's bosses offering him a golden handshake.'

Jamie shuddered. The world outside had gone quiet. In the distance they could hear a lone voice calling out, whooping to the sky in joy. 'Sounds like Georgie's still kicking,' Winston muttered. 'Thinks he's won. I'll see what I can do about that.' He stood up and tossed Jamie a card attached to a loop of string, a pass-out. 'Here. You should go home.'

'What about you?'

Winston laughed quietly, and the laugh became a sigh. 'I might come out too. Don't know yet. Could sure use a few years with my damn feet up before I bow out.' He pulled from his pocket a small pistol. 'See you later, Jamie. I'm off to spoil George's party.'

'Winston . . .' Jamie said. Winston paused in the doorway without turning. Jamie suddenly had too much to say and nowhere to start. He stood mute, trying to find impossible words.

'It's all right,' Winston said in a tired voice. 'You didn't ask for any of this. Neither did I. See you outside some time, maybe. Goodbye, son. Get the hell out of here.'

'Don't forget the priest,' Jamie said. 'Out beyond the fence.'

Winston nodded and left. Jamie wanted to join him, go out there and fight the last part of the battle—but he also wanted to run. What would JJ do? JJ would run. Jamie would let JJ make one last decision for him, and just maybe he'd hate himself for it later. He ran.

He ran in a daze through the bloody swamp that had once been Sideshow Alley. Bodies lay in piles, in pieces. Kurt had done all this in a matter of minutes. Jamie closed his eyes, trying to block the sight from his mind. He passed the 'test your strength' bell, the rotating clown heads, 'shoot a duck, win a prize', and the Ferris wheel, motionless against the artificial sky. When he got to the lift and opened the door, he heard a distant sound: two hollow banging sounds, *pop pop*, a pause, then a third.

'Hope you got him,' Jamie whispered. He pulled the lever for Brisbane city, and went home.


No one told the ticket collectors about the night's events, of course. They lived outside the showgrounds. They set up their booths at the Woomera County Fair, as per their instructions. A few folks were in for a strange day.

# CHAPTER 26

# EPILOGUE

THE country needed an injection of folklore, something grizzly and mysterious to take people's minds off more imminent perils, like the war and terror always in their faces. People camped out, went for bushwalks in search of the fabled circus. Some came back with stories of finding it, which they tried to sell . . . and some succeeded in that. As rumour and superstition grew, the original witnesses stopped talking. Their accounts spread over the internet like wildfire and the tin-foil-hat crowd had a field day, somehow working it into the Illuminati's grand plans for world domination. How could so many people, heads-on-straight farmers, as respectable as people get, swear black and blue to such bizarre sights?

Looked like a circus, they'd said, but there'd been blood everywhere. Bodies everywhere. Like a circus that had been dropped into a blender and tipped all over the ground. There were reports of a black man in a turban, some cheerful black man who'd done some pyrotechnic stunts you'd have to see to believe. Looked like he was shooting comets out of his hand . . .

Witnesses would tend to blank out here, shake their heads, shudder, forget what they were about to say and ask for the interview to finish, please.

It caused some to wonder: that other unsolved mystery that left nine people trampled to death—hadn't that been at a carnival too? Was there some connection?

And what about that guy the police picked up at the Brisbane construction site wandering around in a clown suit? You know the guy, disappeared a while back, he and a friend of his. At the time it was thought to be some kind of gang thing—seedy characters those two, into drugs by all accounts. And here he was, weeks later. He was questioned at length by the police. Psych evaluations had him pegged as the sanest crazy man alive. He didn't know where he'd been, he said, and it seemed he wasn't lying. As for the other guy, the one he'd disappeared with, his ugly mug was all over the news for a week or so. Someone claimed to have spotted him in bushland with some strange woman, but the sighting was unconfirmed.


Once the fuss died down, the interviews with police, psychologists, and the incessant questions of family and friends—none of whom would ever look at him quite the same way again—Jamie's life continued as though a great number of years had been wiped clean from his memory; he felt in his bones weariness from some great ordeal while his mind grasped at shadows. His sense of time seemed shot and the unemployed weeks stretched out like one long day as he busied himself around his parents' house, attempting to learn again the trick of everyday life. He was vaguely troubled and gnawed at by questions asked deep within as though by a stranger. Often he would pause whatever he was doing, shake his head and mutter something to himself in defeat, sometimes the words, 'I don't know'. Other times he would drift off, staring into space, his mind blank and snatching at thoughts like a hand fumbling for a switch in the dark, his mouth hanging open, a book lying open across his knee.

With a fascination bordering on horror he would read the newspaper articles his parents showed him, about those trampled to death, about the toothless priest who mumbled something about a circus then refused to speak another word, about how Jamie himself was found roaming the streets, dressed like a clown, unable to answer simple questions about the flecks of blood they'd found on his shoes.

His mind probed that night gently, looking for answers but not looking hard or long. He remembered staggering around like a drunk, falling face first into the roadside before the cops picked him up, but before that . . . ? There was something there, there had to be. And at some level deeper than thought he knew it was best it remain hidden.

To forget, it had taken one last wish upon fiery stars, with the help of that small velvet bag he'd found in his pocket as he left the showgrounds for the last time. By the time the police picked him up, he'd already blasted the whole episode from his mind.

And the little velvet bag remained in his bedside drawer, half-full. Every so often he would hold it in his palm, a little too heavy for its size, making a sound like marbles clinking together. Then he would drop it as though it had burned him and wash his hands.

For all the forgetting, the nightmares still came. Intense merciless visions of hell, visions of a younger Earth fenced by different rules, of fierce scaled warriors stamping the shivering ground with hooves and howling at the sky, howling from some hidden prison, banging on their cell bars . . .

And there would come a somehow familiar voice in the thick of these horrible caustic nightmares: 'Your time ain't up yet. Hear me, feller? Enjoyin' your holiday up there? Liking these little horror flicks each night? Here's a clue, my sweet, they're *snapshots*, not dreams. Yeah, *now* you know somethin' about the show. *Now* you know. The fun's just started. Chuckles aplenty. You come get your chuckles whenever you're ready, 'cause if they ain't lettin' *me* go, they ain't lettin' *you* go, best believe that. Show's down but not out, you mark my words. We'll be back in town, my pretty, and I don't recall offering you a severance package . . .'

And always on waking was a feeling that overnight, something new had grown within him, then been plucked out and uprooted, tossed away, but was ready at any time to grow back. He would have to be vigilant, but he knew not for what foe.

And he knew there are strange places in the world. It seemed to him the world was a carnival, and that we've all got a free ticket.

And all shows get their curtain call. Eventually.

# ABOUT THE AUTHOR

Will Elliott came to international attention when *The Pilo Family Circus*, his debut novel, won five Australian literary awards. Elliott began working on the book at nineteen, when he dropped out of law school and was diagnosed with schizophrenia. Influenced by writers as diverse as Chuck Palahniuk, Bret Easton Ellis, and H. P. Lovecraft, his writing is at turns creepy, violent, spare, and wickedly imaginative. Now twenty-nine, Elliott is working on a follow-up novel and has recently completed a memoir. He lives in Brisbane, Australia.

# ABOUT THE BOOK

The Pilo Family Circus was the sixth novel-length manuscript Elliott attempted, in what he viewed as a four-year "apprenticeship" period learning the craft. The rough draft was completed in three months, written in very sporadic bursts, sometimes as much as ten thousand words in a single sitting. Elliott was experimenting with sleep deprivation, often staying awake in excess of forty-eight hours, trying to use "cabin fever" as a source of ideas, as well as avoid some of the "slowing down" effects of anti-psychotic medication. Some of the novel reflects this "fevered" state of mind. Subsequent drafts were done over the next two years, in between work on other manuscripts.

The book was chosen for the inaugural ABC Fiction award prize in Australia. It went on to win the Aurealis Award, the Australian Shadows Award, the Ditmar Award, and the *Sydney Morning Herald's* Best Young Novelist Award. It was also short-listed for the 2007 International Horror Guild Award for best novel. Though the list of awards is remarkable, more remarkable is the breadth of the awards—from high literature to horror and back again.

*The Pilo Family Circus* was picked up by UK publisher Quercus. Limited Edition rights were sold to PS Publishing. This edition was produced by Underland Press for America and Canada, the second title on Underland's 2009 launch list.